BEST OF THE WEST 2009

BEST OF THE WEST

2009

NEW STORIES FROM THE WIDE SIDE OF THE MISSOURI

EDITED BY
JAMES THOMAS AND
D. SETH HORTON

FOREWORD BY
RICK BASS

UNIVERSITY OF TEXAS PRESS ◆ AUSTIN

Requests for permission to reproduce material
from this work should be sent to:
  Permissions
  University of Texas Press
  P.O. Box 7819
  Austin, TX 78713-7819
  www.utexas.edu/utpress/about/bpermission.html

♾ The paper used in this book meets the minimum requirements
of ANSI/NISO Z39.48-1992 (R1997) (Permanence of Paper).

LIBRARY OF CONGRESS CATALOGING-IN-PUBLICATION DATA
Best of the West 2009 : new stories from the wide side of the
Missouri / edited by James Thomas and D. Seth Horton ;
foreword by Rick Bass. — 1st ed.
    p.   cm.
  ISBN 978-0-292-72122-7 (pbk. : alk. paper)
    1. Short stories, American—West (U.S.) 2. West (U.S.)—Social
life and customs—Fiction. I. Thomas, James, 1946– II. Horton,
D. Seth, 1976–
  PS648.W4B475 2009
  813'.087408—dc22   2009021566

CONTENTS

I n *The Portable Western Reader*, William Kittredge writes that he knows he is in the West after crossing the Missouri River, but he struggles to articulate exactly what constitutes the differences between the regions. As editors of *Best of the West: New Stories from the Wide Side of the Missouri*, we share Bill's dilemma. The subtitle of this series indicates that we define the geographical boundaries of the West rather broadly, but of course the more difficult challenge is how one describes the uniqueness and diversity of the region's literature. Indeed, while discussing the stories for this volume, we often came across this simple but profound question: "Everyone knows what the West is, but what in the hell *is* it?"

The first volume of *Best of the West* appeared in 1988 and asserted that the West is as much a state of mind as a geographical region. Now, in 2009, we hold this concept to be truer than ever. The characters in the stories collected here seem to tell us that the possibilities of the West are as expansive as the landscape. This West is a place where cowboys wear tennis shoes and bankers wear cowboy boots, a place of mountainous imagination and ambitions as high as the Wyoming sky.

For this volume, we researched more than two hundred and fifty literary journals. Of the thousands of stories that we read, only a handful were permeated with an ethos of the "Old West," a term that historians of the region have used to describe a mythical space that existed mostly in dime novels and movies, where Anglo men, symbols of the country, "heroically" came of age against a backdrop of Mexican and Native American "savagery." Instead, what we have discovered in our research are many protagonists who fail to attain the goals they have set for themselves. We have found stories that emphasize gender issues, suburban topography, environmental degradation, economic injustices, and ongoing cultural disruptions. Regionally, we have read about a West that is intimately linked with Latin America and, to a lesser extent, the Pacific Rim and Canada. Though much of this work has been exciting in that it challenged us to rethink the cultural contours of the region, it is also important to note the most disturbing feature of our research, which was that African Americans and Native Americans, both as authors and characters, were heavily underrepresented.

If contemporary Western writers, then, eschew static and premodern interpretations of the region in favor of approaches that are tentative, partial, and in flux, we hope the *Best of the West* series might serve as a useful archive to reflect these many voices. In this sense, a closer look at our publication history is relevant to these prefatory considerations of Western literature.

The *Best of the West* began as a yearly anthology of short fiction, publishing contemporary authors whose work was exceptional, in five distinct volumes from 1988 to 1992. The first two volumes were published by Peregrine Smith Books in Salt Lake City, one of the largest and best publishers in the intermountain West. The series then migrated to New York City, where W. W. Norton published the next three volumes. Now, after a hiatus of seventeen years, the series has returned to the West, and we are absolutely delighted to be in the capable hands of Casey Kittrell, our editor, at the very prestigious University of Texas Press in Austin. It is our hope that this series will continue both to help Western writers—who have often been marginalized in the marketplace—find as wide an audience as possible, and to help interested readers discover new and established voices of the region.

All of which leads us back to answer the question: What is the contemporary West? It is an important question to consider for, after all, if George W. Bush's "cowboy diplomacy" has taught us anything, it is that Western images and metaphors continue to haunt and illuminate our cultural constructs. The stories that we have selected, as well as the introductory essay by Rick Bass—one of the most gifted Western writers of our time—serve as partial answers. The West, its distinct geography and geology, its inhabitants—both animal and (especially) human—its social history, and its identifiable cultures are all of considerable national (and indeed, international) interest. In literary terms, and specifically regarding short fiction, we believe that what we write, what we imagine, is only a reflection of who we *think* we are, that the characters we create are really only an invention of a society in which we *think* we live. This, of course, is what literature is all about, inventing and reinventing our world and ourselves.

Here, then, are eighteen stories that explore the fictions and realities of the West.

Rick Bass

hat makes a short story? I'm old-fashioned enough to still believe that the classic form is elegant and pleasing to the soul, is characterized by a beginning, a middle, and an end—unless extenuating thematic or aesthetic reasons suggest otherwise—and possesses a resolution at or very near the end, in which something is changed and, more often than not, one or more of the principals recognize that change. It's an ancient and utterly basic scheme.

So what constitutes a Western short story? What particular dialect, tone, inflection, and sensibility might characterize a story to the point where it could be called Western? Of such matters, regarding the Southern short story, I've seen it suggested on numerous occasions, and not always facetiously, that a kind of checklist exists, or once existed, with mules, and front porches, and tobacco, and race relations, and so forth. That's all true, or possibly true—certain elements do tend to recur in any place that is still unique enough to be called a place, repeating themselves until they are studded like inanimate flecks that affect the larger spirit and culture of that place—but the West, fortunately, is so vast as to render such a registry or checklist all but meaningless.

I would, however, not disagree with those who might suggest there is in the West, beneath the flecks—beneath the world of Western things—an underlying spirit, or whatever you want to call it—patterns and rhythms of life, trajectories of personal as well as natural histories—in which isolation—geographic, emotional, spiritual—is assigned a tad greater valence than is the usual case in short stories, where it already typically assumes robust significance.

Further, in a big country, it's easier to feel tinier; and feeling tiny, there might be an occasional propensity to strive or strain against that irrelevance with grand or at least oversized gestures.

A reader can see glimpses, and sometimes more than glimpses, of this response in several of the stories collected here. It's not that Westerners have cornered the market on understanding, with any extraordinary clarity, via the drama of our geology and weather and distance, the ridiculous hubris of our species; but by the same token it's there, a daily part of our heritage. The mastodon hunters didn't have it easy, and the dope growers and real estate brokers of today don't always have it easy.

Is it my imagination, or are there extra teaspoonfuls of loneliness in these stories, extra pinches of desperation?

Shovelfuls of it, of course, in Joyce Carol Oates's violently imagined story about Hemingway's last days: but even low-level background radiation loneliness, steady as the tick of a Geiger counter, crackles in pulses from Ernest Finney's intriguing "Sequoia Gardens," replete with loneliness's almost-constant companion, desperation.

A subset of this kind of thinking: in the South, many stories continue to grapple with the injustice of social inequalities, the horrific echoes and reverberations of slavery. The West is not without a similar negative resonance, a much less discussed yet equally recent legacy of genocide. The whole immigrant story—who's native, who isn't—has yet to even remotely begin to play itself out, and certainly, the socioeconomic tension of the immigrant and the outsider continues to appear frequently and powerfully in these pages.

Again, I want to be clear: I'm not convinced there is a Western short story, yet. The things I've talked about thus far are not so much Western as they are, instead, the universal themes of literature. To claim otherwise would be like trying to call the Bible the first Western. Our beloved West does not own these territories and elements alone, nor even, perhaps, do we possess them to excess. But I can assert that the stuff of literature—the human heart under duress, and the fires of hunger, loneliness, fear, yearning, as well as joy—are strongly felt, here, and when I think of the West, I must confess, I think of how sharply felt too can be the physical senses, particularly in the out-of-doors, and a less-manipulated, still-not-entirely-domesticated, environment.

A story need not be set in the wilderness to be "Western," but unless I am mistaken (it is so hard to speak of invisible things!), I think many good Western short stories tend to possess a kind of intensity or power of the felt physical senses—as if there are certain people who exist a little more vibrantly in the Western external environment.

I want to be clear: I'm not suggesting that characters need to be far from roads or electricity to tingle with this aliveness, this vitality of the physical senses. But we see this so often in the West, coupled with—seemingly paradoxically—this not-at-all-infrequent desperation and loneliness. Antonya Nelson's excellent "Or Else," for instance, pleases me with its elaborate crumbling interiors of characters' psyches that simultaneously reflect the old mountain home in which the story takes place. The mythic mountains of the ski village are described briefly, little more noted than the puff of breath from a speaker on a cold day; yet somehow, some way, the senses, and sensibilities, of the West feel sharp to me in the story.

Specificity in any setting can heighten the senses, of course, north or south, east or west. But what I think I am trying to say is that the culture of literature in the West might—might—lean heavily on the power and value of the physical senses.

Louise Erdrich's sweet tale "The Reptile Garden" combines the ethos of isolation with another element closer to the hidden bone, logistically, of why, or rather how, most of us are here: because the land was wrested away from the people who lived here before us, and in the most violent ways imaginable. It is immoral to sugarcoat or conveniently forget this, and yet, except for the lovely scene at the end, I would not recognize her story as "Western." But it is. Read that last paragraph and you'll see; finally, if even only in that last paragraph, it could happen, could come together, only in the West.

A great sentence begins Annie Proulx's enigmatic and utterly unique "The Sagebrush Kid." Sure, it's muscle flexing, the circus strongman ringing the bell at the top of the pole with a single tap of the sledgehammer; and sure, a story is more than any single sentence, even if it's a great one—but as readers, how we glory in these too-rare gems that scramble the mind like a joyride. We sense vaguely that the sentence is ostentatious—that rather than existing on its own, the sentence is being brought into the world with the aid of a supremely talented writer, and one who is understandably delighted with her talents—but that's okay, we're swept along, would follow her anywhere. So many writers, particularly beginning writers, try to launch a story with similar sis-boom verve, yet fail to imbue their sentences with the requisite associated magic of a steely and committed soul. As such, a reader can scarcely believe his or her great fortune upon encountering the real thing. Voice isn't everything, but my God, when you hear a true voice, and not that of a pretender, you just have to exclaim, have to laugh out loud, like a winterbound depressive venturing out for the first time in months into blue sky and bright sun.

"Those who think the Bermuda Triangle disappearances of planes, boats, long-distance swimmers and floating beach balls a unique phenomenon do not know of the inexplicable vanishings along the Red Desert section of Ben Holladay's stagecoach route in the days when Wyoming was a territory."

Verve, confidence, the illumination and brilliance of an original voice, and an original mind: these things are not "Western," but certainly, in the West—as in any system under pressure—they are capable of flourishing. It's a little as if writers possessing these qualities bundled together and dug a line in the austere sand from which they can then shout against the great infinitude that often looms so near, in the West.

(In the South, similarly, that literary shout went often against the raging injustice, the fear and class oppression that seethed just behind a calcified and genteel code of manners.)

In the case of Proulx's great first sentence, where to go next? Anywhere. This is one of the powers of great writing. The story travels quickly, wonderfully, into the grotesque shadows of human frailty as those shadows encroach upon a disconnected psyche such as the one placed at risk by the chronic geographic (or other) isolation frequent in the West. The first several pages of the story detail a fantastic breaking of the human spirit in breathtaking detail; we're horrified and secretly thrilled at this illumination of how insignificant and lonely we are—at the terror just behind the veil.

A barren, lonely woman tends a sagebrush as if it were an orphan child. Proulx-the-master skates ever closer to a classic denouement—in a conventional story, it would begin to seem that something dire must happen to the sagebrush—but as if bored by such convention, Proulx decides to take the story into out-and-out fantastic myth and surreality; and for what reason, I have been puzzling over for some time. It is a delicious puzzling.

The story leaps with no significant transition or announcement from the improbable to the impossible. It still hews to the germinal truth of that magnificent first sentence, but so outrageous do the next happenings become that some readers might pause and feel they are being spoofed. Why has a masterly work of literary fiction turned essentially into a well-told ghost story, something you might use to entertain children around a campfire? (And if we judge the latter to be inferior, are we not being arch and snooty?)

I think Proulx's gambit here might have to do with the decadence and unsustainability of the Western myth of rugged individualism and self-governance: the ridiculously destructive and unsatisfying story line that has corrupted—for a while—the literature, culture, and politics of the region. White cowboys with big hats and fat belt buckles holding the Indians and blizzards at bay. One can imagine the gnashing and grinding of Proulx's teeth at such stereotypes. How stupid, she might be saying, is any sentence that gives one more puff of breath to this silliness.

Look at her all-important last paragraph: ". . . The man-camp . . . has disappeared." One can almost hear her relief and solace in such a declaration: it, white folks and Western inhabitation, was all but a brief experiment. And then, penultimately, describing the view of the still-standing but maimed giant sagebrush of the title, the mysterious Christ-like symbol, archetype of nonaltered West, icon: "Anyone looking in the right direction can see it."

Maybe at some level the story suggests a ghost dance of sorts, in which the native species outlast the frail and brief immigrants. Or—and this is my own reading—Proulx might be shouting *Fools!* Too many are still too willingly choosing to look in the direction to perceive such folly, such ridiculous perception.

I don't know. It's a story that I've been reading and rereading. It's a story that won't leave me. I think it's an important story, a classic in the West, now and, more importantly, hereafter.

For further examination of this nebulous and, I think, still-developing idea of a "Western" short story, I would turn interested readers yet again in the direction of Proulx, that magnificent immigrant New Englander. In a story the editors were unable to include here due to its length, "Tits-up in a Ditch," Proulx performs a great feat when, near the end, the reader's heart collapses from brief hope into devastation and despair, in the soup of economic and emotional desperation, amidst a so-powerful physical landscape. The fact that part of the story takes Western natives and transports them to Iraq near the conclusion of the story bears further witness, I think, to Proulx's outrageous skills and instincts. Something about the West, something vital and partly horrible, has infected her wonderfully. There are fewer more delicious or exhilarating moments in literature than when a reader realizes, a second after the fact, that something awful is happening or is going to happen to a beloved character in whom the reader has invested his or her heart. Call it a sickness or madness, call it a perversion, no matter: it is literature, and not of any one region but of the depth of chasms and canyons and breadth of mountain ranges in the human heart. It's definitely a story worth tracking down, found in the same collection as is "The Sagebrush Kid," *Fine Just the Way It Is*.

Ultimately, my sense in reading the assemblage of stories collected here is that the Western short story is still very much finding its way—which is, I think, as it should be. Only miracles—like the Sagebrush Kid—can be expected to leap fully formed from the soil, ready, in an instant, to meet our every expectation. A Western short story, in its form and essence, seems to be a work in progress, one which, if I were to place my bets, will continue to be sculpted by the extremes of geography and by immigration: by a ceaseless procession of strangers riding into town, even as other strangers—often magnificent strangers—are going rapidly extinct. Future Western short stories will also continue to be shaped by the yet undefinable, and probably always undefinable, thing—a certain largeness of spirit.

The best and strongest of these stories shimmer with that thing, which, though invisible, somehow yet makes itself known powerfully.

BEST OF THE WEST 2009

A GREAT PIECE OF ELEPHANT

Lee K. Abbott

ven five years after he'd tried to kill himself on the BLM
bladed road just outside the gates to his brother's spread in
the Capitan Mountains almost within a stone's throw of the
birthplace of the original Smokey Bear, L. T. couldn't figure
out why. His life, he'd thought, had been dandy. Well, semi-dandy. Maybe
dandy with an asterisk, which infernal punctuation led you to the finest of
fine print where you learned about the two ex-wives and the ribs he'd busted doing deep-sea salvage out of Astoria, Oregon, and the four years playing softball for the Navy during Vietnam and a bankrupt Baskin-Robbins
31 Flavors franchise and the booze—oh, the lakes and oceans and rivers of
booze: Oso Negro and vodka and Gordon's gin and Early Times and Miller
and Coors and Robitussin and Listerine and, Lordy, any grape or grain that
might take one vale and turn it into another. But suicide? "Seemed like a
good idea at the time," he told the first AA meeting he attended on Buckle
Street in east Lubbock, where he now worked building cabinets and playing
guitar and knocking the golf ball around on occasion while generally trying
to keep his head screwed on straight. Sometimes—the blue times, the times
when the modern world seemed to be missing a handful of its most precious
parts, the times when he felt each of his fifty-five years falling away from him
like old skin—he was tempted to quote one long-gone comic on the crucifix-
ion of Christ: "Just one of the parties that got out of hand."

Still, there he'd been one afternoon the week before Christmas, his pickup pulled across the gravel track leading into Smitty's place, not sixty paces from the house itself—hell, not fifty-five from Smitty himself, who was sitting on his porch rocker, smoking—much of the high desert New Mexico hither and yon snow covered, the light bending white and sharp and hard, sunset about a pony keg from noon. The radio was on, heartbreak being served up and survived by those from the country-western end of the howling kind. You had a girlfriend, it was sung. Or you spent too many hours on too many of the wrong streets looking for one. You had bad dreams, ugly as barbed wire, or you had five kinds of honey and sugar. You honored a God who loved you, warts and all, or you were a faithless pussy doomed to burn in the company of peckerwoods and pointy-headed professors and ruined women who didn't shave their goddamned underarms.

Oh, it was a grand time to have arrived—as if by magic, it seemed—whole at a spot from which, left and right for many and many a mile, rose up hills dotted with juniper and piñon. And then he pushed open the truck's door, the truck still another thing he was indebted to Smitty for, it being wages for five months of hammering up a guest cottage out back by the pump house. Such seemed fair: a Ford F-150, used as a dish rag, with a camper top for the truck bed, given in exchange for six whacked fingers and a saw cut the size of a nail file on the forearm and a Mormon's close-cropped hair and a kept promise to avoid Demon Rum, even demons themselves, for a summer that had seemed to begin in late February the year before.

So he was out, he would tell the AA folks. Standing tall—or tall enough for a fellow with a fifth of swill filling his belly and thoughts flying willy-nilly like pests big as boulders—and getting himself square with Mother Earth, gravity just one phenomenon you could count on, not much between A and B but footsteps and English. The night before, he'd been gambling at the Navajo casino up near Ruidoso—keno, mostly, with some blackjack to loosen the eyeballs—his pockets now miraculously stuffed with legal tender in quantities that made him feel like King Midas or Richie Rich, made him feel, in fact, moneyed as Smitty himself, the big-assed big brother who ran cattle and owned oil and gas properties in Chaves and Eddy counties and was currently in the middle of his fourth consecutive term as a state senator from Lincoln County. And now, as L. T. made his way around the back of the truck, some of that money started floating out his pockets, him a generous man showering an otherwise infertile landscape with seeds and sweetness, which is when it occurred to him to say something. Serious gestures demanded serious talk.

"Hey, Smitty," he said, waving at the several of him sitting there.

"You sleep in those clothes, L. T.?"

He considered himself then: jeans a tad tight in the hindmost, cowboy boots even Roy Rogers would envy, a shirt that had all the appeal of sunrise itself. He turned to study his reflection in the truck cap. The fellow staring back had all the savoir faire of a rodeo clown.

"Vacation," L. T. mumbled, a lot of work in the word. "Had me a night."

Smitty muttered something then—"evidently," perhaps—but L. T. found himself doing a jig with time, one moment made many, and he lost the what and where of himself before he engaged the now again to discover his camper cap open above the tailgate, one hand rummaging in the toolbox before him. He was singing, too, "Sweet Betsy from Pike," hardscrabble Pike now missing its only Betsy.

"Mind if I borrow some garden hose?" he said, holding up a utility knife.

A plan, he told his first AA meeting after he got out of rehab at the VA hospital in Big Spring following his discharge from the state facility in New Mexico. A big plan, he said. With lots of contingencies and fallback. A plan to go to war with, say. A plan you needed Latin for, not to mention high-minded mathematics. A plan to put the heat back and to rub the darkness out of America. But Smitty was standing now, a brother the spitting image of the old man—another cold-hearted, mealy-minded so-and-so—and L. T.'s thoughts went once again haywire, sense more non- than not, and later, utility knife held aloft like Excalibur, he was surprised how quickly he had marched from his bumper to the hose coiled next to the garage.

"Now, hold on," Smitty was saying, all but wagging a finger.

"I'm good for it," L. T. said. He yanked from his pocket another fistful of money, wadded it like a snowball. "You just sit tight and I'll be done here in a jiffy."

And soon enough he was, dragging a length of hose toward the truck.

"Where's Margot?" he called over his shoulder. Smitty, believe it or don't, had a high-water wife.

"Roswell," Smitty was saying, not much brotherhood in his tone. "Visiting her sister."

L. T. took another step, a scary portion of the geography bleeding off into a dump at the horizon.

"How's your buddy, the governor?" This was palaver, is all. Talk without any teeth in it. Shooting the breeze with Smitty was like playing canasta with a hide-a-bed.

"Cruel," Smitty said. "An outright communist. Wants to tax his granny's motorized wheelchair."

"I voted for that son-of-a-bitch," L. T. said, somewhat sure he was breaking the law by saying so.

"You knucklehead," Smitty said. "Come Christmas morning, he's putting a hundred dollars in every stocking in the Land of Enchantment."

This was talk so small, L. T. later said, that you needed tweezers and a preacher's patience to deal with it, so he vowed to keep his mouth shut as he rounded the truck and made for the driver's door. He felt wiry and pinched off, a puddle at the sunken center of him, not a citizen worth rooting for. He was thinking about his first ex-wife, Lucy, now living happily ever after in Birmingham, Alabama, her life easily twenty-eight years removed from his own, tight at the corners and choice as freedom. He'd called her last night from the casino—hell, yes, he had a cell phone, managed to pay for it, too—but found, when she came on the line, that he'd little to say, the very idea of them as cockeyed as chickens that drive. Still, he'd said, "Hey," and got much the same in return, something about the long silence thereafter spooky as gunplay. "You're drunk," she said finally, which observation he tried to deny before admitting he was—Lucy had always been expert at working the truth out of him. "I'm going to hang up now," he'd said, a second or two passing before he could blurt the rest of it: "You were good to me, sweetheart."

And then he'd returned to the present moment, which was all about fitting one end of the hose in the exhaust pipe, which, it was turning out, was work as demanding as rocket science. On the porch, Smitty was lighting his pipe, still more evidence that the old man, the original Leonard Tipp Smith himself, had risen out of the grave, and L. T., his blood moving crosswise and grainy, was briefly tempted to run over there, if run he could, and smack his brother into the middle of next week. But all he did, his business with the tailpipe finished at last, was say, "Democrats are sexy," to which Smitty, nose in the air as if sniffing out misrule itself, said, "What?"

"A bumper sticker," he said. "Saw it on a Cadillac over near Hondo on the highway."

Smitty gave him a blank look, his lips straight as a ruler.

"You had to be there, I guess," L. T. said, another sentence he was unspeakably proud to have left as his estate.

So that's where he quit it—Smitty, these weary hours, the whole in and out of getting by: not sad, just fed the heck up—and eased himself toward the driver's door again, downright goofy that his legs worked and that, by all counts, he was going to get to the end of this drama without passing out or puking most of yesterday into his lap. He shoved the other end of the hose through his window, rolled it up, and yanked the door shut behind him. He snatched up his bottle of rye whiskey from the seat beside him and took a pull. Nectar from the last tree in Eden. Sweat at sixteen. The kissing booth at the county fair. Elixir and ambrosia and fresh-squeezed juice at breakfast. Through the passenger window he noticed that Smitty had come down a step on the porch, shading his eyes against the terrible sun.

L. T. saluted him with the bottle and cranked the ignition. He revved the V-6 twice, the engine throaty and smooth. A minute, he figured. Maybe two. No matter, he always told the AA people. He leaned back into the headrest, in the air something sweet and a touch tired.

"Democrats are sexy," he said to himself and closed his eyes, only heaven to look forward to and the supersonic trip to get there.

Coward. That's the word I was thinking when L. T. wobbled from the tailpipe to the door of his truck. And this, too: *Lush.* Plus, I was darned pleased that Daddy was not alive to observe what he would have called behavior "beneath contempt." And here's the last word I thought: *Quitter.* No, I didn't imagine he'd go through with it. He'd never finished anything he'd started. Quit college. Quit his football team in high school. Quit his job at the Mays Lumberyard. Quit *The Music Man* he was in at the community theater. So I figured he'd sit for a minute or two, come to what few senses he had left, and heave himself into the road to clear his head. I watched, took note of high sky, and puffed my pipe, nothing whatsoever between me and my clean conscience. His creature parts—liver and lungs and stomach and kidneys and all the goo that binds them—were in revolt, I reasoned. For decades, they'd been fed poison after poison, and they'd had enough. More than enough. Anyway, when the radio burst on again, loud with the wails and moans of beasts in pain, I went indoors to call Margot.

"Guess who showed up?" I asked.

"Santa Claus," she said, toying with me.

"Guess again," I told her, still watching L. T.'s truck from the kitchen window. "And it's not George Bush either."

"Oh, Smitty, I don't have time for this horseplay. Libby and I are picking out nail polish. They have one here called Sinful. Me, I'm thinking French manicure. Frosted tips, that sort of thing."

I paused a moment here, reflected on the thirty-six years I'd been married to this sassy go-getter.

"L. T.," I said. "He's killing himself."

I could picture her at the other end of the line, lips pursed, brows knit, thinking I was pulling her still-fetching leg.

"Smitty, stop fooling with me."

I told her then: the truck, the hose, the sad-sack brother with the rain cloud between his ears, me bearing stern witness. "'Look at me,' he's saying. 'I matter,' he's saying. It's pathetic, Margot. I'm embarrassed. He's a goddamned crybaby."

"Smitty," she said, steel in her voice. "You call Mac. Now."

I wasn't going to bother him, I said. He was probably busy.

"He's the sheriff, Smitty. Sheriffs are paid for busy."

Outside, L. T. was working the dial to his radio, squawks and squeals descending upon him from outer space.

"Red," I told her. "Like Valentine's Day. Like passion."

"What?"

The fingernails, I told her. Red like rubies and blood and certain sorts of underwear.

"You call Mac, Smitty, or I will."

L. T. was just angry, I said. At me in particular. Because I'd made something of myself. Because of my checkbook. "He's a dreamer, Margot. Lives in a fairy world where bad is not supposed to happen. It's unbecoming, really."

We shared considerable silence at this point, the air between us too icy for my likes.

"Okay," I said. "I'll call Mac. For all the good it'll do, I'll call the Easter Bunny, too. Man in the moon maybe. The New York Yankees. It won't matter, Margot."

But she'd hung up, her point made, and I did as I'd been told: made the call—took Mac away from his lunch, I guessed—and stormed out to the truck to tell L. T. Smith, sapsucker, how offended I was.

"You're better than this," I told him.

He was slumped in his seat, whiskey bottle between his thighs, his mouth open, his head turned toward the window I was speaking to. He needed a haircut and a shave, scarcely any difference between him and what you could find under a bridge.

"I'm ashamed of you, L. T. You were raised better."

One eye had popped open, unfocused like a fish.

"You're a veteran, L. T. Show some self-respect, some backbone."

He rubbed his face then, too vigorously for my taste, and I could see a lot of our mother in him. Another drunk. Another biped for whom lived life was just one defeat after another, each day another day gone whichaway with self-pity and anger. You'd think he'd know better. Or different.

"What is it you want, L. T.? Somebody to hold your hand?"

That eye closed, slowly, and he brought the bottle to his lips, the gulp he thereafter took big and noisy—theater training, I thought.

"I want you to go away," he said.

I told him to roll down his window some so I didn't have to yell, whereupon the window creaked down a few inches and I got an eye-watering whiff of whatever was coming out of his tailpipe—a cross between burned toast and a firecracker.

"I want you to go back to the porch and leave me alone."

In the distant west, you could hear a siren—Mac Brown, Sheriff, to the rescue—and a part of me, the meanest and driest and most pointed part, wanted to do exactly as L. T. had asked, just wheel on my heel, stroll to the porch and settle myself to watch the rest of this story happen to someone else.

"You remember that dirt bike?" L. T. asked.

I looked at him hard, trying to find what we had in common. We looked no more alike than do dogs and deer. He was a stranger who had sat on the other side of the Smith dinner table for eighteen years.

"In the arroyo," he said.

The summer before L. T.'s junior year in high school—this was the Dark Ages, folks—I was working as our father's land man over in Lea County, where Daddy had spotted some promising parcels, and it was my job to pay as little as possible for the gas and oil that lay under them. I'd been married about a year to Margot and we had a place, small but comfortable, on Birch Street. Early one evening, L. T. appeared on our doorstep. "I hitchhiked," he said. His bike had stalled in the badlands and he'd hoped I'd help him haul it back to civilization. In those days, I was driving an International Harvester Scout, maybe big enough for his motorcycle, so we headed out. A Yamaha 250, I think that bike was. A Suzuki, possibly. To L. T., silly as it sounds, it was girlfriend and God and red meat and breaking the finish line first. So we got to the lineman's road about five miles out of town and the thing wouldn't start. Crunch and cough, was all. We tried to load it into the back of the Scout, but it was heavier than we were strong and bigger than I'd expected. I told him to hide it in the weeds and salt cedars next to the arroyo yonder. "C'mon, Smitty," he whined, "what if something happens?" Nothing was going to happen, I told him. "We'll come back tomorrow with a pickup and a ramp." That night—wouldn't you know it?—we got a gully-washer, more rain in five hours than in five months, rain of the sort you find in the Bible. Next day, of course, no "rice burner." No nothing. Not even the handlebar. Come to find out, it had been washed into town, piece by piece, and until

L. T. walked into the station house on Richardson, the cops had been looking for the body of the rider. A day later, L. T. showed up in my driveway with what he'd salvaged—the frame, twisted like a pretzel, and the dinged-up gas tank—his the expression you see on people at considerable odds with good fortune.

"What about it?" I said to him.

He dug at his ear for a moment, more stage business to annoy the dickens out of me.

"That's on you, brother. That motorcycle is on you."

He had a twinkle in his eye. If you didn't know better, you'd think he had the week's winning lottery ticket in his pocket, plus a soiree to attend in Timbuktu.

"Suit yourself, L. T.," I said, the last words I wanted to be remembered by.

You're right, at this point, to wonder why, on the path from truck to porch, I didn't stop to yank the hose out of the exhaust pipe. Here's the answer: Mac was coming—making good time, it sounded like. Second, L. T. hadn't sealed the hose in the exhaust pipe, another half-assed job. More important, I figured this as a lesson learned, albeit the hard way. He'd get arrested, have his stomach pumped, spend a night in the drunk tank, and thus arrive, dried out and humbled, at a new and lasting appreciation for the straight and blessedly narrow. So, at the porch, I eased myself into my rocker and fished my pipe out of my pocket again. L. T. was singing now, some of the lyrics in Martian.

Democrats weren't sexy, I was thinking. They were gasbags and sob sisters and several degrees of stupid. They had brains like junkyards and no inclination to clean up every now and again. And one of those pea-pickers was blocking my road.

I get the call just as I'm finishing up lunch, the day to that point just about as fine as change from a dollar. I tell Olivia, my wife, that I have to go, some commotion over at Smitty's place, and she gives me the eye, no fan at all of James K. Smith, Mr. Grand High Panjandrum himself.

"Says his brother is committing suicide at the front gate," I tell her.

"L. T.?" she says. "He's difficult, all right."

A minute later I've alerted the EMT squad from Alto. The crew chief figures they can be over there in something under half an hour—good time for a countryside where the roads don't go as the crow flies. I get on the radio, tell my dispatcher the situation, and goose the cruiser pretty hard down my road and over the cattle guard.

I'm out to Smitty's place a good four or five times a year: trespassers (usually folks trying to get to Salazar Canyon or the Baca campsite deeper in the foothills), hunters in the same zip code, a dishwasher or a busted air conditioner left by the industrial trash compactor outside old Lincoln town—piddling matters to grouse about, sure, but well-nigh life and death to the senator: more proof, he claims, of the hell we're hurrying toward. He always invites me in for coffee and a pastry he's baked; we chew the fat and, sometime thereafter, I'm on my way, advised to keep an eye out for the felons and illegals and shifty sorts that America's too soft on. L. T., on the other hand, I only see irregularly—at the County Fair, say, Miss That or Miss This on his arm, or at the VFW in Carrizozo, maybe Mr. Brewer's Shell station. He's got an apartment in Capitan and cowboys for the G Bar F spread out toward Nogal. Last time I saw him, he was across the street from the high school, protesting creationism and the free flu shot program. We talked—me in the cruiser, him walking from crosswalk to stop sign—he sent his best to Miss Olivia, and then he turned around and began singing "We Shall Overcome." Which is how you get, I'm guessing, when life deals you only jokers or the Old Maid. Olivia says he's a big dog that can't get enough to eat.

Anyway, lickety-split, I get to Smitty's road, parking some distance behind the truck. Smitty's on the porch, pipe in hand, something like delight in his face. Procedure says to watch your backside in a circumstance like this—an ounce of prevention and all that; so I punch the siren—a burp, more or less—to get L. T.'s attention, if there's any left to get. Nothing. Just the rumble of the truck, oily smoke squirting out of the tail pipe.

"How long's he been in there?" I holler to Smitty.

"Not long enough," he hollers back. "He keeps rolling down the window to spit. Let him stew a while."

I climb out of the cruiser then, a fair idea that I have no idea what I'm in the blasted middle of. Know this about yours truly: instead of a domestic call, give me a pissant with a handgun and a foul attitude any day.

"Hey, L. T.," I call. "You got a minute?"

More of nothing: just yardage and the creepy knowledge that I have to go one place before I can go any other.

"He's going to be mad, Mac. That's what he does, throws a tantrum."

I'm moving toward the truck now, approaching from an angle so I can see L. T.'s door. I don't want to surprise him, have him do something dumb, though at the moment I'm not sure what the devil dumb is. Dumb, I guess, is trying to sort out in five minutes what got mixed up in five million.

"He's got a knife, Mac," Smitty is saying. "Butchered my hose."

The training manual tells you how to enter a house, how to secure your weapon, how to walk the talk. But nowhere in it does it tell you what to say to six feet of asshole wearing a Stetson. Nowhere in it will you find explanations for heartlessness or idiocy.

Here I see the hose in question, still dangling from the exhaust pipe.

"What's the matter with you?" I ask Mr. James Smith, public servant.

"I had my reasons," he announces, nothing in his voice to suggest that those shouldn't be my reasons, too.

I snatch the hose out of the pipe.

"Go in the house, Senator," I say. "Go in or I'll arrest you right now for aiding and abetting or depraved indifference or God knows what. This is a police matter."

He rises from his rocker, gives one leg a shake. "I have to use the facilities anyway, sir," he says. "Have a nice day." He takes his sweet time, and I'm certain that he and I will never again share an apple fritter across his kitchen table.

At L. T.'s window, I see he's twisted—pretty uncomfortably, it looks like—toward the passenger side.

"Leonard?" I tap the window with a knuckle.

I've seen the dead before: car wrecks, old-timers in their beds, ranchers kicked into the next world by a steer or a mule, those swept away by flood, a tourist lit up by a forest fire. But, until this instant, I've not seen a suicide. Pure happenstance, I reckon. L. T. is gray-faced, his lips pasty, something about the tilt of his chin suggesting an inner life made of wire and bark and dust, and I am struck by how skinny he is—all bones and store-bought dry goods.

I open the door, reach over to turn off the ignition. I feel for a pulse on his neck, but my hand is shaking like a schoolboy's. The inside of the truck smells moldy and old—what's in that box in the back of your closet. Plus, he's got what looks like a year of litter in there: empty cigarette packs, five or six inches of newspapers, plastic cups from the 7-Eleven, a sleeve of Little Debbie cupcakes, a couple of hardback books, a pair of pricey-looking ladies' high heels, the Albuquerque Yellow Pages, and one bat of R-36 pink insulation. Worldly goods, St. Peter might say.

"Tell him to stop."

It's L. T. and he's presented me with one veiny eyeball to concentrate on.

"You hear it?" he says.

I'm breathing again, my heart more or less where it belongs. I can't tell if he's talking to me or to a phantom from dreamland.

"Tell him to knock it off, okay?" L. T. says. "I got a doozy of a head-ache."

I ask him "*Who?*," nothing to hear hereabouts but whatever it is the wind whispers.

"Shit, Mac, the guy banging on the sheet metal," he says. "People are sleeping here."

I need a good minute or so to hoist him out of the cab, little about him working as it should. He's a big dog, all right, mostly dead weight, and I'm a guy whose idea of physical fitness is throwing horseshoes on the Fourth of July.

"You gave me a scare, L. T."

He says *sorry*, word with a remarkable number of syllables to it.

"I'm getting married, Mac. I tell you that?"

He didn't, I say. I have him propped up against a boulder across the drive from his vehicle, and I'm praying he doesn't urp on himself or pee his pants.

"Met her last night at the Billy the Kid. She's a pit boss. A real firecracker."

"That's good, L. T. I'm really happy for you."

He gives me a second eye then, as if I'm a species he hasn't seen before. "Her name is Rita, I think."

I crouch in front of him, give him a thorough once-over. Olivia says I've got a good roadside manner, her notion of a joke. She says I should've been a coach or headshrinker because I give a hoot about our kind. That's true. I hate to see us humiliate ourselves. I'm saddened by the bottom we reach and what we're sometimes content to live with. We're a better tribe, I say. And I say that to myself even though I've spent most of my adult life too often in the company of folks holding the ugly end of the stick.

"I'm in trouble, aren't I?" L. T. asks. His is the voice of a boy caught writ-ing naughty words on the schoolhouse wall.

"I'm afraid so," I say. Then I give him the drill: he'll go to the emergency room in Ruidoso so they can flush him out, sober him up; then, because the statutes work as they do, he'll spend time in the holding cell at the county jail while arrangements are made to ship him to the state hospital in Las Vegas for observation, maybe some treatment.

"That's where the old man sent my mother when I was a kid. She liked it, she said. They treated her with LSD."

The mother—Elaine, she was, always wearing hats that were as much states of mind as headgear—passed some years ago. She seemed pieced together by an evil genius, a creature brought to life by pride and rage, elements awfully common here on planet Earth.

"But she was a drunk, too," D. T. is telling me, "so you couldn't believe a word she said."

We're at the end of it, I'm thinking. The same end we always come to. Life's a series of ends, I think. For L. T., today is just another yesterday, as was the day before that and the day before that. For yours truly, as well. For all sentimentalists everywhere.

"I'm cold, Mac."

I hand him my jacket, and advise him he better not spit up on it. "Olivia hates it when I come home smelling like the job."

"Don't worry." His is the smile he must've given Rita last night: white as new snow itself and easily two hundred volts of hi-de-ho.

I figure the ambulance will be here in five minutes, tops. I figure, too, that Smitty is probably at a window, watching and arranging his grievances in rank order, past to present and small to big. Me, I'm gazing down the valley, the light a glaze shiny as new paint, ours a nature more of right than of wrong. Oddly, a song has sprung to mind—"She'll Be Coming 'Round the Mountain"—and I presume to know exactly which mountain she will be coming 'round. She'll be wearing red pajamas when she comes. She'll be driving her six white horses and waving like crazy, tickled all sorts of silly and pink to have that wretched mountain behind her. Oh, we'll be singing *hallelujah* when she comes.

"Democrats are sexy," L. T. says.

I study him, hopeful the talk has turned to a topic I can understand.

"Bumper sticker," he says.

"Go on," I tell him.

He looks left and right, as if he's about to tell me a secret he discovered when he was in short pants.

"Big print," he says, "'Democrats are sexy.'"

Big print, I think. Just what we need more of.

"Little print underneath," he says, "'Whoever heard of a great piece of elephant?'"

I'm wrong: it's the little print we need to attend to.

"That's funny, isn't it, Mac?"

Yes, I say. It really is.

THE PERSISTENCE OF MEMORY

Aimée Baker

O n the day before the locusts came, Lavinia's daughter died alone in the back room. Lavinia had been heating water, hoping a bath would remove the cherry red stain covering Cecilia's cheeks, arms, and chest. Leaving the water to finish warming, Lavinia went to the small bed where she and her husband slept until Cecilia became sick in that sudden way that made Lavinia hold her breath and pray at night for something she could not name. The room that used to smell like wild grass and lavender sachet began to smell like onions and burnt sugar a week into Cecilia's illness. Lavinia did not want to hold her breath, did not want to admit she found something about her daughter distasteful, but she could not help it. She moved quickly, not wasting movement, not a breath inside the airless room. Before Lavinia reached the bed she knew. Cecilia's skin was parched, the color of cemetery stones, her hand loose, hanging from the bed. Lavinia let out the air in her lungs and breathed in the scent of her daughter, thick and cloying, before leaving. She took the pot of water off the fire, sloshing it on the floor all the way through the house to the front door and outside, where she dumped the scalding water on one of the tomato plants.

Lavinia stayed outside with the empty pot by her feet. Annie, her youngest and then only, played in the dirt, her dress tucked up past her knees, her hands sliding across the ground. The air was stiller than Lavinia thought she could stand and hot enough that sweat dried on her skin leaving brackish trails. Lavinia licked her lips; her tongue extended past to the skin below and tasted the salt there. In New York, it hadn't been like this. Her skin had been moist and her hair damp long after she washed. Annie was too young to remember New York. Less than a year since they left, but it felt like more. Cecilia had remembered it, remembered the lush emerald grass covered in droplets of dew in the morning, remembered the smell of lilacs clutching heavily to the air, the sound of bumblebees almost too plump to fly. Cecilia had recalled all of this, and on nights when the air was too hard she would sit with her mother and make up stories that took place back home, back where she remembered. The story of the man and the black dog who never slept. The story of the woman who lived in the lakes. Cecilia had been able to feel it in every strand of herself that Kansas would never be home.

When Henry came back from Jed Marshall's, where he had been helping dig a deeper well, he found his wife, her skin already pinked from the sun, sitting on the one step that led into their house. His youngest daughter was asleep in the thin strip of shade near the building, bits of grass clinging to her hair. Henry did not ask what happened.

"I'll be in the barn," Henry said. Though his shoulders ached and his fingers were cracked with dirt, Henry went to work on a coffin for his daughter. Henry had done this before, once for his father who drank too much and fell asleep in the snow, and once for his older brother who got sick like Cecilia. Inside the barn, the air was stiff and smelled of the manure he forgot to shovel out earlier in the morning. He left the cow and the mule, a weathered animal by the name of Jules, to stand in it, letting it stain their hooves and legs. In the corner, piled neatly, was the pine Henry had hoped to use on the house. He grabbed what he could, the boards that were straighter, had fewer knots, and began working quickly because Lavinia was still outside in the sun. He thought about bringing her inside the house, but he couldn't, not with Cecilia still on the bed where he knew Lavinia left her.

With the boards set between two sawhorses, Henry began to work, letting the saw tear through the wood, sending fragments into the air where they floated in the thin streams of sun that worked their way into the barn. Henry wanted to ask his wife how big it needed to be because he could not remember the size or shape of his daughter. He tried to recall how tall she was when she stood next to him, but she escaped him. He could see her blonde hair and tanned skin. He could see her straight white teeth and upturned nose, but he could not imagine how long her limbs were. Henry worked faster. With the saw in motion, he kept going, cutting first one side and then the other. Each time he pressed the saw through the wood it swayed and twanged under the pressure. With every board, he looked for a place where the grain was clean and he could slide the saw through without the tight pulling on his shoulders. Henry fashioned the pieces in the size of his wife, petite, strong, thin, but as he nailed the sections together they became larger, man-sized. Henry did not take the time to smooth the boards down, or run his hand over the softness of the wood like he did when he made Cecilia's cradle. He left the boards rough after he settled the finished coffin fully on the sawhorses.

Henry walked toward the house, past Annie who was looking at him, her fingers in her mouth, toward Lavinia who still sat on the step, her hands out before her, palms raised to the sky. As he passed into the house, Lavinia stood and turned toward the open door. Her hair was loosening and falling around her shoulders like it used to when he chased her through fields and she ran, laughing. She took a step but Henry put a hand on her shoulder, pushing on the delicate bones beneath her dress.

Henry left her there and moved forward through the house. He could feel Lavinia watching him as his boots scraped against the plank floor, rhythmic and solid, until they slowed when he reached the threshold of their room. He could see Cecilia inside, just the lower half of her body still covered with blankets. Her face was not something he expected to see, believing as he had that Lavinia would have covered her. Henry took another step until he was inside the room looking fully at his daughter. Even from the door, he could see her face was thinner through the cheeks, that there was loose skin around her neck. She did not look peaceful and calm, worn out and thin as she was, so he went to the bed and covered her face without looking too long. Henry wrapped her in a blanket, swaddling her until not an inch of skin was open to the air. He lifted her from the bed and adjusted her in his arms until her head rested against his shoulder. Moving quickly from the room, Henry walked back past Lavinia, who reached out and tugged at a corner of the blanket with her fingers. He kept going until he reached the barn.

Before he placed her inside, Henry knew she was much too small for the casket, but it wasn't until he eased her down that he realized just how wrong he was. Even with the blanket wrapped around her, there was empty room at her feet and head, inches of space surrounding her shoulders. Henry heard the drag of Lavinia's feet against the dirt floor and he shifted his shoulders to block her view.

Lavinia pushed Henry aside so she could look at her daughter. Henry watched Lavinia's face, waiting for a sign that she noticed that Cecilia looked even more wasted laying inside the pine box, but none came. If he had time,

Henry thought, he would try again, this time going slower, smoothing every-thing to perfection, lining the inside with silk and batting the way they did sometimes back east.

Lavinia placed a kiss on Cecilia's forehead and smoothed back her hair, still bleached almost white from the sun. "She's afraid of the dark," Lavinia said.

Henry slid the cover over his daughter until he could no longer see her face. The skin of his palms caught on the rough lumber, adhering his hands to the casket.

"She's afraid of the dark."

"She'll be fine." Henry pulled his hands away and began fastening the cover into place, gently tapping each nail into the boards.

"You don't understand," Lavinia said.

When Lavinia left the barn Henry stayed behind, raising and lowering his tired arm, hammering in the nails needed to keep Cecilia secure.

Early autumn was hot and dry coming off a summer where the heat had pressed down on Lavinia and her girls, making their skirts feel like lead. Snow barely fell the winter before, and Lavinia wondered if this was what Kansas was like, barely any rain and grass so dry and sharp it left cuts in her skin. They buried Cecilia out in that grass just as the day was slipping into evening. Lavinia was not there when Henry dug Cecilia's grave, but she saw the puffs of dust, dried pieces of Kansas rolling through the air with each shovel stroke, and the pine boards of Cecilia's casket gleaming against the prairie.

She kept Annie with her, like Henry asked her to, but Annie didn't want to be there. She rocked on her heels, her plump legs, still thick with baby fat, kept stiff. Annie held a doll, a fabric one with worn brown hair, by its hand. It used to be Cecilia's until she was too sick to protest Annie playing with it. By then Lavinia had been too tired, staying up at night watching Cecilia's breathing, to stop Annie.

As she rocked Annie sang:

The years creep slowly by, Lorena,
The snow is on the grass again,
The sun's low down the sky, Lorena,
The frost gleams where the flow'rs have been.

Lavinia felt Annie's voice, high-pitched and loud, all the way through her body until her heart and lungs vibrated with the song. Cecilia had learned it on the trail after they left Kansas City from a Kentucky-born woman traveling alone with her sick child. They sang it for hours at a time, racing each other to the end so they could begin again. Two days out the woman's baby died and she held onto it like it was still alive, talking to it and trying to nurse it. "He's gone," Lavinia said the morning after the mother had slept with him tucked to her side. "I'll bury him when I can," the woman said and was still holding the bloating body when Lavinia, Henry, and the children separated from the trail to head south toward Cottonwood Falls. Lavinia's children did not notice the boy's death. Instead, Cecilia had sung the song over and over keeping in time with the woman's voice.

"Stop singing, Annie," Lavinia said.

"But the heart throbs on," Annie sang while she rocked, her toes and heels keeping a rhythm that her voice couldn't.

"Annie, please." Lavinia put her head on the table, wrapped her arms around her head.

"The sun can never dip so low."

"What?" Lavinia kept her head down, closed her eyes tighter.

"Adown affection's cloudless sky."

"Outside, Annie, just go outside."

Lavinia did not move until Henry came in, slapping his hat against his pants. He told her it was time and she stood and walked to the field. Lavinia did not bother to take Henry's offered hand or look for Annie where she was standing in the dirt, her lips pressed tight.

That night, Lavinia could not sleep in her own bed again. The straw ticking felt too warm, the sound of the breeze rustling the dry grass too loud. She stayed awake watching the ceiling, sloped and uneven, and imagined stars there. Lavinia saw the skies of home embracing her. When they entered Kansas, Lavinia felt as though she were under a different sky altogether, a darker one that weighed on her chest, pushing her tightly down.

In the dark, Lavinia thought of Cecilia below the ground, a deep layer of loamy dirt over her, and the grass blending with the roll of the land. The roots from the only tree Lavinia had seen in forever wrapping themselves around the too-big casket, pulling it further down into the earth.

"She didn't suffer," Henry said after he lowered Cecilia into the ground and gave a brief prayer.

"How do you know?" Lavinia asked.

"I just do, that's all."

"How do you know?" Lavinia asked again, but this time Henry did not answer.

Lavinia left Henry in the bed and went to the front room where Annie was asleep. She leaned down and touched her hair, but all Lavinia could smell was sugar and onions sticking to the air and even Annie herself. Lavinia lit a candle, hoping to ward off the night and its darkness. Everything she breathed in, even the dried chamomile and peppermint she opened from her stores, no longer smelled right.

On the table were two cups, set out to tea, like they were on the nights when Cecilia couldn't sleep and they drank from the fragile porcelain. Lavinia could not remember taking them down from the single cupboard. She thought maybe she did, after a dinner of cold bread had with the last of the preserves. Lavinia remembered rubbing her fingers over the chipped handle of one, but she didn't know if it was on this night, or the night before Cecilia got sick, or a night months ago when Cecilia first asked if they were ever going home again.

Lavinia left the cups on the table, though she knew they would need to be washed again in the morning before she could put them away. Every morning a skin of dust covered everything in the room, even the people. The day after they first arrived, Lavinia washed her face in water from their well until the bowl she was using was crusted with dirt. She tried covering the walls in newspaper, but it never did keep the dust out. Instead, the papers made the house theirs somehow, and not the Redcliffs', who left one day without warning. "Readable wallpaper," Henry called the paper Lavinia and the girls had attached piece by piece. Sometimes they read the stories aloud to each other after dinner, though after awhile they were the same ones and Lavinia was too tired to invent stories about who the people were.

"I need your help with the crops," Henry said to Lavinia in the morning. Her head was on the table, her hand wrapped around a teacup. "Chickens need to be fed too."

Lavinia rubbed her eyes and then her cheek where her skin was pressed into the shape of the table. Before she could rise Henry was gone with Annie trailing silently after, Cecilia's doll clutched in her hand. There were dirty breakfast dishes, evidence of fried eggs and salted bacon in the small kitchen as Lavinia called it, even though it was only a corner of the main room. She wondered if it was possible she had slept through all of this, the cooking, the gathering of water, the morning talk. She thought that maybe Henry and Annie did it silently as they tried to do when Cecilia was in the back room, because Cecilia cried out in pain when there was too much noise.

Lavinia didn't eat breakfast or clean the plates. Instead, she went to the chicken pen where the two chickens the Marshalls gave them clucked anxiously at her rough handling. She gathered the eggs, only three small ones that fit in her cupped hand. They were still warm and she brought them to her chest, cradling them. She thought about leaving the eggs with the chickens, Dolores and Mabel, as Annie and Cecilia had named them. She wanted to slip the eggs back into the nest boxes Henry built before last winter, easing them under the birds' thick feathers, even though they would never hatch; the rooster died four months before. So Lavinia brought them into the house and left them in a bowl waiting for their shells to be washed later, maybe by Annie who was old enough now.

Inside, Lavinia heard a noise like the rustling of skirts or dry leaves, the creak of her own bed. Brushing her hands against her sides, across her stomach, she went into her bedroom. There was a new quilt on the bed, put on by Henry the night before. This one had stars in blue; the one before was a log cabin made out of leftover swatches of dresses Lavinia wore as a child. The corner was pulled down in a perfect triangle as though waiting for someone to crawl beneath. Again, there was a sigh like someone shifting. Besides the bed, quilt, and a tiny stand with an oil lamp on top, there was nothing in the room.

Henry was in the corn, only the deep blue of his shirt visible among the stalks. Annie was with him, trailing behind, kicking stones with her feet. Jules, the mule, stood at the edge of the field as though Henry thought he might have a use for him. Lavinia followed the blue into the field. Henry was inspecting the corn, planted late that year in the hopes of more rain. He peeled back the husk, revealing the cob, stunted at the end and pale white.

"Not good," Henry said and Lavinia did not answer. They had this conversation before in July when the thin stalks failed to reach Henry's knee.

Lavinia nodded, though the corn was never her primary concern. By the side of the house she had planted a kitchen garden with the girls. Cecilia had helped dig the holes and Annie had placed the seeds, transported from New York wrapped in Lavinia's quilting squares. During the summer, Lavinia had watered the plants carefully with water from the well that she hoped wouldn't go dry, though Jeb Marshall had assured them it would not.

In the corn, only Annie's head was visible, her blonde hair shining in the sun until she turned a corner and was gone. Henry did not seem to notice his daughter slipping quietly through the field. Lavinia walked forward, roused by the way her arms brushed the corn leaves, how her feet pressed against the dirt. The earth was so hard not one of her daughter's footsteps was recorded in it.

Lavinia heard a voice, soft and gentle, keeping time with the rustling of the corn stalks.

A hundred months, 'twas flow'ry May,
When up the hilly slope we climbed,
To watch the dying of the day.

"Annie," Lavinia called, the name catching on her tongue. The song that Cecilia used to sing. She looked back toward Henry. He was still running the cob through his fingers, sensing the hardness of each kernel. Lavinia remembered how Cecilia used to do this with him, wasting countless cobs throughout the summer, too impatient to let the corn grow. Lavinia kept walking, turning corners in the field, following the voice that kept getting lost in the breeze.

And hear . . . church bells chimed.
. . . watch the dying . . . day,
And . . . distant church bells chimed . . ."

Lavinia turned again and found herself at the far edge of the field where the corn stalks seemed impossibly shorter than the rest, more yellow than green. Just past the edge of the field was Martha Marshall, leaning over a silent and still Annie; Martha's heavy frame bent tightly, her hand placed on her back for support.

"Martha," Lavinia said, surprised to find the large woman this far from her home.

Martha leaned back, moving her body in increments until her hips were pushed forward, her stomach out, her hand still on her spine. By her feet was a quilted bag filled, Lavinia knew, with all the medicines Martha had used to nurse her own children, two boys and a girl who were tall and broad-boned.

"Heard Cecilia was sick. Thought you could use my help," Martha said and extended her hand toward Lavinia, waiting for her to take it like a man.

Lavinia slipped her hand into Martha's and squeezed before leaning down to take the bag at her feet. It was heavy and several bottles clanked dully against each other.

"Is Annie falling ill too? She's not said two words to me," Martha said.

"She hasn't felt much like talking lately. Have you walked this entire way, Martha?" Lavinia started walking toward the house, Martha and Annie following behind her.

"Thought I'd get some fresh air before winter sets in again. Never know when it'll come out here."

"In this heat?"

"Used to it by now I should say."

By the time they reached the house, Martha's breathing was heavy again and her steps slow. Beads of sweat collected on her upper lip, sifting through the downy hairs there. Lavinia let Martha into the house, opening the door wide for her.

"Ah, to be in a wood house again," Martha said as she always did the few times she stopped by. "Sit, sit," Martha directed, gesturing toward one of the chairs.

Lavinia sat heavily, letting her body curve forward, her chest sinking toward her knees. Martha bustled through the house and into the back room while Annie followed, sucking on the four fingers of her right hand like she used to do in New York as a baby.

"Lavinia," Martha called from the next room, her voice calm but loud.

"Yes," Lavinia answered, because she heard the question in Martha's voice, the slight lilt at the end.

"I didn't know." Martha left the back room, her bag tucked against her side.

"She's in the field, by the tree. Henry made a cross to mark the spot. I wanted to make it white so I could find her, even from miles away, but we don't have any paint. We never bought any."

"We'll get you some as soon as we can," Martha said and started a fire so she could heat water for tea. She wiped out the dirty teacups, still on the table, with a corner of her dress.

Lavinia was outside, sitting in the dirt with Annie, twisting weeds around her fingers when she heard the hum. Lavinia had left Martha sitting on the front step, fanning herself with her hands, and shucking the few peas Lavinia had found in the garden. Lavinia had been thinking of Cecilia, how she used to race Annie to pull the most weeds, slowing down so Annie's baby fingers had a chance against her own. They played this game in New York where they knelt in their grandfather's potato fields, gesturing with their hands when they came across a fat, hairless caterpillar chewing on the leaves.

The noise was loud and constant in the way it integrated into her thoughts until she wondered if it had been there since she came out of the house, since she first woke up in the morning, since the night before, since the second she reached Kansas when her back and shoulders ached too much for her to notice the sound. "Do you hear that, Annie? Do you hear it?" she whispered to her daughter so quietly that Annie didn't lift her head from her doll. She twirled the doll in circles by its small cloth hands, singing a song Lavinia couldn't hear, the one she knew in her bones and sang as though she knew what part Annie was on.

> I'll not call up their shadowy forms;
> I'll say to them, "Lost years, sleep on!
> Sleep on! nor heed, life's pelting storm."
> I'll say to them, "Lost years, sleep on!"

Lavinia rubbed her hands across her ears, pushing in on the lobes until they stung, but the noise didn't stop. She could still hear it through her fingers and palms, through the muscles and blood that felt like they were vibrating. "Annie, do you hear that?" she asked again, this time louder than she thought, her own voice muffled by her hands. She could not tell if Annie said anything, but Lavinia could tell her daughter heard it by the way she finally lifted her head to the sky, trying to pinpoint where the noise was originating from.

"Martha?" Lavinia turned toward her. Martha had stopped fanning herself and was trying to stand.

Henry approached from the field. He left Jules, tied to the barn wall with a short, thick rope. The noise was louder then so that Lavinia, standing still, felt the throb run through her feet and shoulder bones. By the time Henry reached the garden to stand beside them, there was a gray cloud in the distance like mist.

Annie raised her left hand and pointed in the distance, her right hand fingers placed in her mouth.

"Rain?" Henry asked.

"Could be," Martha said, making her way to stand next to them.

"The noise, though." Lavinia watched the sky darken in miniature increments.

"It seems so long since we heard rain," Martha said.

Lavinia ran her hand through her sweat-dampened hair. "Doesn't look like any rain I know," she said. Back east it could rain for days at a time until the ground squished when she walked on it. Lavinia wanted it to be rain as much as Henry and Martha, but the hum rattled against her eardrums. "Can you feel it in your feet?" she asked.

Henry looked down at the thick boots he wore. The leather was fractured into lines and pressed tight with earth. "No," he said. Martha shook her head and cupped her hand over her eyes, shadowing her face.

There was a sharp whack on Lavinia's cheek and she raised her hand to touch her face. There was nothing there, but just past her nose her skin was raised into an oval. Beside her, Henry smacked his arm, cursing softly, and Annie crouched on the ground, silently swiping her hair with her hands. Martha rubbed her own cheek where a small red welt was also rising. Lavinia wanted to ask what it was but by then the sound had grown until it vibrated the air around her. She could feel the soil move with the noise. She did not want to look at the sky again.

"Shit," Henry said. Lavinia looked at Henry then turned her head toward Annie. "Shit," Henry said again because they both knew Annie wasn't listening, she was the only one with her head tilted up to see what the sky was bringing.

"What is it?" Lavinia asked.

"I'm not sure." Henry kneeled so he could examine the ground, looking for whatever he had slapped from his clothing. Picking up something between his thumb and forefinger he rose and placed it in his palm. There was an insect, its wing bent, its back leg twitching until it caught on Henry's calloused finger pads.

"Locust?"

"Looks to be."

Before Lavinia could ask another question Annie cried out, the first sound beyond singing she had made since Cecilia died. Lavinia felt it too, when first one, and then another locust hit her face. They pelted her arms and shoulders and head. She grabbed for her hair, pulling them from the pieces that had fallen from the neat bun she had managed to secure earlier that day. No one moved from the corner of the garden, but stood watching the locusts fall like hail.

Annie cried out again, her voice thin, crackling at the edges. "Move," Henry said, pushing Lavinia backward and scooping Annie from the ground where she was covering her eyes. Henry ran to the house with Martha following quickly, her body swaying with the effort. Lavinia trailed slowly behind, letting the bugs hit her back, the sting of their impact pulling her down.

Inside, Henry cleared the locusts from Annie's hair and clothing with Martha's help. Annie's fingers were back in her mouth and she was crying hot sharp tears that fell down her fevered face, dripping from the end of her nose. Lavinia looked toward the kitchen and stopped moving, allowing the insects to crawl across her skin, biting at the sweat that covered her body. It was Henry who finally moved to rid the locusts from her, picking them off and stomping on them with his foot. There were so many that a fine layer of oil, crushed from the bodies of the locusts, coated the floor.

While Henry worked, Lavinia watched the table where once again two teacups were set out. She thought she put them away after Martha washed them, shoving them into the back of the cupboard and shutting the door.

Martha crumpled into a chair, shielding her eyes again with her hand as though she would be able to see through the walls all the way to her home. "My family. I need to get home," she said, but Lavinia did not respond. Outside the locusts were hitting the roof and Lavinia could hear Jules braying, loud and deep. Around her fingers, Annie began singing again.

> Thy heart was always true to me:
> A duty stern and pressing, broke
> The tie which linked my soul with thee.
> A duty stern and pressing, broke
> The tie which linked my soul with thee.

Eventually night came, but Lavinia could not tell its darkness from that of the locusts. Their gnawing was louder than Martha and Henry, who seemed to be having a conversation that Lavinia only heard in fits and gasps. Lavinia closed her eyes only when Annie stopped singing, long after Jules's cries had ceased. When she fell asleep, pressed to the floor of the main room, she did not know if they were gone or still out there, but she could not keep wondering.

In the morning, the sun shone through the one small window in the cabin across Lavinia's bed in silvery streaks, falling across her eyes and face until her lids finally opened. She could hear nothing, not even the wind blowing or her own heartbeat through her pillow. She thought this must be what death was like. Moving from her bed, Lavinia shoved off the thin cotton nightdress she wore. She did not remember putting it on, but sensed Henry had removed her dress from the day before, stained from the innards of the locusts he had crushed against her. She found a clean dress with a hole in the seam below her chest that she was supposed to mend weeks ago. Beneath the dress, Lavinia did not wear any extra clothing and a circle of skin shone through.

Lavinia moved slowly through the cabin, her body moving in small breaths. She looked for Martha's bag in the corner of the main room where she had left it the afternoon before, but it was gone. Not stopping for breakfast, Lavinia continued until she was outside. Before she reached the door, she smelled the locusts. The bitter scent of their bodies creeped into her house like the dirt she could never get rid of.

Outside the door, the sun pushed down on the ground. Lavinia could see the land, now flat and yellow without the slim green stalks that marked the cornfields or the rounded green tomato plants. In their stead, the land stretched on forever, uneven yet empty. Lavinia looked into this distance searching for her daughter or Henry but she could not find them. In their yard the chickens were clucking, moving around and gulping down the pieces of locust. When Lavinia walked toward them, the ground crunched under her feet.

The chickens gulping down pieces of insect and the locusts crunching under Lavinia's feet were the only sounds she heard. Not even the wind could make noise against the ragged bits of grass that covered the ground. Just around the corner was Jules, his body laid out straight, his torso already distended. Flies were collecting near the corners of his nostrils and eyes. Not even the rope that held him tied to the barn was there anymore, eaten away by the locusts.

Lavinia thought when this was done and she could move freely again with the press of the sun, she would write a letter to her family telling them how the locusts came and then there was nothing. How in the morning there was a silence to the air, yet the sky was blue again, filled with white clouds that skimmed overhead.

Lavinia moved past the barn where she thought she might have heard the cow shifting inside and went to the tree where Cecilia was buried. Where there weren't bare twigs the leaves were shredded. Lavinia sunk to the ground beside her daughter. The cross, ragged and quickly made only the day before, was polished like glass by the locusts' jaws. Lavinia slipped her fingers over it, feeling how smooth it was compared to anything Henry had ever made. She could see her reflection there, the rise of her cheekbones, the indents under her eyes. In the empty spaces, she looked for Cecilia and her white-blonde hair.

ELK MEDICINE

Susan Streeter Carpenter

he woman came here from Ohio, twelve hundred miles in her brother's truck, her first time driving so far alone. She brought good hiking shoes and warm clothes; it gets chilly in the mountains even in July. She brought field guides to wildlife and plants; she wants to learn the names of all the trees, all the wildflowers and grasses. She hopes to track animals. And she will see to the drilling of the well.

They need the well before they can build on the land they inherited. Lucky people—the woman, her husband, her brother, her sister-in-law—they will in a few years have a summer place, a time-share in the Colorado Front Range, a mountain cabin with a wooden porch, right where she's parked the camping truck, on the edge of the hill looking out over the valley toward mountains. She teaches biology in a high school, the only one of her family with enough time in the summer to be there for the well drilling.

Time! Solitude! She dials her Ohio number, to tell her husband she's arrived safely, but the call won't go through on her cell phone. She walks to an open patch on the hillside, tries again. Still no connection. The nearest public phone is ten miles away. A rancher she doesn't know lives three miles down the road, but why trouble him? There's no emergency, and she's tired of driving.

The next day, Wednesday, the drilling rig arrives, churning dust and gravel along the jeep trail. She waves the rig through the gate and fastens it with the padlock, and when she's hiked back up the hill, the tractor has been settled, jacked and blocked, on a clump of juniper. The crane rears up slowly until it's vertical, tall as the pines on either side. The woman watches from the slope above as the well-driller unpacks the huge drill bit (450 pounds, he will tell her soon, with perfectly round carbide balls embedded in its head), fastens it to a pulley, hefts it as it swings through the air and lodges above a platform between the controls and the drilling rods. Pulling levers and flicking switches, watching dials, the driller guides a rod off the rack, screws it to the bit, and sends it into the ground. Dirt and gravel rise in a cloud, and the woman hears the clang as the carbide hits rock. The dust becomes finer and pinker, forming a mound around the hole under the platform.

He digs thirty feet. Then he puts a steel casing down the hole and mixes cement in a barrel the size of an oil drum. He has large shoulders and long arms, and he moves with his legs bent, a man accustomed to working on slopes, always with one foot higher than the other. He hooks the barrel of wet cement to a cable on a pulley, raises it, catches it with his back as it swings through the air, rolls it around his shoulder, and holds it as cement pours into the hole around the casing. "It'll harden overnight," he says. The woman has come from her seat on a log to touch the fine granite dust with her fingers. He paws at the mound: "See how it changes color here?" Shows her layers: gray, then pinkish tan. His hand is dark with machine grease; his cap, his mustache, his arms are gray with granite dust. "The first sign that we've hit water," he says, "is that the dust stops."

"How sure of water are you?" she asked, over the phone last winter when they arranged the drilling. The contract says he will drill down at least two hundred feet, and if there's not enough water she can have him pull out and try somewhere else. She—the four of them, really, none with much disposable income—will pay fourteen dollars a foot.

"Oh there's water," the well-driller said. "You're just on the other side of that granite ridge, above the old sea bed . . ." He described the line of the ancient ridge, the fissures in the granite through which water crept, deep under forested hills. How deep? That was the question.

"What if there's water at one hundred and fifty feet—do I still pay for the whole two hundred?"

The well-driller chuckled. "I've dug a hundred-some wells around here since 1988, and they're all at least two hundred and fifty feet. Okay, yeah, there was Arno Loughlin, over to South Park. His place is right on top of a real shallow underground lake, but it's not very big. . . ." He had a relaxed Western voice, telling the story of the Loughlin well.

"Every well seems to have a story," the woman tells her husband that evening. She had to drive into town to call from a little booth outside the Thunderbird Inn, which is a bar full of noise.

"I'm proud of you, driving all that way, staying alone so long," her husband says. "You should be proud of me, too. I biked twenty miles today, after work."

"Did you ride all the way up Devil's Backbone?"

"I had to walk about half of it. By the end of the summer I'll be riding the whole way. But I'm fifty."

"Fifty-one," she says. "Two years ahead of me."

"Oh yes. I forgot." They agree she'll call again when the drill has hit water, or reached three hundred and fifty feet ($4,900)—or on the weekend, whichever comes first. They need to be careful with money. "We can't go much over five thousand on this well," her husband says.

Back at her campsite, she looks out at the meadow below, sees it as ocean—around the edge mammoths and giant sloths move among ur-ferns, palms, sequoias, insects in the warm air—the land was tropical then, millions of years ago. Now it's dry: pines and aspens grip the gravelly hillsides, interspersed with leathery plants—sage, yucca, cactus, mountain mahogany.

On the second day the dust stops at 187 feet. The woman covers her ears against the relentless hammering and sees damp granules spewing out of the hole. *Water!* "Not much!" the well-driller shouts over the noise. He comes close to explain. "There're quite a few fractures—we just hit one, hear it? The spaces change." He thumps his knuckles against his palm in time with the hammering of the drill.

No point in pulling out now. They'll go on drilling. All afternoon she watches, rapt, as the well-driller guides each new twenty-foot rod (he calls them "sticks") off the rack and swings it into position. He has a bucket of thick silver grease and a sort of wand, and while he guides each stick to screw it into the one already in the ground, he swabs the screw threads with grease, first below, then above. Then he throws a wedge over the stick in the ground to hold it while the descending stick screws in. Every move is deft, practiced, economical. He works the groaning rig as though it were an extension of his body—as it is, the woman sees. "Do you get bored doing this?" she asks him.

"Very," he says.

He comes to her camping truck at the end of the afternoon, knocking on the little rattly door, bringing a paper for her to sign to approve his drilling past two hundred feet. She offers coffee and brings the cups outside.

"Look, elk." He points with a coffee cup to the far valley, where dark specks move slowly against the pale green. "They'll all be mamas and babies," he says.

She retrieves binoculars from the truck and looks through the lenses at big elk, little elk, walking across the distant field, stopping to graze, walking again. "Do you see a lot of elk?" She hands him the binoculars.

"I hunt 'em," he says, peering into the valley. "With bow and arrow. Every September."

"Oh." She flinches without meaning to.

"My wife's gotten used to letting me go," he says. "I need it more and more. I can feel right now the urge—doesn't matter if I get the elk, I just need to be out there following 'em through the woods."

After he leaves she's restless, walking the empty land, down the back of the hill through an aspen grove, across a meadow. The sun is behind the hills now; in the clear gray light the flowers leap out, thick, fleshy blossoms, like gentians or paintbrush, but larger, and gray-white, some of them. Others are purple. They fill the meadow like soft cloud. She picks one and sniffs it, chews a thick moist petal. It's vaguely sweet.

You're being hokey, she tells herself, because she is thinking of the well-driller, stalking elk with his bow drawn and his arrow cocked. The hair on his tan muscular forearms glints gold. She's been watching him thrust stiff rods into the earth for two days—*what a macho cliché,* she thinks. There is a welter of thoughts she cannot yet think; she feels them pressing forward in a mass. *I want water to come into the well.* That much is true.

She has walked round the hill; now she's crossing an open slope, and suddenly there are the elk, in the meadow just below her—three of them, no, five, then fifteen, all cows; she creeps closer, down the hill and behind a tree, watching, creeps further. They've gathered in the hollow where wild oats grow dark. The babies bobble along the other slope—four, six, eight calves

herded by three of the largest cows. When she reaches the jeep trail she can
see the herd—fifty or sixty elk—scattered across the meadow, dark heads
dipping to graze, then rising again, rumps pale. The cows and calves call to
each other with mewing peeping sounds. A young cow is looking at her.

The woman looks back. The elk steps forward, as if she were curious.
Her ears sprout from the dark triangle of her face like propeller vanes. The
woman takes three steps and stops. The cow-elk takes three steps, stops, as if
to say, *Let's see you walk again.* The woman steps away from the road. The elk
steps in the meadow above. The woman hears the elk breathing, so she takes
a deep, noisy breath herself. They have that sound in common. Then one
of the larger cows barks—a single shrill yap—and the young elk turns, trots
back to the herd.

The woman walks back to the road and climbs to her little trailer.

"The well-driller's a friendly guy," she writes to her sister-in-law the next
morning. She has promised long, descriptive letters. "I like to watch him
work. He wears filthy jeans with a circle on the pocket from his chewing
tobacco tin, soft muddy hiking boots, a sleeveless T-shirt, a greasy ball cap,
a two- or three-day beard—but oh! Let me tell about my encounter with the
elk-woman . . ." She drives into town to mail the letter, buys five more gallons of water and a six-pack of Diet Coke, and when she returns she hears the
drilling rig at full throttle, hammering rock.

When the well-driller sees her he holds up three fingers. "What?" she
walks down to where he stands. The mound under the platform seems damp.
He walks backward uphill, beckoning with big waves, taking yellow foam
plugs out of his ears. "Three fractures, two of them wet," he says. "I measured when I got here; you got about an eighth of a gallon a minute."

"That's not enough, is it?"

"Ideally you'd want at least a gallon a minute—we're about 248 feet now;
and fractures close together like that are a good sign. That third fracture
was strange—an empty space—the drill stopped completely for about ten
seconds."

"You mean it could start gushing water any minute?"

He shrugs. "I dunno about gushing, but . . . well, yeah, it could."

He returns to drilling. She picks out a ponderosa pine that must be thirty
feet tall, multiplies it by nine and mentally sends it down 270 feet, a long shaft
through the rocks that form this hill, through the rock that lies under the
base, through the clay below the meadow, deeper yet.

The well-driller puts a round white chip into her hand: smooth, cold.
Quartz? "Ice!" he shouts. "The changing temperature down there does this!"

And he explains into her ear about the heat under the drill bit, the long climb up the shaft that freezes moisture.

"How much water?" she calls into his ear, standing on tiptoe breathing on his neck, dusted gray over the tan. He shakes his head, not much.

The thunderstorm hits with force late in the afternoon, ragged streams of rain and then hail bouncing on the slope, pummeling the rig, soaking through her jean jacket. She isn't cold, and the drill bit is 289 feet down. At the end of this stick, 300 feet, he will ask her for another decision: keep going or not?

Then: flash. The hillside cracks and rumbles, and the well-driller turns off the rig. "I'm going to wait in the truck," he says.

"I don't like lightning," he explains as she clambers into the cab of his red pickup. "It got me once. I was closing a gate, holding on to a wire fence, and the lightning hit somewhere down the line, traveled . . ." he shudders.

"What did it feel like?"

"Awful. I was burned, that's all, but lightning spooks me." He pulls the Copenhagen can from his back pocket, opens it, sticks a shred of tobacco into the side of his mouth—the movements as practiced and thoughtless as his working of the rig; it's the first time she's seen anyone do that. The radio plays country and western—smoky bar, golden liquor, a dangerous woman—and the windows of the truck fog in the rain.

The well-driller shoulders himself into a sweatshirt, then pulls a bottle of Mountain Dew from behind the seat, uncaps it. "Want some?" His hand points the twenty-ounce bottle to her left breast.

"No thanks." The woman shakes her head. He takes the bottle back to his lips, sips once, caps the bottle, twists toward her and returns the bottle to its space behind her. Rain hammers the metal and glass around them. Their four thighs, encased in denim, streaked with granite dust and damp with rain, steam on the seat. The woman rakes her wet hair with one hand, then puts both hands in her pockets. The man rests his hands on the steering wheel, drumming with only his thumbs.

The woman sends her mind down to the dry rock under the hill. "I want there to be water," she says.

"So do I," says the well-driller.

The storm passes and he digs eleven more feet, the well spurting rock dust in vigorous clouds. "Maybe you're up to a quarter of a gallon a minute," he tells her in the ringing silence after he's shut off the rig for the day. "We'll test it on Monday."

She drives ahead of the well-driller's red pickup out through the gate and into town, where she parks next to the Thunderbird Inn. He waves as he drives past, heading home, where he has a wife and children. The woman misses her husband, who does not answer the phone. Maybe he's out on his bike, she thinks, hunched over handlebars in a landscape humid and green as a jungle, his yellow biking shirt soaked with sweat.

Inside the Thunderbird Inn she orders a dark draft and drinks at the bar, sitting on a stool watching young people who dress like cowboys and feel comfortable that way. They insult each other and hoot. She thinks of her students in Centerburg. She tries to show them intricate, tender protozoans and they guffaw, or tell her the little buggers are creepy. They would like the Thunderbird Inn.

At the end of the beer she phones again. "Honey?"

"Hey there!" Her husband is cheerful. "Twenty-five miles today; and all but the last fifteen feet of Devil's Backbone. I'm beat." They talk about their daughter, who has landed a job in Japan, teaching English.

"Maybe we can visit her there."

"Maybe we can win the lottery," he says. "We're still paying for college, remember. And now the well."

She tells him about the three-hundred-foot shaft, slowly filling with water over the weekend.

Saturday the sun comes out and stays. In shorts and a tank top she walks through the damp morning grasses, soaking her shoes and socks, identifying sage, yucca, common buffalo grass. She carries a bottle of water and her field guides in a backpack. The white, gray, and purple meadow flowers turn out to be locoweed: cattle eat them and get a little wild. She nibbles again the bland moist petals. No one is here, not even on the neighboring land. She wriggles under the barbwire fence and stretches, then takes off her shirt. Anyone looking into the valley, she thinks, would see a graying woman with sagging breasts and doughy legs—but then she stops thinking about how she must look, because she feels the sun's heat pouring into her through the thin air, and her body knits together, deep inside itself, and relaxes as she walks. She pees in the woods with great pleasure, stuffing the damp Kleenex into the pocket of her shorts. Then she takes off the shorts and walks on. Her whole body wants to be in the warm air, and from her trail, along a hillside among aspens, she can see far enough to dress quickly if a human appears. It is an elk trail; she sees their tracks in the drying mud. They've been nibbling aspen bark, leaving fragrance as well as torn branches and trunks.

A horse and rider appear on the far side of the meadow—too far away to tell whether the rider is male or female, child or adult. The woman puts her clothes on and claws at her hair. She doesn't want to see anyone, so she turns back into the woods, finds a seat on a boulder streaked with yellow and black lichens, drinks some water.

"I want there to be water." "So do I." The exchange seemed to be about the two of them and the well at the same time. *No it didn't,* she tells herself.

He looms close behind her, suddenly; she almost turns to look, but no, it's fantasy of course, his approach, his long arms around her. She would turn. His lips would open to hers; he would stroke her cheek with his thumb. She stops him, tells him no, he does not know her at all, could not really want her, as she does not really want him. She knows what real desire is, and it's not this simple awareness of how soft her T-shirt is, of how his big hand might feel covering her knee.

She gets home quickly, focusing only on her own breathing and the rhythm of her shoes on the earth, and at the door of the camper truck she is grateful to be exhausted and hungry. The afternoon sun is too strong to stay outdoors under, so she eats a sandwich at her little fold-down table and reads a book of American Indian stories, reads about the exploits of Coyote and Glooscap, about the white buffalo, about Uncigela, the monster of the northern plains.

There is a bit about a young man wooing a woman with his flute. The story connects the flute with an elk call. "The elk, wise and swift, is the one who owns the love charm," she reads. "If a man possesses elk medicine, the girl he likes can't help sleeping with him. He will also be a lucky hunter."

Why does she like to read folktales with animals? Her husband has asked her. He reads *The Economist* and Patrick O'Bryan's adventure novels. She can tell him why she loves Annie Dillard or Emily Dickinson, not why she enjoys these stories of people strange to her. Not why these people, who turn into crows and follow white buffalo, do not seem strange to her.

The guidebooks teach her to differentiate between chipmunks and several types of ground squirrels. She learns that male elk "bugle" in the fall, but in July she will hear mostly the piercing peeps and barks of the cow- and calf-elk. She studies crow, magpie, Steller's jay, and the two kinds of woodpeckers. She goes out again at sunset, when the mountain peaks turn rosy with reflected light. The tracks gouged by the drilling rig form dark shadows on the hillside.

The next morning she remembers only a vague image from her dream—a man entering a cool underground room full of baskets—and a sense of intimacy with shapes and half-notions. A lover against her—no one specific; she feels cloth and body, holding and being held, and not knowing who is part of the intimacy. She has a second day of complete solitude ahead.

She remembers Jimmy, without knowing why—he was not the man in her dream. He was a young man in Philadelphia, when she was a young woman. She remembers thinking, as they sat together on the marble steps of the art museum, *Why can't we just have a little sex the way we might have a little ice cream?*

It didn't work: that was the lesson she learned from Jimmy. The sex was complicated by his water bed, and by the lies they told each other—she borrowed Tufts, her brother's college, that night, said she lived in Boston, raised tropical fish, created a marvelous magic version of herself, knowing she was leaving the next day and would never see him again.

She woke at four in the morning to hear him weeping, drunk on vodka, in the grimy flat that smelled of Vietnamese spices and dirty socks—wretched, he told her, because she wouldn't stay. Two months later he found her. She was in Boston, after all, on her first teaching job, with no time to spare for a stranger, which was who he had become to her. There was an ugly scene before he finally left.

It is Sunday. She is in the mountains alone, a happy mature woman, wise from Jimmy-type experiences and years of marriage.

The rig sits, an alien factory among the trees, and the woman walks down the jeep trail to the neighbor's cow pond. No one is around, so she goes in naked, and after the first shock of cold the weeds stroke her breasts and belly, twine between her legs, and she loses all anxiety about water snakes and mud puppies, soaks her head thoroughly and paddles, exhilarated.

Afterward she climbs the hill and spends the rest of the afternoon on the hillside identifying wild flowers, wearing thongs to protect herself from gravel and cactus spines. The air is quiet; she breathes with the faint wind.

The idea comes to her that the earth *wants* them to let flow, that there must be a ritual for a man and a woman to enact that would bring them into harmony with the earth. They would not be their daily selves, of course; they would be . . . oh, earth and steel, male and female principle. And the water would come into the well.

"Why didn't you ask about using a douser?" her sister-in-law says over the phone Sunday evening. The Thunderbird Inn is closed, so the woman eats an ice cream bar from the gas station across the street.

"I did, too late: after he started to drill. They call them water witches around here. Our driller knows a guy named Joe Blowers, who works at the post office in town. Joe charges 150 dollars to walk around the hillside with a bent wire hanger and says he doesn't know how it works, or whether it's better than common sense with a little geology."

"I wish you'd asked earlier," her sister-in-law says. "Sounds to me like a lot of drilling for a puny well."

"Too late now," the woman says. "We have to go down to five hundred feet. Seven thousand dollars. If you folks can pay half, we can pay half."

"Look, I'll talk it over with your brother, okay?" her sister-in-law says. "I can think of a bunch of ways I'd rather use thirty-five hundred dollars."

"We can't just leave the well half-dug," the woman says.

"Hi," says the well-driller, as the woman comes over the hill the next morning. "I'm the bad news guy." He's measured the accumulated water. "Less than a quarter of a gallon, still," he says. "So what do you think: pull out or go on? With a flow this small, if you have a lot of storage, you'll still be able to use the well. You'll have to be careful with water, though."

The woman sighs. "We can't afford to start over," she says. "Keep going." She watches him screw down the thirteenth stick and goes back to her camp. Then she washes, using a basin to get herself thoroughly clean, and drives the truck all the way to Canyon City, where she eats a club sandwich for lunch at a place called Mae's Diner, and visits the public library. She finds a regional geology book and a novel she'd started once and never finished, *Always Coming Home*, and reads: "Serpentine rock is always sensitive. It's from both the water and the fire, it moved and flowed through other rocks to come to the air, and it's always on the point of breaking up, coming apart, turning into dirt. Serpentine listens, and speaks."

In *Front Range Geology* she reads about the granite under her feet, the feldspar conglomerate, the quartz. There is a section on ancient volcanoes. The woman gets a library card and takes both books with her. There's a note under a rock near her campsite: "Stopped @ 400," it says. "Fractures @ 340 and 364."

Solitude takes practice, she tells herself, walking the jeep trail. The locoweed blossoms float like smoke close to the ground. Through the thin rubber soles of her sneakers she feels the vast bones of these hills. Volcanoes formed this granite ridge: the lava erupted and flowed, cooled and cracked, heaved and compressed. The well-driller thrust a four-hundred-foot steel needle into these rocks which withhold their water. She imagines them gasping, thinks: if the rocks would only exhale. . . .

Into the pine grove, over the gate to the narrow valley. The neighbor's cows wheel away in a mass as the woman walks by, thunder up the slope and turn to watch her; she pulls a stem of wild oat and chews the sweet juicy part, walks to the pond and watches its surface dimple and ring with small insects, an occasional fish.

A conviction grows inside her, having to do with the well, its reluctant little seeps of water, its potential for more. She turns and walks back the way she came. A mule deer stands where the trail enters the pine woods—a female with ears as long as her head and khaki-brown fur corrugated over the ribs. Probably she has a fawn nearby. The woman's eyes meet the deer-woman's large brown ones. She takes three slow, silent steps, and the deer turns and walks away stick-legged into the trees.

The sky shows stars as the woman climbs the hill, watching the pale gravel, avoiding the clumps of juniper, pocketing a perfect pinecone. Inside her, the conviction solidifies. A black squirrel crosses the road in a soft, rippling scamper.

She can feel the sore, dry inside of the drilled hole, can feel the energy blocked, dammed . . . when a man and a woman touch moist parts of each other's bodies, then the circuit will be completed; the water will come.

Not exactly lust. Certainly not romance.

We are not ancient people, she tells herself, and the earth has already been penetrated—violated. She thinks of the drilling rig, more than a ton of machinery creeping over the land, scarring just the very surface; underneath, the earth is indifferent.

You're between menstrual cycles, which are winding down, the woman tells herself. You're healthy and rested. You've been watching for days as a man drives steel rods into the ground. Your husband is twelve hundred miles away. And your daughter just got a job in a foreign land.

Four hundred feet, at fourteen dollars a foot: $5,600. She climbs the hill in the dark, following the trail the rig has made. The moon is lopsided, pale and milky, reflecting enough light to show the hillside. The woman sits on a granite outcrop; its nubbly surface pushes cold and hard through her jeans, against her flesh.

She pictures the well-driller's stubbly receding chin; when he takes off his cap he wipes sweat from a very bald head. She thinks of his powerful round brown shoulders. The conviction sits solid within her, against all reason.

A kiss, she thinks the next morning, might be enough moisture. Maybe we don't have to take off our clothes on the gravelly hillside. She washes with water heated on the propane stove. Her ruddy-tan face in the truck's little mirror surprises her; her short hairs curl sun-bleached white on her forehead, dark at the nape of her neck, her skin is loose under her chin, her eyes large and dark. She lotions her arms, her irrepressible belly, her bruised legs, her feet cross-hatched with calluses.

She imagines herself saying, "Would it be all right if I kissed you? I've had this odd thought . . ." He will probably be repelled by this crazy female, older by at least a decade.

Up on the hill he is measuring the water that accumulated overnight: 130 gallons in about fifteen hours, small fractions of a gallon a minute. "I'm worried about the chains," he tells her, "holding four hundred feet of sticks, keeping that bit an inch from the rock."

"How much farther can you go?"

"I dug a thousand feet once."

"Stop at five hundred," she says.

The woman walks to the edge of the hill and looks out. She can see the Sentinel Rock. She can see the silver roof of her own camper truck. With binoculars she can see A-frames on the Ponderosa Estates, five miles away by car, closer by crow flight. Even now, even here, traffic infects the air, thicker and darker near the horizon. At night electric lights interfere with the stars.

You do not know this man, the woman tells herself. She forces herself to imagine him in the Thunderbird Inn with his favorite music twanging and thumping out of the jukebox, wiping the foam of his third mug of beer from his mustache, telling someone, the bartender, maybe, the story of her well. Or going to church, perhaps, mixing up sex with the devil.

She has to test herself like this, to argue hard against what she knows. A crow flies to the ground in front of her. She tosses out a piece of cracker and it hops away. Then it turns, stretches its sleek black head and grabs the cracker. If I don't act, she thinks, I will have spent thousands on a trickle of water, when I could have had a flow.

She finds a boulder, climbs it, looks at the mountain, thinks how much she loves this land—granite, earth, pine and aspen, sage and locoweed.

The rig sings its jackhammer song, and she goes to read the markers on the crane. There is a fracture at 464, damp gravel at 470. At 475 the well-driller turns off the rig. "Time to call for help," he says, walks to his truck, digs out the industrial-sized mobile phone. This afternoon he and his partner will finish the job: remove the sticks, line the well with plastic tubing, cap it off, move the rig out.

The woman holds her elbows with her hands. She feels her body as a charged, humming tube. Power in her hips and breasts.

He's finished his phone call, is tooling around the hill, moving a dead log with his simian arms. "We'll bring the rig up this way," he turns with his arm wide, showing the path for the rig as though he were flinging seed. "You might lose that tree," he points to a small spruce.

She walks to the thigh-high seedling, touches the aqua needles. "We could replant it, I suppose." Then she turns to him. "Well, the last twenty-five feet?"

"Right," he says, with his "bad news guy" expression. He's been giving up hope, she realizes.

"Well," she says, again, and holds out her arms.

He hugs her back. His shoulders are big and warm.

"I had this thought," she says, into his neck, "that if I gave you a kiss it would bring luck to the well."

He smiles and kisses her quickly with small, dry lips.

"Don't get me wrong," she says, as they walk back to the rig.

"This has been as trying for me as it has been for you," he says.

And that's that. He returns to the rig; she stands on the hillside. A chaste encounter, the kind she'd have with the principal of her school, maybe.

The well-driller unhooks things and turns knobs, moving the final stick into position. The woman sits on the log, her inner machinery humming quietly. Please, she thinks to the well, imagining the underground stream, imagining the fractures parting, oh, a quarter of a centimeter to let water through. Please.

The rig sings and clatters as the well-driller swabs the threads inside the descending stick, outside the stick in the hole, brings the two together, wedges the lower one, sets the upper one turning, turning. Then he disengages the gears. Looks up at the woman, walks toward her, beckons her further up the hill. "It could go two ways," he says. "First . . ." The space between them shimmers. She's having trouble hearing the first way the well could go; his words shred in the air. He looks at the rig poised, ready to drill. "And then . . ." he says.

Then he reaches, puts his hand on her left breast.

They come together. His hands are on her buttocks, pulling her in, his hands are between her legs, stroking through her jeans, his hands return to her breasts, to her buttocks. They kiss: she tastes his tangy saliva.

"I'm sorry," he says, and steps back.

"It's the well," she says. "I think it wants us to . . . I mean, it just seems that if we let loose, then the ground would let loose too."

He reaches again, long-stroking her back so her breasts flatten against his chest. She kisses the warm skin inside the neck of his T-shirt, along his tan shoulder. He holds her between her legs. His hand must feel her pulsating. She imagines her cervix softening, forming a closed-lip smile.

"We shouldn't be doing this," he says.

"No," she says, "we shouldn't." And she stands back and grips his hand. "I'm glad you wanted to."

"Yes," he says, pulling the word up by its roots.

She knows that if she turns toward him, takes one step back into him, they will fall to earth, reach under each other's clothes. He will come straight into her, quick and hard. And then what?

She holds his hand and lets the knowing and the not-knowing, the wanting and the not-wanting, rush through her. She shakes, and closes her eyes; she thinks she might cry.

"Let me drill now," he says, and she lets go. She peels her hand away from his and feels a sickening jolt—up from the earth through her legs, along the flaming path between her thighs, through all her organs, her diaphragm, her breasts, her mouth, the top of her head. "Go. Drill," she says, weeping, and drops down next to a juniper bush. Hears the hammering, 476 feet below her, 479 feet below her. Waits for the man to come cover her with his body where she lies. Waits for her body to calm down. Near her face, pushing up through the mat of loose dirt and pine needles are mushrooms, two—three— five of them, large as doorknobs, fat, red topped.

Russula emetica, she learns later, when she finds them in her guidebook. Commonly known as "The Sickener."

There is one more fracture, a tiny seep of water. She walks to the mound of evidence, touches the damp grit. The well-driller keeps his eyes on the chains, which shake from holding the drill just off the bottom enough to keep turning, hammering. At five hundred feet he begins to collect his tools.

"I'll help, after I get my gloves," she says, and when she returns with work gloves the well gushes water.

"I'm flushing it out," he points to his tank full of water with the hose firmly connected to the rig, and turns away.

"Of course. I thought for a minute . . ." She's speaking to herself. The window has been closed. He's dealing with it his way, she thinks. Who knows what that is? The center of her body still throbs.

What if, when he said, "We shouldn't," she responded, "Oh yes we *should*!"

Now she can meet him with her husband, his wife—in the grocery store or the post office, face each other clean and straight-on. She imagines introducing her daughter some day. "This is the man who drilled the well." "How do you do?" All above-board and proper.

If I were to touch him now, she thinks (he has turned the engines off and is standing on the hillside)—just now, this is it—water would flow into the well. A gallon a minute. Two gallons.

She stays where she is, lets the moment pass.

VELOCITY OF MASS

Daniel Chacón

Father Flood rushed through life so fast that Sunday Mass lasted forty minutes, and the daily Mass—which usually took about thirty minutes—rushed by in less than fifteen. He was the oldest priest at Our Lady of Sorrow, and he had been giving Mass for so long and knew it so well that when the laic deacon held open the big, red Holy book during the Eucharist, Flood didn't read from it at all. He had it all memorized, in Spanish, English, French, and Latin. He said it so automatically that his mind wandered to other things and his voice resonated throughout the nave, mumbling words so fast that nobody could keep up. The sound of his voice was heavy and thick, like a cello in a wooden room, like the thud of clay falling on hardened dirt. It resonated and vibrated in the dome of the ceiling, which reached high up and was lined with slats of stained glass. On the outside side of the glass, pigeons nested.

Morning and afternoon sun coming from the windows in the dome was the only light, but when clouds passed and the sanctuary grew dim, Father Flood did not slow down. He didn't need light for speed.

Some parishioners preferred Father Flood over the young priests. They took so long saying each word of the prayers, like a wooden waterwheel, as if they meant to slowly water their garden. They said their words as if they meant them, and that caused the parishioners to think of life. People didn't have to think standing among the flowing sound of the old man's words, they could just submit to the speed of his voice and let their worries run loose from their minds, like children rushing from the house to play in a field. When the Mass was over, they rushed from the house of God into the streets of El Paso, feeling a sense of freedom and purpose they didn't have without his Mass. Father Flood became popular with busy, important people, who, upon entering the nave, would turn around and leave if it wasn't Father Flood presiding.

At first, the young priests ignored the fast Mass of Father Flood, but then something happened that increased their concern.

He began to mumble Mass in other languages, sometimes in Spanish, the language of the parish, but other times in English or French or Latin, and sometimes all four tongues in the same prayer. The young priests got together and decided that there was nothing they could do, that Father Flood was already in his eighties or his nineties or maybe he was over a hundred, nobody knew for sure, but they knew that the most merciful thing to do was nothing. He had no desire to retire, and quite frankly, he couldn't give Mass much longer. He could barely walk. He hadn't ascended the spiral stairs to the bell tower in many years or walked around the neighborhood, which he used to love to do. He could barely see, needing glasses even to discern light coming through the open doors of the church.

They decided to allow him to conduct morning Mass but only morning Mass. He would no longer do Holy Days of Obligation. He would no longer listen to confessions.

But then it got worse.

He got confused about the time of day, and he showed up on the altar one evening in his Mass clothes. It was a Sunday, the busiest, most important service of the church, the bread and butter for the bills. Two young priests were giving the Mass, the youngest reading the gospel, slowly pronouncing Mark 4:22. Father Flood didn't notice. He raised his arms to heaven and began a second Mass. The young priest—so engrossed in the energy of his reading—didn't notice the old man until his voice started to echo his own, and then overtake it.

When he was a middle-aged priest, new to the city, El Paso, new to the life on the U.S.-Mexico border, he used to like to walk around downtown, which were mostly brownstone buildings with ground-level clothes stores and discount shops. All day and night people walked by on the bridges into Juarez— buses passed, taxis wove in and out of traffic. He liked to talk to people, although at first he had to get used to their Spanish, different from his own. He began to like the city, and liked to think of it as a city in Latin America, because everyone spoke Spanish. He liked to browse the art section of the bookstores, looking at the great paintings, at statues and frescoes, at art photography. He liked to sit on park benches or talk to the girl who sold flowers from a booth in a small plaza, and although he never learned her name, over the years he watched her become a young woman. Then one day, when she was in her mid-twenties, the girl was gone, gone was the smell of wet roses, and the booth stood empty for weeks, until it was removed.

After twenty years in El Paso, he could think of no other place as home, and the times he had to travel abroad he was eager to get back to the city he loved to walk. When he became a very old man, and his Masses started to go so fast, he was unable to walk as much. As he grew older still, he didn't enjoy his meals, and when the old woman who worked for the church came to his room with a steaming bowl of hominy and intestines, he would tell her he wasn't hungry. The young priests didn't visit him in his room, because he talked about the past, and he got chronological time confused. He would be telling of when he was a young priest in Rome, giving Mass in Latin, and mid-sentence, his story would take place years later, when he was in Central America and the military came with trucks and guns, how they collected young people they thought were a threat, including a few good nuns and some young priests like him, and he had to hide underneath the church, right under the skirt of the Virgin, a secret place under the altar.

The young priests ignored his senility. He would die soon, and they waited. And waited. And waited for a very long time. More years passed, and the young priests got old. They went on to other congregations, got promoted within the church, quit the cloth for romantic love or doubt or scandal or all three, but Father Flood remained. He gave thousands and thousands of Masses at such high speed that the church became popular with busy people from other neighborhoods. The older he got, the shorter the Masses became. You couldn't keep up even if you were following along in the missal. After a while, morning Mass lasted ten minutes. His following became even bigger, because people who would otherwise not waste their time going to Mass *every* day could certainly spend ten minutes in a Mass so fast that it was like a shot of whiskey.

This is when it happened.

Everyone would talk about it for years. The Vatican would keep an extensive file on it, including eyewitness accounts and expert opinions, and maybe one day they would decide to make it an official miracle. It started one uneventful Wednesday morning when people knew Father Flood would be giving Mass. The aisles were full of businesspeople and some were even standing by the doors. But six o'clock came by, and Father Flood had not come out. The laic deacon, an old man who assisted the Father in giving the Mass, was named Daniel, a retired schoolteacher who lived in the Segundo Barrio. He stood on the altar waiting, wondering, looking at the parishioners and shrugging his shoulders. Father Flood had never been late before.

When he walked out seven minutes later, people could not believe what they saw. What little silver hair he had left was disheveled, and his eyes were baggy and red, as if he hadn't slept in weeks. His undershirt was wrinkled and stained, and he wore no pants, just a baggy pair of boxers. He looked almost dead, his cheeks sunken in, his eyes hollow. He was pale. He walked onto the altar like entering a room he had never seen. Daniel retrieved his robe, and put it over the priest's head. He straightened it out and whispered, "Can you do this today?" The priest didn't answer. He walked to the center of the altar and looked at the people, as if wondering who they were and why they were there.

Every Catholic knows that at the beginning of Mass, the priest leads parishioners into a prayer of forgiveness. Once forgiven, they can go into the ceremony pure. That was not how it happened that day. Father Flood raised his old hands to the dome and said, "The Lord be with you." The parishioners answered back, "And with your spirit," but the father went right into the Lord's Prayer, in multilanguages.

Padre nuestro
qui est dans le ciel
santificado sea
your name.

Everybody knew that his Mass was very fast—the fastest Mass in the world—but they were confused as to why he went from the beginning right to the Lord's Prayer, which was supposed to be toward the end. They looked to each other, maybe hoping that Mass would only last five minutes. They obediently held each other's hands up in the air and recited the Lord's Prayer: "Danos hoy nuestro pan . . ."

But before they could reach the end, he suddenly began to utter words that came right after the readings, "This is the word of God."

The businessmen and women, the housewives and active middle-class moms said, "Glory to you, Lord." They wondered, "Did they already take up

the collection and we didn't notice?" But then Father Flood began to recite
the words to the profession of faith, even though that didn't come at the right
time either. The beginning was the middle was the end was the middle again.
Father Flood went on and on and on and recited prayers over and over again
in different order and in four languages. He held up the cup and repeated
the words Jesus had spoken to the disciples, and then he put the cup down
and began the Lord's Prayer again. He kept saying kneel and stand and sit
and kneel again so that the parishioners moved up and down like frenzied
sports fans. The new young priest across the nave giving confessions didn't
understand what was going on, and he thought that maybe it was he himself
who was losing track of linear time. He held onto his chair like someone on a
bumpy ride. But the Mass went on.

And on. And on.

Some people left after the first twenty minutes. They shook their heads in
disgust, touched their wallets—happy that they didn't give.

An hour passed.

Other people, however, stayed around, as if there were something powerful about the way Father Flood was feeding them, weaving this prayer with
that. Two hours passed. Sentences went back and forth between English and
Spanish and French and Latin, and the swirl of words—the twists and screws
and incomprehensible incantations—enchanted the silence that suddenly
filled the dome.

Father Flood was silent.

The nave was quiet.

The third hour passed.

Then he started again, in the middle or the end or the beginning. According to the Vatican files, one old woman who always wore a red scarf to
Mass, who lived in the building across the street and went to services twice a
day and three times on Sunday, believed that this was a sign from God. Even
as she began to feel hungry and thirsty, she stayed, kneeling and sitting and
standing, according to the words. It was during this time that she realized
something about herself: she knew what the results of her tests would be,
knew it was fatal, but she also knew that it was okay, she was ready to die.

By midnight, not only were there still many parishioners left—as if being
held in the church by a physical force—but curious passersby walking along
the sidewalk outside and hearing Mass going on so long and late felt themselves sucked in, and they peeked into the nave, and some of them stayed.
Then the seasonal rains came to the city, falling so hard that trees grew out
of cracks in the sidewalks and water rushed through the gutters. Homeless

people, wet and without shelter, were happy to enter into the warm light of the open doors.

By three in the morning, the young priests gathered at the far end of the nave and watched the Mass go on and on, but they didn't stop it, because it was clear that people in the neighborhood thought there was something special going on. The church stayed full, and every time the collection baskets went around—every ten minutes or every two minutes or every hour—the redeemed reached deeply into their pockets and gave.

The next morning those who were used to coming to six o'clock Mass thought that they were late, because when they walked in, the prayers had already started. They sat and looked around, confused, but after a while the mixture of the prayers and the nonlinear incantations flowing from Father Flood lulled them into a trance, like a fragrance from a bottle. People prayed like they had never prayed before. And even though this was not a charismatic church—but a very conservative Catholic congregation—some began to speak in tongues. They raised their hands to the Lord and they praised Him in languages they themselves didn't understand. People danced. Others prophesied, yelled out loud what God was saying to them. The voices that filled the church, weaving around the chord of Father Flood's voice— hundreds and hundreds and thousands and millions of voices—were mixing and swirling so fast that the energy almost became Mass and brushed against the doors and the windows, and the pigeons on the dome flew off. People were cured. The blind could see. The young priests couldn't get through to the cardinal, because every time they tried, somehow the phone connection went bad.

In the next few days, so many people had gone in and out of that church, any time of night or day, that it became a pilgrimage, a holy destination not only for Catholics (who would wait all day in line just to see the image of the Virgin in a pizza), but for people everywhere. According to the Vatican files, some Mennonites came from thousands of miles away, just to bask in the spirit, and there were Jews, too, mostly Kabbalists, and Sufi Muslims, and Buddhists. News cameras parked outside, documentaries were planned, magazines sent reporters and photographers.

But Father Flood was old. Other than the host, he hadn't eaten, and other than the wine mixed with water, he hadn't drunk. He began to get weak, and he began to slow down.

He enunciated every word.

As he slowly spoke, he remembered things.

He saw his father killing a chicken. Saw his sister's ankle as she stepped onto a city tram. Saw Rome at night, a well-lit café, a drunk man and woman walking out, leaning on each other and laughing. He saw a pool of water in the cup of his hands, rising to meet his own reflection. He saw the girl who had sold flowers, wrapping a bunch of unsmelled roses in white paper. He saw the snowy mountain that loomed outside of his home village, and from afar it looked like his own face.

And during that time, when things were quite slow, almost quiet, when his voice spoke only one word at a time, people wept. They thought of their lives, and they wept.

Father Flood became so weak that the new young priests had to hold him up, one on each side, so that the old man could continue to raise his arms and weep the words of Mass, like Moses on the mountaintop, looking across the river, looking down on a promise he would never touch.

GREAT SALT LAKE

Jeffrey Chapman

ummer days in Utah were long and hot and dry like sand, even up in the mountains. My parents, always on the edge of poor, tried to take advantage of the heat by selling homemade ice cream from a curious shack in our front yard; I was the salesman from an early age. We only operated it for the summer months, when I didn't have to be in school. I opened it at nine every morning and closed it at seven in the evening—except Sundays because Mom said, *We stick to community principles*, which meant Mormon principles, which meant no work on Sunday. While other kids swam and played during their free days, I worked. I kept a stack of books and magazines in the corner of the shack. I spent the long hours reading and listening to tapes I borrowed from my parents. Mom and I made ice cream every night. Any money went back to my parents, minus my allowance.

The shack was shaped like an actual ice cream cone and painted with glossy paint. The ice cream roof of the shack was pink-strawberry with "Snowy" written across it in white. The cone base was eggshell color: a regular squared-off wafer cone, not a tapered sugar cone. The inside was small—just large enough for a freezer, a tape player and my chair—and in the summer it was hot and cramped. I sold ice cream through a square window in the front. I never asked my parents if they built the Snowy or whether they bought it as it was: a shack shaped like an ice cream cone.

During the summer, the valley dried out and the dust rose from the road and settled on the Snowy so that pretty soon you couldn't tell what flavor of ice cream it was supposed to be. Then I'd hose it down.

Friends rarely came to see me at work, because my mom wouldn't allow me to give them free samples. The only people who ever bought ice cream were families fishing at the lake. Families from Salt Lake City or neighboring towns who'd show up in dusty trucks with kids piled in the back. They'd drive past, brake, back up. Sunburned, greasy faces. Some days there were a lot; some days there were none.

There was one exception: every day a girl stopped at the ice cream stand. Lara. She was the sister of Joe Jensen, who was in my class at school. Dr. Jensen, her dad, stitched my foot when I sliced it scrambling over an old car. Lara was seventeen, two grades above Joe and me in school but only a year and a half older in years. She took music lessons during the summer. She came by on her way home every day, detouring a little to buy ice cream. Joe, proud of her talents because of his own lack of them, said that she was good enough to be a concert pianist some day. I liked that idea. I started listening to classical piano music that summer, imagining it was Lara playing for me. It seemed right to me then, as it seems right to me now, that beauty should be cultivated.

That summer she always showed up wearing overalls or a summer dress. She was tall and thin at the hips. She came in the afternoon, when the sun shined bright on the lake and on the white dusty road. She was silhouetted—a pleasant, cool shape—until she came into the shade of the awning. It took several seconds for my eyes to adjust. She had blue eyes—a lighter blue than the sky. In the desert summer, the sky becomes startlingly blue and far away.

She never said much. She smiled and looked over the day's choices. She would lick her bottom lip. She would point at a flavor. Usually something on the order of blackberry or cherry. Fruity and creamy. I always said, Sure, and pulled her choice out from the freezer. Sure. A large scoop on a cone. A little extra on top. A bit of a present from me to her. Bye then, she said, handing me her money and turning away.

—Bye, I said.

She never came before one in the afternoon, so I would have to bide my time until then, asking fishermen what they caught. They usually had stories to tell. While they talked I pictured them eating the entire Snowy. Some of them—the really fat ones—could have done it, if it had been real ice cream. From one o'clock on I would lean out past the counter every five minutes, looking both directions even though she always came from the right. I bit my fingernails.

Then she would come, buy ice cream, and I felt glorious and annoyed. She was gone again so soon. I held the small and fragile moment carefully in my mind. Then I had the rest of the afternoon in front of me, sitting in my booth, bored. I wanted to leave my post, follow her silhouette, see where she went, but I never did.

That was the last summer that I sold ice cream.

One Saturday Lara walked up as I was closing the Snowy. It was after six and the fish hadn't been biting all day, so all the fishermen had left. I was outside, sweeping dust out onto the road and she walked up behind me. I was preoccupied and didn't notice her until she was standing right there. She coughed quietly.

I couldn't regain composure while standing so close to her. I set the broom against the Snowy and walked around to the door in back. Through the window I said Hi. She was dressed nicely: a silky skirt and a sleeveless shirt. Her hair was combed straight: bronze stretched fine.

—I need an ice cream, she said. She pointed at strawberry.

I pulled out the bucket. I made her a cone, much larger than I normally made, because she looked sad. I was normally very precise about how much ice cream I gave on each cone. If I used too much my mom noticed and closed her eyes in a really tired way.

After I handed Lara the ice cream, I expected her to go away like she always did. But she stuck around. She brushed her feet across the ground several times, startling white dust into the air. She leaned on the counter, resting on her elbows. She didn't look at me, but maybe she wanted me to talk to her. She'd never wanted me to talk to her before.

—You're all dressed up, I said.

—Yes.

—Why? I asked.

—Piano recital, she said.

She took a spoon and used it to poke at the ice cream cone. She took small bites, searching for strawberry bits.

—Piano recital, I said. —How was it?

—Okay, she said. —Good. I scored an excellent.

I didn't know what an excellent meant so I just watched as she picked at her ice cream cone. She swayed forward and back, weight on her elbows.

—John Evans was supposed to come watch me, she said. —But he didn't come.

She looked at the counter, at her ice cream, at the lake, but occasionally her eyes rose and met mine and I saw that thin blue. John Evans had graduated from high school the year before. I hadn't known Lara was dating him. Some people make it their business to know everyone else's business but I just spent my summer days serving ice cream and minding my own.

—You guys are an item? I said.

She shrugged.

—For how long? I asked.

—Five weeks. Now he never calls me anymore. He didn't call me yesterday or the day before either. My parents didn't like him anyways.

I took a little scoop of ice cream for myself. Strawberry. I'd eaten so much ice cream in the past years that I'd lost my taste for it. I almost never ate it anymore. We both sat there and ate in silence.

—Have you ever been down to the Great Salt Lake? she asked.

—Not since I was six, I said.

My family never went anywhere. On weekends we'd sometimes go four-wheeling in the hills up past the monastery, but that was it. Usually we'd stay home and go fishing. Ice fishing in the winter.

—That's where we were going to go today, after the recital. John and me. We were going to go float on the lake.

—Oh, I said.

—I've never floated in the lake. School starts next week, then there won't be time.

She stabbed at her ice cream with her spoon.

—I never do anything different, she said.

—You should go, I said. —If you want.

—Yeah, she said.

She tapped the counter several times and then looked up.

—Are you closing up shop right now? she asked.

I nodded.

—Would you go with me?

Her eyes rested on me and I met them for a second, then I bit my thumbnail. A fly landed near the ice cream and started crawling toward it, so I picked up a swatter and waved it away.

It's most likely she just didn't want to go alone and I happened to be on hand. A small town in summer doesn't provide a choice of many companions. However, part of me managed to imagine—unlikely as it might be—that I was the preferred choice, not John Evans. That she'd wanted to go with me all along. These are the ways we find of blinding ourselves with hope; after all, I'd hardly ever had a true conversation with her. But then, maybe that's what she wanted, to talk with me and get to know me. I was a good listener and I had ideas. Why wouldn't she want to get to know me a little more? Perhaps she'd realized I'd been giving her a little extra ice cream each time she came by and felt I had something real and genuine to offer her. These were all thoughts I had. Hers wasn't a simple and spontaneous request.

—So? she said. I was looking off at the lake.

Throughout life I have had the tendency to remain calm at a moment of crisis; panic arrives later, when I review an event. When Lara asked me to accompany her I looked at her and said yes. Yes, I said. I'd love to go with you. A minute later, as she ran home to get her car, I thought about it. Should I have said no? Should I have said yes but not emphasized that I would *love* to go and *with her*? Would I be able to sit in the same car as her?

I closed up the Snowy and grabbed my swimsuit from my bedroom. —All finished, I yelled to my Mom. —I'm going out.

—Wait, I heard her call, but I was out the door and gone. I knew she would have had another chore for me to do, and she would have said, There'll be enough time for you to go out later, or tomorrow.

Lara arrived in a rusting, beat-up Duster. We drove down through Ogden canyon, sun right in our eyes. In a new setting Lara was a completely different person. She was all energy, bouncing around and talking quickly. She talked more right then than in all the time I'd known her.

—I've never been to the lake, she confessed. She smiled, embarrassed. —I've lived here my whole life, only an hour away, and I've never been there. But I've been reading about it lately. I just got interested all of a sudden.

She started reciting facts. She talked about the size of the lake and the number of people who used to visit the lake and how salty the water is. For twenty minutes she talked. I don't remember the facts she told me, but I remember the flow of her voice, the movement of her lips forming those words. Her cheek was smooth and flushed.

I knew things about the lake too, but I didn't interrupt her. I held my hand out the window, turning it one way, turning it back, feeling the wind pushing up on my palm.

When she finished talking, I said, —Hey, if we put our hands out of our windows and tilt them right, we might fly.

She looked at me.

—Wings, I said. —Hands like wings.

—Right, she said. Both hands stayed on the steering wheel.

So after that I didn't say some of the things I was thinking. I didn't tell her I felt like we were racing the river to the bottom of the valley, all of us heading into the lake. And I didn't tell her the walls of the canyon might fold in on us, like a deck of cards. I certainly didn't tell her that I was silenced by her presence. Mostly we just sat. It was still hot and she had hiked her skirt above her knees to be cooler. I kept looking at her right knee. There was a round scar at the top of the kneecap. How did she get that scar?

When we left Huntsville, the sun was about to set past the mountains, but as we drove down the canyon and the rock walls fell away, I realized that we still had time—maybe an hour, maybe more—before it set on the horizon. The mountains are an artificial horizon, but when you grow up surrounded by them they seem universal. We drove on, the sun sank lower, and all the colors in the landscape grew richer: the yellow grass looked bright white, like snow; a touch of green came out on the mountains that normally looked dry.

She handed me a map and made it my job to navigate to the beach. For almost an hour we drove down through the canyon, which didn't require any work on my part. But eventually we'd have to find our way down back roads. She had marked a public beach with an X and had circled the X, all with thick red marker. I contemplated guiding her onto Interstate 15 and up through Idaho, Montana, and finally into Canada, where we could find a hut in which to live. Lara could play piano for the locals and I could make ice cream to sell at her performances. At night she could play me to sleep. I thought about this while we sat unspeaking, but ultimately I told her the correct place to exit, the correct place to go straight, the right place to turn right and the right place to turn off.

It was warm down out of the mountains. You could see for miles. You could see water stretch all the way to the flimsy flat line of the horizon.

The Great Salt Lake is huge and calm and salty. And lonely. There was no one else on the beach. The white salt-sand was abandoned. Everything is so flat, the slope of the beach is so slight, that from the beginning of the beach to the beginning of the water is well over five hundred yards. Once you begin wading into the lake you can walk for half a mile before the water rises over your knees. That's just how it is.

—You should have a concert out here, I said. —Bring a piano out and play while the sun goes down. It'd be nice.

—I think it would be bad for the piano, she said.

Tiny brine flies skitted over the sand. The lake is so salty that only two animals can live on it: brine flies and brine shrimp. Small, irritating animals.

Lara, next to me, put a finger under her nose and looked out at Antelope Island.

—It smells, she said.

I didn't know whether the lake had always smelled that bad.

—Plug your nose, I said. —You can't smell it once you're in the water.

She looked ahead, doubtful.

—Come on, I said. —You really wanted to swim. You have to swim.

I wanted her to be bold, risky. She looked around. —Where do we change? she said. I looked around. I remembered changing rooms from my childhood but they weren't here.

—Well, no one is here. You can change anywhere you want, I said.

She squinted at me as if to say, Are you crazy?

—Turn away, she said. I turned away and faced the lake. Seagulls circled. I heard Lara pulling off clothes. —I should have changed before we came. Don't look back. You've been here before. You should have told me there was nowhere to change.

—I didn't know, I said.

—I wish I had a tan, she said.

I looked down at the brine flies.

—I'm done, she said. —What about you?

She was wearing a T-shirt over her bathing suit. She turned away while I changed and I stared at the backs of her knees. Her legs were long and smooth and they were tan, I thought.

The water was warm: still, shallow water that'd been in the sun all day, all summer. Our feet sank ankle-deep into silky mud. Lara walked ten feet out and then stopped. Twenty feet out I stopped and looked back at her. Her arms were crossed and she was looking down.

—You don't like it? I said.

—It still smells, she said. —Actually I don't mind it. It feels good on my feet. But I don't want to go any further.

—You're barely in, I said.

—Who knows what's under there. Sharp rocks, animals, glass.

I said, —If we keep going, the mud will disappear. Come on. You have to.

She'd come all this way so it seemed to me that she *had* to come in all the way, and I thought about pulling her in, so she'd change her mind. But she motioned me to keep going.

—Tell me if you get out of it, she said. After a few steps I looked back and she was staring down at the lake.

She was disappointed. The lake hadn't lived up to her expectations. I knew, even then, that her disappointment had nothing to do with me. At that moment, however, it *felt* like it was my fault. I was sure it was my fault. If I could get her far enough out to show that the lake was, indeed, suitable for swimming—then she would thank me. Then I would have given her something. Then she would be happy and grateful, which is what I expected from her.

I waded out, careful now in case of anything under the mud. I went out fifty, one hundred feet. The mud ended after three hundred feet. I waved my arms wildly at Lara. She waved back but she didn't move.

I waved again. —Come on, I yelled. —Come on.

She shook her head and plugged her nose.

I could have walked back to her and taken her hand, or I could have kept walking for another mile into the lake. Instead I sat down in the salty water, lay back until my head touched the water, lifted my legs and let myself go. It's amazing how effortlessly you float on the Great Salt Lake. This, I thought, this is what Lara came here for. This weightlessness. But Lara was standing in a few inches of water, arms crossed, clutching her perfect shoulders.

I've since learned that you almost never convince anyone of anything; people don't want to be changed. In my life I don't think I've convinced anyone of anything significant.

I put my ears underwater and liked the absence of sound. I spread out all my fingers as wide as I could; I spread out my arms and legs. Around me in every direction was water calm as glass, and the sky seemed closer than Lara. We were living in a world of monstrous spaces. Silver-edged clouds slid overhead. It was getting dusky. Lara made no effort to get me out of the water. I only had to raise my head slightly and I could watch her; she had walked away, waiting to return to the car—unmoving, poised but uncomfortable. She had picked up a towel and wrapped it around herself. If she was looking at something it wasn't apparent to me. I lay my head back again.

A flock of pelicans flew overhead. With the gray towel wrapped around her and her thin, awkward legs, Lara looked like one of the lake's great blue herons.

I could be a heron, I thought.

It was true. I closed my eyes, suspended in a featureless water that stole away my senses and dulled any sense of time passing. It was easy, then and there, senseless, bathed in the warm, failing light, to know what it was to be a bird, flying. It seemed as easy to *become* a bird, then and there, as to stay what I was, an improbable boy inside an ice cream shack all summer long. Given all the time in the world, I could feel myself changing, ever so slowly. My skin, which I thought was itchy because of its new salt crust, was actually turning into feathers. It was unnatural anymore to be floating on my back so I stood up on new legs. I extended my arms, and feathers bridged the space below. My wings continued to grow and soon they would be wide and strong; I knew that I would soon be able to take off with two or three strong downbeats. The sun was late in its path but still felt warm and good and I stretched my head back. My new neck was elegant. I spread and shook my wings. Scales of salt sloughed off and fell all around me. To be a bird, that was gigantic. The plane of the lake, to the horizon, was mine.

I opened my eyes again. Lara was still standing there exactly as before, waiting to leave. I don't know how long I'd made her wait, but then I didn't much care. I started to wade back.

As I got close, the low sun glinted and sparkled on her tan legs. It was probably drops of water catching the light; I want to imagine, however, that she was covered with salt crystals left behind after the Great Salt Lake evaporated: like flakes, or scales. Beautiful and still.

THE INHALATORIUM

Tracy Daugherty

obert's father, a geologist, used to tell him that West Texas was once under water. A vast ocean resided here, he said. It receded over the centuries, leaving behind the nutrients that feed the varieties of plant life we find today in the desert, and accounting for the flatness of the land.

"Maybe you're part fish," Robert's father kidded him whenever Robert fell prey to an asthma attack, usually in the middle of the night, waking from sleep. "Maybe that explains your breathing trouble."

Robert's mother, a heavy smoker who'd developed her nicotine habit early, had died of emphysema when he was a baby. On nights when he couldn't breathe, there was only his father to sit with him, rub his back, and hum a song until he fell asleep again.

"Sometimes," his father would say, kneeling beside Robert's bed, "the world is less than splendid. But don't give up on it, okay?"

"Okay," Robert answered. He wasn't sure what "splendid" meant, but the implication was that Robert's mother was one of the weak ones who had given up on life. All that was left of her was the chandelier she had bought for the dining room before he was born, its sharp glass diamonds yellowed from years of cigarette and candle smoke rising from the table.

Robert was twenty-two, and twelve credits shy of a bachelor's degree in American history, when his father passed away of congestive heart failure, a condition that caused excess fluid in the lungs. Saddened and distracted, Robert took a year off from college to travel in the desert, in memory of his father and his work. He'd familiarize himself with the region's contours and surprises: a way of keeping the old man's spirit with him a little longer. He washed and waxed his father's silver Pontiac, and tuned it up for the rigors of the trip.

He put the family house on the market, and left the details of the sale with a real estate agent. On his last day in town, Robert stood in the dining room with the woman, taking stock, making sure he'd packed everything he wanted. "That's a beautiful old chandelier," said the agent, nodding at the ceiling. She was pretty and thin, like Robert's mother in scrapbook photographs.

"Yes," Robert said. Here, as a child, on the dining room floor night after night, he'd sat looking up at his father as his father served supper, usually steak and sweet potatoes. Robert stared out the window, at a perfectly oval beehive just beneath the eave of the house (it hung there like a brittle chandelier). He'd played with his black and white Manx. Katia had never learned to retract her claws when she sparred with him. Robert still had cat scars, whitened now, and hard, on his arms.

"It'll be here long after we're gone," the agent said, admiring the cut glass.

"Yes," Robert said. He turned to shake her hand.

"Nothing to worry about," she told him.

"Yes," he said again, taking one last look around, one last full breath in the house.

On his first day out, in a bathroom in a roadside rest area just north of the Texas-Mexico border, Robert read a faded lyric on the wall:

Clickety clack, clickety clack.
Where you going, where you been?
Clickety clack, clickety clack.
Don't come back, don't come back.

Later that afternoon, tracing a route laid out on a tourist map, he saw the remnants of an outpost where Robert E. Lee had once trained to be an army general. He saw a glass and metal structure built in the late nineteenth century by a man named Will Pruett, whose goal, said the free informational literature, was to "aid sick humanity." The structure, an "Inhalatorium," had been designed for consumptives. They would stand inside it and breathe medicinal vapors. The Inhalatorium was an economic failure, said the brochures, and closed before its effectiveness as a health treatment could be determined.

As he studied the contraption—a tall glass tube in the middle of an old ravine—Robert fell into conversation with a fellow tourist who, it turned out, had suffered from asthma all his life. He laughed when Robert told him his father's old joke. "Well, maybe there's some truth to that fish business," said the man.

Together, they marveled at the fact that a whole generation had vanished from the planet, wars had been won and lost, since Will Pruett had fashioned the Inhalatorium, yet here it stood. A fragile glass booth. "It's like an empty aquarium," the man remarked.

If Robert was really interested in the desert's history, he said, he should read a book called *Commerce of the Prairies*. It had been published in 1844 by a consumptive named Josiah Gregg. "It's the most eye-opening account of this region I've ever found," the man explained. "Gregg came to Texas because he thought the desert air would be good for his lungs. His book convinced hundreds of asthmatics, and people suffering from pleurisy and the like, to migrate here. Naturally, none of them ever got well." The fellow laughed again. "So. It seems a flock of invalids shaped Texas's destiny as much as the battle of the Alamo."

A few days later, Robert ordered a reprint of Josiah Gregg's book through an online bookseller and read it as he continued his travels through craggy moraines and dry fossil beds. In the West, it is "most usual to sleep out in the open air," Gregg wrote, "for the serene sky affords the most agreeable and wholesome canopy" and "seems to affect the health rather favorably."

In one of the textbooks that Robert had tossed into the trunk of the car (next to his father's maps, which he no longer had the heart to look at), he read that Stephen F. Austin, one of Texas's early political leaders, had once proclaimed the "climate of Texas . . . to be decidedly superior in point of health and salubrity to any portion of North America in the same parallel."

Like Austin and Gregg, Robert's father had been an enthusiast for the region. He had always encouraged Robert to look carefully and appreciate what he saw, so he'd know the character of the place that had shaped him. No doubt Robert's passion for history had sprung from his father's excitement.

Utopians, men like this. But Paradise is not a fertile, forested place, Robert thought. Fertility breeds fevers and disease. Instead, perfection is a desiccated emptiness.

This notion troubled Robert's sleep, especially when his daily drive left him far from towns, and he was forced to bed down in the car or on the ground. When he did sleep he dreamed of dark and empty distances. No movement, sound, or air.

The world was perfect. It was Paradise. We decided to change it.

These words swam through Robert's mind just before sleep one night, after he had spent nearly an hour reading Josiah Gregg's book. Robert was staying in the Cactus Glory Motel, just off the Alpine highway. Tires hissed on the road outside his window. Coyotes called in the cooling night air.

After several minutes he drifted. The book fell to the floor. He startled awake, chasing his breath, which seemed to float just out of reach. He coughed, choked, stumbled toward the window and opened its latch. A mild wind flowed into the room. It filled Robert's lungs like water pouring into two tall jars. *Will this sustain me*, he thought, *or is this my last taste of the world?* He leaned out as far as he could, into the night.

The following morning, a warm wind blew in from Mexico, stirring dust devils in the road, coloring the air a thick, chalky brown. Radio weathermen predicted a rough week ahead. The scars on Robert's arms—Katia's old love-marks—itched as he drove (windows up or down, it didn't matter) through the hard and grainy heat.

Because of his weak lungs, Robert had always expected to die young. And yet, whenever breath left him, he was shocked. "Trauma," a doctor said to him once. "The loss of a loved one. Disappointments. They seem to trigger asthma. We're not sure why."

Well, Robert thought. *When the world reveals itself as less than splendid, why keep taking it in?*

"Often, people don't realize how serious asthma can be," the doctor went on.

But don't give up, right?

He stood before a prickly pear cactus next to the highway. At its base, pink and blue flowers.

Robert was waiting for his car, which had overheated on the road, to stop steaming. He would have to find some water.

Meanwhile, he studied the cactus and the flowers: had they evolved from ocean plants? This was not the landscape people envisioned when they thought of the Garden of Eden. But isn't it true, he asked himself, that most of us picture a garden when we think of Paradise?

In the last few days, he had been stopping at small-town libraries and reading old newspapers in the archives, continuing the story where Josiah Gregg left off: articles about hackers and coughers on a limping pilgrimage to the West. Over the decades, they had been accompanied by treasure hunters, railroad magnates, entrepreneurs, electricians, and oil workers. In 1999, the Los Angeles Times reported that Phoenix, Arizona, had become so swollen with people, doctors had coined a new term, "Valley Fever," for illnesses caused by pathogens in the dirt stirred up by continuous human activity. Fatigue. Fungus in the bones and brain.

"Everybody who lives here has a health problem," said one Phoenix resident.

Apparently, the snake had followed each fresh, young Adam and Eve to every new garden. Paradise, no longer seductive . . .

The Pontiac sputtered and let out a sigh, the kind of rattle his father had made in the hospital in the last stages of his illness. Robert turned and looked at the car. Sweat stung the scars on his arms. He went for a jug of water.

The winds grew stronger. One afternoon, in a town called Salton, Robert stopped at a pharmacy. He had been wheezing so badly he couldn't hear the car radio. He had caught only parts of a newscast that said the dust in the air was thickened by smoke from a forest fire north of Oaxaca.

"Don't sound so good," said the pharmacist, a bald man with wire-rimmed glasses pressed tightly to his face.

Fluids moved through Robert's chest. He scanned the shelves for inhalers.

"Strongest medicine's there on the top shelf. Albuterol. Green box," the man said.

Robert brought it to the counter, along with a bag of pretzels and a canned Coke.

"No sir, don't sound good at all," the man said.

Just a taste of what's ahead, Robert thought.

Above the cash register, a small glass chandelier cast weak light on the sales counter and the floor.

"Well, take care, young fellow. Awful nasty out there, with the wind and all."

"I'm good," Robert said. "Thanks."

The light fixture sang three high notes as he opened the door and a breeze caught the swaying glass pendants.

That night, Robert unrolled his sleeping bag on a dirt patch several miles off the road. As the night darkened, the Milky Way spread like powdered glass above the land.

He remembered a camping trip he had taken with his father. He must have been six, maybe seven: one of his earliest rides into the desert with his dad. They had pitched their bedrolls at the bottom of a warm canyon. The air was still. Later that night, Robert shot to his feet, gasping. His father lifted him, pounding his back, toward anything he could suck for strength. . . .

Afterwards, his father had sat and showed him maps, to humor him and keep him calm. "Never give up," his father said. "No matter what. There's always a road out, you understand?"

Smiling at the memory, Robert crossed his arms behind his head. He stared at the stars. A silver satellite drifted across the Big Dipper's bowl. Another movement: a bit of space junk, a second satellite, a silent jet?

No. The object, a single mass made of many parts, dropped several feet and danced above the ground. The hair stood stiff on Robert's arms. He swore it was . . . it seemed to be . . .

The image broke apart. Flashing slivers wriggled in the air, illuminated by a cheddar-yellow moon.

Robert sat up. "All right," he said aloud. "I'm dreaming. This is a dream and I know it's a dream. I'm going to lie down and dream of something else. My father . . . my father and me on the lawn, running, playing catch. Katia leaping behind us. My mother watching from the kitchen . . ."

He lay back and closed his eyes. "Dream," he whispered. What he thought he had seen was a school of blue and yellow fish, darting out at him from the constellation Lyra.

He had lost track of the days of the week. He only understood it was Sunday when he heard hymns from a church down the road as he stood filling his tank with gas. After he paid the service station attendant, a high school kid wearing a "Ski El Paso" T-shirt, Robert drove the car half a block and parked it in a small dirt lot.

He walked to the church and stood on the concrete porch, peering into the open doorway. In a cool, shaded vestibule, a middle-aged woman slouched against a wall, smoking. In her left hand, she held a gold aluminum ashtray, stuffed with butts. The woman nodded at Robert and went on puffing. It was hard for him not to stare at the ashtray, at the smeared lipstick on the ends of the crushed cigarettes. He turned his head to see inside the chapel but it was dark, with just a few candles, and as long as he stood in the sunlight his eyes would not adjust to the shade.

"We will come to understanding by and by," someone said—presumably the preacher. Robert remembered hearing the phrase years ago. His father had not been a churchgoer—"Too much the scientist," he'd say whenever Robert asked him why he never talked of God—but he had taken Robert to mass a few times when Robert was little, thinking, perhaps, that in the absence of his mother the boy needed solace that a working father couldn't offer. Robert recalled sitting in the sanctuary puzzling over the phrase "by and by." Did it mean *next to, because of,* or *all in good time?*

Next to the beehive, through repeated, stinging pain, I learned of loss, Robert thought.

Because of my parents' illnesses, I learned of loss.

All in good time, from traveling and leaving things behind, I've learned about loss.

The smoking woman smiled at him again. He had been staring at her without realizing it. He glanced at his hands, at the lines in his palms. What are you hoping to find, he thought. He rubbed his hands as if to smooth a map.

The flare of a match. A sulfurous smell. The woman kissed another cigarette.

The dreams came almost every night now. Gills . . . whirring fins, yellow tails . . . inches from the ground . . .

Robert told himself to wake up. None of this was real. He sat stiffly in his sleeping bag, wheezing, hugging his backpack to his chest. He rubbed his eyes and shined his flashlight into the dust until the last of the fish disappeared.

"So far, three couples have looked at the house," the real estate agent told him on the phone. "I think one of them may make an offer." Her voice rang high, like a child's, but he remembered how much she looked like his mother. As he slouched in the phone booth, watching teenagers in muddy cars circle a burger joint across the highway, he imagined holding a conversation he never could have had. In his mind, his mother sat in the dining room, beneath the chandelier, wearing a light cotton dress.

"So the house is good?" he said.

"Terrific," said his mother. Confident. Healthy.

"And the lawn?"

"Glorious. I'll be sure to water it again this evening."

"I'm glad."

"Nothing to worry about. Nothing at all."

None of this is real.

"I'll let you know if an offer comes through, okay?"

"Okay," he said.

Across the road, cars went round and round.

As days passed, he feared his mother's spirit had taken possession of the Pontiac, and of him, blowing him aimlessly down paths narrow and obscure. You'll never return, he thought. What remains for you to reclaim?

Abandoned studies of the past.

A house no longer yours.

He hacked. He wheezed. A splendid surrender.

While searching for a place to sit and eat a sandwich, Robert came upon the bones of a bird, tiny as grass clippings, tangled in thorny brush. The bones reminded him of a discovery he had made when he was twelve, out looking for his cat. Katia had been missing for hours and Robert's father feared an owl might have snatched her. Lately, some of the neighbors had spotted a great horned—"unusual but not entirely rare in this part of the world," Robert's father had said.

Sure enough, in the alley behind the house, Robert found bone and hair in a ball: the owl's regurgitated leavings. Robert placed the remains in a pickle jar, like the one in which his father kept his "rainy day" coins. He carried the jar into his room. His father had returned to his office after dinner, to work with his maps. Robert set the jar on a windowsill and crouched before it as the moon rose. Yellow light trailed across the contours of the glass, across the hardened ball. Robert stared, as if this moment, this image, might reveal to him life's liquid motion, the changes, the futures embodied in us all—futures we never saw unless we paused and really looked.

Now, he gazed at the bird's remains. Maybe Katia and this poor flying creature were lucky to leave the world before their bodies betrayed them.

His chest ached. Years ago, a doctor had told him he was utilizing only 10 percent of his lung capacity. "I have half a mind to hospitalize you," the doctor had said.

Robert felt now as he had felt back then, and he knew he'd become dependent on the inhaler. Its effectiveness was eroding. Perhaps he should buy a new one, or maybe even see a doctor in the next town.

On the outskirts of Marfa, Robert sat at a red light. Up and down the street, air conditioners clattered in windows, allowing people to live in this place where otherwise they would perish.

Clickety clack, clickety clack.
Don't come back, don't come back.

He saw a sign for an allergy and asthma specialist. The office was closed. He would return in the morning. The inhaler did nothing for him now. Too much dust. Too much smoke and wind.

He passed a small crowd off the road. They had gathered to see the Marfa Lights, erratic and mysterious flashes in the sky. In a brochure he'd read that the lights had become a tourist draw: some folks believed they were evidence of alien spacecraft, others called them spirits of the dead. Sober-minded observers insisted they were car lights reflected by dust-grains, or traces of glowing swamp gas.

Robert kept going. He turned onto a deserted farm road. Finally, he stopped and spread his sleeping bag in an open field surrounded by mesquite. His wheezing silenced the crickets. He pulled his flashlight and Josiah Gregg's book out of his backpack. He tried to read, but the words floated off the page. All right. He was exhausted. Dizzy from lack of oxygen. Nothing to worry about. Nothing at all. He'd go to the specialist in the morning.

He dozed, and woke to find his flashlight losing juice. He shook it. Inside it, the batteries rattled like fingernails tapping a pane of glass.

He slept again and dreamed of fish.

When he woke, he was encased inside the Inhalatorium.

Water filled the desert.

"This is ridiculous. I'm dreaming," he said aloud. His voice echoed inside the jar. He said no more, for fear of burning up oxygen.

Tap. Tap tap. He turned to see his mother swaying in the water in a splendid green dress. Young and strong. Behind her, a glass chandelier rose in midair, as majestic as a jellyfish. He kissed his mother's fingers through the glass. Katia bobbed past, trailed by exotic plankton. Then Robert's father tumbled into view, weightless and thin. He waved something—a map: the word "Paradise" stamped across its top.

Robert mouthed the words, "I did it." He meant to say, *I've done as you said, Father. I saw where I came from.* His father tried to straighten the map. The night's currents slowed his hands but he wouldn't give up. Watching him, Robert understood, with a swell of excitement and fear, where he'd been headed all along. *Ocean and desert. Sea and sky.* And then he ran out of air.

THE REPTILE GARDEN

Louise Erdrich

I n the fall of 1972, my parents drove me to the University of North Dakota for my freshman year. Everything I needed was packed in a brand-new royal blue aluminum trunk: a crazy quilt afghan that my mother had crocheted for my bed, thirty dollars' worth of new clothes, my *Berlitz French Self-Teacher*, the *Meditations of Marcus Aurelius* (a gift from my father), a framed photograph of my grandfather Mooshum, and a beaded leather tobacco pouch that he had owned ever since I could remember, and which he had casually handed to me as I left, the way old men give presents.

Other freshmen were already moving into their dormitory rooms when we arrived, with their parents helping haul. I saw boxes of paperbacks, stereo equipment, Dylan albums and varnished acoustic guitars, home-knitted afghans, none as brilliant as mine, Janis posters, Bowie posters, Day-Glo bedsheets, hacky sacks, stuffed bears. But as we carried my trunk up two flights of stairs terror invaded me. Although I was studying French because I dreamed of going to Paris, I actually dreaded leaving home, and in the end my parents did not want me to leave either. But this is how children are sacrificed into their futures: I had to go, and here I was. We walked back down the stairs. I was too numb to cry, but I watched my mother and father as they stood beside the car and waved. That moment is a still image; I can call it up as if it were a photograph. My father, so thin and athletic, looked almost frail with shock, while my mother, whose beauty was still remarkable, and who was known on the reservation for her silence and reserve, had left off her characteristic gravity. Her face and my father's were naked with love. It wasn't something that we talked about—love. But they allowed me this one clear look at it. It blazed from them. And then they left.

I think now that everything that was concentrated in that one look—the care they had taken in bringing me up, their patient lessons in every subject they knew how to teach, their wincing efforts to give me my freedom, the example they had set of fortitude in work—was what allowed me to survive.

The trunk was quickly emptied; my room was barely filled. Then, books to my chest, I curled up beneath the afghan and looked out the window. I understood right then that I would be spending most of my first semester in this position.

White girls at the time listened to Joni Mitchell, grew their hair long, smoked impatiently, frowned into their poetry notebooks, and pretended to fuck everything that moved. The other girls—Dakota, Chippewa, or mixed-blood like me—were less obvious on campus, and mainly very studious, although a couple of women swaggered around, furious in ribbon shirts, with American Indian Movement boyfriends. I didn't really fit in with anybody. My roommate was a stocky blonde girl from Wishek who was so dead set on becoming a nurse that she practiced bringing me things—a cup of water or, when I had a headache, aspirin. This was annoying, but we got along. I spent most of my time in the library, anyway. I hid out there and read my way through the poetry section until I hit on my favorites—all writers who had died young or gone crazy or disappeared into war. After Keats and Shelley and Byron, I skipped ahead to Lowell, Wright, Sexton, and Plath. Then I went back to the First World War, found Wilfred Owen, and wandered the campus dazed by "Strange Meeting," thinking about his remarkable use of the verb "groined" and mumbling, "And by his smile I knew that sullen hall." Next, I turned to Rimbaud, Baudelaire, Apollinaire. Searching for clues on how to make my way to Paris, I floundered toward the American expatriates. And then one drizzly afternoon I found her—my muse, my model, my everything. Anaïs Nin.

My attraction was hard to explain—she was so artistically driven, so demure and yet so bold, and those swimming eyes! I was lost in soul-to-soul contact. I checked her out of the library again and again, but when the summer came I found I needed her more than ever. I had to take her home with me. Anaïs. I bought all her diaries—the boxed set—a huge investment. By the time I went back to college in the fall and moved into a beautiful old half-wrecked farmhouse off campus, I was soaked in the oils of my own manufactured delirium.

Like Anaïs, I reviewed every thought I had. All trivia became momentous, my faintest desire a raving hunger. I, too, kept careful diaries now. Each notebook had a title taken from a diary entry by Anaïs. That fall's diary was called "Sprouting in the Void." I wrote long letters to my brother, Joseph, who was studying biology at the University of Minnesota. He wrote short ones back. My third or fourth cousin Corwin, with whom I had been madly in love in fifth grade, had driven me back to college, and I'd read aloud from Anaïs's diary all the way. He'd liked it only when she was having sex; otherwise, he said, she was "way up in her head." But now he visited me whenever his band was in town. He played the fiddle with a mad energy. Our childhood romance was a joke between us. He was a pot dealer and supplied my friends.

I kept Anaïs with me at all times, but every now and then the differences in our lives bothered me. For instance, Anaïs had had servants to feed her and clean up after her. Even her debauched lovers had picked her clothing up off the floor; her dinner parties were full of social dangers and alarms, but when they were over she never had to do the dishes. As for me, I'd moved into a household of local poets and hippies, and everyone was dirty. I tried to be, too, but my standards of cleanliness kept me from truly entering into the spirit of the times. I had learned from my mother to keep my surroundings in order, my dishes washed, my towels laundered. The sagging clapboard house where we lived had one bathroom. Periodically, because nobody else ever did, I broke down and cleaned. It made me hate my friends to do this and resent them as I watched the filth build up again afterward, but I couldn't help it. One night, I had grown so miserable about the bathroom that my fastidiousness overwhelmed my fury. It was past midnight, but I got a bucket, a scrubbing brush, and a box of something harsh smelling called Soilax. I ripped an old towel into four pieces. I wet down the bathtub, the toilet, and the sink, and shook the Soilax evenly across every surface. With a putty knife, I began to scrape away the waxlike patches of grease, hair, soap, and scum, the petrified ropes of toothpaste, the shit, the common dirt.

It took me a couple of hours and the light in the bathroom seemed glaring when I quit, because I'd emptied the fixture of dead flies. But as I contemplated my work a few lines of poetry occurred to me:

My brain is like a fixture deep in dead
flies.
How I long for my thoughts to shine
clear!
Disperse your crumpled wings, college
students and professors of U.N.D.
Let your bodies blow like dust across the
prairies!

I jotted them down in the notebook that I carried in the hip pocket of my jeans, and then headed downstairs to the living room, where a party had just begun. It was a welcome-home party for a draft-dodging poet who'd walked back across the Canadian border and was going to go underground, as he kept saying, loudly. But, first, he was going to take a shower in my clean bathroom. I deserved to drink wine. I remember that the wine we had was cheap and very pink, and that when I was halfway through a glass of it Corwin took a piece of paper from a plain white envelope and tore off a few small squares, which I put in my mouth.

Anaïs had tried everything—she would have tried this! "Spanish dancer," I cried to Corwin. She had been in love with her cousin. "Eduardo!" I said to Corwin, and kissed him. This all came back to me much later. At the time, I was not aware that I had taken lysergic acid, even after all its effects were upon me—the hideous malformations of my friends' faces, the walls and corridors of sound, the whispered instructions from objects, the panicked fear that rendered me unable to communicate at all. I locked myself in my room, which I soon realized was a garden for lizards, geckos, garter snakes, and some exotics, like a hooded cobra, all of which passed underneath the mopboard and occasionally slid out of the light fixtures. I was in my room for two days, sleepless, watching reptiles, moving in and out of terror, unaware of who I was, unaware of how I'd come to be in the state I was in. I should have been hospitalized, I suppose, but my reclusiveness was so habitual and the household so chaotic that no one really noticed my absence.

On the third day, the reptiles were replaced by the occasional amphibian and I began to sense a reliable connection between one moment and the next, to feel with some security that I inhabited one body and one consciousness. The terror lessened to a milder sense of dread. I ate and drank. On the fourth day, I slept. I cried my heart out the fifth day and the sixth. And gradually I became again the person I had known as myself. But I was not the same, for I had found out what a slim rail I walked.

My fear kept returning. It was as though, in those awful days, I'd switched inner connections and now the fear seemed hardwired in me. I couldn't stop shaking at the slightest unexpected movement. I endured panic attacks, momentary breaks with reality, daydreams so vivid they made me sick. On campus, I watched the well-fed, sane, secure, shiny-haired, and leather-belted students pass me by. I was now convinced that I would never be one of them, that I should leave and find my place among the less than healthy.

I got my Psych 1 professor (the course was nicknamed Nuts and Sluts) to help me find a position as a psychiatric aide. That winter, I packed a suitcase and took an empty, overheated Greyhound bus to the state mental hospital, where I trudged through blinding drifts of cold and was shown to a room in a staff dormitory.

My room was small, the walls a deep pink. I had a single bed with an Oriental-print spread—pagodas, winding streams, bent willows. There was a mirror, a shiny red-brown bureau, a tiny refrigerator on a wooden table, a straight-backed blue chair. I took the refrigerator off the table and made myself a desk. I'd met none of the other aides yet. There were rules against noise, against music, because the people on the night shift slept all day. My shift would begin at 6 a.m. So I showered down the hall and dried my hair. I laid my uniform out on the chair, a white rayon dress with deep pockets, panty hose, thick-soled nurse's shoes, which I'd bought at JCPenney. In the room above me, that night, a couple made love over and over. The springs creaked, increasing speed, until there was a crescendo, silence. Then laughter. Each session lasted about ten minutes.

I woke in time to shut off the alarm just before it rang. I boiled water in my little green hot pot and made a cup of instant coffee. It was still dark outside. I put on a long black coat I'd bought at Goodwill, and walked across the frozen lawn to the ward where I was assigned. The nurse coming on duty introduced herself as Mrs. L., because, she said, her actual name was long, Polish, and unpronounceable. She was tall, broad, and already looked tired. She wore a green cardigan over her uniform and a nurse's cap pinned to her fluffy black hair. She was drinking coffee and eating a glazed doughnut from a paper bag. "You're welcome to share this with me," she offered in a dull voice. She turned to one of the other aides coming on and said that she'd had a rough night. Her little boy was sick. She and the aide knew each other well, and the talk swirled back and forth for a few minutes.

"What am I supposed to do?" I asked in a too bright, nervous voice. "Can you give me something to do?"

"Listen to this." Mrs. L. laughed. "Don't worry, there's plenty. None of the patients are up yet."

"Except Warren," the nurse who was going off duty said. "Warren's always up."

I walked out of the office into the hall, which opened onto a huge, square room with green and black linoleum tiles. The walls were a paler green. The curtainless windows were rectangles of electric-blue sky that turned to gray and then normal daylight as the patients rose and slowly, in their thin striped cotton robes, began wandering down the corridor that led into the common room. Everyone looked the same at first—men and women, young and old. Mrs. L. handed out medications in small paper cups, and said to me, pointing, "Go with Warren there and make sure he takes it."

So I went with Warren, the night owl, an elderly—no, really old—man with long arms and the rope-muscled body of a farmer who has worked so hard that he will now live forever, or, at least, beyond the reach of his mind. His tan was permanent, burned into the lower half of his face, his hands, and a V of leather at his neck. He was already dressed neatly, in clean brown pants and a frayed but ironed plaid shirt. He liked to walk. He popped the pills down without missing a step. I watched Warren a lot that first day, because I couldn't believe that he would keep it up, but he didn't stop for more than a breath, filling up on food quickly at the designated times, then strolling up and down the corridors, crisscrossing the common room, in and out of every bedroom. To everyone he met, he nodded and said, "I'll slaughter them all." The patients answered, "Shut up." The staff didn't seem to hear.

The first day's schedule became routine. I woke early to record my dreams and sensations, then I dressed, putting a pen and a small notebook in my pocket, plus a miniature French dictionary I'd sent away for. I noted everything, jotted quickly in a stall on bathroom breaks. At breakfast time, I walked through the underground steam tunnels to the dining room. I ate with the patients—pushed my tray along the line and waited to see what landed on it. Farina, cold toast, a pat of butter, a carton of milk, juice if I was early enough, and coffee. There was always coffee, endless transparent acid in stained and sterilized Melmac cups. Ravenous and forgetful, I ate what they gave me, no matter what. I did the same at lunch. Mashed turnips. Macaroni and meat sauce. Extra bread, extra butter. I began to think of food all day. Food took up too much of my diary. There was nothing new to say about it in English, so I described it in French. Soon there was nothing new to say about it in either language.

I was assigned to an open ward. The patients could sign themselves out if they wanted to walk the ice-blasted grounds. I spent a lot of time making and unmaking beds. Sometimes it was my job to sit with the patients who did not want to go anywhere. If they didn't want to talk, I wrote. Nobody cared—I said that I was training to be a psychoanalyst. I filled a thirty-nine-cent notebook every few days. I knew all the patients' routines, their delusions, the places where their records were scratched and the sounds repeated. More than anything else, I realized, it had to be boring to be crazy, to think the same sequence of thoughts and come up with the same set of bizarre conclusions, to voice those conclusions using the same words, several times an hour, day in and day out. It was hard to get people off their tracks. Because I was new, I kept trying.

One morning, Mrs. L. was in her office, admitting a new patient, a young woman who sat with her back to the door. I paused as I was passing. There was something about the woman—I didn't know what, but I felt it immediately. A heat. She was wearing a black dress. When she swiveled in her chair and smiled at me, I saw that her eyes were black, too, and her lips very red. Her skin was pallid, shiny, as though she had a fever. Her blonde hair, maybe dyed, was greasy and dull. She was about my age. Her teeth had thin spaces between them, which made her look frightening, predatory, like an animal.

"This is Nonette," Mrs. L. said.

I felt a small electric jolt and said, "Is that French?" That was it—she looked French.

The new patient didn't answer, but looked at me steadily, her smile becoming a false, unpleasant leer.

Mrs. L. pursed her lips and filled in her forms. "Nonette can sleep in No. 20. Here's the linen key. Why don't you help her settle in?"

"Fetch my things along," Nonette ordered.

"Evelina's not a bellhop," Mrs. L. said.

"That's all right." I lugged one of Nonette's suitcases down the corridor. She smiled in an underhanded way and dropped the other suitcase once we were out of Mrs. L.'s sight. She waited while I carried it to her room, and watched as I took her sheets, a pillowcase, a heavy blanket, and a thin cotton waffle-weave spread from the linen closet. Her room was one of the nicer ones, with only two roommates. It had built-in wooden furniture, not flimsy tin dressers, and the bed was solid. It even had all four casters on the legs.

"What a fucking dump," Nonette said.

I said nothing. I was supposed to be pleasant.

Nonette's mouth twisted open in scorn. I left.

The next day, she was extremely friendly to me. When I walked onto the ward, she immediately grabbed my hand, as though we'd been interrupted the day before while having some wonderful conversation, and she tugged me toward the freezing glassed-in porch, where patients went to talk privately. I sat down beside her in an aluminum lawn chair. I was wearing a sweater. She had on a thin cotton button-down shirt, with a necktie and men's chino pants. Her shoes were feminine kitten heels. Her hair was slicked back. She was an odd mixture of elements: she looked depressed but also—it could not be denied—chic. Today she wore no makeup except black eyeliner, and her face was prettier, more harmonious in the subdued light.

"What do you want to talk about?" I said.

"I wanted to talk to someone my age, not those jerks, shrinks, whatever. You're not bad-looking, either. That helps. I want to talk about what's bothering me. I came to get well, didn't I? So I want to talk about how really, truly sick I am. I've talked about it, I know I have, but I haven't really told it."

"OK, go ahead."

She paused for a moment, then she leaned toward me, and when she did her whole face sharpened.

"If I could just be born over," she said, "I'd be born neutral. Woman or man—that's not what I mean. I wouldn't have a sex drive. I wouldn't care about it, need it, or anything. It's just a problem, the things you do that you hate yourself for afterward. Like take when I was nine years old, when I had it first. He was a relative, a cousin, living with us for the summer."

"Where?" I asked.

"Not in stupid France," she answered. "Anyway, he comes in without knocking and kneels by my bed. He uncovers me and starts giving it to me with his mouth. And I'm, like, at first I don't know what—ashamed of it. I could get a hook for my door. I could tell on him. I don't, though, because I get so I want it. He strips naked. He teaches me how to jerk him off. And then he does it to me again.

"I'm a little girl, right? I don't even wash very well. Next time, he brings along a washcloth and cleans me first. We have a ritual. Where are my mother and father? They sleep at the other end of the hall, with the fan going in their room. And my cousin is a fucking Eagle Scout! Is he trying for a fucking merit badge? Anyway, he goes home. I already feel different. I am different. There is a smell on me, sex, that no one else in my schoolroom has. I look at the older boys. I know what's coming. I go searching for it." She laughed suddenly, drawing away. "Look at you. You're, like, fascinated."

She stared out the window. "I'm not French," she said gently. "I'm fucked up. I'm in a state hospital. I think I want a sex-change operation. I want to be a man so I won't have to put up with this shit."

"I'm not giving you shit."

Her mouth gaped mockingly. "Oh, look at you, trying to be tough. You're not tough. You're, like, a little college girl, right? Who the hell cares? I'm from the university, too. I have a Ph.D. Pretty Hot Dick. I'm a man, posing as a woman. You want proof?" Then her face closed in, bored. "I'm just kidding. Get the fuck away from me."

"I'm sorry," I said to her. "You're really beautiful."

She wouldn't say anything, wouldn't look at me now.

"You're an Indian or something, aren't you?" she mumbled. "That's cool."

I went back to the common room and played gin rummy with Warren, who couldn't concentrate. I didn't think he was taking all his medication, but if he'd discovered a way to hide it he was pretty slick.

A policeman was standing in the office the next morning, drinking a cup of coffee with Mrs. L. He'd just brought Warren back. The day before, Warren had marched out of town. He took a narrow road that ran west, and was discovered twenty miles away as he crawled into a farmyard. He had fallen and bloodied the side of his head. He was sleeping now, sedated, and it was not until late afternoon that he rose and came out to sit in the lounge, the side of his head swollen and bandaged. I sat down next to him.

"I hear you had a bad day." These words popped out of my mouth. I was curious. Perhaps it was cruel to be so curious. I asked about the voices he heard—if they were hard on him.

He straightened, shrugged a little. He was wearing a yellow shirt that looked almost new. He ran a hand up his face gently, exploring the damage with his fingers. Then he turned to me, his eyes moist and red. "I did it because they told me—" he started, but he choked on what he might have said and his voice was a crow's croak. He rubbed his face with a fumbling hand and closed his eyes. And then I saw, around the edges of his face, in the balled musculature and the set of his eyes and jaw, that he was in a waking dream.

He raised his arms. He recoiled. He sat down in a chair and began taking apart some invisible thing in his lap. Then his hands froze and he lifted his head, gazed off to the side in a fugue of stillness, listening.

Nonette and I were sitting on the frigid sunporch. She had told the story about being raped by her cousin, the Eagle Scout, to every nurse, aide, doctor, and patient available. It was just a conversation opener. Here, of course, it was not supposed to matter whether or not the story was true—the important thing was her need to tell it. I had been trained to believe that. Nonette was wearing a men's black suit and a Charlie Chaplin–style black bowler that were too big for her and comically masculine. Suddenly she reached out and took my face in her palms, leaned toward me, and kissed me. I didn't resist at all. It didn't even occur to me to resist. All I thought was, How shall I describe this in my diary? There was nothing strange about it, not then, or at least it was no stranger than the other occasions on which I'd kissed someone for the first time. There was the same thrill, the same hush of attraction and mutual daring. Only she was supposed to be crazy, I was supposed to not be crazy, and we were women.

"That was nice." She drew back into her chair, crooked one leg up, and hugged her knee. She stared at me, assessing my reaction. I was suddenly and completely charged with an electrifying embarrassment. I forced myself to rise, and stumbled, awkward and big, to the door of the sunporch and the entrance to the ward. She was still watching, smiling now.

Soon the dinner call came, but she was too tired to eat. "I'm sick," she said as she walked past me. "I'm going to bed."

"Are you OK?" I asked. She ignored me.

Later, I was sent down the ward to check on her. She had slid underneath the covers with all her clothes on. I could see her shoes sticking out at the end of the bed. I stood for a long time, watching, hoping that she would move.

I had escorted a patient to the beauty parlor late one morning, and was returning alone through the underground steam tunnels when she was suddenly there, walking toward me with no escort.

"I have a pass." Nonette grinned, stopping when we were face to face.

There was no one else in the tunnel, which was whitewashed and warm, lit by low-wattage bulbs, and branched off into small closets and locked chambers full of brooms and mops and cleaning solutions. Her face was clear and bright, her hair a rumpled silver in the odd light, her eyes calm and free of makeup. She was as beautiful as someone in a foreign movie, a book, or a catalog of strange, expensive clothes. Her eyes were dark, with green in them, brown, every color. I could almost taste her mouth again, fresh with toothpaste. She was wearing jeans, a white sweatshirt, sneakers, and gym socks. I was wearing my cheap, scratchy white uniform with tucks and a front zipper. She put her fingers on the tongue of the zipper at my throat.

"Are you wearing a slip?" she said.

I took her hand and held it around the wrist, my thumb at her pulse.

"Stop, stop." She pretended to resist, but her voice was soft. "Here." She pulled me, but pulled me only because I did not let go of her wrist. I followed her around a corner, then through a door, and we were right in the middle of the pipes, some wrapped with powdery bandages of asbestos, some smooth, boiling copper conduits. My cap snagged, and I let it fall. We ducked under a nest of pipes and walked down some stone steps to the other side, a kind of landing, completely enclosed. Behind us there was a wall of rough flagstone that smelled of dirt, of fields in summer with the sun beating down after a heavy rain. The heat brought out the smell.

"Let's sit down," she said. "I'd like to get you stoned, but I don't have anything."

I was still holding her wrist. There was barely room to stand. The pipes grazed the tops of our heads. We sat down together. I was shaking, but she was very gentle, not like she'd been the first day. And, anyway, it wasn't how I'd thought it would be. After the first few minutes, there was nothing frightening at all about kissing her or touching her. It was familiar, entirely familiar, much more so than if I'd been touching a boy for the first time. Our bodies were the same, and when I touched her I knew what she was feeling, just as she knew when touching me—it seemed both normal and unbearable. We didn't take our clothes off, just felt each other lightly on the arm and throat and kissed. Her face was soft, like flower petals.

She said, "That's enough." Any longer and we'd have been missed.

As I walked back down the corridors and onto the ward, I began to imagine our story. Nonette had come here in obvious need, and I was here for her. I had come here not knowing that she was what, or whom, I'd always needed. And she was here for me. A week, maybe three, and she would be all right. I'd leave with her, go to Fargo or Minneapolis or wherever. She would come with me.

"Nonette said you asked for a patient visit." Mrs. L. sat behind her desk, a stack of forms beneath her spread hands.

"Yes," I said, though I hadn't. But I was smiling, slowly blooming at the idea. Nonette's idea.

"We like to encourage our aides to work with the patients during off-duty hours, and I don't see anything wrong with it, as long as you know that she presented here with some real problems."

"I know that. I've talked to her about them."

"Good."

Mrs. L. waited, watching me a little too carefully. I was not supposed to know a whole lot about each patient's personal history, at least not more than the patient wanted me to know.

"Look," I said, "she told me about her cousin forcing himself on her. I know that she came here out of control, though I still don't know exactly what precipitated it. I don't know what she's dealing with at home, at school, or if she's going back there. The thing is, I really like Nonette. I'm not doing this because I feel sorry for her."

Mrs. L. bit her lip. "Your motives are good, I know that. But you've got to understand: she's on lithium, and we're adjusting her dosage. She's depressive, and then she has her manic spells."

"We're just going to make a batch of cookies."

Mrs. L. smiled approvingly and signed the pass.

There was a small kitchen in the basement of the aides' residence, just one room with a stove and some cupboards, a fridge, an old wooden table painted white, and six vinyl chairs. Nonette and I made molasses cookies, leaving them soft in the middle, then took them upstairs to my room. The cookies were still warm as we ate them, crumb by crumb, sitting on my bed. We drank cold milk. Later, we took our clothes off. It wasn't strange at all, the covers pulled back, the willows bending over streams and bridges. She had small breasts, pointed, the nipples round and slightly chapped because she didn't wear a bra beneath her men's shirts.

She was older than I was by two years and knew so much more. She kneeled over me and spread her legs with a clinical cool, then began to laugh. We laughed at everything I'd never done, and then we did it.

Just before nine o'clock curfew, I walked Nonette back to the ward, a bag of cookies in one hand.

"Do you think about, you know," I finally asked her, at the door.

"Do I think about what?"

Nonette looked at me, her face bland and empty, smiling. She looked like a girl in a ski commercial. Healthy. In my room, when she came, she'd made me look into her eyes, deep with pleasured shock. Now those eyes were scary cheerleader eyes.

"Do I think about what?" she said again.

I looked down at my boots. About what's going to happen to us, I wanted to say. But I didn't. The night was so cold and dark that the snow made squeaking noises as it settled in drifts around the big, square yard. I could hear the trees, tall black pines, cracking. I stood there as Nonette walked into the hospital, as the glass-and-steel doors shut behind her with that movie-ending sound of metal catching, holding fast. The locks were automatic, but I tried them once, anyway, as she disappeared down the bright corridor.

"I'm going home next week," Nonette said one morning. "My parents decided it was OK."

Her parents? Why hadn't I ever seen them? A sudden burst of energy pulsed from the center of my chest. I clapped my hands fast, making sounds to divert the awful feeling, and then I wrung them in the air, shedding the pain like drops of water.

Nonette looked at me and shook her head. "Are you all right?"

I caught my breath, let it out slowly. "Have they been down to visit?"

"Sure. You work days. They drive down in the early evening."

"Next week, next week."

My face stretched into a stupid smile, and she twinkled back. She's not OK, I thought. She's crazier than I am if she can deny this. She must be. I tore my gaze away and felt a deep body flush, as though my ribs were glowing hot, like the bars of a grill. My mind spun a series of wild questions: *If she weren't crazy . . . if this weren't out of the ordinary . . . if it couldn't be helped . . . if I were wrong . . . if people could see . . . if she left here . . . if it meant nothing to her . . . if she didn't care about me at all . . .* I stepped away from her. She had a lovely face, so gentle, a pretty face. A prom queen face. She was wearing a blue sweater, a plaid skirt, and knee-high stockings—ultra-normal Midwest catalog clothes—now that she was well.

"Come and see me," she said.

"Sure! I will!"

She didn't mean it—of course she didn't. I was part of what she thought of as her illness, a symptom of which she believed she had been cured. She, on the other hand, was what I was looking for. I could hardly breathe for wanting her. I walked away with my hands shaking in the scratchy cloth of my pockets. I kept going, without punching out, and walked back down the corridors of the hospital, out the doors, and across the snowy central lawn.

I called in sick the next morning and the morning after that. Two days went by. I couldn't make it to the telephone anymore. I could barely force myself to get up and walk to the bathroom. Once I was in bed again, a kind of black hole gravity held me there. Acid flowed back into my brain, and I could see creatures moving in the Chinese landscape of my bedspread. I threw it on the floor. Gray curtains came down. I put my grandfather's tobacco pouch under my pillow and tried to remember what he said when he prayed. I couldn't think of a single word. The air was painful. I breathed pain in and out, and its residue clung to my lungs like tar, making each breath a little more difficult.

A week went by, and then Mrs. L. came to the door and called, "Can I come in? Can you answer?" I tried. I opened my mouth. Nothing came out. It was such a peculiar feeling that I started to laugh. But there was no sound. I went to sleep again, slept and slept, and, the next time I woke, Mrs. L. was in the room, sitting beside my bed, and she was using the voice she used with the others.

"We're going to move you," she said. "We've called your mother."

Which was how I ended up in Nonette's bed after all.

I was sitting on the cracked green plastic sofa in the common room, wearing my nurse's shoes, only now no uniform to go with them, just baggy jeans and a droopy brown sweater. I'd talked to my mother on the phone and summoned up the energy to convince her that I was all right, that I only needed a rest and would be back in school in time for the next quarter. I'd told my mother that I would use this voluntary commitment as a rest period, but the fact was I was afraid, afraid of losing my observer, the self who told me what to do. My consciousness was fragile ground now, as thin as forming ice. Every morning, when I opened my eyes and experienced my first thought, I was flooded with relief. The *I* was still there. If it went, there would be only gravity to guide me.

Warren walked into the common room and saw me sitting on the sofa. He came over, in his careful and dignified way, and stood before me. He was wearing his yellow shirt, along with a rust-colored jacket, a striped tie of rich burgundy silk, and gray woolen slacks: his best clothes. His shirt had French cuffs. Instead of cufflinks, he had used safety pins.

"You should have cufflinks," I muttered.

"I'll slaughter them all," he said.

"Shut up," I answered.

I lay there for days and more days. I did not get out of bed. I did not read Anaïs Nin—she couldn't possibly help me now. I was past all that, and, anyway, she was the one who had got me into trouble by providing the treacherous paradigm of a life that I was too backward or provincial or reservation-bound to pull off. I no longer wanted adventure. The thought of Paris was a burden. I would never see the back of Notre Dame, and the coffee I drank would always be transparent.

My mother and father came down to see me every weekend. All I did when they visited was cry in sympathy for their worry over me, or fall asleep, but after they left I missed them. I thought about how I had grown up with the certainty of my parents' love, and how rare a thing that was, and how unaccountable and shameful my breakdown was, as was the fact that I had just loved a woman to the point of literal madness. I was just a nothing, half-crazy, half-drugged half Chippewa.

One day, Corwin came to see me.

I was surprised but not embarrassed. He'd learned where I was from my aunt. He remembered the acid he'd fed me, and he felt that he should look me up. He was dressed in a long black riding duster, with a strange orange hunting cap pulled down over his eyes. Under the duster, he was carrying a violin case.

"Sit down."

I gestured with a cigarette. I tried to look bored, but actually I was excited to see him.

Corwin sat in a plastic armchair and rested the violin case on his lap. His face was long, his eyes dark and Indian. He had a short scraggle of unmowed beard. His ponytail flowed out from under his cap.

"So," he said.

"So," I said.

We nodded for a while, like two sages on a hill. Then he opened the case and picked up his fiddle. As he tuned it—an unfamiliar sound—the other patients began to wander out of their rooms and down the corridor. The nurses ventured from their station and stood, arms folded, chewing gum. Their mouths stopped moving when Corwin began to play, and some of the patients sat down, right where they were, a couple of them on the floor, as if the music had cut through the room like a scythe.

After the first run of notes, the music gathered. Corwin played a slow and pretty tune that made people's eyes blur. Warren stood stiff and tall, rooted in the center of the linoleum. Others swayed or looked as if they might weep, but that changed quickly as Corwin picked up the tempo and plucked out a lively Red River jig. At this point, Warren began to walk around and around the room, faster and faster. The music ticked along in a jerky way, and then something monstrous happened. All the sounds merged for a moment in the belly of the violin and filled the room with distress. Alarm struck us. Warren stopped walking and backed up flat against the wall. But Corwin drew some note out of the chaos in his hands, and then drew it farther up and up, until it was unbearable, but at the very point where it might have become a shriek that note changed a fraction and broke into the most lucid sweetness.

Warren slid down the wall, his hand over his heart as if he were taking a pledge. His head slumped onto his chest. The rest of us sat down, too. Calm rained upon us, and a strange peace slowed our hearts. The playing went on in a penetrating, lovely way. I don't know how long it lasted. I don't know when or if it ever really ended. Warren had fallen to the floor. A nurse plodded over to check his pulse. The violin was the only thing in the world, and in that music there was dark assurance. The music understood, and it would be there whether we stayed in pain or regained our sanity, which was also painful. I was small. I was whole. Nothing mattered.

When the music was just reverberations, I stood up. The nurse was checking her watch and frowning first at it, then down at Warren, then at her watch again. I stood next to Corwin as he carefully replaced his violin in its case and snapped the latches down. I looked at my cousin and he looked at me—he gave me his wicked, shy grin and pointed his lips in a kiss, toward the door.

"I can't leave here," I said.

And I walked out of that place.

When I left the hospital with Corwin, I took my purse and my diary and nothing else. I left behind Anaïs—the entire boxed set, annotated. I didn't . know if I could actually bear leaving the safety of the hospital, but I just kept going until we reached Corwin's car. I'd lost a lot of weight and hardly exercised, so I was dizzy and had to ask Corwin to stop the car once so that I could puke. He told me that he had stopped selling drugs. He was straight now, he said, which gave me an opening.

"Well, I'm not. I'm a lesbian," I told him.

He said that I couldn't be. I didn't dress like one.

"Like you'd know," I said.

He said that he did know. He'd been around. "They dress like me, aaaay."

We drove along quietly for a while.

"I'm really sorry that I gave you that acid, man," he said. "Did it, you know, change your head around?"

"You mean did it make me a lesbian?"

He nodded.

"I don't think so."

We drove some more. We'd known each other stoned, sick, and drunk. We'd beaten each other up in Catholic school. So the silence between us was comfortable, even a relief. I looked out the car window. The world was beautiful all along the road. The fields were great mirrors of melted water. And the light was clear and golden, blazing on the slick surfaces. I started to feel better. It was as if telling my news to someone I'd known my whole life had lifted a great weight from me. Every morning in the hospital, I'd awakened and felt normal and then remembered about Nonette. Corwin's taking my confession in stride removed some of the dark glamour from my feelings.

"Do you actually know any lesbians?" I asked.

"I've played in bars all over, but I don't know any just to talk to," he said. Then, a moment later, "Or any I could set you up with, if that's what you want."

A heated flush rose along my collarbone.

"Hey," Corwin said after a while, "you don't have to go anywhere with this thing just yet. Take it easy."

I didn't answer, but after a while I felt happier, thinking that he was right.

As we passed onto the reservation, I saw that the ditches were burning. Fires had been set to clear the spring stubble, and a thin glaze of smoke hung over the road in a steady cloud. After Corwin dropped me off, I sat outside with my grandfather Mooshum, drinking cool water from tall galvanized water cans. It occurred to me that I'd be all right. I didn't have to do anything, not right away. I didn't even have to record my sensations in a diary. I could just sit with Mooshum, drinking water. As the sun went down, light shot through the smoke and turned the air around us a dark gold that cast an unsettling radiance on the trees and houses. Mooshum and I watched as the light began to recede. It was very cold, but still we sat until the darkness had a brown edge to it, and my mother came to the door, expressing no surprise at seeing me there.

"Come in here, you two," she said, her voice gentle.

SEQUOIA GARDENS

Ernest J. Finney

California. From the back window of the van it was a world made out of cement, a tangle of freeways streaming with cars, of aqueduct-like overpasses. Once you merged it was like you were propelled along in your slot among the other vehicles by some mastermind computer. Everyone gaped from the tinted windows when Arturo said, "This is LA," though nothing looked very different from before. There were twelve of them plus the driver; no one spoke, they just looked. He jumped when he heard the sirens. The sound got louder and then there were flashing lights. "Fire trucks," Arturo said. "Something is always burning in LA." But it was police cars, one two three four five, passing them in the fast lane as they and all the other cars slowed and moved to the right. Was he going to end up in the back of one of those cars, handcuffed, bleeding from a gunshot wound? "Don't worry," Arturo said as if he could read his mind. "I've got your IDs: born in the Golden State, all of you. You haven't committed a crime. Yet." He and the driver started laughing their heads off. At sundown they started climbing: the city lights ended and the freeways faded into black except for the taillight streams of red veering off and the white cones of light ahead from the van. They still watched.

A week ago he'd been sitting in his uncle's appliance store in Mazatlan—it was something to do before he started hotel school in Mexico City in the fall—when opportunity knocked. That was his mother's favorite expression. It had knocked when she'd signed up for cosmetology school. Again when she'd applied to work at the hotel in Acapulco. But the sound could be false, they both knew that: there had been a very loud knock when she'd met his father, then the assistant night manager at the hotel. He had always wondered himself if you'd actually know at the critical moment each time opportunity knocked. What if you failed to heed it?

His mother had a first-row seat as manager of the hotel salon and kept a minute-by-minute record of who got ahead. Every night she came home with more information. It was the maître d' in the restaurant who made the most money, more than the concierge. But it was the manager who met all the most important people. The chef got a write-up in an international newspaper. The couple who had the jewelry store concession netted a hundred thousand dollars one quarter.

By the time he was nine he was working after school in the hotel kitchen on cleanup. He saw for himself how the El Conquistador operated. It took him until he was eleven, the same year he'd joined the recreation director's Boy Scout troop, to decide for sure what direction he wanted to go. He would aim for the top, hotel manager. No one got yelled at or worked up a sweat in the manager's office. He'd taken all three English courses offered at his school because of that, and also because he liked British movies. He was going to learn Japanese, too; they were the world's most dedicated travelers. When he got tall enough he moved from the kitchen to outside maintenance and then to housekeeping, which was more efficient than maintenance, and the reason for the 405-room hotel's 93 percent occupancy rate, according to his mother. At fifteen he became a bellhop, which meant big tips.

His mother's younger brother Jorge had worked in maintenance at the hotel too, but later went north and opened an appliance store in Mazatlan. After school ended in May every year he took the bus to Mazatlan and stayed with his uncle's family for the summer. He knew his uncle felt it his duty to make a man of him because he had no father. And because his mother was his mother, a strong woman, as Jorge said. He enjoyed being with Jorge. "Raul, machismo is the code of the simpleton. Use your head, not your huevos." When they went out on repair calls he worked right alongside his uncle. He could replace a washing machine pump almost as fast as Jorge. He liked figuring out what went wrong. They'd stop for a beer on the way back to the store. "You see this?" and his Uncle Jorge made a fist out of his hand. "God made this so you won't get any girls pregnant until you're ready to be a man." They both broke up laughing. Jorge was funny; he always said, "Don't take yourself so seriously. Life is a comedy; laugh at it."

Luz, his cousin, oldest of Jorge's three daughters, was not funny. She was worse than his mother when it came to yelling. Aunt Claudia never yelled: how did Luz pick it up? They were both almost eighteen but she treated him like he was ten years old. "Raul, when you work back in the repair shop, pick up after yourself." He'd just replaced the belt on a washing machine motor, and she was scowling at him and throwing the dirty rags he'd used in the drum. "And it's your turn to clean the bathroom, too." He swept out the whole store and then shook some cleanser in the toilet and wiped out the sink. He heard Luz yelling again and went out front. A man was just going out the door; he mouthed something through the front window at Luz, drew his forefinger across his throat, and went over to the restaurant on the other side of the street.

"That *estúpido* was looking for the crew that's going north." Luz started laughing. "How dumb can you get? He'll work until his back breaks up there in the fields in California. Or spend twelve hours in a motel laundry and get paid for eight and kick back half of that to the guy that got him the job. Get spit on by the gringos and called names by the old wetbacks and probably get knifed outside some bar by some Indian from Chiapas. It's better to make fifteen dollars a day down here than fifty up north. That's if you even make it up there. If you don't suffocate in the back of some truck or die of thirst crossing the desert and owe some recruiter for the rest of your life. No thank you."

He went out the back way and crossed the street toward the restaurant. He'd just heard opportunity knock, but he wanted to find out more before he opened the door. A cousin of his father who went up north and worked for eight or nine years in a fancy restaurant in Montreal had gone from dishwasher to chef. Sent his money home to his mother and came back when he had enough to build a house and marry his sweetheart. But the thing he remembered him saying more than once was, "For Americans money is an illness; they always want more." He didn't want a lot of money; only enough to enroll in the European program at the Geneva site of the hotel management school, where you got to spend six months each in Italy, France, and England, interning at different hotels. The thought of London girls made him almost run down the street.

They went north in an old ex-tuna boat. You could still smell the odor of fish in the cabin. The Pacific for once lived up to its name and remained calm for the whole trip. The food was good, and all twelve were allowed up on deck in the evening to get some exercise. They never saw a plane or another boat. They slept and played cards; a few swam one evening. It was like a four-day vacation. On the last night, Arturo, who was going to be in charge up in the mountains, brought two cases of beer up to where they were all sitting on the forward deck. "Enjoy this," he said; "this will be the last booze you get for the next five months."

The four Indians, who didn't speak Spanish, didn't understand what Arturo was saying, but each took his two beers. Miguel and Juan, the two brothers, didn't drink and Arturo took the bottles for himself, whispering to the others that they were Jehovah's Witnesses. Everyone knew that already. They didn't gamble either. Neither did the two Guatemalans or the Cuban. The Argentine, Ernesto, was the one who had come into his uncle's store in Mazatlan. His Spanish sounded strange and he drank and gambled and got into a fistfight with one of the Indians. His uncle always said, "Judge others as you would hope to be judged," but then Jorge went to mass every morning at six a.m. also. Keep your mouth shut: that was his own proverb, at least until he knew what was what.

The boat put into shore while it was still dark. Everyone filed across the sand and got into the van. There were no problems. He didn't know what he'd expected, but this was California. It was like sitting in the cine watching a movie about the place and then being asked to step into the scene. Like he was one of the actors now. He knew the geography of the state, shaped like a sock: they'd landed somewhere near the toe, he thought. The van stopped at an empty warehouse where they waited a long time for the trailer they were to pull. Then hours through L.A. and the drive through the night and now through flat country that all of a sudden changed to hills. They were taking back roads, going up now, and suddenly the van stopped in a grove of trees. They were given box lunches and let out to pee. It was still too dark to see. It was getting colder; the heater was turned on, but it was still cold. He fumbled around in his bag until he found his sweatshirt.

Back in the van again, he fell asleep thinking of the girl from London who'd come with her parents to the hotel that winter; she had played tennis with him, and he'd let her beat him, once; and then of Luz, who was going to keep his mother from worrying. He'd left a dozen postcards, each with a different scribbled message, that Luz was going to send to his mother, one every couple of weeks. His mother would probably phone, but Luz was ready for that. He would owe her, but he was going to make a lot of money: $4,700 U.S. a month, plus a bonus when the crop was in. Jorge thought he'd got lucky, hired on as deckhand on a fishing boat, and would be back in October.

He woke up when the van began to brush against branches as it went up a dirt track. It was getting light now, and he could see the shape of trees and what looked like mountain peaks. Everyone was coming awake. The van was slowing now, and it came to a stop at a flat place and they got out. If it was cold before, it was freezing now. He put on his jacket and his wool cap. They had been told about the weather and the clothes they'd need. And when Arturo had gone through everyone's things to make sure they didn't have any radios, cameras, cell phones, or guns, he'd checked the clothes they were bringing, and their shoes too. He'd loaned money to the Indians to buy boots and the Argentine a heavier jacket and gave them all leather gloves on credit until they got their first pay. They all watched the van maneuver around the flat place until it faced the way they'd come, and then it went down the track. They were left standing there, shivering. He wondered if this was such a good idea.

"Gentlemen," Arturo said, "this is where you earn your money." Looking at the mountainside in the morning light, he didn't think it could be done. They'd have to go straight up. There was no trail. They had unloaded the trailer and lashed the equipment onto their packboards; each of them had to be carrying over fifty kilos: supplies, hoses and shovels, food, plus their own gear.

Arturo led the way and the rest of them followed. There were jokes at first about mountain goats, but there was no talk after the first ten minutes. It was too hard to breathe. He'd estimated the flat where they'd started at around a thousand meters. There were trees at first, dense, and then only brush and more brush, taller than they were: you couldn't see where you were going. They stopped at a wooden sign—an unpronounceable word followed by NA-TIONAL FOREST with USFS underneath it—and rested.

He thought it would be Arturo who'd have a hard time—he had a big belly and must have been in his forties, but it was one of the Indians his own age who wouldn't get up after the rest. He was surprised at how patient Arturo was. He reminded everyone about the contracts they'd signed and the amount of money they'd receive each month. Then he took the Indian's pack and distributed the cans of food to everyone else to carry. "This was too heavy for you," he said to the Indian. The Indian still wouldn't get up. The Indian said something to Arturo in his dialect, and Arturo answered him, translating in Spanish to the rest of them. "He wants to go home." They spoke some more. Arturo was trying to reason with him, speaking asides to them in Spanish like an interpreter. "We all have to fulfill our agreements. The *padrón* will be upset if we don't." Arturo must have gotten tired of talking finally because he went over and yanked the Indian to his feet. The Indian tried to get away

then and Arturo pulled out a pistol. The Indian stopped dead. "Raul, go dig
a hole over there," and he pointed off the trail. They were in the tall trees
again, and they were all using their shovels as walking sticks. Arturo cocked
the hammer of the pistol. The sound seemed to echo in the quiet. The Indian
came back fast and started up the trail ahead of everyone else.

On the way up he thought about why he had come. The money, of course.
When he'd gone into the restaurant it was Arturo he'd seen with the Argentine, laughing at something Ernesto had said. It sounded like a roar; people
turned to look. Arturo was a big man and his manner was larger still, like he
was five meters tall and it wasn't just a job interview but a new life you were
signing up for and he'd show you how to live it. He'd watched them for a
while before going over to the table, but when he did he knew what he was
going to say: yes, and yes again to anything. Even when Arturo told them
what kind of crop they would be growing he had said yes.

They reached where they were going at dusk and everyone got into their
sleeping bags, exhausted. He was too excited to sleep. He kept adding up the
money he'd have at the end of the contract and wondering how much the
bonus would be. He knew Arturo wouldn't have shot the Indian, but he had
scared everyone with his "Dig a hole." The man was a good actor.

He must have fallen asleep because the next thing he knew it was getting
light and he could see the sharp points of the mountains around them. The
long narrow meadow, overhung with trees, was almost flat. A little stream
ran down the higher side. He had woken up inside a nature movie this time.
Instead of meadow grass, there were long rows of little plants coming up in
the turned-over dirt. Arturo would tell them what to do next.

It was cold outside and it was freezing in the water, building the dam across
the creek. Arturo sat on a log and explained. The seeds had been planted
weeks ago, and now it was up to them. "The plants need water, they thrive on
water, and that's why we're building the reservoir. The more water, the faster
they'll grow." They worked all morning fitting the boulders into place until
the water started backing up. Then the two-and-a-half-inch hoses took the
water by gravity to the garden. The whole program was very well thought-
out. Arturo had done this before, and he knew the rules. No fires after dark.
When you hear an airplane, hide, then freeze. If you see anyone, report it at
once to Arturo.

It started to snow that afternoon, big flakes that floated out of the sky, still
blue in places, like pieces of white lace. The two Guatemalans ran around

trying to catch them in their open mouths and made everyone laugh. They were short and squat and were hopping around like two chocolate toads. The Cuban had been a ship's steward and quit early to do the cooking for the big meal in the afternoon on a two burner portable gas stove fed by a small propane canister. They ate big tin platefuls of pasta with meat sauce and bread, and dried fruit for dessert. For supper—no fires allowed—they had sandwiches and bowls of sweet U.S. cereal.

The week went by like an hour-and-a-half feature film. They'd dug irrigation ditches around the rows of plants and positioned the water hoses coming down from the reservoir. It all worked: you could almost see the plants grow as you hoed around them. There was a good feeling among the crew, too, as if that were written into their contract. No one complained when it rained hard and most of their sleeping bags got wet, or when the Cuban burned the rice. They were so tired after work they lay like they were in a stupor listening to Arturo, who was full of stories. He had been to the university and had two degrees. Played professional soccer for Puerto Rico. Taught school. Made a CD. Been married; had children. Lived in Chicago. Owned a trucking company. "If you're so rich, why are you here?" the Argentine asked.

"For the same reason you're here. Because I need the money." Then after a pause he added, "Or I'll go bankrupt." No one talked after that. Everyone was probably thinking, like he was, about the money.

Sunday afternoon they were supposed to have off, but Arturo yelled, "Boy Scout, you and the two Witnesses get your packs; we're going down." Once when he was lashing together some tree limbs with nylon rope, making a chair for himself, Arturo had asked, "Where did you learn that?" and without thinking he'd said as a Boy Scout. Arturo had thought that was hilarious. He'd been calling him Boy Scout ever since. Arturo had a way with words, and he was funny. He would hold up pretty well in an argument with his mother.

It took only an hour and nine minutes to get down to the dirt road and the cache where the week's food was hidden, but four hours and forty minutes to climb back up to the garden, which was a lot faster than the first time. The food was light this time: freeze-dried meat and vegetables, the sweet cereal that everyone liked. Only the sugar, dried milk and flour, and the propane weighed anything, and Arturo carried that. They stopped often to just stand, breathing hard, looking back over the way they'd come. They all agreed it was a beautiful place. No one ever mentioned that what they were doing was illegal or that they could go to jail for years if they were caught. He hardly ever thought of that.

It was really not hard work once the routine was established. The plants told them when they needed more water; they began to droop. Then Arturo, who was always checking, would yell, and they'd start running down the dry irrigation ditches to change the hoses. By the third week the plants had doubled their height to almost half a meter and were becoming bushy. Miguel, the older Witness brother, turned out to be a better cook than the Cuban and sometimes would get up early so they'd have pancakes with their coffee instead of the usual jam and crackers. Arturo made sure there was a pot of hot water so they could wash their tin plates, once he'd suggested it. None of them needed to shave regularly except Arturo, and he was growing a beard.

He'd also taken it upon himself to dig a new latrine further away from the camp than the old one when it began to smell, and he picked up all the refuse and buried it every morning. The recreation director at the hotel, their troop leader, had never tired of saying that to shoulder responsibility before you're asked was the sign of a good scout. Arturo asked him to make him a chair. He found an old dead tree with limbs as hard as steel to use for the frame and then took his time and wove a yellow nylon rope seat. "It's a goddamn throne," Arturo said when he sat on it the first time. He looked like a king, too, bearded, holding the thick crooked walking stick he used on the steep slopes.

After Arturo told all his stories, Juan, Miguel's younger brother, told them stories from films he'd seen when he worked in a movie house. He would half listen in his sleeping bag, staring up at the sky, letting thoughts go through his head like shooting stars. He'd like to come back to California as a tourist some day and really see the place. Even come back here. It was sort of funny to spend a month in a foreign country and never see a single native person.

There was a rock outcropping just above the reservoir where Arturo set up a spotter scope on a tripod. He lay there by the hour, looking over the country. When his eyes got tired he'd tell someone else to take over. It was a job everyone liked, lying flat on the rocks, watching, heads nodding after a while, trying not to get caught snoozing. You could see for miles across the other ridges to the higher mountain peaks. When he remembered, he brought some of the cereal to feed the birds. There was a dark blue bird with a black crest who made loud squawks and pecked at his shoes if he didn't get fed. The air was so clear you felt you could see forever.

Up there in the quiet he would daydream his future life as if he were reading it on his résumé. Graduate, Swiss Hotel Management School, Geneva, and Mexico City. Promotions all the way: desk clerk to director of the Conquistador hotel chain. Memberships: Lions Club International and Toast-masters. Marriage: a beautiful wife crazy about sex but one his mother liked too. Pastimes: foreign films; shoots par weekly on the hotel's golf course.

No one would own up to it, but someone had nailed up a little picture of Our Lady of Guadalupe on a tree. It looked like it was from a calendar. His mother had never insisted he go to church; he wasn't even sure he was bap-tized. For the tourists the hotel sponsored a traditional religious procession each year that went through one of the old neighborhoods. Last year he'd helped carry the platform with the giant Virgin on top, all the cameras aimed at her, into the church. His mother had whispered to him during the collec-tion, "Raul, who is the fattest person in this building? Who eats the most?" He had looked at everyone. The three priests were all fatter than even the heaviest tourists. His mother poked him and snickered, "Wait until you see the bishop."

Arturo ignored the picture. It was the Argentine, Ernesto, who yelled, "Who put that superstitious crap up there?" and started to walk toward the tree. No one answered, but one of the Indians picked up the big ax. Arturo stood up too. "Leave it, Ernesto; it may bring us luck. Think of it as just a picture of some woman." And he went over and grabbed the ax away from the Indian.

Whoever left the food down on the road made sure that the few glass jars were wrapped in crumpled newspapers so they wouldn't break. When no one was looking, he saved the papers in his pack to read later. A lot of times it was just the advertisements, but sometimes there were comics or stories. A couple of times there was almost a complete paper. He wasn't sure he'd ever read a whole newspaper before in English. It was like the news on TV: violence interested people, and in this newspaper a war was occurring daily in the cit-ies of California, more people were killed on the streets of L.A. than in the Middle East. There were murders in Acapulco too, but not like California. Little kids, shot down for fun by gangs.

It was Arturo who found the other camp two ridges over with the spotter scope. They built a fire one morning and he saw the smoke. "Los locos," Arturo called them. "The government has fire lookouts; this is a national forest." If you looked long enough you could see the workers moving in the open. That garden was much smaller than theirs, about ten hectares, and their own crop was better hidden, more under the canopy of trees. For some reason it gave him a kind of comfort to see other people in the wilderness.

At first it was interesting to watch the deer come around the garden. Sometimes a doe and her fawns wandered down, and once a whole herd of twenty-seven, five of them with antlers. It was Miguel who noticed they were grazing on the far side of the crop. Arturo had two men sleep on either end of the patch, then, and strung fishing line with empty cans with rocks inside to rattle when the deer came down to feed. It worked; the deer didn't like to be disturbed while they had dinner.

And then it was June first: they'd been up in the woods for a month and it was payday. Arturo woke him and the brothers before dawn to go down with him. So they wouldn't leave a trail, all four took different paths, ten meters apart, for the hour slide down on their backsides. The sun was trying to fit between the two highest peaks as they got to the road. He was surprised to see the van. "Wait," Arturo said, and went over alone. He and the driver spoke in English about the crops, how tall the plants were. Arturo handed him a plastic bag of leaves. They laughed at some joke he didn't understand, shook hands and the van moved off.

He wondered if it was the thought of the money that made them stronger; they took only one break all the way back up. And the food was changing; there were cold cuts and hunks of cheese. Sacks of cookies. Everyone was waiting around the stove when they finally puffed into camp. No one moved while they caught their breath. He noticed Arturo had lost most of his belly and his beard had some gray. They all must have changed somewhat, he thought, but not so much as Arturo because they were younger. Someday they'd all be as old as Arturo.

No one formed a line, but after Arturo took out a blue plastic bag from inside his shirt and unzipped it, the Cuban took a step closer. Arturo counted out forty-seven hundred dollar bills into the Cuban's right hand, and then put a new white cloth money belt to wear around his waist into his left. "We're going to fill that," he told each person. When everyone had got his money, the Argentine asked, "Did I get my turn? I forget." Everyone laughed. Arturo surprised them: he handed each one a tall can of beer. The brothers drank theirs this time. Arturo made a toast, raising his can. "Hard work pays," he said, and everyone agreed.

The money didn't change anything; there was nowhere to spend it, and Arturo had confiscated all the cards because of the arguments, so there wasn't any gambling. It would be nice to have a new jacket; the zipper on his old one didn't work any more. He kept his roll wrapped in a plastic bag in the left front pocket of his pants and filled the money belt with folded newspapers. He had walked in on Miguel by accident as he was digging a hole up by the reservoir. Miguel had stopped what he was doing and walked away.

It was getting dark later, so he was able to read after supper. He usually went up by the spotter scope to be alone. He tried not to read any of the political articles in the newspapers he'd saved: his mother could go on for hours about politics, his Uncle Jorge too; all adults were too ready to tell you their opinions. "Raul, you can read the *L.A. Times?*" Arturo asked him in English. He hadn't heard Arturo come up the trail.

"No, I just look at the pictures," he answered back in English, and they both laughed. After a minute he said, "Arturo, how could they have elected the Terminator to be their governor?" He thought it a question that would interest Arturo.

"Because it's a beauty contest up here, like anywhere. If you say all the right things to the different groups and the very rich support you, you win. You have to be older, to have seen it happen over and over, to understand how flimsy any system is. Just because they say democracy this and constitution that doesn't mean that the people with the most money don't run things."

"My mother says the minute the candidates' names get printed on the ballots they are corrupted and they all become the same person."

"Your mother's a smart woman. I know someone who votes up here. You know what he says? 'If Jesus Christ came back to the U.S.A. they would call him a terrorist and give him a lethal injection, and if Judas came back they would say he had learned from his mistakes and elect him president.'"

Arturo stopped talking to look through the scope. "This country has made too many bad choices," he went on. "That's what catches up to you, just like in a person. It won't be around in fifty years. It has no memory. The U.S. chooses not to remember what happened to the other empires in the twentieth century—Great Britain, France, Russia. All gone, and it's going to go too."

It was the first time he'd ever really talked to Arturo. He wondered what his mother would say about him. A know-it-all? A man who would never be anything more than a night clerk? Arturo was more than that.

The second month went faster than the first. He got the black-crested bird to hop on his finger when he fed him. He built a cage out of sticks and mosquito net but decided not to shut the bird inside after Arturo said it would die. One of the Indians killed a fawn with a shovel but the meat was too strong, no one would eat it, and they ended up burying the carcass. They all took turns using the big pot of hot water on the stove to wash their clothes, scrubbing them with bar soap and a stiff brush, then rinsing them in the creek and hanging them on a line under the trees. They dried in a couple of hours when the sun was out. All of them dressed in their clean clothes on Sunday as if they were going somewhere. He moved his sleeping bag for the fourth time, cutting fresh pine boughs for a mattress. The new place was under some manzanita brush at a distance from the garden. He wanted to able to get away if something happened. He'd noticed Arturo went off by himself every evening, to a different place each night. The Indians stayed by themselves in the pines. Everybody else slept near the stove.

He was amazed how well things were working out. There was plenty to eat; no one stole any food; you could take what you wanted. If you needed something, ·toothpaste, you told Arturo and he'd write it down and you'd have it by the next week. There was no reason to argue, but everyone was too tired to, anyway. The Indians had made flutes, a rattle and a small drum, and sometimes entertained them after dinner.

The last Sunday of the month the four of them went down. He'd made the mistake of suggesting to Arturo that he ought to take someone else, to give the others a turn; there had been some grumbling. He'd said it in English to Arturo: he only did that when there was no one else near. "I'll make the decisions," Arturo said.

The same driver was in the van waiting, but someone new stepped out of the passenger side. When Arturo saw who it was, he started cursing in English. You didn't have to understand the language to know what he was saying. The passenger started laughing and yelled, "You know what you can do, Artie," in English.

The driver of the van said something to the passenger, who yelled again to Arturo, "Tell the goats to get back to work; time is money," before he lurched back to the van. The man was drunk.

Arturo was red-faced with anger. The driver came over to Arturo. "I couldn't stop him from coming up," he said.

"The deal was, he was not to be part of the operation. I was promised that. He's bad news." The two of them moved away, talking quietly, but he could hear enough. "If they even think he's around here, much less see him, they'll guess about our operation. I don't care what his father said. He's not the only one who put money up for this. It's going to be bigger than last time."

The passenger got out of the van again, unzipped himself and started pissing in Arturo's direction, laughing his head off, yelling, "Come and get it." Arturo went for him; the driver ran to shove the passenger back into the van; he and the two brothers held Arturo back. It was like trying to stop a horse. But the van took off, finally.

No one said a word all the way back up; they never rested once. Everyone was waiting around the stove again. Arturo didn't seem to understand what they were there for and walked up to the latrine. From there it looked like he was going over to the scope. Everyone was watching him, waiting. The brothers must have told the others what had happened down at the road. He pretended he was going to take a look at his wash on the line and passed close enough to Arturo to whisper, "They're waiting for their money; it's payday."

Arturo seem to come awake then. He went back to where everyone sat. "Something's come up. I can't pay you this week. Next Sunday." No one said a word. Arturo walked back to the point to look through the scope.

The weather turned warm and the plants liked that, gaining height like they were trying to reach the sun. They were taller than he was now and had spread out, like the stand of bamboo in front of the hotel. He hadn't thought of the Conquistador in a month. He was moving the hose at the far end of the patch when Ernesto came running. "Come on," he said, and they ran back up the slope toward the reservoir. The Argentine had confided that his real name wasn't Ernesto but Daniel, and that he was from Paraguay. He had changed his name to honor Che Guevara the same day he'd gotten the tattoo of Che on his arm. When they got close to the pond Ernesto shhhed and put his forefinger against his lips, and they crept up through the boulders. At first he didn't understand what he was seeing. The two Guatemalans were in the water up to their waists. One was washing the other's back. They all bathed there. Then the first turned around with the bar of soap. She had breasts; she was a woman. Then Ernesto made a snort and the two Guatemalans saw them.

It didn't take long for everyone to know. He'd gone and found Arturo; Ernesto had told the others. He knew this was going to change things, cause trouble. The Cuban was combing and recombing his long hair. Even the brothers were acting lively, rubbing their palms together in anticipation when Arturo came back down followed by the two Guatemalans.

Arturo took his time; he seemed amused. He said in Spanish first, "Betty and Armando are husband and wife. They have been married for three years." Looking at them with their clothes on, he couldn't tell which was which until Betty held up her left hand with a gold band around her finger now. The two of them did as much work as all four of the Indians, who were lazy. The Indians were awaiting an explanation too, with big grins. Arturo spoke to them next. He must have explained two or three times in different ways, but the Indians still were smiling. Then he said in Spanish, "If anyone even thinks of interfering with Betty, he'll answer to me." They all went back to what they were doing, but their thoughts were their own.

It was Saturday, an important day because it was one more day to Sunday, when they got their fresh food supply, and the day Arturo told them they'd get their back pay. He was up at the lookout, watching through the scope. It was too early, there wasn't enough light and the mist made it worse, but he still liked looking at the mountain for the changes. There was always something: the oaks were leafing out, the snow on the peaks was receding, the meadows were colored with wildflowers, the streams growing larger. As he watched he heard an unfamiliar sound. Then he heard Arturo running, yelling, "Down, get down, turn off the stove." A helicopter appeared above the next ridge, and like a computer game, men started to slide down a rope. You didn't need the scope to see, but he watched through the glass anyhow for the finish, men running away and right into the arms of a group of police wearing helmets who had come down the ridge. Shots. He closed his eyes; he didn't want to know.

No one said anything but everyone was thinking the same thing. What was going to happen to the men? They were going to prison for a long time. The drug laws were harsh here. And not one would talk, either, to make it easier on themselves, because they wanted their families to be safe at home. Everyone knew this without ever being told it by Arturo or anyone else. That's why he'd said he lived in Guaymas and had given a false address. But Arturo probably knew that too.

Everyone was subdued for the rest of the day. There was no talk of building a house for their families at home with the money. Or getting married. Or buying a car. Or getting drunk. No one was even bothering to stare at Betty when Armando wasn't looking. She wore loose clothes, but at certain angles you could see the shape of her breasts, and when the afternoon breeze came up and blew her hair aside, her ears were small, like a baby's. The weather was getting even warmer; the mosquitoes came out before dark for their dinner.

The four regulars went down for the food. There was no van this time, but the supplies were hidden in the usual place. They loaded their packs up. He and the brothers were watching Arturo to see if the money had been left this time. There was no telling. He was too clever for them. Laughing, he said, "Look," holding up a big stack of dark green towels. The brothers were always complaining about the others using their towels. There was a case of beer, too. That would make everyone happy. There were bags of cookies and six packs of pudding and the bars of chocolate with hazelnuts that everyone liked. It was going to be a feast tonight.

They made it back in record time. They were all used to the climb and the altitude now. Watching Arturo, you could see what he must have looked like when he was their age. Tall, built like one of those athletes who could do eight or nine different events, decathlon. He was carrying twice as much as they were and almost running up the trail.

The Cuban met them at the bottom of the garden, holding a dirty shirt to the side of his head. "I didn't do anything," he told Arturo, and went into some long story as they all broke into a run. Betty was nowhere in sight, but her husband puffed out like a rooster when he saw the Cuban, who, it turned out, had picked a bouquet of wildflowers—it must have been a big one, because they were scattered all over the ground—and presented it to Betty at breakfast. Armando had taken offense when she accepted them and clubbed the Cuban from behind with his stick, cutting the top third of his ear loose: it hung like a flap from the side of his head. Then he'd gone after Betty, who climbed a tree and was still up there.

Arturo took this all with a shrug like it happened every day. He got out the big metal first aid kit and then examined the Cuban's ear. It looked awful, limp, blue, like it had turned color when it died. He gave the Cuban a pill, cleaned the wound well, then sewed the severed part of the ear back where it belonged with a curved needle. "Good as new," he said, washing his hands. He tried to get Betty to come down from the tree but she wouldn't. Armando got the ax, intending to chop down the fir, but Arturo wouldn't let him. A study in patience, his mother would have said.

It wasn't until then that Arturo noticed. "Where are the Indians?" No one answered him. Arturo walked over to where their sleeping bags were. Then up to the flat place, where all four of them were laid out, stupefied. For the last three weeks they had been picking the dry bottom leaves from the plants and smoking them on the sly. They must have overdone it this time. Arturo kicked the Indian the others listened to; everyone called him Dogman because his head looked like it was solid bone, shaped like a Doberman's. He came awake, his chin covered with drool, his eyes unfocused. Arturo reached down and picked him up by the hair. Shook him like he was a pet. The Dogman came around fast, reaching for the knife at his belt. Arturo backhanded him to the ground, then lost control, kicking at the Dogman with his heavy boots. He was yelling in English, he was so angry. "You want to get us all caught, do you? Answer me. Smoke that stuff. I told you. I warned you."

The Indian tried to roll away but took a boot in his face and spit out two side teeth. Then Arturo stopped, breathing hard. The Indian stayed where he was on the ground until Arturo left.

When all the excitement was over and everyone was calm again, Betty came down from the tree when she saw the package of cookies Arturo was holding up to her, the ones shaped like little animals coated with pink and white frosting and covered with colored sprinkles that were her favorite. She apologized to Armando for accepting the flowers. The Cuban said he was going to get even. The Dogman came back from where he'd been hiding when he saw Arturo was handing out the cash. Everyone got their forty-seven hundred dollars and then five additional bills for waiting an extra week. That made everyone happy. Then Arturo passed out the beer. That made almost ten thousand dollars now: what would his mother say?

The more the plants grew the more water they needed, and everyone was on the run. Some animal, Arturo thought it was a bear, chewed up twenty-five meters of hose near the reservoir. The Indians voted among themselves and decided to go home after breakfast one morning. The Dogman and the other Indians talked to Arturo a long time before they decided to stay. That same day a rattlesnake bit Miguel on the back of his left hand.

They all stood around in a circle to watch as Arturo cut a line of x's up Miguel's arm with a razor blade, the way it used to be done years ago. That was a mistake. The tourniquet was above the elbow, just like the first aid book said, but he knew cutting the x's was worse than doing nothing because they could get infected. Then Arturo used the old-fashioned small red suction cup over each cut. Miguel kept saying it didn't hurt. What Miguel needed was a shot of antivenom serum, but it was already too late because you had to administer that within twenty minutes after the bite. He knew all that from his first aid merit badge, but he didn't say anything. What was there to do?

That afternoon Miguel couldn't get up and his arm was turning yellow. "We have to take him to the hospital," his brother kept saying.

"It's nothing," Arturo said. "He'll be better tomorrow." The Cuban agreed and told a story about his dog getting bit, how his head swelled up like a cantaloupe first, but he lived.

"Miguel is not a dog," Juan yelled at him. But the next morning Miguel's arm was swollen and the skin was splitting, like you'd peel a peach, and he was barely conscious and kept moaning.

It was only when Juan said he was going to take Miguel down by himself that Arturo agreed to get him to the hospital. "Raul, take an end," Arturo ordered, and they half-carried and half-dragged Miguel down the mountain in his sleeping bag. On the way, Arturo pulled out a cell phone when it rang inside his shirt and started talking. Arguing. The ringing had made them all jump. He hadn't known there was a cell phone in camp.

When they got to the road the van was there and the driver was angry. He spoke in English to Arturo. "You should have handled this differently." He made his hand into a pistol and snapped his thumb twice against his forefinger.

"This is the only option, if you don't want to abandon the product," Arturo answered.

They drove down the mountain, broad daylight on a Saturday afternoon. They passed other traffic once they got on to the blacktop, and then went by houses and then small towns. When the van stopped behind a two-story building they helped Juan put Miguel on his shoulder. Arturo grabbed Juan's jacket front. "Listen, amigo, you were sleeping in a ditch, looking for work picking fruit when the snake came along. You don't say anything else. And don't flash your money around. We'll keep in touch. We expect you to come back and finish the job." He let go of Juan's jacket and patted his cheek.

The driver started swearing again as Juan hurried with Miguel toward the door marked Emergency. "Relax," Arturo said. "They don't even know where the place is. They can't lead anyone up there to us. They think we're coming back for them. And they know the rules."

He had been dozing, but he woke up when the van stopped in a parking lot behind a bar. Arturo and the driver got out and he followed. The driver ordered a double shot and a draft and Arturo said, "Make it three," to the bartender. They sipped the whiskey but drank off the beer and Arturo ordered them another. He did what they did, but he didn't feel a man of the world, the way he did with his Uncle Jorge. When he picked up the whiskey he saw his hand was shaking.

The place was full of men, some wearing rubber boots like they'd just come out of the fields. Only a few women. This bar could be on almost any street in Acapulco, away from the tourists' section. The driver said he was hungry, and they walked over to the restaurant in back. He told them he had to use the toilet and went down a hall, then out the back door. This is where he was going to resign, get out before it was too late. He'd finally got it through his head he was in trouble: this business was too dangerous. It wouldn't be a problem to go south and get across the border. He could pass, speaking English, thanks to his mother, who had an ear for languages; she'd picked it up at work and brought it home like a cough. He'd studied it at school, but she'd taught him more. She'd got so good that she would correct other staff, and a couple of times even an English-speaking guest. People used to run from her. It made him feel calmer, thinking of his mother.

He stopped at a drugstore first, with a sign in the window advertising ice cream cones, bought a dark green hooded sweatshirt and a triple-decker cone, broke a hundred dollar bill, and went back outside and started walking. He had to find the bus station. A shiny new car full of men pulled up alongside him. They looked Mexican, but the man in the passenger seat yelled in broken Spanish, "Hey you, stop," and leaned out the window and showed a big badge. "We want to talk to you." He dropped the cone and started running. Down an alley first. The car followed. He jumped a fence, went through someone's yard and down a sidewalk. The car came around the corner after him. One of the men got out of the back and started chasing him. He ran across another yard and out into an orchard of walnut trees. He was making good time on the man who was chasing him, but he could already see the car turning ahead of him. He doubled back toward the main street.

He found the bar and saw the van. Arturo was standing there, smoking. He could barely breathe. He leaned forward, hands propped on his knees, trying to catch his breath without showing it. "I didn't feel like eating either," Arturo said. The car that had been chasing him pulled up and the same man stuck his badge out the window, yelling, "El sheriffo." Arturo ignored them. Then someone in the backseat yelled it again. Arturo dropped his cigarette and carefully ground it into the blacktop with his heel. Then he opened the car door and pulled the man out of the front seat by the collar and took the badge away from him. "Raul," he said in English, as if explaining a simple procedure to the crew, "they buy these in the toy stores and then rob illegals, who can't do anything about it." None of the others in the car got out. A couple of them were urging the driver in English to go. Arturo reached over and stuck the badge on his new sweatshirt. "Now you're a cop, Raul." The man didn't look so tough next to Arturo, who was still holding him by the neck. He was too angry to aim well; he missed with his first kick, but the second and third time his boot landed right where he wanted it. Squealing, the man doubled over and grabbed his crotch. Then Arturo stuffed him back into the front seat headfirst through the open window as the car was backing away.

On the return the driver played American music on the radio. It was soothing, and he watched the scenery slip by as the van followed the road back into the mountains. He was feeling safer by the minute. They hadn't realized he had been trying to get away. On the hike up he decided he was glad he hadn't quit. He could make the other ten thousand.

"Raul," Arturo said. He had stopped and was sitting on a stump, waiting for him to catch up. "We've got to talk. I feel I can trust you, Raul, so I'm going to tell you the facts. There's a thirty-five million dollar crop up there at the camp. Over ten thousand plants. All we have to do is hold out another six or seven weeks. But this was a big investment, too; it costs money to start an operation like this. A lot of capital."

He tried to look interested, pay attention. He wasn't looking forward to being an adult if these were the kinds of things they had to say. He wished he hadn't had to throw his ice cream away.

"It's not just our pay, or the equipment or food, but the land up there is costing us big money to use. A whole office full of people had to be paid off not to know what we're doing. And if we fail, we'll be in more trouble than if we got caught by the law. The people that are financing most of this operation are not easy to get along with."

His mother talked to him like this sometimes when things weren't going well at the hotel. He hated it when older people took you into their confidence. It was never a happy situation.

"You remember that Sunday when that drunk came up in the van and made that scene?" Arturo said. "He's the son of the man who is financing us. We used to be friends. He was in charge of one of these operations two years ago and got caught. Everyone nabbed. There was some shooting. He got out of jail on bond and jumped bail, three hundred thousand dollars. The others are doing twenty years to life. Life, man. Think about it. And they were lucky. One was going to snitch and he got his head cut off in prison and so did his two sisters at home.

"You have to help me, Raul. I have to be able to count on you. And I'll make it worth your while. Your pay is chicken feed, compared to what I'll give you."

They started back up. He wasn't sure why, but he was getting that hopeless feeling again, that this was going to end in disaster. He hoped Miguel was going to be all right. Maybe he and Juan were the lucky ones.

They finally got back to the camp. It had taken much longer than usual because Arturo kept stopping to discuss all his problems in running the operation: the workers were always a bunch of dummies, animals. At other camps the workers were whipped when they got out of line, chained up at night, but he wanted to be fair, democratic. Arturo went on and on.

The four Indians were gone the minute Arturo was out of sight down the trail, Ernesto told him. Arturo didn't say a word about the Indians. "Let's eat," he said, and he took a stack of frozen pies out of his pack, one for every-one with four left over. He got chocolate; it was still frozen a little and that part was like ice cream, but the thawed part was like pie. They sat around eating, the only sound the scrape of their spoons against the aluminum pie pans. The sun had disappeared but it was still light.

"It means more money," Arturo said the next morning at dawn. "We can split the Indians' money between the five of you."

"But it's more work," Armando pointed out.

He felt he should add something, but he didn't know what. "The crop is almost ready to pick," he finally said. "We can do the extra work for a split of thirty thousand; that's the four Indians' money plus Juan's and Miguel's."

"Raul's got a point," the Cuban said. He had stopped looking at his ear so much in his pocket mirror. It had grown back almost like the other one.

"What if the Indians tell?" Betty asked.

"Who in California can understand them?" Arturo said.

Nothing happened for eight days. Everyone was on the run doing the jobs the Indians and the brothers had done. But he noticed that, like everyone else, Arturo was jumpy. At any sudden noise he reached for the pistol that he kept in a shoulder holster under his jacket. There was little talk even at din-ner. The Cuban was cooking again. But no one was eating much; it was as if they'd all of a sudden lost their appetites.

The next Sunday was a payday. Arturo asked him to pick one person to come down with them. He asked Ernesto. They took turns carrying a plastic garbage bag stuffed with leaves that probably weighed thirty kilos. It was nothing, carrying the load downhill. "These are samples," Arturo explained. "They'll get passed around to buyers that are interested, so they can bid on the crop after they see the quality. This is important. We planted the best seed that money could buy and science could develop. Quality means a few dollars more per kilo, which can add up to a substantial improvement in the profit margin." Arturo had taken to making these statements to him all week, like he was some junior accountant trainee. And in front of Ernesto, now, in English.

The driver was in a bad mood. He yelled at Arturo, "Do you realize how much money is invested up there? There can't be any question about fulfill-ing the contract." When he paid Arturo it was less the amount for the broth-ers. They argued. He moved over to the cache of food and started loading his pack, but he could still hear them. "They did the extra work. You owe them," Arturo was shouting. "Go complain to the Mexican Embassy if you don't like it," the driver yelled in parting.

The trip up took a little more than two hours now. In the food sacks there were a couple of dozen hamburgers from one of the fast-food places. They had their fill, and french fries too. "Isn't this the life?" Arturo said.

No one answered until he did. "You can say that again." Arturo had split the Indians' pay between the five of them. It didn't seem to make anyone happier. Betty wanted to know how much Arturo was being paid on his contract, but Arturo didn't answer.

Knowing Sunday afternoon was free made you lazy. They were lying around after lunch on their sleeping bags, too full to move. His eyes kept sliding closed. He thought he was seeing things when a man in a uniform stepped out from behind the pine tree that one end of the clothesline was attached to. He had a pump shotgun without a stock, like a cop's. "Now don't get excited," the man said. The shotgun muzzle was pointed up toward the sky. His pistol was still in his holster. Everyone was too surprised to react. "I'm alone, just passing through, and I thought I'd stop, say hello. My name is Jack. How are you folks?"

There was a patch on his shoulder, USFS, like on the sign, and he wore a small copper badge in the shape of a shield. Arturo said, "We're okay," and then started translating what the man had said. His uniform wasn't a *soldado's*; it was more green, like a senior scout's. "What I was wondering," Jack went on, "is if any of you'd like to make an investment." Everyone watched him like they could understand what he was saying without Arturo's translation. "Say, five thousand apiece. I usually ask newcomers seventy-five hundred, but for you I'll offer a special deal. I've been watching since the crop was sown, and of course the last Sunday in the month is payday." The amazing thing was that the man seemed so sure of himself, as if his words would convince them of anything. It wasn't working on Armando, who was inching his stick with the big nail wired to the end toward his right hand with the heel of his boot.

"You're probably wondering what you get in return for this investment. What you get is no problems." He winked at them. "You harvest your crop and get your bonus and you go home. Everyone's happy this way. I'm not a greedy person."

"Let me translate that," Arturo said, who'd been forgetting the others couldn't understand. Why was this Jack so confident? Was he like those salesmen who came into the hotel and believed in themselves so much they overwhelmed you? His mother would hide from that type. He didn't catch himself; he asked in English, "Why should we trust you, Jack?"

"You have my word."

Arturo started laughing at that so hard he choked, so he had to translate for the others. Everyone started laughing. Jack became angry. "I could have reported you months ago, but I wanted to treat you fairly." There was a long silence; no one looked at each other. At home you paid the bribe and joked about it later with your friends. Here he'd thought it would be more subtle. But Jack seemed to feel he was only taking what was his; that was a new concept.

Beside him, Armando was getting a grip on his stick, ready to throw. Armando practiced by the hour, and at ten meters he could pin a beer can to a tree; he'd killed a gray squirrel. He slid closer and gave a hard punch against Armando's upper arm, and the stick slid away. Armando swore. Jack noticed. Pointed his forefinger at Armando. "I left a note on my desk and also on my computer about where I'd be this afternoon, and about my investigations. I better get back before someone reads them," he said.

"How about twenty-five hundred?" Arturo said. "You can see this crew is not first-rate. A month's wages. We were supposed to be protected from any added costs. You must be aware of that, but I'm willing this one time to make this investment to gain your personal protection." Arturo said that with a straight face.

"I get it now; there's been a misunderstanding here," Jack said. "The money that you folks paid before was for the management team in the other forest. You see, there are two national forests here, side by side; the stream is the dividing line." Jack was speaking from the heart. "The pond you made is in my forest." The others were unable to follow; no one was translating. "I'm glad that's out in the open now. I'm really sorry, but I can't change my price. I thought there were more of you. I've given you my lowest figure."

Arturo explained to the others that everyone would have to pay the man five thousand dollars. He could hear Betty whisper to Arturo, "Shoot him; kill him." Arturo unbuttoned his shirt to get at his money belt. The others did too, counting out the Franklins, fifty of them.

Jack leaned his shotgun against a tree and crouched down, using the ground as a table, recounting the bills into five thousand dollar stacks. They all watched. He noticed the Cuban was counting with him too, moving his lips. When he got to the last pile and the last bill, Jack announced with disappointment in his voice, "We're four hundred dollars short." Arturo looked disgusted and undid his shirt again, but reached his hand under his jacket. Everyone tensed up. He was already hearing the gunshots echo. Jack stiffened too and unsnapped the strap over his pistol. He had to do something. He counted out four more hundreds and crumpled them up and threw them at Jack's feet. Arturo relaxed.

Jack took his time smoothing the bills out and adding them to his last pile before scooping all the cash up and putting it in a green canvas bag slung over his shoulder. "Well now. Business done. I should have asked before: when are you going to harvest the crop? Three or four weeks? Same crew?" Arturo nodded. "Well. That means trucks. That's going to complicate matters. But let's not worry about the future. I'll get back to you on that; you can't keep semis secret up here." In the silence Jack clapped his hands together twice, like applause, as if they had been performing for him. "Well, I better be off." And he was gone.

The others argued for days about who had not given his full share so that he had to pay the extra four hundred. No one would admit it. Ernesto said the man couldn't count and had got more because of it. Arturo acted like he had lost interest in the whole project. He disdained to speak in Spanish to the crew and spoke only a few words in English to him. He sat in his chair all day, smoking the stuff rolled up in toilet paper. Sometimes when they woke up he'd still be there.

Arturo wouldn't go down Sunday for the food. He went with Ernesto. And the next Sunday, too. The driver waited for them that time. "Where's Arturo?" he asked in English. He could speak correct Spanish, too, like the foreign businessmen who stayed at the hotel.

"He's working his ass off up there. The stream is drying up. We're running lines down from a spring we've found." The driver didn't believe him, he could tell. He didn't say that he'd had to take Arturo's cell phone away, he was always phoning to argue with these people, and then his pistol, too; he was going to hurt someone or hurt himself. He told the driver about Jack. They both had a good laugh over the incident. They would all get a bigger bonus because of it, the driver told him.

"You have to expect the unexpected in a deal like this," the driver said, and added, "I like you, Raul. We should have a talk later. I've already mentioned you to the others. There's always a need for a man with a good head on his shoulders."

Betty came around when he was alone at the spotter scope. She had started wearing lipstick and glasses that magnified the green in her brown eyes and saying she wanted him to teach her English. She whispered as if there was someone else nearby, "It was me, Raul. I just couldn't give that thief the last four bills. I didn't miscount." She waited for him to say something.

"It doesn't matter, Betty, it's past. Forget it." He really didn't care. The driver had slipped him an extra ten bills last Sunday. It wasn't the money for him anymore. It was like a game he had to win. He'd stopped thinking about the hotel school, too. Why should he consider going to school when he could buy his own hotel?

"It was me. Here." She held out her hand. There was a tight roll of hundreds. He waved her away, shaking his head. She sat down on the ground near him. "I came north with Armando because it was the only way I could get here. We're not married. I'm done with him, anyway. To play the man and the rest, that was my idea. Take the money."

He shook his head. He couldn't help smiling at her. "Okay, I'll keep it here for you," and she stuffed the bills into the pocket over her heart. "It's there when you want it," she said, taking her finger and rubbing it across his bottom lip. "You have cookie crumbs," she said, getting up.

Arturo stayed in his chair all the time now, silent, smoking, with an unopened paperback in his lap. There were no more arguments. They waited, counting the days until the harvest. There was less work to do now; the plants were three to four meters and had reached their full growth. They choked the weeds out and their roots went down deep enough to get their own water. The plants fit in now, looked like they were part of the autumn underbrush in the forest. They stopped cooking: for lunch and supper they ate cookies and fistfuls of cereal from the boxes.

It got light a little later in the morning now, but the sun never seemed to want to go down at night. He couldn't wait for dark sometimes, and would crawl into his sleeping bag in his clothes and boots and fold a towel over his eyes so he wouldn't think about helicopters, or Jack and what he said about the semis, or the driver, or what would happen to Arturo. It was only in the dark that he felt safe from everything. The other four would be watching, waiting, and they'd join him right away. All slept close together now, head to head, feet out, like a five-point star. He had read somewhere that soldiers did that at night when the enemy could come from any direction.

WILLOWS VILLAGE

Dagoberto Gilb

I needed the favor because I wasn't doing well and I'd ran out of places to stay and mostly money. I didn't really like it that my Aunt Maggy would know about my life, unless it was how great I was doing. I'm not sure where my embarrassment comes from, or if it's only a man thing. Could also be my mom and the years of gossip, and since my mom was my favorite mom, I always want to side with her no matter what. So Maggy was an all spoiled this and did all bad that but got away with everything because of her looks—men lined up to do whatever she whined for. Even now, she was supposed to be close to fifty, and she did not look fifty. I don't think many women looked much better than her after thirty. Could be my mom didn't want to tell the truth about Maggy's age because, well, if my mom wasn't as pretty, she was probably a better cook. Maybe Maggy was a lot younger. It was possible, if you ask me. I was here looking at her.

I wouldn't have recognized her if I weren't at her kitchen table. Last time I saw her I was at most fifteen. She'd visited our house in El Paso a few times but you know how that is. I didn't stick around for the family things once I was older, and even when I kissed her hello and good-bye, I didn't see or hear her. I was a teenager then. Now I was a man, with a wife and a baby and another one coming too. I was a man, and I realized my aunt was a woman who, well, was hard to not look at.

"I'm trying for everything," I told her. "I only want a job that I can count on." I'd told her about the three I'd already had. Two were in construction, which I didn't really want and didn't last more than a week, and the last, in a restaurant, I only took it to have something, but it went from early morning to early evening, and I couldn't look for one better.

"You listen to Jim's advice when he gets back, Guillermo. He won't be away that long." Jim was her husband. He was in Chicago and on his way to Brazil and he'd be gone for a couple or even a few weeks. I didn't ask her what he did. He had a last name that I couldn't pronounce. My mom would get mad at my dad for saying this, but he would call him a rich *gabacho* son of a Zabludovsky—that *chilango* newscaster—living it up inside Mexico. My mom didn't like him making sexual remarks about Maggy, even if everybody did. I think Maggy'd had at least two other last names too since she'd been married at least two other times. Her family name was Santamaría, which also made my father wink sarcastically.

"Billy," I told her. "Everybody always calls me Billy."

"Guillermo is much better," she insisted. "It's more mature, and it's a manly name." The jewelry on her arms and ears tingled like in a breeze that also swayed her long black hair.

I preferred Billy. I didn't like to be formal. I didn't want to sound like I just crossed. I liked people to know I was American, born and raised. I had an uncle, who was one tattooed *cholo*, who called himself Memo, and I didn't want that. Besides, wasn't she a Maggy? A grateful guest, I didn't say more.

She was drinking wine. It was from a big jug, not that there weren't plenty of those others you usually saw in a restaurant—a rack of them and others sitting on the table and counter. I'd already said no thank you. I didn't really know how to drink wine. It wasn't just the wine, but the entire kitchen was loaded up like a mall gourmet store. She had the complete set of copper pots and pans, and a lot not copper, hanging from above the stove, she had another rack of wine glasses, she had so many utensils it was more like a tool shop to me. There were appliances too. Not one blender but two. A food processor and an industrial toaster. A bread maker. A pasta machine. New, new, new. She had knives in several wooden blocks, towels, and the counters were weighted with so many plastic and glass bottles of this and that you wondered what could be in the cabinets. On the space above them, Mexican pottery, Mexican dishware. On the table where I was sitting, a floral bouquet, a setting. It was beautiful and it looked real but it wasn't—I smelled them and she told me. On the table and on the floor near it a pile of unread beauty magazines, half in Spanish, a couple which were the same but one was American, the other from Mexico—or Spain, or wherever, I didn't know.

"A beer then?"

"Sure."

She opened a side of the silver refrigerator. It seemed like things would fall out it was so stuffed. She dug around—I felt like I should get up and help her take stuff and hold things—until she found a green bottle and somehow seemed to know right where an opener was. She gave it to me and I probably shouldn't have stared at it first and then so long. It had foil around its top and I don't think I could read the language it was in.

"Jim loves it, thinks it's the best."

I stopped what I was doing and drank. It had a strange taste to me. "Wow, yeah, really good. Thank you."

"I have to tell you about Lorena."

I nodded and I sipped the strange beer.

"She's been staying here too. Downstairs. It's where I'd have you stay if she wasn't here already. She's been having trouble. We're very good friends."

"Sure," I said. "I'm really thankful for your help."

"We're family. You're my sister's son, so you're my son too."

I had a room up the carpeted stairs. It was a girl's room, teenager, or like that. It was confusing looking. She said it was her playroom, and she was sorry it was a mess. I told her to not be sorry, that I didn't care. I didn't either. Though it was a girl's room, and there were two big boxes of little boxes of dolls—not all in their store boxes—and a few facedown and sideways on shelves, and knitting boxes and an antique sewing machine and makeup jars and compacts and brushes and lipsticks, and all in shoeboxes piled and stacked, and photos everywhere, all in more shoeboxes but also in a pile on the floor. It was hard to know where to put my suitcase except in the middle of the room. And the walls were wallpapered. That was more old-ladyish to me, a pink, with red velvet roses. The kind of bed had a name that meant it wasn't just the bed. It was also considered a couch, she told me. To me it was a bed and only a bed and it had lots of pillows, girl pillows, and a frilly cover. It was fine. I was happy. I needed a place to sleep. And the TV on the floor, like it didn't work and wasn't really supposed to be in there, it worked. I think there was another bedroom next to this one, but that door was closed and I didn't look. There was a bathroom and then there were double doors, right across from where I was, that opened to the master bedroom. One of those doors was open. It was a huge room, as beautiful as any hotel, a king-size bed that didn't even take up too much space. There was still plenty between it and all the dressers and mirrors. It was a lot better than a hotel.

I was up in the morning early. I decided to dress as nice as I could. I wore a white shirt and put on a tie. I didn't have a sports coat. Besides, though it wasn't hot, it wasn't cold enough. And I didn't own one. Aunt Maggy's was in a tract development and it was called Willows Village. I don't know why I thought about it so much even before I drove in, when it was only part of the directions. I did. And then the actual image of the sign on the block wall entrance to the village burned my eyes. It was trapped in my head and when I would think of Aunt Maggy, I'd see a droopy green tree and those words. Her house was right next to the freeway. Which was a good thing if you were driving to work and had to get on the freeway, which maybe most everybody else did. We had highways in El Paso, nothing like this one right next to the village. Even in the morning, or maybe especially, it was loud. I couldn't really believe how loud it was. It almost made me stop. But there was nothing to look at, to see. The freeway was just above and on the other side of the houses across the street. You couldn't see the cars or trucks or motorcycles. Their sounds, though, they made like shadows my eyes wanted to see but couldn't. So I got in and rolled down the windows and joined the noise too, the looking-for-the-job driving noise, and I drove past the Willows Village sign and into the job world.

There were lots of jobs in Santa Ana and around it when you looked in the paper. There were lots of construction sites but I saw so many car dealerships I finally decided, I really made up my mind. I wanted to be a car salesman. I had a high school friend from El Paso, up a couple of streets and right near Fort Boulevard, who told me that when he moved out here, that he started at car sales and the next he knew, he was making a really great living and he loved it. I tried to find his new address before I left El Paso. He'd grown up with his grandma, and when I went over, she didn't live there. The people who did said they bought the house after she died, and they had no idea where he was. I just thought what he did was original and smart. Not that it was. Everybody had heard of car salesmen. What was original was to be one. And after the other jobs, it was even more original. So I started stopping at dealers on Harbor Boulevard and I went right in, shaking hands, saying I was looking for a job as a car salesman. I filled out applications, and I talked to a couple managers too. I think that I spoke Spanish was a definite asset. Definitely at two places. One used, one new. The new car dealer manager asked if I had a coat even, a couple even. I said I did. I think he didn't like my white shirt or my tie, something in his eyes—so I decided that if he called back, I'd get something. I'd borrow the money. I thought I had a really good shot.

I wasn't sure if I should get back to Aunt Maggy's so early in the afternoon or not. I wasn't sure if she would like it if I didn't, say, look for a job until the evening. I also didn't know where else to go besides there. When I stayed with an old friend and his wife for a couple of weeks, those days I didn't work, they were. I could watch TV. I didn't know if Maggy had a routine or not. I had a key but the door was a little open. I mean, it wasn't closed. Still, I rang the doorbell.

"Hello!" Aunt Maggy yelled.

I went ahead and pushed the door open.

"What are you doing ringing the bell? Just come in! You live here!"

I kind of nodded and muttered a thanks, okay. They were at the table and it was that jug of wine. Maybe even another one just like it. It was hard to see them though. There was a big glass window behind them, and the sun was out. I was afraid I would be looking funny at them as I got to the table.

"How'd it go?" Aunt Maggy asked. She was wearing a one-piece bathing suit. She was a *chichona* woman and it was hard not to know that, especially when she was wearing a bathing suit. I still saw the Willows Village sign, which I'd just passed again, in my head too. It didn't feel right.

"Pretty good," I said. "I really think I'm gonna get one."

"*¡Qué bueno!*" said Aunt Maggy.

"One doing what?" the other woman said. I knew it was Lorena.

"Oh," my Aunt Maggy said, "this is Lorena."

I shook her hand. "I'm Billy," I said.

"Guillermo," Aunt Maggy said.

"Doing what?" Lorena said.

Aunt Maggy started laughing. "I didn't even ask what." She laughed and so did Lorena. They thought it was funny, and they each took another drink and giggled.

"Do you want some wine?" Lorena asked. Besides on a rack, there were a few clean wine glasses on the counter near the kitchen table and she reached over and got one and she poured me a glass.

"He doesn't drink wine," Aunt Maggy told her.

"I'm sorry," Lorena said.

"I can." That made her feel better. I sipped some. I didn't really like wine, I guess.

"So tell us," Lorena said. "What kind of job?"

"Car salesman."

I think they wanted to laugh. Maybe. Except they didn't.

"Is that what you want?" Lorena asked.

"I think you can make good money at it." I almost was going to tell her about my friend in El Paso. I didn't really like the wine, but I drank some more.

"Good for you," Aunt Maggy said. "I think they'll be lucky to get you."

We clinked the wine glasses. We all took drinks for a toast and Maggy refilled Lorena's, then hers.

"I bet you're hungry," Maggy said to me.

"I'm hungry," said Lorena. "What can we make?"

"There's so much," she said.

There was, too. The kitchen was so full of everything.

"Let's just get takeout. Chinese? Italian? How about subs?"

"Yum," said Lorena.

We were all supposed to pick, until Aunt Maggy said she'd get three kinds and we'd share. She got on the phone and she was ordering.

"What about you?" I asked Lorena. "What do you do?"

She didn't answer quickly. "I fight for a woman's rights. I fight against dirty husbands."

Maggy, still on the phone, made eyes at her and shook her head.

I decided not to ask.

Lorena was in a bathing suit too, but she had a towel bathrobe over her. Hers was a two-piece, a bikini, because once in a while it opened. It was a good bet that all of her figure was good too. She had an accent. I couldn't figure it out. It might have been Mexican, but if she spoke Spanish, then they would be speaking Spanish. Her eyes were hazel but also green. Maybe her shoulder-length hair was dyed. It was brown with yellow in it. I thought her hair should be dark brown. She was my age, give or take a few years.

Off the phone, Aunt Maggy took another gulp of wine and got up and then so did Lorena. Too much to look at, so I looked down and out the window to the big backyard. I listened as Maggy took out plates from a cabinet and brought them to the table. Lorena went to the sink and came back with a dishrag and wiped the table. Both of them brushed up against me when they came back. It was that I was in a chair that was in the way, the one I sat in without thinking when I walked in. I considered moving.

"Would you rather have beer with your sandwich?" Lorena asked me. "If you really don't like wine."

I decided I had to look up when I answered and she was very close to me, her robe loosely closed, and she was standing, and I was sitting. It was hard to keep my eyes steady. "Well," I said, "no, I think I should stay with the wine." I finished my first glass and then she leaned across me and got the bottle and filled it back up. The jug was almost empty, so then she put the last of the wine in hers. She was warm.

"Open another if you want," Maggy said. "Open this one." She handed Lorena a smaller bottle and she looked around for the wine opener. Lorena handed it and the bottle to me.

The truth is, I wasn't sure how it worked. It had the curled screw, but also something else. I don't know if they watched me, but I pulled the cork out the only way I knew. "So you guys went to, like, the beach?" I asked. I left the bottle on the table because all of the glasses were full.

"My neighbor Paula has a pool," said Maggy. "You want to go swimming? I'm watching it for her while they're away."

"It's delicious!" said Lorena. "It's so nice over there. You have to go."

Ready for the food to arrive, Aunt Maggy started cleaning the kitchen. "I don't know how I get such a mess all the time," she said.

Lorena sat down again, looked over at me, drank wine and sighed. "Are you as hungry as I am?" she asked me.

I was trying to be quick to answer.

"Don't be so shy," she said. "Just say yes."

"Okay," I mumbled.

"Yes yes yes," said Maggy near the sink. "We say yes!"

"Yes!" said Lorena more loudly. They laughed. Then Lorena got up from her chair and put her arms around me and hugged me. "Please don't mind us drunk women."

"What did she say?" Aunt Maggy asked over there.

"I told him not to mind us drunk girls."

"Mind us? What man is going to mind drinking with us? Right, Guillermo? You better say yes!"

They laughed, staring at me. I made myself laugh along with them, but I wasn't sure what else to do. I was doing more than sitting there but it couldn't look like much. I drank more wine and was feeling it, not noticing the taste so much. I was thinking of how warm Lorena was when she hugged me and I still felt her breasts pressing on me too, stuck to me like that sign was.

The doorbell rang. As I turned back to look, Aunt Maggy yelled "Hello!" It was a young delivery guy and he was holding a white bag. The door was wide open but not because he opened it but because it was wide open. I guess I forgot to shut it.

Maggy came around the corner from the kitchen. "Come on in!" she told him. She was in the kitchen, then went through another door. "I can't find my purse!" she yelled.

He stopped near the table. Lorena took the bag from him and was pulling submarine sandwiches out. Lorena's robe wasn't even tied anymore. I was standing for a minute and then I sat but I moved my chair, making more room to pass. The guy didn't talk. He was staring blank. I wondered what he was thinking about them in their bathing suits. Maybe he was more used to it than me.

Suddenly Lorena yelled. "It's over here, Maggy!" She held the purse, which had been in the corner.

"I am so dingy," Aunt Maggy said when she came back in the kitchen. When she opened the purse, it exploded money like a jack-in-the-box. Bills popped out everywhere, a fountain of crumpled greenbacks. Maggy made a loud sigh and an "*¡Ay, Dios!*" and rolled her eyes, like it was the fault of the purse. Lorena picked up the cash and I helped too and when Aunt Maggy started counting out a few—"How much?" she asked the delivery guy—I was already making a neat stack of mine. I was going to do the same thing with what Lorena piled on the table but I didn't. They were of all kinds of denominations and I thought they could be sorted too and I didn't do that either. When the guy left, Aunt Maggy stuffed them right back without a second thought and clicked the purse closed.

I knew I was going to get one of those jobs. I mean, I applied at more dealers too, but my gut feeling told me that it was going to happen with those first ones interested in me. I was trying to figure out which would be better money, used cars or new car sales. I didn't have enough information about either, so I just thought about it. One strong guess was that the new car job would require better clothes. Maybe a suit, but at least a couple of good coats and pants, but for both some dress shirts. Ties too. I felt it even more when I dropped in on them again telling them I was still looking, still hungry for this work. I think both of them liked me, I also felt like they might have been seeing that I was wearing the same white shirt and tie. I could not go there again in the same shirt and tie, and if they did call, I had to have something else, no matter what. So I stopped at a store afterwards and bought another of both. They weren't the most expensive, but I was almost out of money, and that wasn't good. I needed to buy a few shirts. And the rest. I could get some money from home, from my parents. My wife Suzie was living with my *suegros*, her parents, so we wouldn't have to be spending on rent.

This time I got in late. I took a long drive once it got to be afternoon, got stuck in a lot of freeway traffic I didn't know how to get out of, and I had to go to a few stores to find the shirt and tie once I found a mall. I had to put gas in my car too. I went to a drive-through and got a large soda and stayed parked in the lot a while. It made me feel bad that I would have to borrow from my parents again. My mom anyway. She wouldn't even tell my dad. It was nice sitting. I needed it. I even turned off the radio. I think I was there a long time. I thought of going to a bar, but that didn't seem right to buy beer too. And there was plenty of beer and wine at Aunt Maggy's. I missed home and wished this would stop. It was getting dark. The automatic lights were already on the Willows Village sign when I drove in.

"Did you get a job?" Aunt Maggy asked.

"No, not yet."

"You're so late. I thought maybe you found one."

Lorena came to the kitchen from her room. She looked concerned too.

"Are you hungry?" Maggy asked.

"What'd you buy?" asked Lorena, interrupting. I had the shopping bag in my hand. "Let me see," she said, reaching for it.

"It's just a shirt and tie."

She already knew it because she took them out before I answered. I don't think she thought much of them.

"You have to be hungry. Sit with me." Aunt Maggy sat down at the kitchen table. It was full of all kinds of stuff, not only the wine bottles and glasses, but a stack of folded towels and women's colorful underwear, top and bottom. Even a full grocery bag not unloaded. "Lorena, can you serve him that Chinese food? I think there's a lot."

"I can do that," Lorena said. "Of course." She kind of stepped into the kitchen like it was too dark to see, even though the bright panels of ceiling lights were on. "Where is it?" There was so much everywhere.

"It's there. Somewhere. Maybe I put it in the fridge. I don't remember now."

Lorena opened the refrigerator door and stared, then she stuck her hand in like touching any one thing wrong might tip over something else. "Way in the back somehow," she announced. "But it is here."

"Are you okay? ¿*Todo está bien*, Guillermo?"

I guess I was grouchy. For one, I felt like being called Billy. "I think I'm a little tired is all. I'm fine."

Lorena was trying to get to the microwave. She had to move lots of things.

"You have to put it on a plate," said Maggy. "Those takeout boxes have wire."

"I already know. I already have it on a plate."

Maggy stared at the mess on the table like it was someone's fault. "Do you need your clothes washed?"

"I was going to ask. I sure do."

She picked up the tie I just bought. It was on the table too. "Do you need some ties? Jim has so many ties. I think he has some shirts that would fit you too."

I couldn't believe it! "That would be so great, *tía*," I told her.

To make room on the table, Aunt Maggy had Lorena take the towels and underwear and my two things upstairs. I really liked the Chinese food too. It was the best I'd ever eaten.

When I woke up I couldn't think of what else to do really. I had gone to every new and used car dealer in Santa Ana and north, south, east, and west. All those streets and neighborhoods that looked exactly like each other, passing so many tract developments that weren't named Willows Village but could be. So many restaurants to stop at or drive through and eat so much food, so many stores to shop in, so many gas stations to get gas. I wore my new shirt and a tie Aunt Maggy gave me, even a sports coat I told her I would only borrow, and I'd gone back twice to those dealers and one more that I thought maybe about too but nobody called back. My good mom sent me money by Western Union fast, no questions. I didn't need it that way but it was what she wanted. I felt bad about it. I didn't like it. She didn't want me to have to borrow or take anything from her sister. I think she felt jealous and she didn't want Aunt Maggy to think she didn't have plenty too. I felt bad asking for help but what could I do? I did really believe that, especially that one used car place, especially, that guy wanted to hire me. It was about me speaking Spanish. He didn't, none of his salesmen did. He said they really needed that because they got so many Spanish Mexican people. That's how he said it. He called me Guillermo and I thought that was fine if I got the job. Then again I wasn't sure of anything since he hadn't called or the other place either when I felt like it was such a sure thing.

Yeah, it was strange to be in the girl's pink room. At first, to be polite, I didn't want to make any moves, any changes in it. The cute little pink and red and white pillows stayed in the bed with me when I slept. Then I stacked them in a corner of the bed, and then I left them in a pile off the bed. Though I kept a couple, sort of extra cushions for my feet, my head. I finally picked the TV up off the floor and put it on the sewing machine cabinet. Once I started opening makeup compacts—she had so many in this one box. I was looking in the little mirrors when I started laughing at myself. What if someone saw me? Very very funny! I wondered what it'd be like to have to stare at my lips putting on gloss. I looked at the lines in my own lips. Funny! I pushed boxes around and made room for my suitcase, but I was neat, tried to be. My own clothes looked heavy and dark in the room on the floor. Even my socks. I'd spilled a perfume, or something like it, and the room really stank of it. At first I was embarrassed that I'd gotten it on the rug. But it didn't stain. Aunt Maggy didn't say anything about it. At first I kind of didn't like the smell, but then I did. By now I was sick of it, tired of it being in my nose when I slept. I thought it would go away fast and it never seemed to. I even worried that I might have the smell on me or in my clothes, so one day, before I took off, I went into Aunt Maggy's bedroom when she wasn't there and I borrowed some of Jim's men's spray. I saw a couple of bottles on his dresser there when she took me up for ties and shirts. I was sick of that perfume smell in my room but what could I do?

I woke up and I didn't feel like going out there so I fell back asleep and it was later in the morning. It was the first time this late in the morning I was still here. When I woke up this second time, a couple hours later, I needed to pee. I opened my door and, across, Aunt Maggy's doors were both open and she was standing near the king-size bed completely naked, drying her hair, looking toward the long mirror I couldn't see across the set of sinks on the wall over there. She didn't hear me open the door—she had a radio on—and so I closed it. Not all the way. I left it open enough to see. Oh my God my aunt was a Playmate of the Year! It was shocking to me, and I couldn't believe it. She was too much. I couldn't stop myself from looking, even though I knew it was sick, or something kind of bad, but I didn't want to not watch. She finally rolled her hair into the towel and then she sat to put panties on. Then she stood and put on a bra, kept playing with this or that around her breasts, but she didn't like it so she took it off and dug in a drawer and then she found another. She kept this bra on and when she went toward the sinks and mirrors I closed the door and breathed and shook my head quietly for at least a minute. I didn't know what it would mean that I just watched my own aunt so much and so naked. No way she was an older woman! Though I felt like I'd done something wrong and gotten away with it, or maybe because I'd gotten away with it, I felt kind of good. Better than I did before, a lot. I made noise this time when I opened the door. The cabinet near the bathroom, where there were bath towels and linen, was open so I took one out and closed it hard and then I closed the bathroom door and I even took a shower. When I was out, she had closed one of the two doors, though the other was open like normal. I heard her downstairs, a TV set on, and talking to Lorena.

I saw this guy painting a house a few houses from the Willows Village entrance and he said yeah it would be great if I worked with him, so it was me and this Gabe. It was his mom's house and it was for sale and he wasn't really a house painter either, but while we were working, first one, then another woman in this village stopped and asked if we wanted more work. We both looked at each other and said sure. He bid what seemed to be a ton, and we agreed to split it. We were knocking out his mom's so fast it was amazing. It's because the house was a single story and there wasn't that much brush or roller work, it was 95 percent compressor. Three days is all it took and when we would do the next one we both knew it would only take two because now we knew how to do it and we had the drop cloths and all of it. The two-story we said yes to too, even that, well, we'd have to rent an extension ladder or maybe a scaffold but after that, nothing to it either. It wasn't like I was going to be rich, but it felt good to have some money and more coming. I even told Suzie and she felt better about me being out here too. I didn't usually tell her anything that wasn't good because I didn't want her to worry or to worry her parents either—they didn't want her and their grandchildren to leave El Paso. I told her I was sure we'd get another couple before we finished and that soon I'd get a real job. I wasn't ready to give up. I just wanted the opportunity to make more money than I knew I ever could there.

On Saturday, Gabe and I drank a few beers, and I got back to Maggy's tired and I fell right asleep. I woke up at around three in the morning and I was hungry. I didn't want to treat her house like it was mine so I never went into the refrigerator unless she said to. But I was hungry. I went downstairs and I turned those bright lights on until I opened the refrigerator. There was light in it so I could turn off that big one. Then I looked inside. Impossible to know what was there because there was so much. Who ate so many pickles? I had never seen my aunt or Lorena eat one. And mustard jars. Who knew there were so many brands of mustard? Salsas in jars, so many, and I knew they would all be bad and I wondered if my aunt could eat that too. I had to put things on the floor. I tried to be organized and quiet too. So many things in foil that didn't look like food. One thing could have been beef once upon a time, and there was maybe a chicken though it was too small and it smelled wrong. There was some ham and I thought that would be it. I started looking inside plastic cartons and I found some *chile* that tasted real next to some tamales that were rock hard. And then I found a plastic container with wide noodles. They had a white sauce on them and they were really good too and so then I was putting things away when Lorena, in a huge T-shirt, scared me.

"I wondered what that light was so I had to wake up," she said.

"I was trying to be real quiet."

"You were, you were," she said. "It was one of the reasons I decided to get up and look, because it was just a light."

"Sorry."

"Don't say that. Did you find anything in there? She has so much."

"Really, huh?"

"It's that she never eats. She takes a bite, and that's it, in the fridge. But she wants everything anyway. What'd you find?"

"Noodles."

"Oh, those are the ones she made. She bought that pasta machine. She said Jim likes pasta." She shook her head and made a face. "And so she bought it and we made pasta one day. Like she'll ever do it again. It is really good. We ate some right after she made it, or I did. I forgot it was there. I'm the one who saved it. I'm also the one she told to."

I was standing not sure how to eat it since now eating seemed to involve Lorena, but she read my mind.

"With a fork, eat, stop thinking. She doesn't remember it's there, and she wouldn't care if she did."

"It is good," I said.

"Fresh. Fresh cheeses too. Always the best at Maggy's."

I poured a little *chile* on it.

"That's right, make it Mexican." She leaned against me as though she always did.

"What're you anyway?"

"My dad's Greek. He barely speaks English. My mom's from Mexico, but she's half Greek too. She grew up in a restaurant in Mexico City, but came here for college and never left."

"Greek. I would've never thought of it."

"Let's go sit. Bring your food."

She didn't mean the table, she meant the den where there was a couch. I sat. She lit a candle and then sat more close to me than I would've expected. I really loved the *chile*, as much as the noodles, and I decided I'd eat all these noodles, so I poured it all over it. Lorena laughed at that.

"How come you never come down and talk to me or watch television with me?"

"I don't know. It's my aunt's house." She'd scooted closer, and it was impossible to not like it. "I'm married. My wife's pregnant and we already have a daughter."

"I'm married too," she said. "I still love my asshole husband."

I ate. She got closer to me and then she was leaning against me. The candlelight jumped from wall to wall. I finished and put the container on the table in front of me. Lorena cuddled against me after that. I could feel her so warm and then I put my arm around her on her shoulder and she kissed my neck. It made me have goosebumps. Then she started kissing me more and moving into me and we were kissing and her T-shirt was so warm and I started feeling her under it too and it didn't stop.

Gabe started getting moody with me. He wanted to get to this other job the next weekend. I'd proudly sent money to both my mom and Suzie from the one we just finished because I was expecting more. We had another house come up too and a few more people had asked about our prices and availability. He was being something and he wouldn't say. I was starting to think. I didn't even know where he lived, and he never once asked me about where I lived, where my aunt was, on which street. I only knew where his mom used to live. I told him more than he told me. I was a little worried too because I told him about Lorena right after that night and I wished I hadn't. I don't think he was shocked or disapproving, or anything. But he had that on me. It was then that I noticed it was more than a bad day. Not me, but him being selfish, and I didn't matter enough to get an explanation. He even left me alone for a long time and came back and no explanation for that either. I was having to think what I had to do if I didn't have this work. He had the phone numbers. He had a truck. I was hoping that man who wanted the next house would drop by, and I could get the job on my own.

"We've been kind of fighting too," Lorena said when I got back. Aunt Maggy wasn't even there. "She drinks too much and she gets all bitchy."

"You drink a lot too."

"Probably. But I don't get all bossy at her like she does me. It's not like her to go out alone. Usually she sends me on errands she doesn't want to do. When she takes me with her shopping, she always buys me something pretty. Lately she acts like that makes her mad, like I'm asking her to. I'm not. I don't care."

I was upset when I came in but Aunt Maggy was worse, like she was drinking the wine straight out of the bottle. It was like she was waiting for me to get here, even though I was so early.

"I had to ask Lorena to leave," she told me. "It is so disturbing."

"What happened?"

"She said horrible and mean things to me. I am still so upset." She drank from her wine glass.

"Were you guys drinking when this happened?"

"What do you mean by that?" She stood up. "I am not going to be criticized by you too." She had her wine glass in her hand, but she put it down in the kitchen and paced around.

"I'm sorry," I said. "That's not what I meant."

She didn't want to listen. I went up the stairs, into the pink bedroom. I sure didn't want this. I didn't even ask about dinner, even though I was starving. It was the first time she didn't bring it up. I guess I was being punished. I would just go get something. I wanted to apologize, but I heard her go into her bedroom. She got on the phone too. I was getting mad. Everything was making me mad. All these people had things, good jobs, everything. I was in the pink bedroom. I was thinking I should just go out. I was glad that Lorena was gone. That was a relief. I wanted to call Suzie. I wanted her to tell me she missed me and our baby was good. I wanted to talk to her about this work, about Gabe burning me. I couldn't tell her though. I didn't want to tell anybody really because I was embarrassed by how much trouble I was having. I didn't imagine this. I could go back to El Paso. I could say I didn't like it here. I didn't really. All of it made me mad and I was tired of the driving and the gas money. I was going to tell Maggy what happened, and I would have.

I went to a chain fast-food place and I ate a chicken burger with jalapeños and fries and some bad ice tea. I called and I called that Gabe, but he didn't pick up and he was not going to pick up. I couldn't do anything, not one thing I could think of. I was thinking I would just go back to El Paso. I went back to the Willows Village. Aunt Maggy was around the corner from the kitchen and watching TV—I peeked around the corner and she never looked up, like she didn't even hear me come back in, though I knew she did. I went up to the pink room and thought of watching TV too and packing up my clothes but instead I started looking at those photos she had everywhere, that I'd shoved under the bed and put in an empty doll box. Pictures of so many people I had never seen and not one of my family, of my mom or dad but especially my mom. My mom who talked about Maggy all the time. Even if she were jealous of her, she admired her like a hero and envied her life. I wondered if I should tell my mom when I got back. So many photos of so many people and so many families and not one of our own family. Where did she get them all?

Then I heard Maggy's car go out of the garage, the automatic garage door opening and closing. Since her room looked over that driveway, I hurried to look out the window to make sure and it was her. It was nighttime, it was dark, but she left a light on by the bed and that's where I saw what I am sure nobody would ever see ever. It was a pile of bills, of money. Not one that was stacked, in any way organized, but a crumpled pile. Each one crumpled in its own way even, individually. And it was a big pile, big as birthday cake—no, for a wedding. It was tall and it was wide. At first I just stared, even as I got closer to it. I didn't want to disturb anything. Since it was close to the edge of the bed, I went to my knees like I was going to pray but only to get my eyes closer. It was dark. I wasn't believing my eyes. They were hundred dollar bills. I couldn't imagine how many hundred dollar bills there were. It was uncountable to me and maybe because I was so nervous about being there and awed both. I kept looking to see if there were other bills and it did not seem like it, not one wasn't. She could not know how many there were, it couldn't be possible. Hundreds of hundreds. It was more like she'd had these in a grocery bag and she dumped them all out onto the bed. I went ahead and picked one off, carefully, from the top. I couldn't believe it was real, that anyone would have so many, and then like this. Then I was thinking. And I did it. I took five of them. Because she wouldn't even know! And it didn't look even a little different after I did. It would be like taking five pennies from a jar of them. Then I went to the pink room. At first I was throwing my stuff around and bumping things. I wanted to pack my suitcase. I already wanted to leave before but I needed the money and if she had so much, well, come on! I don't know how long I was more confused. I thought I shouldn't run out, like I did this. That I should wait a day or two but tell her as soon as I could that I decided I had to go back home, it just wasn't working out. Maybe the day after tomorrow. I don't know how much time passed but I was afraid she would be back any minute. I couldn't do it. I had uncrumpled them but I crumpled three of them and rushed back in and . . . it looked no different with or without those. I hoped it would make me feel better and it did a little. Now I had gas money, I told myself. Enough to drive back and so I wouldn't have to borrow. The better feeling was for a few minutes is all. So much I never done before Willows Village. I was trying to think smart. Because she wouldn't know. She would never know.

Then the automatic garage door was opening. It was done, there was no turning back. I closed the pink bedroom's door and I turned on the TV and I sat on the bed like it was a couch. I wasn't watching or listening to it, only for her, to hear her. I think I heard her in the kitchen. I think I heard her coming up the stairs. And then she knocked on the door. I got up and said come in at the same time.

She didn't say anything at first. "I know I have so many of those. Probably drives you crazy, doesn't it?"

I was holding one of her dolls. I didn't even realize. "It accidentally fell onto the bed from above and I guess I didn't put it right back." I tossed it back on the bed.

"Well, it seems like you," she joked.

I nodded, more ashamed than embarrassed. I looked over at the doll like I shouldn't have tossed it like I did.

"I want to apologize to you," Aunt Maggy said.

"For what?"

"Today. I was upset about Lorena."

"I understand. It makes sense. I'm sorry too."

"Should I close this?" She was talking about the bedroom door.

"I guess, yeah."

It was just about closed. "Oh," she said, reopening it. "I think you have good news. A phone message. It was a man asking for Guillermo."

"That car dealer," I said. "One of them."

"I think so. Do you know how to listen to the messages on the machine?"

"I can figure it out."

"Good night then," she said, and she closed the door.

A MEMORY

Lucrecia Guerrero

igo and Marisol lie on the army surplus blanket that he's thrown over a patch of desert sand; their faces shine eerily pale in the light of the vast and starry skies. Rigo runs the point of his muscled tongue into Marisol's ears, her mouth, her nose. Lick, lick. She's his lollipop. He insinuates his arousal, restrained behind his Quickie Lube work pants, against her jeans-protected thigh. The blanket itches and Marisol squirms.

What's wrong? Rigo says. His heat pulses against her night-coolness. Are you ready, Mamita? he says. He presses his weight on top of her. The sand shifts beneath the blanket.

Lick, lick in her ear. Sounds are muffled. Lick, lick in her mouth. Words are sucked away. Lick, lick in her nose. Breath is blocked. She places one hand on his chest. His heart is pounding. Close. Too close. She pushes.

Don't you like it, Mamita? he says.

Maybe, she says, coy. If he keeps licking there'll be nothing left of her but a sliver of cherry-flavored candy.

Hey, what's your game? he says, and sits up. You're no virgin. He stretches his legs, adjusts the bulk inside his pants. Are you? His back is to her, and he turns his head slightly to the side as he awaits her response.

Maybe, she says, coy.

Rigo's twenty-five; at fourteen his father took him across the line into Mexico, away from downtown, up into the hills and the red-lit Canal Street. The professional women would teach Rigo what was what. He was a natural, a real hombre, the paid lovers said. Marisol has hinted at a dark and mysterious past in her sixteen-year-old life. After her nightly prayers, she asks the Virgencita to forgive her imagination. She lies in bed and gazes out the window and wishes on a falling star. She touches herself, and wonders, Is she a real *mujer*?

Marisol strokes Rigo's arm. I'm ready, she says.

He groans. She groans. I want you, Mamita, he says. I want you, too, she says. She wants and wants. The blanket itches; the sands shift.

Marisol stares up and over Rigo's shoulder, finds the brightest star. So far away from Nogales. Tonight she won't have to fib to her diary. She will imprint a spot of her blood on the page, make sure it dries before she closes the book. She doesn't want the blood to seep into the blank pages.

Un Recuerdo Que No Olvidaré, Rigo writes the next day on the flyleaf of the white Bible Marisol once received from Vacation Bible School. A Memory I'll Never Forget, he has written, and below those words last night's date. He's going to save that blanket, stain and all. They'll keep it after they're married. Right, Mamita? he says.

Marisol looks out the windshield of the Chevy Nova, gazes beyond into the Sonoran Desert. It reaches far, far. Maybe, she says.

OR ELSE

Antonya Nelson

y family owns a house in Telluride," was his favorite, most useful line. And it was a particular kind of girl or woman he used it on, somebody with whom he could not foresee a future. She would one day perceive him truly, with X-ray eyes, and move on. In the meantime, he could take her for a long weekend to Telluride.

She would be impressed by the modesty of the place. "It really is a shack," he would insist during the drive from Arizona, the desert falling away mile by mile, shrubbery and rocks transforming subtly as he ascended, from prickly saguaro and desiccated scrub oak to piñon, then aspen and spruce, those more gracious, greener trees, an escalation of markers by which David had measured his own evolution, from nagging anticipation to delighted arrival, for over twenty-five years. Not much had changed, on that journey: neither for David, nor in the world around him. Yes, traffic in Tucson was worse; sure, Show Low had made a comeback; sadly, a piece of the petrified forest was on fire; and some gaudy casino had suddenly landed on the vast moonscape of the Navajo Nation. In Cortez, you detoured through the endless engineering endeavor to straighten out that highway, which used to be sexy 666, but now was newly, inoffensively numbered. Trout farming had become a going enterprise along the Dolores River, square plastic-lined pools

in which writhing motion could be detected, as if someone were boiling rather than breeding a great roiling stew of fish. But: the most important things
remained faithfully themselves, and David watched them pass as if they were
winking at him, confirming their talismanlike confidence in his fortune.

"You're giddy," his current companion noted, in her peculiarly deep
voice. When would this voice cease surprising David? "Very cute," it said.
On the phone, you might mistake it for a man's voice. Its owner had not seen
him this way before, unguardedly enthusiastic, and he knew joy made him
appealing, as joy always did, like a child's smile, and also somehow vulner-
able, for the same reason. She could hold his joy, that child's smile, in contempt. "You're like a little boy," she said, opening the two windows on her
side of the car so that she could smoke. Meanwhile he held tight to the wheel
and adhered to speed limits because he wanted nothing to interfere with his
momentum, no rules to be broken, no winking signposts dissolved. Then
they were at the penultimate turn, the box canyon just ahead, and the little
town corralled within, its waterfall tumbling reliably at the precise backdrop
center, a landscape painting by a sentimental artist.

"Telluride," he announced in a tone that said *ta da*! "The most beautiful
place I've ever been."

"But," she exhaled, teasing, "where have you been?" And he was too
drunk with pleasure to do anything but laugh.

He narrated the noteworthy city sites as they rolled past, those milestones
of adolescence and young adulthood: the former train station, where he'd
watched, one night in the late seventies, as the firemen set flame to an out-
building and then extinguished it, which was their tradition. Only later had
they discovered that a member of their volunteers had suffered heart failure
in the drunken hubbub. And this man was the father of one of the children
watching, one of the boys rolling his eyes at the antics of his elders, which
were not so different from the antics of the youngsters, who crowded a furtive
campfire, smoking cigarettes on what had been, then, the rugged other side
of the river.

"That's where we used to hang out on Friday and Saturday nights," he
told his passenger, pointing at the marble steps of a former bank, its stately
window now cluttered with sunglasses. "Waiting to see where the party was.
And that's the bar that never carded, and up there is the historical museum,
which we knew how to break into."

"Why?"

He left his wistful repertoire to study her. "Why?"

"Yeah. Why break into a museum? I mean, did you steal stuff?"

"No." Well, yes. But not important stuff. Danielle, he considered, was maybe different from the others he'd brought here. She was older, forty-two to his thirty-nine. Had she outgrown not only brattiness but the memory of its allure? Maybe. Once, in the middle of making love, he asked why she had closed her eyes. "I'm pretending you're someone else," she said. David had ceased motion, no idea what to say; that was what was wrong with him, he was often left in a lull, unsure of his rights to indignation or hurt feelings, of how a person was entitled to react. "Who?" he finally asked.

"My last boyfriend," she told him, slipping away, pulling a pillow into an embrace between them. "He was a married man, and a lot older than me. He died a couple of years ago, of a heart condition. I don't think of him the whole time, hardly ever, actually, I just was then, when you asked." She'd stared at David frankly, pillow still clutched in her arms. "I sometimes miss him," she added.

"And there's the house," David said now, making the turn that led up to the little home he loved more than any place in the world.

"The house that caulk built," the family fondly claimed. It was dwarfed, these days, by mansions on either side. Forty years earlier, Jack Hart had purchased this property upon the birth of his first child, Priscilla. They'd been campers, the Harts, until Pris was born. Mrs. Hart then put down her foot; she said so whenever the story was retold. "No infants in tents! No diapers in the wilderness!" And so a small house was found, there in a glorious dying mining town, in the heart of that place, on a hill, with views shockingly symphonic from the crooked front porch. The Harts abided by the academic calendar; they fled the heat of Tucson and discovered Telluride, a summer respite, and in it a tiny miners' den with walls made of something called beaverboard, sagging into the ground, there atop a fading community of similar structures, occupied or abandoned by drunken miners and eccentric bar owners, Masons, shopkeepers, future ghosts. "The salt of the earth," Professor Hart would extol. He taught American studies; his interests were wider and perhaps more catholic than many of his ivory tower cohorts. He thought his summer town unpretentious, gritty, endearing. He became an Elk; he agreed to be deputized for the annual invasion of Hells Angels on the Fourth of July. He invited his friends to visit; his offspring did the same. Their home was small, and shabby, but filled with impromptu dinner parties, bridge games, storytelling sessions over the sticky kitchen table on which always sat a large bottle of red wine.

At the house—like a house in a cartoon, wedged between big bullying structures on either side—David parked, smiling in greeting to his hemmed-in old friend. Whatever the loss of open space—the dog pen, the falling-down shed, the horseshoe pit, the clothesline—nothing for him had changed about the sacred spot that remained, porch slats raggedly grinning. The air was bracing; the lack of oxygen might mean that your breath was literally taken away. Around him the peaks rose in their familiar battleship formations, proximate and daunting. They seemed poised to move, shift on their haunches and shrug the tiny toy town aside. No man-made object could detract from them. It was May and they were still snow covered; the aspen wore their nascent green, and on the streets below a resonant silence. Off season. The collective reverent rest between tourist onslaughts.

Up the crumbling concrete steps David led Danielle; the doors would be locked, their keys long ago lost, but the west living room window would be unlatched. It would squeal when he yanked it up, and then, to prop it open, he would require the use of a tubular cast-iron counterweight that sat, year after year, in a cluster of other rusty or glass objects found on hikes and scavenging adventures, as porch decor. Then, nudging aside the desk that sat before the window, he would crawl through. Inside, David took a moment to breathe in the peculiar scent of this house: coal dust, which still filled the inner walls and pooled at the base of the spongy paneling; stale sunlight as it had been captured through the wavering glass of the western windows; a very faint odor of natural gas from a leak that could never be located; and the simply unique smell of the Hart family itself. Home.

Then David went to the front door, on the other side of which waited Danielle, who was shivering, staring cross-eyed at the door handle rather than at the monstrous mountains all around her. The elevation was nearly nine thousand feet; from bake-blasted Tucson, you had to bring sweaters and wool socks as an act of faith. It was cold up here. At night, the stars devastated the clear, clear sky.

David Chalmers was a liar by nature, and now, by long habit. He lied when it wasn't necessary, when it wasn't even advantageous. He lied to amuse himself, to excuse himself, to camouflage himself. The Harts were not his family. He'd been an honorary member, once upon a time, and then he'd been banished, albeit gently.

He had found the family through Priscilla, the eldest daughter, who, at age nine when she was asked, insisted that he was the friend she wished to bring with her for the summer visit. Priscilla was a tomboy, and David was her partner in crime. In Tucson, they were prohibited from being in the same classroom at Sam Hughes Elementary. It was they who'd broken into the Telluride museum, along with some local miscreants. At night, they'd occupied the front upstairs bedroom, with its cracked window view of town, the bats that dipped all night long at the green streetlight outside. Late enough, they'd tiptoe through the back bedroom, where Priscilla's little sisters slept, and exit the window there, onto the hillside and into the night. For five summers she'd invited him. And then they were fourteen, and the invitation did not come.

"What happened to your girlfriend?" his father asked that fateful June first, smirking behind his beer and sunglasses. "Have yourself a lovers' spat?" David had no desire or even ability to explain, it was the exact opposite of what his father suggested, not a lovers' spat but the taint of loverly possibility. Pris had never been his *girlfriend*. Until this summer, she hadn't been a *girl*. And now suddenly she was, and she'd invited another girl to accompany her.

David spent the summer daydreaming and imagining himself there, wondering what project Dr. Hart was working on this year.

Dr. Hart had always enjoyed having David around, and David listened with unskeptical, uncritical attention to whatever Dr. Hart taught him. He'd memorized the names of the vegetation, the difference between flower and weed; he'd read whatever novel Dr. Hart handed him, reporting back on his confused progress, scandalized, mystified, ashamed; he learned to drive on those dirt roads, his own parents busy eviscerating each other, impatient with him, unable to fathom what it was the Harts liked about him, resenting his ability to escape Tucson for weeks at a time while they were forced to remain, their jobs not ones that permitted long holidays, their friends not likely to have summer homes in the mountains, and the existence of their son a complicating factor in their shared wish to part ways. David only reluctantly introduced them to the Harts, hustling the conversation along as he retrieved his duffel bag on the morning of the first departure. He'd been highly aware of Dr. Hart's taking in his family living room, the giant television, the absence of books or art, and, mostly, his mother's china doll collection, its pantheon standing rigid on their perches, staring back with their ice-cold eyes.

Meanwhile, his mother had studied Mrs. Hart, glaring at her tall thinness, her long hair falling in a braid down her back, the easy smile on her tanned face. Mrs. Hart was a potter; her hands were tools, unbeautiful, clay beneath her nails, calluses on her palms. She set her own schedule and followed arts fairs around the Southwest. Her three daughters blinked unafraid beside her, Priscilla, Violet, Lydia. Their white hair was tangled, their knees dirty; the older two already read above grade level and sassed the teachers, and so would the youngest, when it was her turn. They were occasionally kept home "to play in the dirt," Mrs. Hart said. "Just in case they start getting infected by the catty crowd. You know how girls can be," she appealed to David's mother.

"No," she replied. "I just have David." *Just*. And as if she'd never been a girl herself. As if she'd been born the hag she was now, lumpen and unhappy, suspicious of the lifestyle of her neighbors, those hippie Harts. She and her husband let David go because they had no better options for his summer freedom, and expected the worst of him: delinquency, slovenliness, eventual arrest. They didn't provide spending money: if the Harts wanted him, they could have him, but his parents would never regard it as a favor to them.

Mrs. Hart from then on treated David with a small degree of pity—the moist glance, the gentle pat—which he accepted like any rescued creature. He was not proud, he knew that. She kissed him goodnight as she did her girls, the four of them tucked in upstairs where the cabin's air was stuffy and warm, the pitched ceiling directly overhead, decorated with their own child-ish artwork, the very walls their canvas, naughtiness and eloquence, criss-crossed by webs, and spiders, which the Harts never killed, the old records of folk songs spinning on the player set before the open doors of the two bedrooms, the girls singing along to all the shocking lyrics. In the morning, Mrs. Hart would ask how they had slept and serve them pancakes. Every day, pancakes, studded with berries; David hadn't known pancakes came from anything but a box, or that there was such a thing as butter instead of margarine, or that syrup from its maple source ran thin and tart, nothing like the gluey stuff he got at home.

Then they were set free, out the front door to rush wild in the empty town. Down to the river, out to the mine, up the hills, into the few businesses that lined Main and where all the shopkeepers knew their names. David pretend-ed to be the brother. He wished it with all his heart. At night they played kick the can with the local children, hiding behind sheds and burn barrels. When the curfew siren sounded, they'd head home, spend the next hour or two all four riding the propane tank in the side yard, that warm echoing horse, or rocket, or motorcycle, while the air cooled around them.

For five years the weeks he would spend in Telluride stood for David as an annual pinnacle, time that he anticipated and then consumed. Those summers were when David felt most fully himself, trotting alongside Priscilla down the rocky streets, climbing at midnight up the slender path beside the stream to a large flat stone they considered their own, reclining there shoulder to shoulder, talking without thinking while stars fell overhead. Priscilla encouraged frankness in him; perhaps she encouraged it in everyone. He hadn't spoken without forethought since his early days as a liar. And he hadn't done it since.

David pulled the cord for the kitchen light, a foreign familiar coin cool in his palm, beneath which sat the house's modest hub, the table. Here was where he'd learned the rules of bridge, Mrs. Hart always recognizing his anxiety just before he made a fatal error in play. Here was where, after a morning of painting or plumbing or weeding or roofing, he joined Dr. Hart for lunch. Sandwiches on bread made by Mrs. Hart, soggy combinations David's mother would never have dreamed up, and his father wouldn't have tolerated. Hummus. Shredded carrot. Basil leaves. What the Hart family called stinky-feet cheese. Beer. And afterwards the afternoon, a warm haze, a certain kind of clicking bug hopping drunkenly through the air . . . So strong was the sense of the past, so deep was his desire to have it restored, David for a moment forgot with whom he'd come today. Danielle. She was asking in her hoarse voice about the bathroom, about making a fire, about what they might do for dinner, which she called, like a man, "chow." David immediately set to work with the necessary homecoming moves: plugging in the refrigerator, pulling sheets from the upper cupboards, running the water long enough to clear rust from the lines.

"This is a cozy room," Danielle said, after she'd emerged from the bathroom, toilet gurgling behind her. She stood at the door to Dr. and Mrs. Hart's bedroom.

"My room's upstairs," David said. He had never yet spent a night on the adult Harts' bed. He was willing to break into their home, but he was superstitious about sleeping where they had slept, having sex where they had had sex. "The view is better up there," he said, which certainly must be true, now that the mansion next door had blocked any kind of view or light from the elder Harts' bedroom window.

He and Danielle went up together, single file on the steep, noisy treads. In the front bedroom, where he'd spent five summers with Priscilla, and then one, in secret, with teenage Lydia, when he'd been her brief lover, he sat on the edge of the bed and creaked open the window. Cool air poured in like water. The moon was rising over the mountains, a glow there opposite the lingering glow of the setting sun.

"Once I found a bat hanging in here," David said, "before we put up screens." This story wasn't his but Priscilla's. She'd screamed, the black thing attached to her wall like a leather glove.

"It's incredible," Danielle said, blinking as her face encountered a web. "Smart investment, buying this back when."

"It wasn't an investment," David said, bristling as he always did when this dull observation was made. "They didn't buy it to make a profit."

"Yeah, OK, but most people wouldn't have hung onto it. Most people would have cashed in." And then, backing up, she asked, "'They'?"

"Before I was around," he said.

Dr. Hart had allowed David the use of the house one winter when David had tried to move to Telluride. He'd failed at college, been refused at both his mother's and his father's now-separate homes with their newly constituted second families, the fleet of stepsiblings he scorned. He found a job with the Telluride transit company, driving away three days a week in a truck he could barely control, returning the next day with the goods he had accumulated down in the larger towns. Film reels, liquor, coal, hardware, groceries. Without him, Telluride might fail to function. He had felt like a legitimate local for the three months that this idyllic situation stuttered along, like Santa when he arrived and threw open the truck's back doors to reveal its bounty. Then, in November, he crashed, rolled off the hillside on black ice, a delivery of beer cans and lumber spilled four hundred feet, and that was the end of his time as town hero. The men who worked at the gravel quarry at the bottom of the hill made off with the spoils; David could only crawl from the cab and shout ineffectually, clutching his broken arm, gasping around bruised lungs, "Stop, thief!" Although his rent was free, he had no money for utilities or food or fun. He'd had to return abjectly to Tucson, gas for his own vehicle siphoned with a section of garden hose from somebody parked in the street. He'd not known how to leave a house in the winter; the pipes froze and burst, and a brood of skunks moved in under the floor. When the Harts returned, as they always did, on June first, they'd had to stay in a hotel for a few days while the plumbing was replaced and vermin evicted. David also came to understand that he hadn't been particularly tidy, as a tenant, either. "I don't blame you," Dr. Hart assured him. "But I wouldn't bring any of this up when you see Judy or the girls." With horror, David remembered the pornography he must surely have left under the upstairs bed. Who had discovered that?

Beside him Danielle sneezed, five loud times in a row. "I may be allergic to your house," she said. "And don't you ever bless anybody when they sneeze?" As she stepped cautiously, duck-footed, down the steps ahead of him, David had an ugly temptation to plant his foot squarely between her shoulders, deliver a powerful kick.

"Why's your room painted purple?" she was asking. "You some kinda gaylord?"

He'd known the Harts' schedule so well as to have engineered a pity pickup, one season. They always arrived on the first of June; he'd positioned himself, as hitchhiker, on the highway just east of Rico. This would permit neither too much nor too little time with the family.

He envisioned their drive as he made his own journey. He hitched from Tucson days earlier, accepting a long, lucky ride on a band bus with a blue-grass group booked at a bar in Telluride. Although that was his ultimate destination, he begged off at Rico, spending two nights camping on Scotch Creek. It snowed both nights; his small holey bivouac sack was frozen every morning as he hatched himself from it. By the time the Harts' white van appeared, David had been offered a half dozen rides; had the Harts driven by without stopping, he might have later sought them out for revenge, torched their little piece of paradise.

But they pulled over, as he had trusted they would, and he managed to hide his exhausted lingering and near-hypothermia long enough to pretend utter astonishment at this incredible coincidence. This was two years after his stint as Telluride transit driver; he claimed he had a job awaiting him, a place to crash, friends looking forward to his arrival.

Lydia and her best friend were along with the parents, that year. The other Hart girls were coming later; they had jobs, boyfriends, summer school. Only Lydia was still fixed in the family routine. She would be a high school senior in the fall; her best friend was a dark beauty who greeted David with an automatic seductive move of her knees as she made room for him and his damp belongings. Swinging himself into the vehicle, he witnessed an exchanged glance between the Hart parents; he wished he could convince them he was someone worth admitting back into the warm circle of their family. Prodigal? Wasn't that a role he might claim?

"Pris is getting married," Lydia informed him over her friend's presence. "At the house. Me and Violet are maids of honor."

"Violet and I," said Mrs. Hart.

"Wow," David said, trying to hide his hurt feelings. Nobody had notified him. And now nobody was inviting him. A pregnant pause filled more than a few miles. The teenage beauty allowed her bare thigh to rest against David's, although all he could think of was Priscilla, his old best friend. When they left him at the bakery—No, he wouldn't take money, although he might stop by for a drink, later on—he began immediately devising some way to become integral to the wedding. Lawn boy? Caterer? He had until the summer solstice to figure it out.

The friend, because girls were cutthroat, would be the key, leading Lydia to sneak him into the house, through that same back window, and into her bed, in the purple room that had once been Pris's, in order to claim victory in having seduced him. Twenty-four to her seventeen years, he closed his eyes during sex, an apology running in his mind like a prayer. For a couple of weeks, he lived upstairs without the Hart parents' knowledge, like a stray cat, padding softly across the floors, climbing in and out the back window, eating the food Lydia and her friend brought for him, crawling into bed beside her and lying when he said he'd always liked her best.

In the morning, David's eyes flew open. He'd heard the west window screech downstairs. He looked to the pillow next to him, where he expected to find Danielle, snoring mannishly away, but she was gone. Maybe she was climbing out of the house, finished with him.

Before he could pull on pants he heard the women meet, the vague scream of surprise on either side, the confrontation. This was backdrop to his swift calculations—through the upstairs window he would go, down to the car, out of town. But wait: no key! Then another flashing plan, the one story that would convince two people of his innocence. Palms flattening his hair, he wondered which sister it was, hoping for Lydia, who was the naughtiest Hart, the spoiled baby with whom he'd had shaming sex. He arrived at the bottom of the stairs just as its door was thrown open. Violet.

"David! What the *hell*? I wondered whose car that was, with the Arizona plates."

He moved to embrace her, which would have been acceptable to placid Violet, except that she seemed somehow armored, wearing a backpack and carrying a shoebox.

"You're early," David chose to say, hoping that bluster might cover his trespass long enough to hustle Danielle out of earshot. "It's usually not until June first. This is Danielle, but I guess you met, I heard the yelling." Meanwhile, he made a whirl of himself, filling the kettle, lighting the gas. "I told your dad I was coming but maybe he forgot to mention it?"

Violet didn't respond for a moment. She wasn't as fast on her feet as her sisters. Finally, she said, "When did you tell Dad?"

"Maybe a month ago?"

Violet turned to Danielle. "What's your name, again?"

"Danielle. Danielle Graham."

"I'm Violet, and this is my family's house. Welcome," she added, looking down at Danielle's long bare legs under her nightshirt.

"Coffee?" David asked, having the absurd thought that this might not end badly, that Violet might allow him to escape utter humiliation. She had asthma, and sometimes disappeared from social exchanges in order to attend to her own respiration.

"Sure," Violet said, collecting breath, returning to them. "I don't know why I decided to drive all night."

"Lotta wildlife on the road?" David asked, fussing with filters, cups, potholders, avoiding Danielle's curious expression. Unlike other women, she had a patient observing personality, the same one that had been bemused by his childishness yesterday, the one that today studied him for clues as to what was going on. She was a nurse, and she didn't panic, not at the arrival of an emergency, not at the sight of any human facial expression. She had seen them all. Would that get him off this hook today? Or more fully snag him?

"I almost hit a dozen deer," said Violet. "I was starting to think it was the same one, following me, throwing itself out in the road like a joke." She set the shoebox on the table, shrugged out of the pack, then pulled her knitted duster around her, and fell sighing into a chair. As a middle child, she'd been accustomed to being left out. She was neither oldest nor youngest, and neither was she a boy, which would have been a Hart novelty. Perhaps she felt redundant. David had been Pris's friend, not hers. Violet had read books; sometimes she'd grown bored and tattled. David had always thought her the dud Hart, the least necessary of the bunch. Along with the asthma, she had a wandering eye, her left, that nudged toward her skull. Because of these imperfections, she'd always seemed approachable; she'd seemed to be a *nice* person even if she wasn't actually a nice person. People were misled by the wandering eye, as if her attention or intelligence or humanity also wandered, as if she had only to be half-attended to.

Violet let him serve her coffee. Via chitchat, she and Danielle had discovered they were members of the same twenty-four-hour gym in Tucson, although Violet, lazy, rarely used the place, and Danielle's routine there was odd, given her shifts at the hospital.

"I'm here to plan for Lydia's wedding," Violet addressed David. He forced himself to focus on the eye that reliably strayed. "Mom and Pris and Lyd are coming tomorrow, and then Pris's husband and kids the day after, with the fiancé."

David had seated himself at the head of the table, aware suddenly that his feet were bare and frozen, that he ought to have started a fire, that Violet hadn't mentioned her father's arrival time, that he was looking away from her face to the box she had set on the table, and that the label on it was from a mortuary. There would be the wedding in a week, Violet was saying, but before then, before the men and children arrived, the women were going to spread Dr. Hart's ashes.

"What?"

"Dad died," Violet said, adding apologetically, "last December. Pancreatic cancer. It was very unexpected." She was studying her coffee cup, which was one her mother had thrown, years earlier; almost all of the cups and plates and bowls and trivets were of her making, mismatched seconds that she hadn't been able to sell. There was a mug in the cupboard that had been David's, once upon a time.

He blinked at the white box. The box could have held shoes, or a pastry, perhaps letterhead. He felt specifically as if his body were repulsing the news of its true contents, like the wrong end of a magnet. The box on the table, the table in the house, the house in the town, the town in the canyon. And the man, in the box. David was dizzy. "Christmas was awful," Violet was saying, "but I think we're all getting used to it. We thought we'd take him up to Blue Lake. He always said that was his favorite spot. Although I'm not sure Mom can make it up there, anymore. Arthritis. She's a potter," she explained to Danielle, "so it's really especially cruel to have arthritis."

"I didn't know," David finally uttered. Cruel, he noted; maybe Violet had found religion, believed now in some figure who'd *cruelly* afflicted her mother with arthritis, Violet's own peculiar brand of rebellion against passionate atheist parents. "Why didn't you tell me?" he finally said, interrupting an exchange the women were having. Danielle, he'd overheard, learning it for the first time, was an orphan.

This time Violet performed her unique blink, one eye closing just before the other. "His obituary ran in the paper," she said at last.

They should have notified him, he thought, he should have been personally told. How was it they could not understand his affection for them all, his need especially of Dr. Hart?

Violet said, gently, "I think you probably ought to get out of here today. I don't really care that you're here, but it's not going to be cool with Mom or Pris."

He never got away with anything, David thought. If it wasn't an officer of the law actually pulling him over, it was a ticket in the mail, the indisputable evidence of his vehicle, flying by a camera, traveling many miles over the limit. What a person might eventually ask himself was why he felt a need to break rules, tell lies, have things to get away with? Why he couldn't, in some definitive way, exhaust or outgrow childish defiance.

Upstairs, bundling their belongings back into their bags, David preempted what he believed would be Danielle's outrage by saying, "Don't say anything, OK? Just don't say a fucking word." She was his responsibility, witness to his humiliation, a woman with a horsey face—big, square teeth, oversized jaw, hair she tossed like a mane—five hundred miles from Tucson, where she belonged. When he first saw her, he'd wondered if she was a former man. And now she was stripping the bed, methodically removing what they'd just last night spread out together.

"We have to wash these," she said. "It's the least."

Downstairs, she assured Violet she would return the sheets by noon, leave them on the front porch. David glanced at the broken-handled mug atop the refrigerator, where the quarters were kept for the washateria, and then his gaze crashed into Violet's, whose eyes had also gone automatically to the money.

While the sheets churned, David took Danielle to his favorite bar. The bartender was the same as previous years; she said hello without true recognition of him, the generic hospitality of a tourist town. He began to tell Danielle about the local character who rode his horse through these very doors, reliably, every year, when she stopped him.

"You already told me about that."

"I did?" He wondered if he'd also told her about being beat up behind this bar, if he'd trotted out that particular tall tale, the explanation for the divot in his forehead, from the time he'd taken a header in the alley. He touched his scar and raised his eyebrows.

"Yeah, I heard all about that, too. You know, I'm beginning to feel like I could diagnose you."

"I don't want a diagnosis." But then he discovered he'd rather know it than not. "Alright, what?" He was ready to deny being a compulsive liar.

"You perseverate."

"I don't even know what that means."

"Not knowing doesn't exempt you. You live in the past, you revisit the same things over and over. This place is nothing but a big nostalgia trip for you. I don't know what the story is with you and that family, but—"

He inserted himself here, "Messy breakup with Violet," he lied. "The others—"

"I. Don't. Care," Danielle said. He could tell from her expression that she
didn't. The details bored her. Neon beer lights turned her face green, then
yellow. She was as mechanically unmoved as one of the machines she manned
at the hospital, merely charting a human condition. "Just for a change, how
about you ask me something," she proposed. "How about that?"

"OK." David thought a moment. "How old was that other boyfriend?"

"Seventy," she said.

"Wow."

"My parents were spinning in their graves, a man as old as them. But I
loved him with all my heart."

"Why?"

"Why?" Danielle leaned back, focusing on David's face. "Two questions
in a row. It's a record. But whatever. I'd rather visit my weird situation than
hear about yours. So I loved Franklin because, when we talked, I always
felt as if we were wandering around in a big house, a big house with endless
rooms, and every time we came to a closed door in one of those rooms we
were able to open it. Open doors, open doors, one after another. That's why
I loved him."

David imagined the house, the wind circulating through those rooms,
doors swinging on hinges.

"You can't smoke in here," the bartender came over to tell her, as soon as
Danielle had lit up. "New law."

Danielle suddenly laughed. "I love drinking before noon," she declared.

"It's a great high," David agreed. "The altitude really helps." He was
tempted to tell her about the BIOTA club—blame it on the altitude—but
was afraid he already had.

Back at the washateria, they couldn't locate their load of sheets and underwear. Every machine was empty. "What the fuck?" David said. The floor
was damp and smelled of chlorine. There was nobody to appeal to, the business a self-service one; upstairs were apartments, blameless tenants. "*You* tell
her," he said to Danielle. She shrugged, willing. Her record was still relatively
clean. He watched from the street as Danielle banged on the front door.
When Violet answered it, she sneezed into the sunlight.

"*Bless* you," David heard. Then the two women went inside, the door
banging behind them. David waited. He studied the garbage can, latched the
clip so that bears wouldn't overturn it, swiped his hand on the creosote-treated
light pole just to have the odor on his fingers. Finally, Danielle emerged.

"What took so long?"

"None of your beeswax. I wrote her a check, she can buy six hundred thread count. And then we exchanged numbers. We might share a trainer this fall."

"I don't actually know what you're talking about."

"You're in shock," Danielle said. "I've seen it before."

"Shock?"

"The dead dad?" *Duh,* her tone said.

Dr. Hart. David saw him suddenly at the kitchen table, a few of his university cronies alongside, bearded and complaining around the glowing wine bottle—bastard politicians, pretentious films, popular potboilers, historical rogues, critical tirades turned into a competitive sport—while Mrs. Hart floated around humming, serving food, salving childish wounds, providing pajamas and lighters and answers to all manner of esoteric inquiry: Who the hell was that poet? Where, oh, where was the blankie? Even then, when David was a young boy allowed to sit beside Dr. Hart, to sip at the wine if he wanted, to occasionally receive a fond pat on the back, he had recognized the difference between Dr. Hart and those others. Concerning a certain slim confounding novel that Dr. Hart had just the day before handed to David, one particular colleague had sneered, "Is that any good?" A gauntlet, made of contempt.

"Oh, my God," Mrs. Hart murmured, rolling her eyes indulgently.

"Dad's trash habit," Violet sing-songed.

"Well," Dr. Hart had confessed, "I did like it."

"I liked it, too!" David had declared, heart swollen with pride, confoundedness forgotten, pledging loyalty to his king. Everyone in the room laughed, even little ignorant Lydia, and he felt himself shrink back to size: skinny boy on quaking stool, squawking sidekick to the great man.

Still, he *had* been a great man, hadn't he?

"Keys?" Danielle said, out of nowhere. Apparently she had been waiting, palm out, fingers wiggling. "I should drive."

It snowed that night. They stayed at a lodge on the edge of town, down by the river, by the former train station where an outhouse had once burned. David opened his mouth to tell the tale, then couldn't remember whether he'd already told it, and didn't want to be scolded for perseverating. Diagnosis, indeed. He did appreciate Danielle's accepting the change in plans. She did not seem shocked by his deceit, and she had a functioning credit card to

offer at the front desk. David himself was consigned to cash, which he read-
ily provided—what he had of it—promising to make up later what he owed.

"No reason to ruin the weekend," Danielle had said. ER nurse: David had
to admire her unflinching willingness to roll with the punches. This, too, reminded him of a man. When she undressed he watched from the back, mentally sheering off her long hair so as to see only the wide swimmer's shoulders
and narrow hips, calves overmuscled, feet perhaps flat, certainly large. Then
she dropped her hair and swung around, her breasts dispelling any lingering
sense of manliness.

"I think it's only fair to tell you that I'm not using protection," she said, in
the middle of sex.

David laughed, relieved to be in the throes of someone else's story, whatever weave of fabrication that allowed her to think her admission, at this late
date, honorable. "Duly noted," he said.

"I was pregnant before, with the married man, and I aborted. I really wish
I hadn't. It's my big regret. Franklin," she added.

The image of that man had been taking shape in David's mind, a dead
man like Dr. Hart, and that's who he was thinking about as they finished
having unprotected sex.

Danielle wore one of David's jackets when they went out walking on their
third and last evening in Telluride. He was glad to do something for her,
clutching at any small favor. They stopped by the trash cans outside the Hart
house, snow falling once again around the warm glow of the window. The
tentative green of spring would not be killed by this storm. It was a harmless
piece of winter, an errant cold cloud making a pit stop here, inflicting no permanent damage. Inside were the women, the mother and three daughters;
Judy Hart still wore the braid down her back, her hair silver now against her
bronze face. She smiled, sitting at the head of the table, facing the window,
where she would see only her own reflection. Others crossed the small space,
moving from stove to sink to refrigerator, a tight choreography with which
David was intimately familiar. Then strangers filled the room, two men and
two little boys, Pris's children, who would no doubt be sent to sleep in the
back bedroom upstairs, under the drawings made by their mother and their
aunts. And by David. His scrawls were up there, too.

"Looking in like this reminds me of a snow globe," Danielle said, quiet
and low. "Except we're in the snow, and they're in the globe." There had
been drinks with dinner. David held her hand happily, quietly. He wished

that Priscilla would step onto the porch and discover his happiness; he needed to display it, to prove it.

He saw Lydia embrace one of the men, from the back, lean over him and put her face beside his. Her hair was the same bleached straggle from childhood.

It had been Mrs. Hart who had discovered David and Lydia in bed together, one morning long ago, only days before Pris was to be married, when David was officially an adult and Lydia officially not. Mrs. Hart had opened the door after rapping briefly. "Lyd?" Then closed her eyes at the sight of David's bare chest. She hadn't been angry; she was a kind, kind woman, whose disappointment was far harder to bear than her anger. "Let's not tell your father," she'd suggested to Lydia, still standing there at the door, eyes averted. "I'm afraid he won't understand."

Danielle asked David now, "Do you wish you were in there instead of out here?"

"No," he said. And then he reviewed his response. It was a lie—or else it wasn't.

PAPA AT KETCHUM, 1961

Joyce Carol Oates

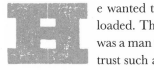e wanted to die. He loaded the shotgun. Both barrels he loaded. This had to be a joke, both barrels he loaded. He was a man with a sense of humor. He was a joker. Couldn't trust such a man, a joker in the deck. He laughed. Except his hands shook and that was a shameful thing. His head had filled again with pus. His head had to be cleared. His head was leaking. And you could smell it: greeny pus. His brain was inflamed, swollen. He was a stealthy one. Soundlessly he moved. Barefoot on the stairs. Had to be early morning. Downstairs he'd come from bed. The woman would think he'd groped his way into the bathroom. He'd located the key in the kitchen on the windowsill. He had the shotgun now. He was fumbling to steady it. This was the new shotgun and it was heavy. He was fearful of dropping it. He was fearful of being discovered. When he drove into town, only just to the liquor store, he was observed. The license plates on his pickup were noted. In the liquor store, a hidden camera photographed him. He'd bought the new shotgun in Sun Valley. The dealer had recognized him. The dealer had said it's an honor and shook his hand. The gun was a twelve-gauge double-barreled English shotgun with a satin-nickel finish and maplewood stock. He was sorry to defile the new shotgun. Clumsily he was positioning the muzzle beneath his chin. There his throat was wattled and stubble grew in wayward clusters like a porcupine's quills.

With his bare big toe he groped for a trigger. His toes did not quiver and quake like his fingers but the nails were badly discolored and thickened. Beneath the nails, black blood had coagulated. His feet, his ankles were swollen with edema. He prayed God damn, God help me. You did not believe in God but it was a good bet to pray. He was determined to do this job cleanly and forever, for even a joker does not get a second chance. God was the joker in the deck, of course. You would have to placate Him to execute the job perfectly. This meant all of the brain blasted away in an instant. He feared that there might be some remnant of a soul remaining in some area of the brain not blasted away, or that the brain stem would continue to function, in some hospital there's Papa in piss-stinky pajamas stuttering his ABC's out of a thimble of brain left intact somewhere up inside the skull mended like broken crockery where they could trail a shunt into it. And TV would broadcast this, and a voice-over intoning *The wages of sin is living death.* How many sleepless nights here in Ketchum and at the hospital in Minnesota he'd ground his teeth over this fear. For he feared being pitied as he feared being laughed at. He feared strangers touching his head. Rearranging his hair. For his hair was not thick any longer, the bumpy scalp showed. If the head was to be destroyed it would have to be cleanly. He was not altogether serious about some of these fears yet you could not know: even the wily Pascal could not know: if you make your wager, make your wager one you cannot lose. He thought this might be a principle. His body had grown strange to him, clumsy and uncoordinated. Sometimes he believed he had wakened in his father's old body he'd scorned as a boy. It is a terrible thing to wake in your father's old body you have scorned as a boy. There is something very cruel in such a joke and yet it is fitting too. For now he was having difficulty steadying the shotgun for his hands shook. The satin-nickel finish was damp with sweat from his hands. There is an unmistakable odor of sweat on gunmetal. It is not a pleasant odor. He recalled that, yes his father's hands had shaken, too. As a boy he had observed this. As a boy he had scorned such weakness. Yet his father had managed to hold his gun steady and to kill himself with a single bullet to the brain. You would have to grant the old man that, beyond scorn. His father had used a pistol which is much more risky. A shotgun, skillfully maneuvered, is not risky. A shotgun is a wager you cannot lose. Except if he could see his bare foot, he would be more confident. If he could see his big, bare toe. Positioned as he was, muzzle beneath his stubbled chin, he could not see the shotgun at all, nor could he see the floor. A misfire would be a tragedy. A misfire would alert the woman. A misfire would bring an ambulance, medical workers, forcible restraints and a return to the hospital where they would shock and fry his brain and catheterize his penis that already leaked piss and blood. That joke had gone far enough. He fumbled for the trigger with his big, bare toe. He tried to exert pressure but something was in the way. His eyes were open and alert. His eyes moved frantically about like a fly's multi-faceted eyes yet his vision was blurred as if he were staring through gauze. He could not be altogether certain if in fact he might be staring through gauze, recuperating from a head wound after the accident. It might have been the plane crash, or the other. He was facing a window and the window was splotched with rain. He was in the mountain place: in Idaho. He recognized the interior. There was a pine needle smell here, a wood smoke smell, he recognized. He'd come to die in Idaho. What you liked about Ketchum was that there was no one here. In Sun Valley, yes. But not here, he would not be leaving this time. If the woman tried to interfere he would turn the gun on her. He would drop her with a single shot. In midcry the woman would collapse. She would slump wordless to the floor and bleed out like any dying animal. He would turn the gun on himself, then: he became excited imagining this. His hands trembled in anticipation. His truest life was such secrecy and fantasy. The truest life must always he hidden. As a boy he'd known this. As a man he'd known this, amid bouts of drinking, partying, hosting house-guests, playing the Papa-buffoon everybody loved. He'd known this lying gut-sick and insomniac in sweat-stinking bedclothes. *Always you are alone, as a man with his gun is alone and needing no others.* It was an erotic imagining beyond sex: that explosion of pellets up into the head cavity, powerful as a detonating hand grenade. Jesus! This would be sweet! What remained of his life was pent-up in him like jism clotted up into his scrotum and lower gut. Pent-up so it has turned to pus. He would blow out the greeny pus. His sick brains leaking down the oak-paneled wall. Shattered bits of skull and tissue embedded in the oak-beamed ceiling. He laughed. He bared his teeth in wide Papa-grin. The explosion was deafening but he'd passed beyond hearing.

To get to Ketchum you drove north from Twin Falls. You drove north on Rt. 75 through Shoshone Falls and beyond the Mammoth Caves and the Shoshone Ice Caves. Beyond Magic City, Bellevue, Hailey, and Triumph. Into the foothills of the Sawtooth Range you drove. In this range there was Castle Peak at nearly twelve thousand feet. There was Mt. Greyrock barely visible on misty days. There was Rainbow Peak. Not far from his sprawling property was the Lost River Range. There were such settlements as Rocky Bar, Featherville, Blizzard, Chilly, Corral, Yellow Pine, Salmon River, Warm Lake,

Crouch, Garden Valley. There was Black Canyon Dam, there was Mud Lake, Horseshoe Bend, Sunbeam, Mountain Home, and Bonanza. There was the Salmon River and there was the Lost River. There was also the Big Lost River. The cities were Little Falls, Butte City, Boise. Mornings when work did not come to him he uttered these place-names aloud and slowly as if the sounds were a mysterious poetry, or prayer. He studied local maps, some of them dating back to the 1890s. Nothing gave him more happiness.

Mornings when work does not come are long mornings.

You do not give up until 1 p.m. at the earliest.

From the window of his second-floor workroom facing the Sawtooth Mountains he was watching a young stag at the edge of the woods that was behaving strangely. He'd been watching the young stag for some minutes. Like a drunken creature it stumbled in one direction, then reversed course abruptly and stumbled in another. The stag was perhaps one hundred feet from the house. He could not work with such a distraction within his view. He could not hope to concentrate. He went downstairs. The woman had driven into Little Falls, no one would call after him. His skin was heated, he had no need for a coat but he pulled a hat onto his head for his thinning hair left his scalp sensitive to cold. He did not take his gloves, which was a mistake, but outside as he approached the young stag at the edge of the clearing he did not want to turn back. Softly he called to the stricken creature as you might speak to a horse, to calm it. He approached the stag cautiously. His breath steamed. His feet (he was wearing bedroom slippers with woolen socks, he'd forgotten and hurried outside without boots) broke through a dry crust of snow on the grassy slope. The stag was so young, its body lacked the muscular thickness of the older stage and its antlers were miniature antlers covered in velvety down. When he was about fifteen feet from the struggling stag he saw that it had caught the miniature antlers in a wicked strip of barbed wire. The wire had cut into the stag's head and into its slender neck. Blood glistened on the stag's dun-colored winter coat and was splattered on the trampled snow. The stag shook its head violently, trying to dislodge the wire that seemed to be cutting into its flesh ever more deeply. The stag's eyes rolled white above the rim of the iris and frothy liquid shone at its muzzle. It was panting loudly, snorting and stamping the ground. He knew: you did not ever approach a mature stag or even a mature doe, for their hooves were sharp and ideally suited for stomping an adversary to death, should the adversary make the blunder of being knocked to the ground. Once down, the adversary would very likely not get up again. A deer's tooth was also very sharp, like a horse's tooth. Yet he continued to approach the young stag, extending his hand, making a rhythmic clicking sound with his mouth meant to command calm. For he could not bear to turn aside from the beautiful struggling creature, that was bleeding, and terrified, and in danger of dying of shock. It was heartrending to see a short distance away, partly hidden in the woods, a ragtag herd of deer, some of them with ribs showing through their coarse winter coats, watching the young stag in distress. The closest was a mature doe, very likely the stag's mother. Cautiously he continued to approach the stag. He was a stubborn old man, he would not give up easily. His heart pumped so he could feel it in his chest. This was not an unpleasant sensation, you only just hoped the heartbeat would not kick into tachycardia. The last time, the woman had had to call an ambulance to take him to the ER at Little Falls, where they'd managed to bring the heartbeat down with a powerful dosage of liquid quinidine into his bloodstream but the woman was not here now and he had no idea when she would return. Damn, to come outdoors in bedroom slippers! He did not so much mind the cold, which was a dry, mineral cold that cleared the head. He was warm with excitement, heat on his skin. The stag had seen him by now, and had smelled him. The stag was making a panting-snorting noise that was a noise of warning. The stag staggered backward, its hooves slipped, it fell heavily to the ground. Immediately it scrambled to get to its feet but he was too quick, crouched over it, cursing and grabbing at the threshing neck, the antlers. Something pierced the fleshy base of his thumb, sharp as a razor blade. He cursed, but did not release the panicked stag. He saw that it was bleeding from several wounds, including a deep gash beneath its chin, which could not have been far from a major artery. Another time he cursed the young stag as it kicked at him. Its eyes rolled hack in its head, the snorting was loud and quickened as a bellows. Yet he'd managed to get behind the creature, out of range of its flailing hooves and bared teeth. His hands were bleeding. God damn, he cursed the young stag, that would not surrender sensibly to let him help it. Skeins of frothy saliva flew into his face, his hands were cut again, after what seemed like a very long time he managed to tear away the damned barbed wire, that had gotten twisted around the antlers. He threw it away, and released the stag that leapt up immediately, making a moaning-whinnying noise like a horse. At the edge of the clearing, the mature doe had come closer and had been snorting and stomping as well but as soon as the young stag broke free, the doe backed off. God damn, he'd been knocked back onto his buttocks. On his bony old man ass in the snow and one of the bedroom slippers was missing. His heart continued to pound in angry rebuke of such folly. He knew better, of course he knew better, his heart was leaky and had become his adversary in recent years. His body was now his adversary, his father's cast-off body. Yet he watched anxiously as the young stag teetered away, still shaking its head, glistening blood, and another time slipped, and he prayed that the stag would not fall because if it fell hard, if it could not right itself, it would soon die of shock, or cardiac arrest; but the stag managed to right itself, and at last trotted away into the woods. The rest of the ragtag herd had vanished. Except for the hoof-trampled snow, and the blood on the snow, and the old man on his ass in the snow wiping deer blood and deer spittle on his trousers, you would not have guessed that there had been any deer at all.

Mornings when work does not come.

Mummy had been Mrs. Hemingstein, sometimes just Mrs. Stein he'd called Mummy for any Jew name was a joke between them. He himself had numerous school nicknames, including Hem, Hemmie, Nesto, Butch. His own favorite was Hemingstein, sometimes just Stein. Mornings when work did not come that final winter he heard *Hemingstein, Stein* faint and teasing in a husky female voice that made his lips twitch in a smile of childish pleasure or in an adult grimace of pain he did not know.

Sirens.
    In Ketchum, Idaho, he came to know sirens.
    Emergency rescue van. Ambulance. Police siren. Fire department. Vehicles speeding on Route 75 out from Ketchum, careening past slower traffic. In this place you became a connoisseur of sirens: broken and looping and breathless-sounding it's the Camas County emergency rescue van. Higher pitched, it's the Ketchum Medical Clinic ambulance or private-owned Holland Ambulance. Frantic-beeping siren, sheer belligerent fury like a shrieking elephant, it's the Camas County Sheriff's Department. A lower-pitched whooping shriek punctuated by a rapid wheezing noise like a horn, it's the Ketchum Volunteer Firefighters.
    At first the siren is distant. The siren could be moving in any direction. Gradually, the volume increases. The siren is headed in your direction. The siren is turning off the road and into your driveway and up the hill, emerging from a dense, clotted woods, and the siren is inside your skull, the siren is *you*.

Maybe he'd been drinking and smoking sprawled on the leather sofa downstairs, TV on but sound muted and maybe a shower of sparks had fallen from his cigarette, he'd brushed away with his hand not noticing where and next thing he knew, smoke, stinking smoke, and the woman in nightclothes screaming at him from the stairs. Or maybe he'd fallen on an icy step at the back of the house, rifle in hand (he'd been alerted to someone or something at the shadowy edge of the woods) and the rifle had gone off and next thing he knew he'd cracked his head and was bleeding so badly the woman thought he might have been shot. Or, fell on the stairs, broke his left foot howling in pain like a wounded monkey. Or dizzy in the tepid bathwater, Seconal and whiskey, his heavy Papa-head slumped forward as if he were broke-necked and the woman could not revive him. Or, middle of the night, how many nights, hadn't been able to breathe. Or, chest pains. Or, abdominal pain. Kidney stone? Appendicitis? Stroke? Internal hemorrhage? Or, what the woman would report to the medics as "suicidal ravings"—"suicidal threats." Or, Papa had threatened her. (Had he? Papa denied it vehemently in the midst of collapse and spiritual wreckage, face gnarled and twisted as if in a vise, Papa was yet eloquent, convincing.) The woman dared to struggle with him for the shotgun shells that went rolling and skittering across the floor, and for the heavy Mannlicher shotgun. *Get away! Don't touch!* Papa could not bear to be touched and so he shoved the woman away, stumbled from the room and locked himself in a bathroom, pounding his fists against the mirrored door of the medicine cabinet, broke the mirror, lacerated his hands, and out of spite the woman dialed 911 and yet another time—how many times!—a siren began to be heard in the distance, one of the looping wails, furious shrieks like a wounded charging beast, how many times careening up the hill to Papa's house on its remote and desolate promontory and the woman outside in the driveway disheveled and lacking in all wifely restraint and dignity crying *Please help us! Help us!*

Papa had to laugh: *us.*

Especially if you married them, they began to think *us.* As if the world gave a shit about *us.* It was Papa who mattered, not *us.*

This one, he'd married. The one he'd loved most, the most beautiful of his women, Papa had not married for she'd been married to another man. But this one he'd married, the fourth of Papa's wives and his widow-to-be. A female is essentially a cunt, the pure purpose of the female is cunt, but a woman, a wife, is a cunt with a mouth, a man has to reckon with. It's a sobering fact you start off with cunt, you wind up with mouth. You wind up with your widow-to-be.

He limped out to the grave site. Always there was the faint anxiety that somehow it would not he there. The rocks would have been dislodged. The pine trees would be missing. The trail would be so overgrown, he would lose his way. The idea of outdoors is so very different from outdoors. For the idea is a way of speaking but the outdoors has no speech. You are often startled by the sky. Your eyes glance upward, quizzical and hopeful. God damn, the left foot dragged. Swollen feet, ankles. He was using a cane. He would not use the crutches. He inhaled the odor of pine needles. It was a sharp, clear odor. It was an odor to clear the head. It was an odor you could not quite imagine until you smelled it. And there was the sky, shifting cloud vapor. His weak eyes squinted but could perceive nothing beyond the cloud vapor. The anxiety was returning, a sensation like quick, sharp needles. And in the armpits, an outbreak of sweat. Why, he did not know. The grave site was a place of solitude and beauty. The grave site was a place of peace. The grave site was at the top of a high hill amid pine trees facing the Sawtooth Mountains to the west. Papa was particular about his grave site, you did not wish to excite him. He had positioned rocks to mark the grave site and on each of his walks he took the identical route up the hill from the house and along the ridge at the edge of the woods and he paused at the grave site to lean on his cane and catch his breath. His weak eyes squinted at the mountains in the distance. For he was a vain old man, he detested glasses. Papa had never been a man to wear glasses unless the dark-tinted glasses of an aviator. Here at the grave site he breathed deeply and deliberately. His lungs had been damaged from smoking and so he could not breathe so deeply as he had once breathed. At the grave site his agitated thoughts were flattened and lulling as a lapping surf. At this site he was at peace, or nearly. *Promise me. You will bury me here. Exactly here.* Reluctantly the woman had promised. The woman did not like him to speak of dying, death, burial. It was the woman's pretense that Papa was yet a young vigorous man with his best work ahead of him, not a sick broken-down old drunk with quivering eyelids, palsied hands, swollen ankles and feet, a liver so swollen it stood out from his body like a long, fat leech. It was the woman's pretense that they were yet a romantic couple, a happily married couple and such talk of death was just silly. *Like a bat out of Hell I will return to torment you, if you betray me.* This before witnesses. The woman had laughed, or tried to. He wasn't sure if he could trust her. Most people, you can't trust. God damn he'd meant to include an item regarding the burial site in his will.

At the burial site he remained for some minutes, breathing deeply and deliberately. He did not *believe* in eternity and yet: in this place, in such solitude, amid such beauty and calmness, you could almost believe that there were eternal things. There was a hell of a lot more than just Papa and the interiors of Papa's brain churning like maggots in a ripe corpse. You knew.

(Maggots in corpses he'd seen. Whitely churning, in the mouths of dead soldiers, where their noses had been, their ears and blasted-away jaws. Most of the soldiers had been men as young as he himself had been. Italians fallen after the Austrian offensive of 1918. You do not forget such sights. You do not unsee such sights. He himself had been wounded, but he had not died. The distinction was profound. Between what lived and what died the distinction was profound. Yet it remained mysterious, elusive. You did not wish to speak of it. Especially if you did not wish to pray about it, to beg God to spare you. It disgusted him to think of God. It disgusted him to think of prayers to such a God. Fumbling his big, bare toe against the trigger of the shotgun he was damned if he would think, in the last quivering moment of his life, of God.)

That summer he'd turned eighteen. That summer in northern Michigan at the summer place at the lake. He'd known, then. Observing his father through the shotgun scope. Observing the turnip-head through the scope and his finger on the trigger. His young heartbeat quickened. There was a warm-thrumming stirring in his groin. His lips parted, parched. His mouth was very dry. *Do it! And it will be done.*

Early on, you know to love your gun. Your gun is your friend. Your gun is your companion. Your gun is your solace. Your gun is your soul. Your gun is God's wrath. Your gun is your (secret, delicious) wrath. This was his first shotgun, he would never forget. Twelve-gauge, double-barreled Winchester. There was nothing distinctive about the secondhand shotgun but he would remember it through his life with a throb of excitement. His birthday was in July. He'd only just turned eighteen. They were at the summer house: "Windemere." This was Mummy's name. Most names were Mummy's names. He avoided Mummy, he was eighteen and did not wish to be touched. Mummy was fleshy-solid with big, droopy breasts and a balloon belly even a whalebone corset could not restrain. Mummy had been his first love, but no longer. He had no love now. He wanted no love now. He would fuck any girl he could fuck but that was not love. He liked it that he was unobserved by his father as he was observing his father as you observe a hunted creature through the scope of your gun and the creature has no awareness of you until the shot rings out.

The old man, weeding in the tomato patch. Still, stale heat of July. The old man oblivious of the son's finger on the trigger. The son's excitement. The old man stooped amid tomato plants he'd tied upright to sticks. Squatting awkwardly on his heels. He wore a straw hat that Mummy sometimes wore. Against the fabric of his shirt his bony shoulder blades stood out like broken-off wings. His head was bowed as if reverently. His jowls were fatty ridges of flesh. His skin was weak like melted-away wax. In the shed at the foot of the garden the son observed the father calmly and objectively. Very much he liked the firm weight of the gun's stock against his shoulder. The strain of the heavy double barrels against his forearms that nonetheless held steady. The delicious sensation of his finger teasing the trigger. The delicious sensation in the region of his heart, and in the region of his groin. The father's lips twitched and moved as if the father were speaking with someone. Smiling, coy. The father was winning an argument. The father moved along the row of tomato plants on his heels. The father's shoulders were hunched. The father's chin had melted away like wax. Like a turnip such a head could be blown away very easily. For where a man was weak, a woman has unmanned him. It would be a mercy to blow such a man away.

His finger against the trigger, teasing. His breath so quick and shallow, almost he felt he would faint.

That summer he'd turned eighteen, he ceased being a Christian. He ceased attending church. Mummy prayed for his soul. The father, too. *May the Lord watch between me and thee while we are absent one from the other.*

From father to son, the gun would pass.

Not the Winchester shotgun but the Civil War Smith & Wesson "Long John" revolver the father used to kill himself eleven years later in his home in Oak Park. When the son was twenty-nine, long married and himself a father and a quite famous writer and living far from the old man and Mummy and rarely inclined to visit. Profoundly shocked he'd been, impressed, astonished, the weak-chinned old man had had the guts to do it.

Or, Daddy was a coward. Daddy had always been a coward. You were ashamed to think of such cowardice, blood of your blood. He'd been worried about his health, Mummy said. Many frantic worries Daddy had had. An unmanned man has many worries as a way of drawing his attention from a single, shameful worry. Yet he'd had unerring aim. He had not dropped the gun at the crucial moment. He had not hesitated. You would think that at such close range you could not miss your target but it can happen that in fact you miss your target inside the brain and must ever afterward endure a shadow-life of brain damage and utter oblivion and so the old man's act was a risky one, or a reckless one. Perhaps it was courageous. Or, more likely it was *the coward's way out.*

The son was in anguish, he could not know which. The son was never to know which.

The mother was no longer Mummy but Grace by this time. The son so despised Grace he could not bear to remain in any room with her. He could not bear conversation with her unless he was damned good and drunk or could console himself with the imminent possibility of being damned good and drunk. The son returned to Oak Park, Illinois, to oversee the funeral. The son who'd ceased to be a Christian let alone a member of the Congregational Church returned in the somber outer guise of a dutiful son to Oak Park to oversee the funeral services in the First Congregational Church. Afterward he did in fact get damned good and drunk and the drunk would last for thirty years.

Afterward he requested of his mother that she mail to him the family heirloom "Long John" revolver that had originally belonged to his father's father and this Mummy-Grace did, with a mother's blessing.

For a long time his favorite drink was Cuban: "Death in the Gulf Stream." Dash of bitters, juice of one lime, tall glass of Holland gin. He liked the poetry of the name. He liked the taste. He liked the glass chilled, tall and bottomless as the sea.

More recently, in Ketchum, he had no single favorite.

He'd practiced with the (unloaded) Mannlicher .256. Sit in a straight-backed chair barefoot and place the butt firmly on the floor and leaning forward he would take the tip of the gun barrel into his mouth and press it against his palate. Or, he would settle his chin firmly on the muzzle, leaning forward. He would concentrate. Always now there was a roaring in his ears like a

distant waterfall and so concentration was difficult but not impossible. He
would breathe deeply and deliberately. It was a careful procedure. There is a
technique to using the shotgun for the purpose of blowing off your head. You
would not wish to fuck up, at such a moment. Like fucking, like writing, the
secret is technique. Amateurs are eager and careless, professionals take care.
No pro trusts to chance. No pro tosses the dice to see how they turn tip, a pro
will load the dice to determine how they turn up.

With his big, bare toe he fumbled for the trigger. The *click!* was deafening
to him. The *click!* echoed in the oak-paneled room where on the walls were
glossy framed photographs of Papa with his trophy kills: gigantic marlin, fall-
en but massive-headed male lion, enormous antlered elk, enormous grizzly
bear, beautiful slender leopard with tail stretched out at Papa's feet and Papa
cradling his high-powered rifle in his brawny arms, bearded Papa, grinning
Papa, squatting above his kill. *Click! click!* It was against his chin he'd pressed
the shotgun muzzle and for some time he rested his head against it and his
eyes fluttered shut and his wildly accelerated heart began gradually to slow,
like a wind-up clock running down.

Summers in northern Michigan at the lake. His first kills and his first sex.
Sighting the old man's head through the shotgun scope and that night with
the slutty Indian girl drinking whiskey and fucking her how many times he'd
lost count. Sticking his cock into the girl, deep inside the girl, any girl, the
rest of it did not matter greatly, the face, the name of the face, it was purely
cunt that excited him, his cock deep inside the fleshy-warm, slightly resistant
cunt that opened to him, to his prodding, thrusting, pumping, or was made to
open to him, and coming into the cunt left him faint-headed, stunned.

Sweet as your finger on a trigger, squeezing so there's no turning back.

. . . *greatest writer of his generation* and he'd set down his drink bursting into deep-
chested laughter, rose to accept the award, the heavy brass plaque, the check
and the excited applause of the audience and the handshakes of strangers
eager to honor him and he was still laughing to himself after the ceremony
amid a flattering melee of camera flashes convinced what he'd heard in the
citation was *the greatest hater of his generation.*

Had to concede, that might be so.

The woman was uneasy asking, Why? This remote place where no one knows us, when you've been having health problems, why? The woman was one in a succession of cunts in defiance of Mummy-Grace. She was the fourth wife, the widow-to-be. Naively and with a childish petulance she spoke of *us* as if anyone other than Papa mattered.

Mornings when work did not come, and there was no drama of a slender young stag desperate to be rescued by him, Papa brooded: if the woman interfered when it came time, maybe he'd blow her away, too.

Thirty years, the Papa-spell held him in thrall.

Before even his father killed himself, as a young man in his late twenties he'd been Papa in the eyes of adoring others. Why this was, why he seemed to wish his own life accelerated, he had no idea. Papa was intoxicating to him: sexual energy, joy. Joy mounting in a delirium to euphoria. You drank to celebrate, and you drank to nurse your wounds. You drank to nurse the wounds of those you'd wounded, for whom you felt a belated and useless and yet quite sincere remorse.

There was his writer friend, his fellow Midwesterner he'd denigrated in his memoir of their youth together in Paris. His friend he'd unmanned after his death with sly Papa-gloating and scorn: claiming that his friend was so sexually insecure he'd asked Papa to look at his penis, to tell him frankly if his penis was inadequate as his wife claimed. In the memoir Papa described the two mildly inebriated men entering the men's room at the Restaurant Michaud and unzipping their trousers to "compare measurements," and Papa portrayed himself in a kindly if condescending light, assuring his anxious friend that his penis appeared to be of a normal size, but Papa would not add how stricken with tenderness he'd felt for his friend at that moment, how the rivalry between them seemed to have faded in the exigency of his friend's vulnerability, what emotion he'd felt for the man, how badly he wanted to touch him; to close his fingers reverently about the other's penis, simply to utter aloud *I am your brother, I love you.*

This confession Papa would never make. In the cruelly bemused pages of his memoir, tenderness had no part.

Why, the woman wondered. As others wondered.

Why leave Cuba where he was Papa to so many, admired and adored. Why leave the warmth of the Caribbean to live in isolation in Idaho. From a millionaire "sportsman" and fellow drunk he bought an overpriced property of many acres in the beautiful and desolate foothills of the Sawtooth Mountains. Close by was an old mining town called Ketchum. Here he would do the great work of his life as a writer, for he believed that the great effort of his soul was yet to come; no single work of his had yet embodied all that he was capable of. Though the world acclaimed him as a great writer, though he'd become a rich man, yet he knew that he must go deeper, deeper. Descending into the ocean through shimmering strata of light, sun-filtered greeny water darkening gradually to twilight and to inky-blue and finally to night and the terrible obliteration of night. In accidents, in mishaps, in tropical illnesses and in the drinking bouts for which Papa was fabled he had worn out his health prematurely and yet: he was capable of this descent, even so. He was capable of descending into the terrible obliteration of night and of ascending in triumph from it. He knew!

Nights when he could not lie in his bed but, for the wild erratic pounding of his heart, had to sit up in a chair in the darkness, he heard the murmur *May the Lord watch between me and thee while we are absent one from another* that had once so enraged him, filled him with a son's contempt for a weak-womanly father and now he was sixty years old and nearing the end of his own life made to realize that his father had loved him tenderly and passionately and those words he'd despised were words of paternal solicitude, how had he so misunderstood his father! How had he attempted to replace his father with bluff-blustery Papa, who scorned masculine weakness! He was stricken with remorse, his eyes stung with tears like acid. He was made to realize how much older he was than his father had been when the distraught man had killed himself in Oak Park, Illinois, in 1928 with that single bullet to the brain.

His life was stampeding past him like a herd of maddened wildebeest. So many thunderous hooves, such a frenzy of dust the hunter would not have time to reload and shoot quickly enough to kill all that he was meant to kill.

Belatedly he'd come to love his father. Or some memory of his father. But Mummy-Grace, he would never cease to despise. Mrs. Hemingstein he had a sinking feeling he'd be greeted by, with the bitch's reproachful smile, in Hell.

Drinking is the affliction for which drinking is the sole cure.

The sirens had come for him. The woman had betrayed him. He'd been strapped down. Electrodes had been attached to his head. He'd been shocked. He'd been zapped. His brains had fried and sizzled as in a skillet. What they'd dripped into his artery stung like acid. There was talk of a lobotomy. There was talk of an ice pick being inserted into his eye socket. At angle upward: frontal lobe. There was talk of "miraculous cure for depression." There was talk of "miraculous cure for alcoholism." He was restrained in his bed. Papa was the greatest writer of his generation, restrained in his bed. Papa was awarded the Nobel Prize for Literature, restrained in his bed. In his bed he would piss. He would void his bowels. He would flirt with the nurses. Papa was one to flirt with the nurses. *Here is Hell nor am I out of it.* Papa entertained the nurses with his classy Brit accent like Ronald Colman. Papa won their admiration and their hearts. The last and most ignoble of a man's vanities is his wish to entertain and impress the nursing staff that they will remember him kindly. They will say that he was brave. They will say that he was generous. They will say that he was a damned good sport. They will say that he was a remarkable man. They will say you could tell he was a great man. They will not say he was a pitiful specimen. They will not say that he was a wreck. They will not say that his penis was limp and skinned-looking like a goiter. They will not say he was so frightened sometimes, we had to take turns holding his hand.

They will not say *He was raving, praying God help me.*

Such adventures he had! Slipping from his captors.

On their way to the Mayo Clinic in Rochester, Minnesota, they'd landed in Rapid City, South Dakota, to refuel; Papa walked briskly out onto the runway. Papa walked with purpose and unerringly. Papa did not appear to be limping. It was a fine clear windy day. The airport was small: a single dirt runway. Papa had not known why he was slipping away from his captors until he saw: a small plane landing on the runway. Taxiing toward the airport. A single-propeller plane taxiing in his direction. More rapidly he began to walk. Almost, he broke into a trot. The pilot could not have said if Papa was smiling at him or clench-jawed like one clamping down on a towel. When Papa was about three feet from the noisily spinning propeller, abruptly

the pilot cut the engine. The woman was crying *Papa, no. Papa, please.* They
came for him then. Very still Papa stood in front of the slowing propeller. He
knew not to resist, his defeat would be but temporary and his revenge would
come in time.

Back in Ketchum she'd locked the guns up in the cabinet downstairs. She'd
locked the liquor cabinet, too. The woman was his jailer. The woman was
his succubus. The woman was his widow-to-be. The woman had tricked him
with legal maneuvers. The woman had managed to get him "committed."
The woman had allowed FBI technicians to enter the house and to wiretap
the telephones. The woman had turned over his income tax records to IRS.
The woman spoke frequently with "his" doctors. The woman kept a diary
of his behavior. The woman colluded with the sheriff of Camas County and
his deputies. The woman alerted these deputies when Papa was driving into
town. For Papa's driver's license had been revoked. For Papa's eyesight was
so poor, the headlights of oncoming vehicles at dusk glared in his squinting
eyes like deranged suns. Papa had reason to suspect that the woman was in
intimate communication with Fidel Castro, who had been her lover at one
time and who had expelled Papa from Cuba and appropriated Papa's property there. He had reason to suspect that the woman knew more than she
would acknowledge about Papa's mail that was opened and crudely reglued
shut when he received it. Nor did the woman acknowledge the deceit of his
lawyers, or his publishers in New York City who'd defaulted on his royalty
statements, or officers at the bank in Twin Falls where he kept his money.
The woman refused to drive out with him to check the several billboards
on the road to Boise another time, that made cryptic use of Papa's famous
likeness, in gigantic posters containing mysterious words and numerals per-
taining to Papa's masculinity and his association with the Communist Party.
Though the woman did not object when Papa wore dark-tinted glasses in
public or when, at Papa's favorite restaurant in Twin Falls, Papa insisted
upon sitting in the most remote booth, the brim of his hat pulled low over
his forehead.

   Revenge is a dish best served cold, as the Spaniards say. The sweetest revenge,
the look in the woman's face when he blasted her back against the wall.

This most delicious revenge: Papa's new love.

   At the Mayo Clinic he'd seduced the youngest and prettiest of the nurses.
How like Papa this was to seduce the youngest and prettiest of the nurses.

Gretel was the girl's name. Papa and Gretel were in love. Papa and Gretel had plotted, how Gretel would arrive in Ketchum and come to work for him. How Papa and Gretel would be married and Papa would change his will and leave Gretel all his money. How the woman, Papa's aging-bulldog wife, would be furious. How Papa would deal with the aging-bulldog wife. Gretel had come to Papa in the night in his private room. Gretel had pleasured Papa with her mouth and with her soft, caressing hands. Gretel had sponge-bathed Papa's body that reeked of his sweat. Gretel had laughed and teased, calling him *Grand-Papa*. But also there was Siri. Papa was not certain which it was, Gretel or Siri, who would come to Ketchum to work for him. He could not recall the last names of either Gretel or Siri and only vaguely could he recall the Mayo Clinic where his brain had fried and sizzled as in a skillet and his penis had been so crudely catheterized, he passed blood with his leaky urine.

Mornings when work does not come are very long.

My father shot himself, he'd used to joke, *to avoid torture.*
In his delirium strapped in his bed he'd tried to explain to the young nurse, or nurses. How his father had worn long underwear and so rarely changed it, the underwear stank of his father's sweat even after being laundered. Tried to explain to whoever would listen to him, that it was not a cowardly act to kill yourself to avoid torture for if you were tortured you might inform on your comrades and a man must never betray his comrades, that is the single unforgivable sin. *May your soul rot in Hell forevermore if you betray a comrade* he'd begun to thrash against his restraints and to shout and he'd had to be sedated and would not wake for many hours.

Mornings here in Ketchum. Seeking words he leafed through the dictionary. For words did not come to him now, he was like one trying to pick up grains of rice with a pliers. He avoided the typewriter for a typewriter is so very silent when its keys are not being struck. In longhand he meant to write a love letter to Gretel, or to Siri. It had been a long time since Papa had composed a love letter. It had been a long time since Papa had composed a sentence that had not disgusted him with its banality. The composition of a sentence is a precise matter. The composition of a sentence is akin to the composition of steel: it can appear thin, even delicate, but it is strong and resilient. Beyond the sentence was the paragraph: an obstacle that confounded him like a boulder that has rolled down a mountain and into the road, blocking the way of your vehicle. At the thought of a paragraph he began to feel dizzy. He began to feel light-headed. His blood pressure was high, his ears rang and pulsed. He could not recall if he'd taken his blood pressure tablets and he did not wish to ask the woman.

So many tablets, capsules, pills, he swallowed them in handfuls, unless he flushed them down the toilet. His silver flask, he carried with him in his jacket pocket. The woman had locked up the liquor cabinet but he'd been buying pints of Four Roses from Artie, who came out to the house to do repairs.

Like such place-names as Sawtooth, Featherville, Blizzard, and Chilly, that exerted a curious spell on him when uttered aloud, like fragments of poetry, the words of the dictionary were mysterious and elusive and required a fitting-together, a composing, of which Papa was no longer capable. The neurologist at the Clinic had said that his cerebral cortex had shrunken as a consequence of "alcohol abuse." The internist had said that his immune system and his liver had been "irreversibly damaged." The psychiatrist had diagnosed him as "manic-depressive" and given him oblong green tablets he had mostly flushed down the toilet, for they made him groggy and coated his tongue in gray scum and the woman shrank from him, his breath so stank. In the mirror at the Clinic he'd first seen: the shock of his father's face. For there was his father's terribly creased forehead. There was his father's heavy-lidded vacant eyes. There was the curved set of the lips. There were the clenched jaws, the strain in the cheeks. His hair was whiter than his father's hair had been. His hair was dismayingly thin at the back of his head (so that others could see his scalp, but he could not), though still above his forehead. Anguish shone in his face. Yet it was a handsome face, the face of a general. The face of a leader of men. The face of a man crucified, who does not cry out as the nails are hammered into the flesh of his hands and his feet. It was an astonishment, to see his father's face in his face and to see such anguish. And how strange, the wave of the hair, the waved furrows of the forehead, even the dense wiry wave of the beard and the mustache were all *to the left*. As if his body yearned *to the left*. As if a cruel, powerful wind were blowing relentlessly *to the left*. What did it mean?

So badly he wanted to write of these mysteries. The profound mysteries of the world outside him, and the profound mysteries of the world inside him. Yet he waited, patiently he waited, and the words did not come. The sentences did not come. His stub of a pencil slipped from his finger and rolled clattering across the floor. Clotted and putrid his desire was backed up inside him. He must discharge it, he could not hear it much longer. Old burn wounds, old scars. His flaking skin itched: *erysipelas*. There was a word!

Downstairs, there was the woman on the phone. Which of them she was betraying Papa with his time, Papa had no idea.

. . . a nice private life with undeclared & unpublished pride & they have shit in it & wiped themselves on slick paper & left it there but you had to live with it just the same, such shame was not a construct of artfully chosen words that came to an abrupt and inevitable end but more in the way of the damned wind out of the mountains that seemed never to cease, by day, by night, at times a raging demented wind, a bitterly cold wind, a wind to snatch away your breath, a wind to make your eyes sting, a wind to make outdoor walking hazardous if you were stumbling with a cane, a wind tasting of mineral cold, a wind smelling of futility, a wind to penetrate the crudely caulked window frames of the millionaire's mountain retreat overlooking the Sawtooth Range, a wind that penetrated even sodden drunk-sleep, a wind bearing with it muffled jeering laughter, *a wind of no rest.*

At the grave site between the tall pines this melancholy wind would blow, forever. In that he took some solace after all.

By the rear door he left the house at 6:40 a.m. He'd had a bad night.

The woman had taken him out to dinner, with Ketchum friends. They had gone to the Eagle House in Twin Falls, which was Papa's favorite restaurant. Papa was suspicious from the start. Papa distrusted the woman in all things. Papa was nervous, for all that day work had not come to him. What was pent-up inside him, roiling like churning maggots, he did not know. At the Eagle House, Papa wished to be seated in a booth in a far corner of the noisy tap room. Once Papa was seated in the booth with his back to the wall, Papa became agitated, for he was facing the crowded tap room, and was being observed. The woman laughed at Papa, assuring him that no one was observing him. And if someone was observing him, glancing at him with smiles, it was only because Papa was a famous man. But Papa was upset, and Papa insisted upon trading places with their friends so that he could sit with his back to the room. But, once they'd traded places, Papa became uneasy for now he could not see the room, he could not see strangers' eyes upon him, but he knew that strangers were observing him and of these strangers several were FBI agents whose faces he'd been seeing in and around Ketchum since the previous winter. (Certain of Papa's old writer-friends-turned-enemies had denounced him as a Communist agent to the FBI, he had reason to suspect. Hastily typed-out letters of accusation he'd sent to his enemies had been handed over to the FBI . . . a terrible misstep on Papa's part he could not bear to acknowledge.) Papa could not eat his T-bone steak, Papa was so upset. Badly Papa needed to use the men's room, for his bladder pinched and ached and of all things Papa feared urine dribbling down his leg, from the poor lacerated penis that dangled useless between his shrunken thighs. Somehow it happened, on his way to the men's room, being helped by the woman and the Eagle House proprietor who knew Papa and revered him, Papa was approached by smiling strangers, visitors to Idaho from back east, and paper napkins were thrust at Papa for him to sign, but Papa fumbled the pen, Papa fumbled the damned paper napkins, crumpled them and tossed them to the floor and afterward Papa began to cry outside in the parking lot, in the pickup, the woman was driving, the woman dared to take hold of Papa's fists where he was grinding them against his eyes, his eyes that were spilling tears, and the woman said he'd be fine, she was taking him home and he would be fine, and the woman said *Don't you believe me, Papa?* and Papa shook his head, wordless in grief, for Papa was beyond all belief, or even the pretense of belief.

The woman said *So many people love you, Papa. Please believe!* Now by the rear door he stumbled from the house, Papa was eager to get outside, and away from the house which was his prison, where work would not come to him. He was not certain of the exact date but believed the day to be a Sunday in early July 1961. His sixty-second birthday loomed before him icy-peaked even in summer.

He'd found his cane, one of his canes. It did help to walk with a cane. Papa's daily walk. Sometimes, twice-daily. Locally, Papa was known for his walk along a half-mile stretch of Route 75. An old man but vigorous. An old man but stubborn. An old man who'd bought the millionaire's hunting lodge house outside Ketchum, that had a curse on it.

What is this curse? You are such a bullshitter.

Bullshitter is my occupation. Hell's my destination.

Damned uphill climb to the grave site on the hill. Papa's lips twitched, his revenge would be this climb, pallbearers straining their backs, risking hernias. There was no visible sun. Papa wasn't sure if the season was summer. He was wearing a black-and-red-checked flannel shirt, haphazardly buttoned. He was wearing a cloth cap, for he disliked the sensation of cool air at the crown of his head, where his hair had grown thin. No visible sun, only a white-glowering light through skeins of rapidly shifting cloud vapor overhead. Beyond this cloud vapor there appeared to be no sky.

His weak, watering eyes could not make out the mountains in the distance, but he knew that the mountains were there.

At the grave site he paused. He breathed deeply, here was peace. This place of beauty and solitude. The world wipes its shit on most things but has not yet despoiled the Sawtooth Mountains. He saw that one of the heavy rocks he'd positioned to mark off the grave site was out of place by several inches and his heart kicked in fear, and in fury. His enemies conspired to torment him into madness, but he would not succumb.

What had happened back at the house, when the woman had called to him in her harpy voice. He would not allow it to upset him.

For the grave site was *his place*. There was a purity and a sanctity here, of all the places of the world.

It was rare Papa and the woman went out with friends any longer, as they'd done the previous night. For Papa did not trust his so-called friends, who were the woman's friends primarily. More rarely did houseguests come to Ketchum now. You did not have time and energy and patience for the bullshit of playing host. No more interviewers. No more "literary journalists" with straying eyes. No bloodsuckers. For there were bloodsuckers enough in Papa's family, he did not require bloodsuckers from outside the family. Much of the large house was empty, unoccupied. Rooms were shut off. The purchase of the house in Ketchum had been Papa's idea and not the woman's, yet it had come to seem to Papa, the woman had manipulated him into making the purchase, to have him to herself. The woman was a harpy, the woman had a beak. That thing between a woman's legs, inside the softness of the woman's cunt, was a nasty little beak. You did not need so many damned rooms where there are no children in a family. The woman had hinted of children, that the woman might be a triumphant rival over Papa's previous wives who'd borne him children. Now the woman was too old, her uterus was shrunken, her breasts sagged on her ribcage. Papa would have his children with Gretel, or with Siri. But Papa had grown up in a five-bedroom Victorian house in Oak Park, Illinois, that was crowded with children, for Mrs. Hemingstein had been a brood sow, who'd devoured her young.

Mummy-Grace! Papa liked to think Mummy-Grace was buried in the ground in a Christian cemetery in Memphis, Tennessee, and could not get loose. Damned glad Papa had been when he'd been awarded the Nobel Prize in 1954, for Mummy-Grace had "passed away" in 1951 and had not been alive to gloat and boast and give coy interviews in which the mother of the famous writer spoke with veiled reproach of her genius son. Mummy-Grace knew nothing of the genius son's great fame nor even of the son's present whereabouts unless in Hell this news had spread.

Papa laughed, a deep-gut laugh that hurt, it would not surprise Papa that his name was known in Hell and in Hell his most ardent admirers awaited him.

He walked on. He walked using his cane. By degrees the day was warming. His mind worked swiftly. Stopping by the grave site gave him hope as always. He would continue to ascend this hill for several minutes and then at the crest of the hill he would seek out the faint, overgrown path that looped downhill, now gravity would ease the strain on his heart and legs, and then the service road out to the state highway, and so back to the house. He did not wish to return to the house but there was no other destination.

Before the woman had called to him on the stairs, he'd had a painful time on the toilet. Swirls of blood from his anus, bloody little turds hard as shrapnel. The pus had gotten into his bowels. Very possibly, he was being poisoned. The well water that came with this accursed property. The woman had every opportunity to mix grains of arsenic into his food. The silver flask he carried in his pocket, the woman had surely discovered. He'd been wondering what had become of his father's Long John pistol. That crude firearm! Civil War artifact. Maybe his brother Leicester had it: they'd joked, Papa and his younger brother, the good uses you could put that gun to. Papa himself would not have wished to use it, for it was a crude firearm by modern standards. And you would be a reckless fool to risk a single bullet to the brain even if your aim was steady.

Since he'd returned from Minnesota, the woman had kept the gun cabinet locked and the key hidden away but now, more recently, the woman had been leaving the key on a windowsill in the kitchen.

Saying, a man has to be trusted. A man has to be respected, in his own house. A man like Papa who has grown up around guns.

The key he'd taken, closing his trembling fingers about it.

On the stairs the woman called to him *Papa no!*

The positioning of the shotgun. The angle of the muzzle. You must rest the stock firmly on a carpet, not a hardwood floor, to prevent slippage. He would sit in a straight-backed chair. He would sit in a straight-backed chair in the living room in front of the plate-glass window overlooking the mountains.

The living room had a high oak-beamed ceiling and oak-paneled walls covered in animal trophies and framed photographs of Papa with his spoils, dead at his feet. The living room was a drafty room even in summer with a massive stone fireplace inhabited by spiders and matched leather furniture that had come with the house that farted and sighed with mocking intent when you sat in it.

It was crucial to lean forward enough. To rest your chin firmly on the gun muzzle, or to take the muzzle into your mouth, or, more awkwardly, to press your forehead against the muzzle even as with your bare, big toe you grope for the trigger and exert enough pressure to pull it yet not so much pressure that the gun is dislodged and the muzzle slips free and the blast blows away only part of your head and damages the damned ceiling.

After the Austrian offensive he'd been astonished to discover that the human body could be blown into pieces that exploded along no anatomical lines but divided as capriciously as the fragmentation in the burst of a high-explosive shell. He'd been yet more astonished to discover female bodies and body parts amid the smoldering rubble of a munitions factory that had exploded. Long dark hair, clumps of bloody scalp attached. He'd been nineteen. This was in 1918. He'd been a Red Cross volunteer worker. They had given him the rank of lieutenant. Later, he'd been wounded by shrapnel. Others had died near him but he had not died. Two hundred pieces of shrapnel in his legs, feet. They'd given him a medal for "military valor." He had to suppose it was the high point of his life at age nineteen except there was the remainder of his life awaiting him.

The woman shouted *Papa no!* struggling with him for the shotgun and he'd shoved her away with his elbow and turned the barrels on her and the look in her face was one of disbelief beyond even fear and animal panic. For that was the cruel joke, not one of us truly expects to die. Not me! Not *me*. Even creatures whose lives are a ceaseless effort to keep from being devoured by predators fight desperately for their lives. You would think that nature had them with the melancholy resignation of stoicism but this is not so. Terrible to hear are the shrieks of animal terror and panic. The shrieks of the mules at Smyrna where the Greeks broke their forelegs and dumped them into shallow water to drown. Such shrieks Papa can hear in the night, in Ketchum. The shrieks of the wounded, animals hunted down for their beautiful hides, their trophy heads, tusks, antlers. Hunted down because there is such pleasure in the hunt. In his life as a hunter he had shot deer, elk, gazelles, antelope, impala, wildebeest, elands, waterbucks, kudu, rhinos; he had shot lions, leopards, cheetah, hyenas, grizzly bears. In all these, dying had been a struggle.

The hunter's excitement at the kill had been fierce and frankly sexual as the wildest of copulations and he recalled with wonder now in his broken body how he had been capable of such acts. Snatching life out of the heaving air, it had seemed. Devouring life with his powerful jaws. Yet their dying screams had lodged deep inside him, he had not realized at the time. Their dying, expelled breaths in his lungs he could not expel. For the breath of the dying had passed into the hunter and the hunter carried within him the spirit-breaths of all the creatures he had killed in his lifetime from the earliest years shooting black squirrels and grouse in northern Michigan under the tutelage of his father and his father's death too was part of the curse.

On safari, he'd always brought a woman. You needed a woman after the excitement of the kill. You needed whiskey, and you needed food, and you needed a woman. Except if you were too sodden-drunk for a woman.

Walking in the woods above Ketchum, God damn he was not going to think about *that*.

In this place of beauty. His property. He did not want to become agitated. The need to drink he preferred to interpret as a wish to drink. It was a choice, you made your choice freely. In the hip pocket of his trousers he carried the silver flask filled with Four Roses Whiskey, its weight was a comfort. On this walk he paused to remove the flask, unscrew the lid and drink and the old pleasure of whiskey-warmth and its promise of elation rarely failed him.

For a long time he'd carried a single-edged razor blade in a leather holder, in a pocket. You make the cut beneath the ear and draw the blade swiftly and unerringly across the big artery that is the carotid. In Spain, at the time of the civil war, he'd acquired the razor blade, for it was a way of suicide more practical than most, he had been assured that death would come within seconds and that such a death if properly self-inflicted would involve no pain. But he had not entirely believed this. He had witnessed no one dying in this way and did not trust the reputed ease. And the matter of swiftly bleeding out was doubtful: you surely would not die before registering the enormity of what you had done and that it was irreversible and you would not die without witnessing a gushing loss of blood and in those terrible seconds you would peer over the edge of the earth into the chasm of eternity like the cringing mongrel dog in that most horrific of Goya paintings.

He could not bear it, the mere contemplation. He drank again, the whiskey was a comfort to him. *Spirits* is the very word, you are infused with spirit that has drained from you.

In his pockets were loose pills, capsules. No damned idea what they were. Painkillers, barbiturates. These looked old. Lint stuck to the pills, if you were desperate you swallowed what was close at hand but Papa wasn't desperate just yet.

High overhead geese were passing in a ragged V-formation buffeted by the wind. Canada geese they appeared to be, gray, with black markings, wide powerful pumping wings. The strange forlorn honking cries tore at his heart. The great gray pumping wings and outthrust necks. For some time he stood craning his neck, staring after the geese. Their cries were confused with the ringing pulse of his blood. He could not recall if the woman had cried out, in that last moment. The scolding whine of the female voice, bulldog-Mummy voice was most vivid in his memory. The woman's hand feebly raised to repel the buckshot blast from a distance of six inches. You could laugh at such an effort, and the expression of incredulity even as his finger jerked against the trigger. *Not me! Not me.* The kick of the shotgun was greater than he had remembered. The blast was deafening. Instantly the soft woman-body went flying back against the wall, an eruption of blood at the chest, at the throat, at the lower part of the face and what remained of the body softly collapsing to the floor and blood rushed from it and instinctive]y he drew back, that the quickly pooling blood would not touch his bare feet.

He glanced down: his feet were not bare, but in boots. He was wearing his scuffed leather hiking boots he'd bought in Sun Valley years before. Yet he could not recall having taken time to pull on boots. Or to pull on this shirt, these baggy trousers. This was a good sign, was it? Or a not-so-good sign?

On the service road through the woods, he'd emerged onto Route 75. The woman did not like Papa "tramping" through the woods. Especially the woman did not like Papa "making a show of himself" on the highway. What brought Papa happiness here in Ketchum in his old man broken body was begrudged by the female in her heart. He'd blown out the heart. Bitterly he laughed, there was justice in this.

It was nearing 7:30 a.m. On Route 75, on the shoulder of the roadway he walked. In the wake of a passing flatbed truck bearing timber his cap was nearly blown off. He felt that the wind might stagger him if he did not steel himself against it. His custom was to walk facing oncoming traffic, for he needed to see what was coming at him, passing beside him at a distance of only a few yards. Trucks, pickups, local drivers, school buses. Sometimes on both his morning walk and his afternoon walk Papa would see carrot-colored Camas School District buses hurtling past him and without wishing to betray his eagerness he would lift his hand in greeting like one conferring a blessing, he would hold his breath against the terrible stink of the exhaust and smile at the blurred child faces in the rear windows, for such moments brought an innocent happiness. To smile at the children of strangers whose faces he could not see clearly, to see himself in their eyes as a white-haired and white-bearded old man who carried himself with dignity though walking with a cane, an old man of whom their elders had told them *That is a famous man, a writer, he has won the Nobel Prize,* gave him pleasure, for there had to be some pleasure in this, some pride. And so he anticipated the school buses and tried to time his walks to coincide with their passing and at the appearance of the carrot-colored vehicles at once Papa's backbone grew straighter, he held his head higher, his frowning face relaxed, he thought *All their lives they will remember me.*

But today there were no buses. Vaguely he recalled, this was a Sunday. How he disliked Sundays, and Saturdays. He would not let his spirits ebb. He had been feeling good, optimistic. He would not let the damned woman ruin that feeling. There were conspicuously fewer vehicles on the highway into Ketchum. In some of the cars there were child passengers to observe him, smile and wave at him, but Papa was no longer in the mood. Papa was limping, muttering to himself. Papa was stroking the bulging leech-liver at the small of his back. Papa had drained the flask, not a drop of Four Roses remained. Papa was feeling very tired. Shards of broken glass, shrapnel lodged too deep inside his body to be surgically removed were working their way to the surface of his skin, why his skin so badly itched. His broken health was a joke to him, with a straight face the neurologist tells you inflammation of the brain yet "shrinkage" of the cerebral cortex. You could not believe any of it, the bastards told you things to scare you, to reduce you to their level.

Goddamn he could not bear it, he could not return to that life.

He was in the roadway, suddenly. Stepped into the path of an oncoming police cruiser. Papa's weak eyes could yet pick out these gleaming white vehicles with green lettering CAMAS COUNTY SHERIFF DEPT., like vultures cruising the stretch of Route 75 in the vicinity of Papa's property. The cruiser skidded, braking to a stop to avoid hitting Papa. Quickly two young deputies climbed out. They recognized him: Papa saw. He was trying to explain to them what had happened at the house that morning. He'd become excited, he was stammering. He'd had a "gun accident." He had "hurt" his wife. He'd been holding a shotgun, he said, and his wife had tried to take it from him and it had "discharged" in the struggle and the shot had struck her in the chest and "cut her in two." Cautiously the deputies approached Papa. Traffic on Route 75 slowed, drivers were making wide berths around the deputies' cruiser partly

blocking the southbound lane. Papa saw, neither of the deputies had unhol-
stered his weapon. Yet they were approaching him at an angle, alert and prepared. Asking if he was armed, and calling him *sir*. Asking if he would object
to them searching him, and calling him *sir*. Papa was partly mollified by the
young deputies' respect for him. He was agitated but would not resist. One
of the deputies searched him, briskly patted him down, discovered in his hip
pocket the empty silver flask but did not appropriate it. Next Papa knew, he
was being helped into the rear of the cruiser. He'd dropped his damned cane,
one of the deputies would bring it. In the rear of the cruiser behind a protective metal grill Papa sat dazed and unsure of his surroundings. The pulsing
in his ears was loud, distracting. The pulsing of his heart that beat hard and
tremulously like a fist inside his ribcage. It was a short drive to the turnoff at
Papa's graveled driveway and with a stab of gratification Papa thought *they*
know where I live, they have been following me.

The driveway was a quarter-mile long. The pine woods on either side
were thick. Papa had himself posted numerous signs warning NO TRESPASS
PRIVATE PROPERTY KEEP OUT. As soon as the cruiser pulled up in the driveway below the house, the woman appeared outside on the first-floor deck.
The woman was wearing a housecoat, her graying blonde hair blew in the
wind. She was not a young woman, the deputies would see that at once. Her
skin was very pale. Her face was doughy. Her waist was thick. She would
be their mothers' age. In short, clipped sentences the woman spoke to the
deputies. One of the deputies was helping Papa out of the back of the cruiser,
as you might help an old man. Gripping his arm firmly, and calling him *sir*.
Papa was grateful, the young men were respectful of him. That is really all
you wish, to be treated with respect. He felt a tug of sympathy for the young
men in their twenties, as he'd once been. There was an unspoken brotherhood of such men, Papa had been expelled from this brotherhood and keenly
felt the loss. He had never comprehended the loss, all that had been taken
from him. The woman had come down the steps from the deck, to take hold
of his arm, but he resisted her. Tears of alarm and exasperation shone in the
woman's eyes. Her face was lined, yet you could see the faded girl beauty
inside the other. Her lips had lost their fullness, though, as if she'd been sucking at them. In a bright voice the woman thanked the deputies for bringing
her husband home. Her husband was not well, she told them. Her husband
had been hospitalized recently, he was recuperating. He would be fine now.
She would take care of him now. The deputies were asking the woman about
guns and the woman quickly assured them, all his guns are locked up. In disgust Papa turned away. The woman and the deputies continued to speak of

Papa as if he were not there, he felt the insult, he would walk into the house unassisted. He did not need the damned cane. Not the steps, he would not risk the steps to the deck, he would enter the house by the ground floor. In her self-important way the woman continued to speak with the deputies. The woman would laugh sadly and explain another time that her husband was a very great man but a troubled man and he had medical problems that were being treated, the gist of it was that the woman would take care of him, she was grateful for the deputies' kindness in bringing her husband home but they could leave now.

Ma'am, are you sure, the deputies asked.

Yes! The woman was sure.

Papa slammed the door behind him, he'd heard enough. A few minutes of peace he hoped for, before the woman followed him inside.

Note: Though *Hemingway* by Kenneth S. Lynn was consulted frequently in the composition of this story, and passages from Ernest Hemingway's "A Natural History of the Dead" are included here, "Papa at Ketchum, 1961" is purely a work of fiction.

For George Jones

THE SAGEBRUSH KID

Annie Proulx

hose who think the Bermuda Triangle disappearances of planes, boats, long-distance swimmers and floating beach balls a unique phenomenon do not know of the inexplicable vanishings along the Red Desert section of Ben Holladay's stagecoach route in the days when Wyoming was a territory.

Historians have it that just after the Civil War Holladay petitioned the U.S. Postal Service, major source of the stage line's income, to let him shift the route fifty miles south to the Overland Trail. He claimed that the northern California-Oregon-Mormon Trail had recently come to feature ferocious and unstoppable Indian attacks that endangered the lives of drivers, passengers, telegraph operators at the stage stops, smiths, hostlers, and cooks at the swing stations, even the horses and the expensive red and black Concord coaches (though most of them were actually Red Rupert mud wagons). Along with smoking letters outlining murderous Indian attacks, he sent Washington detailed lists of goods and equipment damaged or lost—a Sharp's rifle, flour, horses, harness, doors, fifteen tons of hay, oxen, mules, bulls, grain burned, corn stolen, furniture abused, the station itself along with barn, sheds, telegraph office burned, crockery smashed, windows ditto. No matter that the rifle had been left propped against a privy, had been knocked to the ground by the wind and buried in sand before the owner exited the structure, or that the dishes had disintegrated in a whoop-up shooting contest, or that the stagecoach damage resulted from shivering passengers building a fire inside the stage with the bundles of government documents the coach carried. He knew his bureaucracy. The Washington post office officials, alarmed at the bloodcurdling news, agreed to the route change, saving the Stagecoach King a great deal of money, important at that time while he, privy to insider information, laid his plans to sell the stage line the moment the Union Pacific gathered enough shovels and Irishmen to start construction on the transcontinental railroad.

Yet the Indian attack Holladay so gruesomely described was nothing more than a failed Sioux war party, the battle ruined when only one side turned up. The annoyed Indians, to reap something from the trip, gathered up a coil of copper wire lying on the ground under a telegraph pole where it had been left by a wire stringer eager to get to the saloon. They carted it back to camp, fashioned it into bracelets and necklaces. After a few days of wearing the bijoux, most of the war party broke out in severe rashes, an affliction that persisted until a medicine man, R. Singh, whose presence among the Sioux cannot be detailed here, divined the evil nature of the talking wire and caused the remainder of the coil and all the bracelets and earbobs to be buried. Shortly thereafter, but in no apparent way connected to the route change or the copper wire incident, travelers began to disappear in the vicinity of the Sandy Skull Station.

The stationmaster at Sandy Skull was Bill Fur, assisted by his wife, Mizpah. In a shack to one side a telegraph operator banged his message key. The Furs had been married seven years but had no children, a situation in those fecund days that caused them both grief. Mizpah was a little cracked on the subject and traded one of Bill's good shirts to a passing emigrant wagon for a baby pig, which she dressed in swaddling clothes and fed from a nipple-fitted bottle that had once contained Wilfee's Equine Liniment & Spanish Pain Destroyer but now held milk from the Furs' unhappy cow—an object of attention from range bulls, rustlers and round-up cowboys, who spent much of her time hiding in a nearby cave. The piglet one day tripped over the hem of the swaddling dress and was carried off by a golden eagle. Mrs. Fur, bereft, traded another of her husband's shirts to a passing emigrant wagon for a chicken. She did not make the swaddling gown mistake twice, but fitted the chicken with a light leather jerkin and a tiny bonnet. The bonnet acted as blinders and the unfortunate poult never saw the coyote that seized her within the hour.

Mizpah Fur, heartbroken and suffering from loneliness, next fixed her attention on an inanimate clump of sagebrush that at twilight took on the appearance of a child reaching upward as if piteously begging to be lifted from the ground. This sagebrush became the lonely woman's passion. It seemed to her to have an enchanting fragrance reminiscent of pine forests and lemon zest. She surreptitiously brought it a daily dipper of water (mixed with milk) and took pleasure in its growth response, ignoring the fine cactus needles that pierced her worn moccasins with every trip to the beloved *Atriplex*. At first her husband watched from afar, muttering sarcastically, then himself succumbed to the illusion, pulling up all grass and encroaching plants that might steal sustenance from the favored herb. Mizpah tied a red sash around the sagebrush's middle. It seemed more than ever a child stretching its arms up, even when the sun leached the wind-fringed sash to pink and then dirty white.

Time passed, and the sagebrush, nurtured and cosseted as neither piglet nor chicken nor few human infants had ever been—for Mizpah had taken to mixing gravy and meat juice with its water—grew tremendously. At twilight it now looked like a big man hoisting his hands into the air at the command to stick 'em up. It sparkled festively in winter snow. Travelers noted it as the biggest sagebrush in the lonely stretch of desert between Medicine Bow and Sandy Skull Station. It became a landmark for deserting soldiers. Bill Fur, clutching the handle of a potato hoe, hit on the right name when he announced that he guessed he would go out and clear cactus away from the vicinity of their Sagebrush Kid.

About the time that Bill Fur planed a smooth path to and around the Sagebrush Kid, range horses became scarce in the vicinity of the station. The Furs and local ranchers had always been able to gather wild mustangs, and through a few sessions with steel bolts tied to their forelocks, well-planned beatings with a two-by-four and merciless first rides by some youthful buster whose spine hadn't yet been compressed into a solid rod, the horses were deemed ready-broke to haul stagecoaches or carry riders. Now the mustangs seemed to have moved to some other range. Bill Fur blamed it on the drought, which had been bad.

"Found a water hole somewheres else," he said.

A party of emigrants camped overnight near the station, and at dawn the captain pounded on the Furs' door, demanding to know where their oxen were.

"Want a git started," he said, a man almost invisible under a flop-rimmed hat, cracked spectacles, full beard, and a mustache the size of a dead squirrel. His hand was deep in his coat pocket, a bad sign, thought Bill Fur, who had seen a few coat-pocket corpses.

"I ain't seen your oxes," he said. "This here's a horse-change station," and he pointed to the corral, where two dozen broomtails stood soaking up the early sun. "We don't have no truck with oxes."

"Them was fine spotted oxen, all six matched," said the captain in a dangerous, low voice.

Bill Fur, curious now, walked with the bearded man to the place the oxen had been turned out the night before. Hoofprints showed where the animals had ranged around eating the sparse bunchgrass. They cast wide and far but could not pick up the oxen trail as the powdery dust changed to bare rock that took no tracks. Later that week the disgruntled emigrant party was forced to buy a mixed lot of oxen from the sutler at Fort Halleck, a businessman who made a practice of buying up worn-out stock for a song, nursing them back to health, and then selling them for an opera to those in need.

"Indans probly got your beasts," said the sutler. "They'll bresh out the tracks with a sage branch so's you'd never know but that they growed wings and flapped south."

The telegraph operator at the station made a point of keeping the Sabbath. After his dinner of sage grouse with rose-haw jelly, he strolled out for an afternoon constitutional and never returned to his key. This was serious, and by Wednesday Bill Fur had had to ride into Rawlins and ask for a replacement for "the Bible-thumpin, damn old goggle-eyed snappin turtle who run off." The replacement, plucked from a Front Street saloon, was a tough drunk who lit his morning fires with pages from the former operator's Bible and ate one pronghorn a week, scorching the meat in a never-washed skillet.

"Leave me have them bones," said Mizpah, who had taken to burying meat scraps and gnawed ribs in the soil near the Sagebrush Kid.

"Help yourself," he said, scraping gristle and hocks onto the newspaper that served as his tablecloth and rolling it up. "Goin a make soup stock, eh?"

Two soldiers from Fort Halleck dined with the Furs and at nightfall slept out in the sagebrush. In the morning their empty bedrolls, partly drifted with fine sand, lay flat, the men's saddles at the heads for pillows, their horse tack looped on the sage. The soldiers themselves were gone, apparently deserters who had taken leave bareback. The wind had erased all signs of their passage. Mizpah Fur made use of the bedrolls, converting them into stylish quilts by appliquéing a pleasing pattern of black stripes and yellow circles onto the coarse fabric.

It may have been a trick of the light or the poor quality window glass, as wavery and distorting as tears, but Mizpah, sloshing her dishrag over the plates and gazing out, thought she saw the sagebrush's arms not raised up but akimbo, as though holding a water divining rod. Worried that some rambunctious buck trying his antlers had broken the branches, she stepped to the door to get a clear look. The arms were upright again and tossing in the wind.

Dr. Frill of Rawlins, on a solitary hunting trip, paused long enough to share a glass of bourbon and the latest town news with Mr. Fur. A week later a group of the doctor's scowling friends rode out inquiring of the medico's whereabouts. Word was getting around that the Sandy Skull station was not the best place to spend the night, and suspicion was gathering around Bill and Mizpah Fur. It would not be the first time a stationmaster had taken advantage of a remote posting. The Furs were watched for signs of opulence. Nothing of Dr. Frill was ever found, although a hat, stuck in the mud of a playa three miles east, might have been his.

A small group of Sioux, including R. Singh, on their way to the Fort Halleck sutler's store to swap hides for tobacco, hung around for an hour one late afternoon asking for coffee and bread, which Mizpah supplied. In the early evening as the dusk thickened they resumed their journey. Only Singh made it to the fort, but the shaken Calcutta native could summon neither Sioux nor American nor his native tongue to his lips. He bought two twists of tobacco and through the fluid expression of sign language tagged a spot with a Mormon freight group headed for Salt Lake City.

A dozen outlaws rode past Sandy Skull station on their way to Powder Springs for a big gang hooraw to feature a turkey pull, fried turkey, and pies of various flavors, as well as the usual floozy contingent and uncountable bottles of Young Possum and other liquids pleasing to men who rode hard and fast on dusty trails. They amused themselves with target practice on the big sagebrush, trying to shoot off its waving arms. Five of them never got past Sandy Skull station. When the Furs, who had been away for the day visiting the Clug ranch, came home, they saw the Sagebrush Kid maimed, only one arm, but that still bravely raised as though hailing them. The telegraph operator came out of his shack and said the outlaws had done the deed and that he had chosen not to confront them, but to bide his time and get revenge later, for he too had developed a proprietorial interest in the Sagebrush Kid. Around that time he put in a request for a transfer to Denver or San Francisco.

Everything changed when the Union Pacific Railroad pushed through, killing off the stagecoach business. Most of the stage station structures disappeared, carted away bodily by ranchers needing outbuildings. Bill and Mizpah Fur were forced to abandon the Sandy Skull station. After tearful farewells to the Sagebrush Kid they moved to Montana, adopted orphan cowboys, and ran a boarding house.

The decades passed and the Sagebrush Kid continued to grow, though slowly. The old stage road filled in with drift sand and greasewood. A generation later a section of the coast-to-coast Lincoln Highway rolled past. An occasional motorist, mistaking the Sagebrush Kid for a distant shade tree, sometimes approached, swinging a picnic basket. Eventually an interstate highway swallowed the old road and truckers used the towering Sagebrush Kid in the distance as a marker to tell them they were halfway across the state. Although its foliage remained luxuriant and its size enormous, the Kid seemed to stop growing during the interstate era.

Mineral booms and busts surged through Wyoming without affecting the extraordinary shrub in its remote location of difficult access until BelAmer-Can Energy, a multinational methane extraction company, found promising indications of gas in the area, applied for and got permits, and began drilling. The promise was realized. They were above a vast deposit of coal gas. Workers from out of state rushed to the bonanza. A pipeline had to go in and more workers came. The housing shortage forced men to sleep four to a bed in shifts at the dingy motels forty miles north.

To ease the housing difficulties, the company built a man-camp out in the sagebrush. The entrance road ran close to the Sagebrush Kid. Despite the Kid's size, because it was just a sagebrush, it went unnoticed. There were millions of sagebrush plants—some large, some small. Beside it was a convenient pullout. The man-camp was a large, gaunt building that seemed to erupt from the sand. The cubicles and communal shower rooms, stairs, the beds, the few doors were metal. A spartan kitchen staffed by Mrs. Quirt, the elderly wife of a retired rancher, specialized in bacon, fried eggs, boiled potatoes, store-bought bread and jam, and occasionally a stewed chicken. The boss believed the dreary sagebrush steppe and the monotonous diet were responsible for wholesale worker desertion. The head office let him hire a new cook, an ex-driller with a meth habit whose cuisine revolved around canned beans and pickles.

After three weeks Mrs. Quirt was reinstated, presented with a cookbook and a request to try something new. It was a disastrous order. She lit on complex recipes for boeuf bourguignonne, parsnip gnocchi, bananas stuffed with shallots, kale meatballs with veal ice cream. When the necessary ingredients were lacking she did what she had always done on the ranch—substituted what was on hand, as bacon, jam, eggs. After a strange repast featuring canned clams, strawberry Jell-O, and stale bread, many men went outside to heave it up in the sage. Not all of them came back and it was generally believed they had hiked forty miles to the hotbed motel town.

The head office, seeing production, income, and profits slump because they could not keep workers on, hired a cook who had worked for an Italian restaurant. The food improved dramatically, but there was still an exodus. The cook ordered exotic ingredients that were delivered by a huge Speedy Food truck. After the driver delivered the cases of sauce and mushrooms, he parked in the shade of the big sagebrush to eat his noontime bologna sandwich, read a chapter of *Ambush on the Pecos Trail*, and take a short nap. Three drillers coming in from the day shift noticed the truck idling in the shade. They noticed it again the next morning on the way to the rig. A refrigerator truck, it was still running. A call came three days later from the company asking if their driver had been there. The news that the truck was still in the sagebrush brought state troopers. After noticing spots of blood on the seat and signs of a struggle (a dusty boot print on the inside of the windshield), they began stringing crime scene tape around the truck and the sagebrush.

"Kellogg, get done with the tape and get out here," called a sergeant to the laggard trooper behind the sagebrush. The thick branches and foliage hid him from view and the tape trailed limply on the ground. Kellogg did not answer. The sergeant walked around to the back of the sagebrush. There was no one there.

"Goddamn it, Kellogg, quit horsin around." He ran to the front of the truck, bent and looked beneath it. He straightened, shaded his eyes, and squinted into the shimmering heat. The other two troopers, Bridle and Gloat, stood slack-jawed near their patrol car.

"You see where Kellogg went?"

"Maybe back up to the man-camp? Make a phone call or whatever?"

But Kellogg was not at the man-camp, had not been there.

"Where the hell did he go? *Kellogg!!!*"

Again they all searched the area around the truck, working out farther into the sage, then back toward the truck again. Once more Bridle checked beneath the truck, and this time he saw something lying against the back inner tire. He pulled it out.

"Sergeant Sparkler, I found this." He held out a tiny scrap of torn fabric that perfectly matched his own brown uniform. "I didn't see it before because it's the same color as the dirt." Something brushed the back of his neck and he jumped, slapping it away.

"Damn big sagebrush," he said, looking at it. Deep in the branches he saw a tiny gleam and the letters "OGG."

"Jim, his nameplate's in there!" Sparkler and Gloat came in close, peering into the shadowy interior of the gnarled sagebrush giant. Sergeant Sparkler reached for the metal name tag.

The botanist sprayed insect repellant on his ears, neck and hair. The little black mosquitoes fountained up as he walked toward the tall sagebrush in the distance. It looked as large as a tree and towered over the ocean of lesser sage. Beyond it the abandoned man-camp shimmered in the heat, its window frames warped and crooked. His heart rate increased. Years before he had scoffed at the efforts of botanical explorers searching for the tallest coast redwood, or the tallest tree in the New Guinea jungle, but at the same time he began looking at sagebrush with the idea of privately tagging the tallest. He had measured some huge specimens of basin big sagebrush near the Killpecker dunes and recorded their heights in the same kind of little black notebook used by Ernest Hemingway and Bruce Chatwin. The tallest reached seven feet six inches. The monster before him certainly beat that by at least a foot.

As he came closer he saw that the ground around it was clear of other plants. He had only a six-foot folding rule in his backpack, and as he held it up against the huge plant it extended less than half its height. He marked the six-foot level with his eye. He had to move in close to get the next measurement.

"I'm guessing thirteen feet," he said to the folding rule, placing one hand on a muscular and strangely warm branch.

The Sagebrush Kid stands out there still. There are no gas pads, no compression stations near it. No road leads to it. Birds do not sit on its branches. The man-camp, like the old stage station, has disappeared. At sunset the great sagebrush holds its arms up against the red sky. Anyone looking in the right direction can see it.

SPIN

Aurelie Sheehan

The BLM auction took place at the county fair. In the corner of the world stood five sorry-ass enclosures with about twenty or thirty animals inside—mostly horses, but then a few burros, too, carted over from Yuma. It would be my horse, technically. I was just going to keep it at the Arizona Home for Girls as part of an "enrichment program." They could call it anything they wanted for all I cared.

The website had featured two kinds of animals: sad little hopeful ones, waiting to be adopted, and robust thriving productive picture-book horses—the before and after of it all. I knew it had to be more complicated, but even so I wasn't prepared for what I saw. Behind those green bars the yearlings and the two-year-olds, mostly bays, were like wind, captured. They moved together. One heard a pin drop somewhere in Idaho, and they all skated to the other side of the enclosure, a whoosh and a rumble and then there they stood, in the new location. Side by side, facing the world as one, ready to go.

Still fenced in, however.

Let's just say it was hard to choose. They wanted blind bids, anything over a hundred and twenty-five dollars. I stared into each pen, mares on one side of the lot, geldings on the other, half ignoring and half catcalling to each other. I could be reasonable about this. I could check their legs, eyes, conformation. But I didn't want to be reasonable. I saw one who'd been in some kind of accident and had a scar running the length of her nose, I wanted her. I saw a beautiful dun who looked like he'd come from a herd far from the others, I wanted him. I saw two chestnut yearlings huddled nearly on top of one another, and I wanted them, too. I wanted every horse the BLM could sell me. I had to give up. I had to get away from there.

Then I saw him staring through the slats, looking at me, as if we'd made an agreement a long time ago and I was about to run off and forget all about it. He was a bay, probably just under two. The tattoo under his mane looked like Chinese lettering. All the wild ones had these markings, white fur filling in the shapes of letters and numbers burned into their necks or haunches, a precaution against slaughter.

He looked away. I looked away. I looked back. He looked back.

The BLM cowboys were sitting in front of their trailer, shooting the shit and squinting at me, a horse gaper. I wrote down my offer. If you're not a gambler, you want to offer everything. If you find what you want, you're liable to offer it all. Not a hundred and twenty-six bucks, not two hundred. How about five hundred or a thousand? My horse, Number 433 from Elko, Nevada. I could see his ribs when he breathed out, short, anxious huffs. He had a good coat, somewhere under the dirt and the burrs, and his legs were strong. He moved with the others, jammed together, but he kept one eye on me as I held on to the rail. Fifty thousand, a million? Still, he wouldn't come close to the fence. *It's all right*, I told him telepathically, *we'll talk later.*

I turned in the bid—just about what I had in savings, not quite as much as you'd hope for—and got a few *Thank you, ma'ams*, and, *You'll get a call in forty-eight hours.*

The girls at the center weren't as attractive as they are on HBO: little jail-baits, the blonde, troubled sexpot and her dark-haired, smart sister. These girls came stumbling out of the building and into the sunlight, eight lost souls in some kind of gym outfits. Jesus, they didn't need gym clothes for this—I'd told Jack Jones that. And couldn't he let them wear sunglasses? It was god-fucking-forsaken Arizona. They huddled together at first, the girls did, even in the heat. They had to stick together, form a large body to combat me: a new problem.

"Hi girls," I said, and waited. No response. "I'm Dr. Laura Benjamin, and I'm really glad to be here, glad to have this chance to be together."

"Glad someone's glad," said a girl with bangs in her eyes. I couldn't read her expression, but I can assure you it wasn't "winning," "happy," or "eager."

I launched in anyway. "As you know, the Bureau of Land Management culls the wild burro and horse herds in Arizona and across the United States, and these animals can be adopted. I've adopted a two-year-old, and today we're bringing him here. This is an opportunity for us to raise him together."

"Horses are dumb as hell," said someone.

"What makes you think horses are dumb?" I asked. Still fresh, still inquiring.

"I grew up on a ranch, Doc, and horses were just about the dumbest animal, just about as dumb as—"

"Dumb as dumbass you?" said a compatriot.

"Shut the fuck up."

"You've got to be dumb as hell to end up here," said another girl. Her arms were crossed over her chest; she had long hiding hair.

"Look, ladies. I don't really care if you think horses are dumb or not. You signed up for this program—right? It's better than PE or whatever. It's better than watching, what, *Oprah*. So you're going to learn something about an animal. About taking care of the horse. You're going to help me train this beauty, and, over time, he's going to be a good companion for us. It's going to be something to see."

"So you like took this horse from the wild, out where he was free? You took him from the place he grew up and you're dropping him here? What's the point of that? What makes that so great?"

"What makes that so great? Well, for one thing, if they get thirsty out there and can't find water, that's it, they die a long, gruesome, dehydrated death. If they break their leg, they fall down and rot. If they get sick—it's a slow, miserable road to horse hell. It's the end of the little pony story. That's what makes it so great. It's better here. All right? Better to be alive, don't you think?"

They looked blankly at me. Eight girls, mostly a little overweight, some too thin entirely. Most were brunettes; half were white, half Hispanic. All wore mesh shorts and teal T-shirts that read *A Better Day*.

"All right. Here's the trailer." Take a deep breath, doctor. "Now, listen. The horse is going to be pretty freaked out at first, all right? So you can watch us get him out of the trailer, but you've got to step back, back by the fence there, and don't make any sudden movements or noises, OK?"

"Now she's telling us what to do," a girl said.

"Stay away from the horse," someone else said slowly, replete with irony.

"He's going to need patience," I said, under the bluest sky imaginable. "But the first thing he needs will be a little space."

"What's his name, Mrs. Doctor?"

"He doesn't have a name yet," I said. The trailer was backing up to the gate.

"Call him fucking Lucky," I heard behind me.

"Fucking good idea," I said. I wasn't here to be a disciplinarian.

When I opened the trailer door there he was, sad as a creature can be, huddled up against the side of the stall. Once the light hit him, he started knocking at the trailer with his front hoof, as if he'd scramble up the aluminum if he could. Then he slammed the side with his body, and the whole trailer trembled and the din drove him crazy. He lurched back, pulled sideways, hit the end of the rope, swung toward the wall, lurched, knocked, swung, shook like a baby. It was a complete disaster, worse than when we got him from the BLM site to the clinic; worst I'd ever seen. "What do you think?" said Jan, from the clinic—she'd driven him out for me. "Tranqs?"

"No. Jesus. I'm trying to show these girls a better way." Eight juvenile delinquents and I'm going to pull out the drugs immediately?

He was back to climbing the wall; he was quaking in the corner.

"I can take care of this."

"Don't get hurt now," said Jan.

"Man, that horse's totally mad!" said one girl.

"He hates it here!"

"Don't worry," I said—full of bravado, right? "It just takes a little time. Getting in and out of the trailer is the hard part. If he could get it through his head that my being here means his freedom, things will start going our way. I'm just going to open these windows, see? Open these windows on the side."

I was stalling, is what I was doing. Baffled completely. I wasn't a horse trainer by profession, just someone with my head filled with hay.

"C'mon, let's go over here," I said to the girls. "Sit."

I was met with a chorus of mumblings about sand and scorpions, but they all sat down. The horse stood stoically, ass to me, like we'd never met before, like he was in the process of getting sentenced for a crime against the country.

Finally he turned his head and looked toward us. Briefly curious—then he turned his head back. A couple more minutes passed. He looked again, a longer scrutiny. After he turned back to the wall, he stomped a foot: not fury this time, but impatience. I got up; I started back in. *Come on, come on, come on. Do me this favor, little one.*

I got a hold of the halter and unhooked him from the trailer. Leaned on him, leaned on him hard, and one step back, two steps back, I was in a storm. A rush of noise from all directions, hooves on metal, wooden slats groaning, and we were at the edge, down the plank, turned around.

I released his halter and he was gone. Pissed right off. Pissed at me and everything I stood for. He ran to the far end of the corral, jammed up against the fence, snorted, ran again—this time full tilt to the other end. No luck there, either. He raised his head high as love. He was never going to look our way again.

"OK," I said, brushing my hands together, pleased with myself.

I turned to the group of girls standing by the fence. A couple of them were comparing tattoos; one had lifted her shirt and was looking at her stomach. A girl with short red hair, red as in Bozo red, watched me with an unnaturally mild expression, like she was the best pickpocket in the world.

So the girls were right. So maybe the horse wasn't as happy as he might have been elsewhere. The BLM culls the healthiest, the "adoptable" horses. In other words, the good ones are taken from their home, away from the landscape they've memorized under their hooves, tracing and retracing their geography, their history. So what was I supposed to do, object to everything? Say *no, fuck it, I'm going home*?

The next day I sat for a couple of hours against the shade structure (to call it a barn would be going way too far). Lucky was walking. He walked and walked, staring down into himself, down into a dark and empty well. When I first ducked under the fence and slid down to sit, he'd swished his tail and trotted to the other end of the corral. Now he was mostly ignoring me, but every once in a while I'd catch his eye—and then we'd both look away again, like we were back at the auction.

This technique, Magazine Reading in Vicinity of Corralled Animal, didn't look fancy, it wasn't in the books, but I didn't want to rush him.

"Is he lonely, do you think?"

"What?" I asked, turning around. It was the girl with clown hair. She had a tattoo around her neck, I noticed this time, like a black chain choker.

"He knows I'm here," I said. "You're in the class, right?"

"Yeah." She showed me her profile then: proud, lucky.

I should have asked if she had a pass or something—the place was teeming with rules of every kind. I'd been sitting in the heat, not rushing the horse, for a long time by then.

"You want to come in?"

"So it's some sort of feel-good program?" Jack Jones had said on the phone, when I'd first pitched him the idea. "The girls get in touch with themselves?" I explained that it was more than that. Better, even, than that. "As long as you keep the disruption down," he'd finally said, after a meandering rumination on the school's thirtieth anniversary, on extracurricular this and that, and on what the goddamned hoity-toity delinquents were doing up in Phoenix.

Girl-units. He used the term *girl-units* once.

This girl—her name was Kris—sat down next to me and pulled her knees up close to her chest. Her regulation khakis were blown out and frayed at the knee. Right away she started worrying the hole with her finger.

Lucky was standing by the westernmost fence, staring out past the school's property, a half-dozen saguaros and some mesquites and scrub brush and some old equipment (torture devices, for when punishing the girls had more range?). *Go west, young pony!* And actually, yes, west was the way home—three hundred miles west and six hundred north and he'd be back where he began.

"He's nervous," she said.

"It's going to take a while to get used to it here." I glanced at the girl. Her home was some kind of Stephen King nightmare building, nothing really wrong that you could immediately put your finger on.

"Yeah."

"Do you like animals?"

"Who doesn't like animals?"

"True," I said, too quickly. You want to ask, "So what are you in for?" But that question seems like a lie, and everything else is a mistake.

"I used to have a horse," she said after a while. She was watching the pony watching us.

"Did you? Neat." Now I was a moron. "Neat" was an anesthetized little word, like I was trying to cozy up to a Mouseketeer. "When was that?"

"At my first dad's. Long time back." She started twisting a hunk of her hair. "Of course, at this hellhole, no pets allowed."

"Yeah."

"But now we've got Lucky."

I smiled into the sun. "We do," I said. "That's right."

Every Tuesday and Thursday the lady administrator handed me a sheet of paper, eight names altogether, and on the other days I just came out at lunch or after work, whenever I could squeeze it in. Lucky and I stared across the corral making monkey faces at each other. Kris joined us maybe half the time. She'd see my truck, I guessed, though I never really asked. In a few minutes there she'd be, a red comet ducking under the fence.

"What was she *like?*" Kris said one Wednesday afternoon, responding to yet another of my grown-up drone questions. She laughed, threw a pebble. "Well, it depends."

"Yeah? On what?"

"Once she made me this amazing dollhouse. She found this bookcase on the street, you know? And fixed it all up with these little rooms and with lamps and curtains and all this? It took her like a whole week to do it."

"Nice."

Kris was staring at the horse, her eyebrows completely, as in Clint Eastwood, scrunched. It really was fucked-up that they wouldn't give the girls sunglasses, for Christ's sake.

I said, "So, that was a while back?"

"Yup."

Somewhere a sun-stroked dove was calling, as if it had forgotten the time of day.

"When you were just a kid," I said, half to myself, all pissed off.

"She got us back one time, for about six months. Then she lost custody again. It was mostly the drug thing."

I blamed Jack Jones. I didn't have anyone else to blame so I thought I'd blame him.

"She's out there somewhere, doing her own thing I guess," said Kris, dropping her head back to rest on the fence. A Roman warrior in repose, red hair, tattooed choker unaccountably moving, like she was holding something in or something down.

I hated talking, I really did. I've always hated talking. "How long have you been in here?" I asked the ground.

"Since Christmas."

I drew a line in the sand with my finger, erased it again.

"I want to stay," she said.

"Stay here?"

"I saw this show on TV, where they trained a horse in like two hours. It's not like that really? It'll take longer?"

Lucky: the name was a way to trace him, to run your hand along his mane, his back, his black tail.

"Yeah, we're just going to take it easy with him. I want him to get to know us first, you know? Get to know his surroundings. We'll get him used to us, and then we'll teach him on the lunge line, and then try the saddle and bridle. It could take years—months, anyway."

"I want to stay for all that," she said, and then looked at me as if I'd just said something harsh—like it was going to rain or something might rip—but I hadn't said anything.

Sometimes the heat here becomes a shape, as if it's hauling itself into the form of an apparition of some kind, and then you sigh, or pass out, and everything is muted/normal/gone again.

A couple of days later Jack Jones called me into his office.

"The animal benefits from human interaction—that's the whole point," I tried to tell him. "And the girls, they benefit—"

With his hands, he made a little fascist church. Here's the steeple. "That's terrific, Doctor, but Kristine G. Wick and the others must, first and foremost, adhere to the rules of the Arizona Home for Girls. Then and only then does your animal therapy program come into play."

"The corral is, what, ten feet from the building? So, what? They're not allowed out of the building during the day? Did Kris miss a class or something?"

"She missed recess. She missed lunch."

"Recess, Jack? I mean, I can see the issue with lunch."

He kept his eyes leveled at me then, practicing his Intimidation Stare—good for the headmasters of girls' detention centers. I kept my mouth shut for a minute. I could do this, I thought.

"I'll talk to her," I said, just to get out of there. Jack swung his bright white sneakers up onto the desk and leaned back, head resting in his palms.

"You better do more than that."

"Well, but—I didn't actually miss lunch, I mean, I ate my food and everything," she said to me. We were sitting by the fence in the corral.

"Really?" I said. "Figures. Okay, just keep an eye out for Jack, got it?"

"Right."

Bureaucratic bullshit.

Lucky had gotten pretty comfortable with us by then. He didn't balk and snort when we came in under the fence, a young one and an old one, dodging the splinters in the railing. Sometimes we'd both read magazines, sometimes we'd talk. After I'd dispensed with my message from Jack, I handed Kris *Veterinary Medicine*, and I had some newsletters to read. She was reading the drug ads at the back of the magazine when I suddenly had this feeling.

"OK, Kris, you ready?"

"Ready for what, Dr. Benjamin?"

I'd already told her about the all-important "join-up," the moment I'd read about in some of the training materials, seen on a video that came to us at the clinic. I believed it could work. You had to believe in something. If you weren't going to truss up their legs and hobble them into submission, you had to have a back-up plan.

"I don't know, I mean—you said he wasn't ready," she said, when I told her what I was thinking. "Aren't we supposed to wait for him to come to us or something?"

"We can't wait forever, right? May as well meet him halfway. Just go out there, go out a little ways."

"Well, OK," she said—seesawing up, awkward. I got up, too. She ran her hand through her hair. We were both pretty excited then.

"Go on," I said. "I'll stay back here, by the fence."

Standing, you become smaller in a corral in the middle of nowhere, save one monolithic building on your right and a tilted sign at the end of a long driveway—pockmarked, actually, with bullets. Arizona Home for Girls. What would the Road Runner do here? Probably side with the administration and clock Coyote with a piece of lead. You become small, under the sun. Weak, little, not much breath to speak of. But Lucky stood strong, magnificent.

Kris put one soft foot in front of the other. She stretched her arm out in the gentlest arc.

The horse stopped his phantom chewing and looked at her, his head still close to the ground. She moved a little closer, stopped again. Ten feet between them. She stood for the longest time. She wasn't looking at Lucky anymore, but at the ground.

The sun went up another mile, radiated outward, a nuclear pinprick. The horse sighed, swayed forward on his front legs and went back to center. Blinked. Kris was standing alone in the dirt corral, like the red bull's-eye of the universe. Finally Lucky dislodged himself from his lonely place, his famous last stand, and took one, two steps, toward her outreached hand.

I drove home unbothered by the traffic on Oracle, on Ina. I was driving into the wind, my windows open, the radio loud. I didn't know what I'd do for dinner. Pizza, I thought. I didn't know who to call, what to do with the daylight left. Seemed only right to keep driving—to drive, and sing, until it was night.

Two weeks later things were still going great with the horse. After Kris got him to come up to her that first day, I joined the two of them. We stood on either side of him for a few minutes, touching his body like we were blind. I pulled a burr out of his mane. The next few days—OK, with a little reluctance, a little backtracking—we were able to lead him to the fence, lead him around the corral. The girls started grooming him with me Tuesdays and Thursdays. You should have seen them with that horse. At first, they were like, "Ew, disgusting," but then it was as if I'd gotten them the biggest Barbie in the store, and they brushed, and primped, and combed him to a shine.

Kris had forgotten that part where she wanted things to go slowly. She was greedy for the horse, wanted to get her hands all over him. She still couldn't quite get the hand-over-hand motion to trot him in circles with the lunge line, but she'd been walking him close, up and down the fence, and in some figure eights of her own. I told her I thought we'd be able to ride him by fall. "You up for some hard work?" I'd asked. She'd said, "Nothing's hard with Lucky." We'd sort of started ignoring the whole missing-lunch thing. She didn't bring it up again, and neither did I—and pretty much I had been avoiding Jack Jones.

Then I got a call from him. Five in the morning, some girls had tripped an alarm sneaking back into the building. They'd been out with the horse; they'd given him some food. Now he was sick—lying down. *I thought I told you this had to be a no-problem situation? A see no evil, smell-no-pony-shit kind of deal?*

Manny the non-English-speaking maintenance man met me in the driveway. He gestured toward the *caballo*. "Muy mal, señora."

Muy mal, indeed.

Lucky was in the corral. Above the mountain, a tide of pink disappeared into the flat light of dawn. His neck was hot. His stomach was strained and bloated, his eyes rolled to the side. I threw open my bag and took his pulse and temperature. Cheese puff bits were everywhere, orange confetti. A domesticated horse would eat himself sick too, but a horse that's gone from meager roughage in the desert to this? How many bags of cheese puffs did they find in that goddamned kitchen? How many cheese puffs does it take to choke a horse?

"Can you help me?" I said to Manny—shouted, really.

I got the equipment from the truck and Manny held the horse's head while I forced the tube down. Behind me I heard Jack Jones shouting at the girls who'd come trotting out, shorebirds to the wave's edge. Later I'd remember seeing Kris there, in her Tweety Bird nightgown and big untied sneakers, her arms crossed tightly against her stomach.

They'd called me in time. Within an hour, he was standing back up. Drinking water, too, before I left for the clinic. When I came back a few hours later, it was as if nothing had ever happened. The crazy horse wanted food more than anything.

On the way out Thursday, I rehearsed a full-tilt speech on responsibility and horse care for the girls. Now I *thought* I'd gone through this before, but I guess the message hadn't really sunk in. (Though the girls had looked terrified the other morning, horse down.) I'd go over the fact that Lucky was a wild animal, dependent on us now. I'd use Kris as an example. I'd say, *Look what she's done.* The ground around the building was tamped down, dark and hardened by an early monsoon the night before. The rain had released a smell from the greasewoods and mesquites, bitter and strange.

"What does this mean?" I asked—two times. Luanne and Twila looked at each other. They weren't surprised by it, by anything. But I, the teacher, self-appointed horse angel, didn't get it at all.

Hall, Luann
Lauterio, Lisa
Rivera, Dorothy P.
Roan, Enriqueta
Smitt, Libby Rebecca
Torrez, Maria
Villareal, Twila

And instead of "Wick, Kristine G.," there was a new girl at the bottom of the list.

There she was, *White-Eagle, Donna,* standing at a distance from the others, holding her arm with the opposite hand. Her elbow was bent in the wrong direction, double-jointed.

I turned and went inside to talk to Jack. He looked up from a phone call, gave me some kind of glamour-actor smile and waved me to a chair until he finished talking.

"What can I do you for? How're all creatures great and small?"

He said she'd been reassigned.

"Re-fucking assigned?"

"You want to get reassigned too?"

"You can't reassign everything," I said, unknowing.

The girls were waiting for me when I got back outside, quiet, faces screwed up in the sun. I didn't go through with my speech.

They took turns grooming Lucky, first Twila and then Donna and then Luann. Each girl had her own scent. I knew this from standing near them, helping them figure out how to care for the horse. Each had her own personal blend of grief, Suave shampoo, and perfume. Each girl, too, had a little different way of holding the brush, holding her own hair so it didn't fall in the way. Lucky, the luckiest horse in the world, let himself be groomed. Then the forty-five minutes was over and all the girls went inside and I was alone.

He stood, brushed to velvet, believing that I had won.

I snapped on the lunge line, a twenty-four-foot green tether, and we walked together to the wide part of the corral. His gait was smoother now; he didn't as often trip over invisible stones. *Your honor, I must disagree,* I would say. *Your honor, as a doctor of veterinary medicine and an instructor of young girls—*

The saguaros stood guard around us, wouldn't let us go. I began to let out the line, hand over fist, backing away from the pony. Tension animated the rope, drew it taut between us. He sighed, threw his head down for a moment, then stumbled into a trot. Two years old, fourteen point two hands, bay. Dog food.

I followed him with my eyes, and then my body. My arms and hands held the rope, and he began to whirl around me. I followed him, circling, circling, my footprints a hash in the sand.

AMANUENSIS

Stephen Tuttle

Later, when the storms had stopped, they began to discover what so much snow could do. They saw the way it had collapsed roofs and bridges and trees, how it made roads impassable and telephones useless. And they saw that wild animals, deer and raccoons and foxes, had been forced to look for food at lower and lower elevations until the hunt had brought them to the streets of their town, where they found no better luck. For days after, they found carcasses all through their streets: gaunt and empty and wasted away. And if there were many among them who saw so much snow as a sign from heaven, there were none who saw it as a blessing. They called it a trial or a purification or a mystery of God, but they couldn't say they were grateful for it. And no one said anything about the drought they wouldn't have to worry over, no one said anything about the reservoir that would be filled to capacity for the first time in a decade.

They endured twenty-six consecutive days of heavy snow, one storm beginning before the last had ended, one storm overwhelming another. Nearly a month of constant snow, nearly a month inside their homes, weeks during which their churches were empty, their schools locked tight. They knew snow well enough, living as they did at the northern end of the Wasatch Mountains, where they could expect to buried under for a day or two every season.

But they also knew that this was something much greater than they had ever experienced. When it was nearly over and the sun began to shine through, they came out of their homes as though for the first time in their lives. The clouds thinned and the sun shone down and began the weeks-long process of condensing so many feet of snow, compressing it into mounds of hard ice veined with oil and soot. It was then, having come out to inspect the damage, to see what had collapsed, what had burst, what had failed to endure, that word of Dumond began to circulate. One of their neighbors was missing. Their junior high school science teacher had disappeared into the snow and hadn't returned.

What they heard was that a day or two earlier, when one storm had started to fade and another had not yet come to replace it, Dumond had left early in the morning, on foot, intending to photograph ice crystals and falling flakes. This was a hobby of his and it came as no surprise to them that he would head to the foothills on a day when anyone else would have stayed inside his warm house. Dumond's wife waited through most of the day, she said, before she decided that enough was enough. Her husband had a tendency for losing time, she knew, but the snow had continued to fall that whole day. If it was tapering off, it was still immense and still fell so heavily at noon that she regretted his decision to leave. She was left to suspect that he had gotten himself stuck in a snowdrift or worse.

They admired Dumond and respected him. Those children who had sat through eighth grade earth science, hearing again and again how lucky they were to live here on what was anciently the northernmost shore of Lake Bonneville, were nearly unanimous when they called him a favorite teacher. His close neighbors called him a credit to society. And they wasted no time organizing themselves. They used every means at their disposal to rescue a man who had thought, just prematurely, that the weeks of snow had finally come to an end. But if they worked swiftly, after an initial search revealed nothing, they did not hope for success. A day turned into a week. But after so many storms had buried them under they couldn't hope they were going to find him, not in so much snow, not for months. Say what they might about hope, theirs was a town of farmers and hunters and survivalists who knew what it meant to be alone in the elements. They were slow to say so, but each of them knew that no one, not even Dumond, could have survived an entire week exposed to such conditions.

They asked his wife if it would be alright for them to honor her husband, knowing that she was unlikely to abandon hope until she had some concrete evidence, even if it was clear to them that he was gone for good. They suggested that this was for the best, for her and for everyone. They took her silence as permission. They made the arrangements because they knew that she was in no condition to do so and that there was no one else to do it for her. The service was a matter of course. They gathered in a Mormon chapel, took turns telling each other just how much they had respected this man, just how much his absence would be felt. When they talked about him, they nodded in the direction of an empty casket. They held the memorial service in a building he hadn't entered in years, and understood when his wife didn't join them.

The Dumonds had been a part of this town for as long as anyone could remember. The schools here were rarely without a Mr. or Mrs. Dumond, and neither were various boards and civic committees. A Dumond had been the mayor once, one had been postmaster, and no less than four had stood in front of them on Sunday mornings, wearing a dark suit and tie, saying again and again what they had heard so many times before. But this Dumond was the last. Over the previous decades the family had dwindled: no children replaced those who grew old and passed. Dumond's parents were both dead, killed years earlier and in the same instant, when their car and another collided on Highway 91 inside Sardine Canyon. His two brothers were also dead: each a victim of his own, untreated depression. Neighbors had watched as the Dumond family, this constant in their town, turned slowly away from them until they were left with only this couple: blood and then marriage making them the last Dumonds. They had had no children of their own and they politely ignored every hint that it wasn't too late to change that fact. They had stayed to themselves more often than had previous members of the family: his parents and theirs. Even before the snow had started to fall, neighbors had noticed that these Dumonds, these last Dumonds, were not as neighborly as they might have been, not as likely to visit over a fence. They rarely saw him outside of school, they hardly saw her at all. They regretted the distance that had grown between them and this family, how they had said nothing when he disappeared from ward meetings so many years earlier, how they had never invited her at all.

Former students who attended the memorial service were quick to announce their fondness for a man who made science fun. He had taught them so much without making a minute of it seem like work. And as a kind of excuse for his final hours they talked and talked about how much he loved the snow. They recalled their collective fondness of a year's first snowfall, how it meant that Mr. Dumond would cancel whatever he had scheduled, even a test, to take them outside where they could examine those early flakes. They recalled the things he taught them about snow crystals, how the popular wisdom about their inexhaustible variation was true, but that there was more to the story. He told them that each snowfall contained millions of crystals that were nearly identical to each other and that any distinction was not a matter of creation but of environment, that each was formed minutes or hours earlier, far above the earth, and that these crystals collided and joined and broke apart in the air, that what they saw in their hands, falling onto their tongues, captured on sheets of glass to be viewed under a microscope, were indicators of atmospheric conditions. The infinite patterns were there, but did they notice the consistency of their shape, the perfect hexagonal symmetry of each flake? These were the results of a specific wind speed and humidity and temperature. He showed them photographs of snowflakes he had taken, photographs they could hardly believe were of naturally occurring phenomena. The complexity was incredible, the balance surprising. They couldn't see the world the same way after Mr. Dumond taught them to look at snow. They were indebted to him forever.

It was late spring, when the snow was melted and gone, when the damage of the storms was largely repaired, that children—playing where they had been told not to—first learned that the empty Dumond house was not empty at all. Grown bored with their own backyards and the quiet routine of empty fields, the children examined the locked doors and windows of the house until something gave under pressure and allowed them inside. Dumond's wife had left without so much as a good-bye. She had hired a moving company and was gone before they had had the chance to offer help. Neighbors had told the children to stay away from that house, that it wasn't theirs to creep around in, that sooner or later someone would buy the place, and that they could ask the new owner for a tour. But they also suspected the house might never sell, that it might sit there, empty for years, surrounded by its weeds and already brown lawn. And if they didn't show it—to maintain consistency, to appear disappointed by a rule not obeyed—the parents of those children were delighted to know that someone, finally, had explored the space where the Dumonds had lived. And what their children told them, when they reported, sheepishly, what they had done, was that in the basement of the Dumond house they had found an entire city.

Where they had expected to find nothing more than broken furniture not worth hefting into a moving truck, their children had found a series of tables filling the vast middle of Dumond's basement, and on those tables there were miniature chapels and miniature stores and miniature houses in cul-de-sacs. And when neighbors finally came to inspect that basement, they saw that this was not just the scale model of a town, not just some three-dimensional, plastic landscape on which children might arrange toy cars, but it was a model of their little Utah town with their homes and their hardware store, their bakery, and their supermarket, and it was large beyond anything they had ever seen. No map, no model, no miniature of anything they had known had been so enormous in its scope and so precise in its detail. They stood there amazed, stood and admired the size of their town and how large it seemed now that it was so small, how it stretched out around the low hills surrounding them, how it filled the long space of its valley. They stood in awe of Dumond's scale model, they stared at themselves as though they were each aerial photographers.

There was a swell of pride in those first encounters with Dumond's model town, a sense of confidence that this place was worth a scale replica, as though it were the site of a Civil War battle or the example of visionary city planning, architecture well ahead of its time. Neighbors and citizens, former students and their parents, everyone came to Dumond's empty house. They came to see the model and they came to see how accurately it was built, to see which details were included and which were not. They found the movie theater and the dry cleaners, the record shop and the sporting goods store. They found the library, the dinosaur museum, and the cemetery with its vast, open park. They even found the model-train shop, a scale model of a store that sold scale models. They applauded Dumond for his attention to detail, they clapped their hands and smiled, impressed by the painstaking hours he must have dedicated to this work.

It was only later, when they were returning for a fourth or fifth visit, that they began to notice small mistakes that hadn't caught their eyes before. He had correct numbers on their houses but the paint Dumond had chosen for any given door was often the wrong color. The headstones in the cemetery were blank. The marquee above the old theater was beautiful, but the jumble of letters there said nothing at all. The wide variety of trees that lined their streets and filled their yards (elms and maples, willows and catalpas) were represented by a largely scattershot arrangement of one tree, a dummy version of some generic thing that corresponded to nothing they had ever seen. The precision that had impressed them at first was only a broad and general accuracy. The close detail they had seen was never truly there. This map was not the impressive reproduction they had taken it for. It was large, of course, and clearly the result of long work. But still, they had taken it for something greater, something immense and impossible. They tried to remind themselves that they had never created anything close to this themselves. They reminded themselves that no map is as precise as the one they hoped for.

What bothered them more, however, were the markings they found all over this miniature town of theirs. There, among this reproduction of their landscape, was a network of colored dots placed inexplicably on the corner of this roof or on a window of that building. They hadn't noticed them at first, but now they could see little more than the markings that filled the map, markings that corresponded to nothing they knew of. There were colored dots and nearly invisible numbers and letters, filled shapes and empty shapes, and dozens of icons they couldn't identify at all. Some of the markings they could guess at. They could tell, for example, that the various colored lines that ran along their streets corresponded in some way to their traffic patterns: a busy street was nearly filled, while the streets they lived on, and especially the dead ends, were almost empty. But their homes were also covered in markings, laid out in such a way that they appeared to be embellishments at first, as though this series of symbols might have been an architectural flourish, some contemporary design. They began to document the marks on their homes and compare them as though they were Boy Scout merit badges or baseball cards they had collected. They attempted to translate Dumond's cryptic language, identifying which of them shared a red dot, which had the symbol of an opened eye, who had three yellow slashes and who had two overlapping circles.

By the time they discovered the key to Dumond's symbols they had already invented one of their own. They had decided that certain markings were desirable and that others were not. They had begun to clap each other on the back when two houses shared a mark, when two neighborhoods on either side of the model town were found covered in matching symbols. They had determined that the markings were indications of certain verifiable facts: who drove which cars, who worked which jobs, whose property value had increased the most over recent years. They were right in their first general assumptions about the markings, but wrong in nearly every particular. It was a substitute teacher at Dumond's school who finally stumbled upon the key, filed away in the back of a cabinet Dumond had filled to capacity and that the substitute teacher had never felt was hers to use. After so many months and such dwindling space, that teacher had decided, finally, to empty the storage Dumond was clearly never coming back to use. The key itself was handwritten and covered in smudges and corrections, originally typed but covered by ink from a dozen pens. It was ten pages of marks and their translations.

The key made the map seem innocuous at first. They had been right about the markings of traffic and walking routes, they had been right that certain markings indicated water lines, power mains, and shared resources. They were right that other markings indicated the value of their real estate or identified their tax bracket. But they couldn't have guessed at most of Dumond's symbols. He had markings to indicate their faith and the regularity of their attendance at church, how much debt they carried, what politics they endorsed, what bias they felt. His map showed things he would have had to watch them to know, and things he shouldn't have known even if he had watched. He had charted out their lives in the most intrusive ways. He knew the secret routes their children took to school, he knew how much time their teenage daughters spent on the telephone, he knew which houses had the most valuable heirlooms. He knew which of them had trouble sleeping, which used medications for sexual dysfunction, which had been unfaithful to a spouse. They knew, almost immediately, that Dumond's information was invented, that it was faulty. He couldn't have known about attempts to defraud insurance companies, he shouldn't have known just how many of their children were left unattended in the late afternoon when any stranger might walk into their homes and have his way with them.

If they denied each revelation Dumond's map seemed to make of them, they were also eager to spend more time in his old basement. They said very little to each other about what they saw there, except to scoff at a ridiculous hobby. They were quick to forget the praise they had had for Dumond. They were quick to recall just how much they had always disliked him.

Notwithstanding the history of the Dumond family, the people here could rarely remember that Dumond's wife was named Kathleen. They called her Catherine, Kelly, Karen, Carolyn, and even when they stumbled upon the right name they were never confident that they had found it. They attempted her name without conviction because many of them had not met her, and many more had never seen her. She was foreign to them the way a distant relative might have been, she was someone who had lived many years on the periphery of their lives. They knew she was often sick. But the severity of her illnesses ranged, in their many accounts, from a series of colds and allergies to rare viruses and incurable diseases known only to specialists. She was anemic, frail, and on her deathbed, they said. She got migraines and bloody noses, they said. They knew, without knowing how they knew, that she often slept sixteen hours a day, couldn't stand direct exposure to the sun, and had no capacity for digesting certain, common foods.

They knew next to nothing about Kathleen Dumond. They were unable to admit that they had embraced the accounts of her illness because they had wanted some excuse for the distance she kept from them. The people of this town were close to each other, knew each other well, and for Dumond to have married a woman who seemed unwilling to share in their closeness, unwilling to be a part of their society, was something that needed explaining. If they were prepared to believe any account of frailty they did so out of a kindness they couldn't escape: no one in this town stayed away from the community of it unless they were compelled to. And so they talked about this woman, got her name wrong, refused to admit how unlikely their stories were, and prepared a set of excuses for the disappointment they felt.

What they never said, what seemed beyond saying, was that Dumond's wife was inferior to them, came from weaker stock, was less well prepared for living than they. The people of this town worked hard, didn't get sick, didn't like to think about the various ways a human body might falter, leaving them incapacitated for any significant period. They were strong, reminded themselves how strong they were, and set about their lives with a sense of earned confidence. Dumond's wife, on the other hand, was a transplant and had come here only after Dumond had spent some time in Salt Lake City, returning, half a dozen years later, new wife in tow. They talked about what might have motivated such a move, why Dumond should have chosen to look elsewhere for what was clearly to be found here. What was worse, though, was that she wasn't even from Salt Lake, and she knew virtually nothing of life in what they once heard her call a flyover state where it was always either too hot or too cold for her. But they were forced to admit that for as little as they knew about his wife, they didn't know much about Dumond either. They knew that their children couldn't stop talking about Mr. Dumond, the science teacher, the one who always had a game or a clever way of making science fascinating. This was the same Dumond who didn't seem to enjoy his hometown enough to hang around in any weather. And it was the same Dumond who traveled every summer, who disappeared for months at a time and never thought to say good-bye, who never thought to apologize for his absence.

Their children seemed to know the Dumonds had been around the world, that they had seen the pyramids, the Great Wall, and the Leaning Tower. They seemed to know that Dumond and his wife saved and saved on his meager salary so that the two of them could travel. Their children were jealous, they said, they regretted the things they hadn't seen. But parents and teachers were quick to remind the children that there was more to the world than sightseeing could provide. They recalled the many virtues of this place, of the camaraderie they felt, of the life-lessons they'd learned right here, in this town, in these streets, in that garden. They reminded the children that life was richer and more rewarding when one invested oneself in a place, in a community, and that globe-trotting was simply a means of escaping responsibility. They said that Dumond may have filled the classroom with fun and games, but that he was a mercenary who saw those fun-filled hours as nothing more than a means of going away. Think about it, they said, not even our snow was good enough for him.

Some were not as quick to begrudge the Dumonds their travels, but suspected, and had suspected all along, they said, that Dumond's map was accurate only in as far as it was autobiographical. They argued that the map was an indication that a pervert had lived among them, that they were fortunate to be rid of that influence. They argued that they all ought to be counting blessings in the absence of the Dumonds, that a wicked influence was gone from among them. They argued that God had protected them from an evil they had been blind to and that they ought to sing praises for that. Did they need any more evidence than Dumond's conspicuous absence in their Sunday services? Did they have to look any further than his carnal behavior to see that he was wrong in the head and certainly an influence toward all that is misguided? Some were slower to condemn. They asked everyone to recall that Dumond and his wife had, in fact, been churchgoers even if their church was not the same that most in this town attended. They remembered that Dumond and his wife had belonged to some church, that they had been seen entering a small chapel on the edge of town. They remembered that Dumond had said something once about marital unity and not wanting to make waves.

All through that summer, there was hardly room to stand in Dumond's basement at any hour of the day. They regularly filled that space and shouted at each other about what should be done. Self-appointed guards stood watch over the long series of tables to protect the map from vandalism and destruction. They said that no one was going to touch Dumond's model until everyone agreed what they should do with it, that if it were to be dismantled they would do it systematically. They said that it needed to be protected from those who would destroy what they couldn't understand. Others set to work transcribing the map, making detailed copies of Dumond's markings. They took photographs and argued that this thing was the work of a preservationist, that it froze a particular place in time and could be thought of as a historical document or as a time capsule. They said it was impressive to think that such an artifact could so enliven a community, could so effectively hold a mirror to a people. But this was wrong, of course. So many said so. They asked if they were expected to believe, as the map suggested, that their neighbors cared so little for their children, or that they were surrounded by the depressed, the financially destitute, the immoral. This map, they said, was filled with lies. This map was the product of a stranger and a skeptic. He was a scientist, they said, and not a good one at that. After all, he did no better than a job at a junior high school in a district notorious for low standards. Some agreed that Dumond had hardly reached the heights of his profession, others said they were appalled to hear such criticism of themselves, the teachers who ate lunch next to Dumond, those who felt owed a certain respect, they said, for choosing to teach in this place.

There were those who found themselves conflicted. They were impressed by what Dumond had done, impressed by the stir he had caused, but also suspicious of his facts. They believed, they said, that this map was a rudimentary attempt, that it represented a first, broad sketch of this town. And if the details were wrong, the idea was right. They said that perhaps the map should be used as a template, but that they should feel free to make corrections and alterations to fit what they knew to be true. They argued that the map could be useful but that it could also do them harm and that they needed to be careful. They said that no one could deny that Dumond had hit a nerve and that they would be wrong to simply ignore the significance of his act. This was an opportunity to understand their community better than they had and they would be foolish not to take what was given.

One man got a black eye when he said to another that people like Dumond didn't belong in this town. A second man had asked what kind of person the first man thought Dumond was and if this had anything to do with politics. The first man said it was obvious and the second man took that as his cue. A woman admitted that she couldn't speak for the rest of her neighbors but that she could verify that Dumond got everything right about her house. She wasn't proud to admit it, she said, but facts were facts. Another woman said that one of two things was true and either Dumond was a regrettable human being or her husband had some explaining to do. Several parents said that they had altered their schedules because of what the map had shown. They believed the map had been wrong, they said, but now they had made sure it was. One man said that he would not allow himself to be slandered by the speculations of a dead man. The map may have been right in some few generalities, he said, but it was filled with lies all the same. He had daughters to think of, he had a wife, and he wasn't going to rest easy while that map said what it did about him. Many of them apologized for wrongs they had committed and others forgave sins that had never been confessed. Still others refused to let their children play with the sons and daughters of neighbors who had once been close friends.

They decided to protect themselves from the map and prohibit anyone from entering the empty house. They locked the doors and windows and said they would give the keys over to the new owners, if anyone were willing to buy the house. And if it sat there in its vacancy, if the house were inaccessible to them, it still occupied much of their thinking and most of their conversations. They recalled what they had seen, and argued about details. They disputed what markings had been on what properties and what the key had revealed. They fought among themselves until many of them refused to speak to one another ever again. They returned to their homes and their lives and said that time would tell, that eventually the basement would be opened and then they'd see who was right and who wasn't.

Some of them talked about opening Dumond's house and fixing the map, adding to the work they saw as incomplete. They might repaint the doors to match the colors of their own, they could find model trees that more accurately represented their real trees, they could paint small human figures and fill the map with the people Dumond had forgotten to include. But their most important addition would be no addition at all. They could remove all of Dumond's markings that did not correspond to something they could see with their own eyes. They could return his key to his filing cabinet and clear the model town of the symbols that had so bothered and confused them. It would be better, they said. The map was a beautiful thing that anyone but a fool would admire. They would reinforce the tables Dumond had worked on and place a velvet rope around them. They would have electricians install a series of ceiling lights to best allow inspection of each wonderful detail. For years they could come and be impressed by the map. They argued for intervention, saying that the map would erode with time, that they needed to keep it free of dust. They said it would take years, but that eventually the map would show signs of age, that it would fail. If they could look after it, however, if they could care for it, they could save it.

Some of them claimed to have seen Dumond wandering in the darkness of their homes and backyards. Some said they had seen him watching from a distance through binoculars. He wasn't dead at all, they said, and he wasn't gone. If he had disappeared into the snow, he had only gone into hiding.

They recalled the body they never found, they recalled the wife who disappeared in the night. They recalled the map Dumond had made and how it had infected them.

Some considered dismantling the map and hiding it away. They might gently separate it into parts and scatter the pieces throughout their town. They might take each miniature church and lock it in a cabinet in a real church. They might take the miniature model of their movie theater and lock it away in the projection booth of their real movie theater. They might slide the models of their homes beneath their beds in the bedrooms of their real homes. They might spread the map to the far extremes of what it represented, hiding its parts as close as possible to the things Dumond had copied. They told themselves this would be a way to remember, and that later, when they felt comfortable reconstructing the map, they would have little trouble finding it constituent parts. But they knew, even if they didn't say so, that they would never reconstruct the map even if they were successful in their plans to disseminate its parts. But they knew that by exploding this map they could save it, that they could make it real. Dumond's map would be safe, they knew, if they could bury it inside their town, every piece where it needed to be.

Then, after the long heat of August was gone and the leaves had begun to turn, some of them destroyed Dumond's scale model. They overwhelmed those who would have kept it and protected it. They tore it apart and crushed it, smashing it onto the hard concrete floor of that basement. They ran from the house carrying large sections of the map, dragging long sheets of plastic and pieces of green felt behind them. They soaked everything in gasoline and watched it burn in the middle of the street. They tore the key to Dumond's map into shreds and then burned the shreddings. They congratulated themselves on a work completed, on an evil banished. They smiled and said that now, at least, they could relax, knowing that nothing of Dumond was left among them. They wouldn't make eye contact with those who had fought so hard to stop them, they wouldn't speak to those who had opposed their plans.

Eventually, their conversations returned to the things they had always talked about: a football game the previous weekend, a problem at work, a series of storms the meteorologist had predicted. They rarely said anything to each other about the long months during which they had grown angry with each other about this thing that had invaded their lives. And if they mentioned Dumond from time to time, it was only the name of a man who had once lived in their town: a good man from a good family they were sad to have lost. They remembered the garden he'd kept, they remembered how their children had been invigorated by his teaching, they remembered that he had had a peculiar hobby.

Dumond's house was still empty that winter. It was emptier than it had ever been. And when the first heavy snow came, they watched it from behind the windows of their homes. They watched as snow slowly amassed on their lawns and in their streets. They watched the branches of their trees grow heavy with the weight. They watched Dumond's house disappear beneath the first real snow of the season.

DON'T LOOK AWAY

Urban Waite

I heard about Eddie on the news. Of course they didn't say his name or list anything more than what happened. There was a police raid on a farm outside Seattle: about ten dogs were seized and a man had been arrested. For a long time I sat there. Shocked. Bathed under the dull flicker of the television, recounting the newscaster's words. And then, after a while, I got up and stared out the window at nothing in particular. The weatherman was talking about rain, and as I watched, the wind kicked out the branches on a nearby tree, the water coming down out of the sky, highlighted and then lost in the shadows of the tree branches and leaves.

Anyone who knew Eddie Vasquez knew what he was doing out there with the dogs wasn't right. "A man's got to have his delights," Eddie said, his hands on the steering wheel. This was many years ago in a Safeway parking lot.

I had asked him straight out, "What are you doing, Eddie?" The cat piss smell of his truck wafting up through the cab, ammonia and dog hair mixed into the fabric of the seats. I hadn't seen him in years. I was twenty-five. Newly married with a son beginning to take his first wobbly steps.

"How long has it been, Raph?" Eddie said, more exclamation than question. I was standing in the parking lot, with my elbow up on his passenger door and a bag of groceries for the baby in my other hand. "Jesus, Raph! How long has it been?" he said again.

I put a hand through my hair and stepped back from the truck. "Ten years."

"Ten years," Eddie repeated, as if it were something giant and wonderful.

"What are you doing here?" I asked.

I asked because the last time I had seen Eddie was just before we moved out of Long Beach, a month or two after my father had left and my mother decided she didn't want to be in California anymore. We were fourteen and standing at the counter of a Walgreens, stuffing cheap silver Casios into our pockets. And as Eddie stuffed the silver bands down his pants, he listed them off in dollar amounts, five dollars, ten dollars, fifteen, like he was putting together an inventory.

"What does it look like?" Eddie said, turning a hand over the backseat of his truck, and motioning to about thirty pounds of beef on the floor of his cab. "I'm shopping."

I looked at the meat and then I looked at Eddie. A wave of guilt passed over me, like it did whenever I thought of Eddie. I hadn't even jaywalked in ten years, and here I was talking to my former partner in crime. It made me want to step back away from his truck and run all the way home. But for some reason I didn't.

Eddie was listing off the various cuts of meat: a few chucks, a strip, some loin, and even a few miscellaneous bones.

"Are you having a barbecue?" I asked.

Eddie laughed. "No," he said. And then after a little while, after he had stared off at the end of the parking lot, where the cement sloped down and entered the street, "Come on, I'll show you something."

I thought about not getting in, I thought about my baby at home. I thought about my wife. But what I did was get in the truck with Eddie. He was my brother, or as close to a brother as could be, without being related by blood. He had lived down the street from me all my life, right up until we moved to Seattle, and in the dusky nights of our childhood, we had run around on the Bermuda grass, playing soldiers with the other neighborhood kids. And no matter how uncomfortable I was with him, I knew he would never purposefully hurt me.

We turned out onto the street and took the on-ramp for I-5; we passed through downtown and headed south on the freeway. I was still holding a grocery bag full of diapers and baby food in my arms when I asked, "What is all the meat for?"

"Dogs," he said, not turning from the windshield, as he hit the turn signal and merged onto the 167.

I looked at the meat in the back of the truck, measuring the dollar amount in my head, estimating numbers inside the plastic bags. I thought about the meat. I thought about what Eddie had said—dogs—and then I asked, "What are you doing, Eddie?"

"Good and evil," my mother had said. I traced a finger along her nurse's name tag. The twin snakes of health and sickness, the winged staff of Hermes, these two forces fighting for balance; it was all part of it. "It's like night and day," my mother said. I was sitting in the front room of our house in Long Beach; my mother had quit her job at the hospital and was home at all times now. She had been working the night shift, while my father taught math out at Fullerton, a strange stability evolving out of this. And in her way she was telling me about my father. "Night and day," she said again, crossing through the front room on her way to the kitchen. There was anger in her words, the way she walked, spitting off insults as if I were her husband. I thought about how things can change. I thought about sons and fathers, happiness and sadness, love and hate, marriage and divorce.

I stood at my living room window for a long time. The house quiet around me, and it had been like this for more years than I cared to remember. My wife left me when I was midway through my thirties, taking my son. They live across the Sound now in a small town, where she sells croissants, breads, and pastries from her bakery on Main. And most of my nights are spent in this fashion, watching the weather come in, or sitting for hours in front of the television, although, if asked, I could not tell what I had watched the night before, or any night this week.

I couldn't believe it. I looked out into the darkness beyond the windows, my own empty house reflected across the pane. I couldn't believe that they were talking about Eddie. And I thought about all the things that had surprised me in life. I closed my eyes and felt the emptiness of my house, the pure and simple fact of its failure. I thought about Eddie, knowing that he was the one they had taken from the barn, the one they would not name, but hoping all the same that he was not.

Eddie was a good person who did bad things. This is how I had always known him. When we were kids we snuck into the El Dorado Country Club and stole balls for a profit. And when we couldn't sell them all, we went to the park under the guise of batting practice and hit them, high-flyers, over the street and into the surrounding neighborhood, to which we would listen, waiting for the sound of glass breaking, or the echo of tin reverberating as golf balls hit garage doors.

We exchanged looks of surprise, half wary of our wrongdoing, while Eddie talked about the batting angles of stance and posture. In the few months that remained of Long Beach, after my father left, Eddie would say, "Point your foot," standing at the pitcher's mound in the middle of the diamond. He tossed the white ball up in the air, waiting for it to swivel then fall into his hand. I felt the chalky earth at my toes, the way the rubber caught in the dirt, and turned up like two black-felt erasers clapping against each other. "Arch your back, get under it." He tossed the little ball up into the air again; shielding his eyes from the sun as the ball fought gravity, then fell back into his hand. "Get this one," he said, picking his leg up off the mound and throwing the ball, arm over shoulder, closed hand swinging until fingers released, and the little white ball shot across the space in between.

The bat made a sound, the ball floating up into the air as if it were being pulled up on a string. Fast at first, and then as it gained some distance, slow, seeming to float out above us. Finally falling, hundreds of feet in front of us, faster and faster toward the earth.

There was no sound; the ball simply ended. It went down over the roof of a house, and Eddie said, "Je-sus," in that dreamy, drawn-out way people sometimes use when something has happened that is hardly believable. "That's a home run for sure."

. "Did you hear anything?" I asked.

"Slick as a whistle."

I stood on the first-base line and waited. I didn't hear anything. It was a sunny day with a high, pale blue sky. Out on Stearns Boulevard cars were passing. Across the street I saw a woman come out of her house and pick a newspaper out of the grass. She stood for a moment reading the headlines, then turned, not looking in our direction, and went back into her house. Nothing happened, and Eddie tossed another ball up into the air, a big silly grin on his face, waiting for me to take another try.

My mother said there was something wrong with Long Beach. We were in the car on the 405. I turned to look back at the city; my father was out there somewhere, my aunts and uncles, my house, my friends. I heard the car shift down, the bend of a corner curving up, and then the city disappeared. We were leading a large, silver trailer behind us. Everything we owned was inside, pictures of my father and mother, my baseball bat and glove, my brother's toys.

"You're my little man now," my mother said.

I didn't know what to say. It wasn't like the old times when my mother would rush through the house and hug my father, saying over and over again, "You're a lucky man to have a wife like me."

No, it was not like this. She said it in a way that made me feel sad about it. And I pressed myself closer on the seat, looking for the familiar buildings of my city but finding only the haze of things I could no longer recognize.

And what I hated most of all was that my father had let her down somehow. I could hear it in her voice when she asked, "You'll be my little man, won't you?" Taking a hand from the steering wheel and running it down the back of my head, until it came to rest on my neck, and I could feel the weight there, like the question, waiting for a response.

Eddie's barn was south of Seattle in a place called Auburn. In the distance I saw the high stands of a horse track, and in every direction there was the flat, low-lying fog of farmland. I smelled the dogs before I saw them. The odor about the place was that of a kennel, earthy and sweet, like urine left to dry in the sun-warmed dirt. "This is it," Eddie said, climbing down out of the cab and facing the burnt-red building, with its gray tin roof and slumped walls, which leaned close against each other.

There was an eerie feel to the place. It felt as I must imagine the aftermath of war felt. The sleepy tightness of a place that had once been in motion, and now sat slumbering in waiting. There were all the smells, cow dung, hay, and grass seed. The muddy earth below my feet showed multiple paw tracks, and from the shadows I could see the slight movements of animals within the barn, tucked away below the doors, back into a place Eddie was walking to, and that I feared to follow.

"What is this place?" I asked, following close behind Eddie, pausing as he entered the shadows of the barn.

"I'll show you."

I could see the animals in there, the pacing of their bodies against the cages. But what disturbed me the most was that there were no sounds. Not a single animal made a noise. The dogs simply paced, back and forth along the edges of the cages, like a cat at the zoo, waiting for its opportunity.

And what I saw—what Eddie had brought me to see—was a long line of cages, built roughly along the edges of the barn. I counted twelve in all.

Chain-linked and squared up against the wooden walls of the barn. And in the center I could see a ring, built of wood, and lined along the bottom with sod and packed earth. I came to a stop at the center of the barn, looking down into the ring, seeing the red splatter along the walls, the rouge of dried blood at the edges, where, after staring down into the pit for a long while, I assumed the dogs had gone to die. "Jesus, Eddie," I said. "What have you gotten yourself into?"

"It's a terrible thing," Eddie said. "Almost an addiction."

And I could see from his face that he meant it, but that he could do little or nothing to stop himself. "Why am I here, Eddie?" I felt the dogs all around me. I smelled them. I heard their feet pacing in the cages. The hairs on the back of my neck had risen, and I felt their eyes on me.

"It's my business," he said, as if this would satisfy all the questions.

"You're a dogfighter?"

"I know," Eddie said, shrugging the idea off his shoulder. He looked around at all the cages, taking a few steps over to a milky white pit bull, letting it run its nose across his knuckles as he leaned down and put his hand to the fencing. "It's a horrible, brutal thing to fight dogs. It's bloody, it's mean, it's everything that is evil in this world." And he paused, looking back at me from the crouched position he kept by the dog. "But it's what I'm good at."

"This is what you do," I said, and I realized I was almost yelling. I realized I was scared and that it had been a long time since I had been scared. "I sell insurance," I said. "That is a normal job, that is a job you can tell people about. I don't want to know about a job like this."

"I don't want to know about a job like this either, but I'm good at it, really good," he said, standing now and rubbing his two hands together, his knuckles into the palm of his hand. "And I know people don't want to know that a person like me exists, but you know me, and there is no changing that."

I looked around at the dogs, at all the cages, at the ticked-out holes of sunlight coming through the walls. "You're lonely," I said.

"Yes." And he looked me straight in the eye, until I turned my eyes away.

I didn't know what to say. We had been friends once. But I didn't know if we were anymore. "How long have you been here, Eddie?" I asked

"A year."

"And you've been doing this the whole time?"

"I run fights on the weekend," he said. "I take a percentage of the winnings. I kennel a few dogs for a little extra cash. And, yes, this is what I've been doing." He walked over and put his arms down on the rim of the dog pit, his toes touching the boards where they met the earth. "Haven't you ever been good at something?" he asked, his eyes skipping over me before coming to rest on the floor of the dog ring again.

I thought about my marriage, I thought about my son. I thought about all the things in life that I had been a failure at, classes, jobs, women. But what I thought about most was that I was a father. "I have a son," I said.

Eddie made a low whistling sound; he leaned back from the walls of the pit, finding the shadows of a beam of wood above. "That is something special," he said.

But what I know now is that as much as I wanted it to work, my marriage failed, and in the midst of all this I lost my son. And that it has been life's cruelest agony knowing I will never have him back the way that I had always pictured, the way I was picturing him then, with Eddie leaned back away from the dog pit, and me dreaming about all the things in life that I thought I was talented in, that I thought I had natural skill in. And knowing this, having faith in myself and my son, I knew what Eddie was talking about when he said he was good at it, that there is little to nothing that would separate me or him from our desires.

Eddie took a moment and after a while he said, "A son." Giving the same slow whistle. "How old is he?"

"Eighteen months."

"And when was he born?"

"April first," I said.

Eddie looked off down the barn. I could see a door at the end of the building, it was open a crack, and within I saw a single mattress, a few pieces of clothes thrown out along the floor. "Fools' day," Eddie said.

I didn't see Eddie much after that. It was the last and only time I would go to his barn. And in the years that followed, I believe he became respected in his field, in his art, with his gift for terrible things. But I never saw it.

Instead we would meet from time to time at a bar, or to grab a little food, never more than three or four times a year. In short, we became as acquaintances become, simply tolerant of each other, civil toward each other, like a pair of old lovers when there is little but history left over. From what I gathered, Eddie was still a lonely figure, as he must be in his profession. And I can imagine that his time, like my own, was dedicated to the pursuit of that one desire which so easily and totally overcame his schedule.

Our relationship was one of convenience, one in which we avoided the things in our lives that made them ours. It went without saying that I would not ask Eddie about the things he did in that barn down south, and he would not ask me about my family. Instead we preferred to talk about the casual, convenient topics of men. Over burgers, we talked of football, we ran statistics back and forth across the table. We talked about baseball: batting averages, RBIs, home runs, stolen bases. And if it rained, or the fog settled into the hills, we talked of weather. It was that simple.

And then Eddie asked one day, while I sat close up to the bar with a pint in front of me, "Isn't your son's birthday coming up?"

I pulled back, straightening the crease of my pants with my hand. "Yes, the first of April," I said.

"I thought so."

Eddie didn't say anything after that, and I waited, trying to act nonchalant about the game on the television, but then I asked, "Why'd you think of that?"

"No reason," he said. "Just thinking."

And in a week I had my answer. I was in the kitchen talking over a few bills with my wife. It was my son's sixth birthday the next day, and the counter was covered with party decorations, streamers, and open cookbooks. My wife's hands were white with flour, and the kitchen had the smell of burnt sugar and lemon zest. I was talking with my hands, adding figures one at a time on my fingers, my wife with her hands buckled back on her hips, the whites of her fingers held out from her clothes, when the doorbell rang.

I knew who it was before I got there. What Eddie had asked me at the bar had been on my mind; his question hadn't sat right with me. It was an intrusion. It was an unnecessary part of our friendship, a malignant bump, threatening something, although what I did not know.

And so Eddie was there, a big smile on his face. It was the same smile I recognized from our time as boys, watching the golf balls sail high over the neighborhood, waiting for their time to fall. I said, "Eddie," following the tilt of his grin toward his arm, and then along his arm to his hand, in which I could see a leash, and at the end of this a small puppy. From the size of the puppy, I guessed it was a month old, maybe a week or two more. "What are you doing here?"

"I'm sorry," he said. "I wanted it to be a surprise."

"I'm surprised," I said flatly. "What are you doing here, Eddie?"

"I brought it for your son."

I turned to look back at the kitchen; my wife was standing in the door, looking at us. She was cleaning the flour from her hands with a dishtowel.

I pushed Eddie back and stepped out onto the front lawn, closing the door behind me. I raised a hand to my forehead. "I wish you would have said something, Eddie."

"It's a puppy," Eddie said.

"We don't want a puppy."

"How can you not want a puppy?"

I looked down at the dog at Eddie's feet. It had a blond coat, feathery and light, like newborn hair. "I'm sorry," I said, "but I can't take it."

Eddie took a step back. "You know what I do for a living," he said.

"I know."

"Well, it's not a nice thing."

"I know," I said.

"There is nothing glamorous about what I do. There are no rewards. It is about money, it has always been about money. And I'm good at it."

"Eddie, I can't—"

"It's a dirty business. But there are little things," he said.

"I can't be a part of this."

Eddie looked down at the dog. "You know what will happen to him if you don't take him. He might be the next champ," Eddie said. But he paused here, the look in his eye: downward, studying the grass at his feet, and then after a while he said, "Or he might not."

"I'm not going to be the one to decide that," I said. "You've got a sickness," I said. "It's not right." I took a few steps back toward my house, a distance opening up between us. Eddie was standing in the grass, his truck parked at the curb.

"It is the one good thing—" Eddie started to say.

"I can't, I have a family," I said. "These things you do, they don't wash off because you want to give up a dog." I watched him standing there. I couldn't take the dog. I didn't want the dog. But something in me wanted this dog, too. I wanted to know about Eddie, about the things he did. I wanted to know why he did a thing like dogfighting. How a person could be good at it. I wanted to help him. I wanted to understand. But in the end I knew that Eddie might have had a gift for the things he did, but so did I, and I was barricading against Eddie's to protect my own.

I didn't see Eddie anymore after that. And in the years that followed I thought about how I stood in my front lawn, watching him drive off around the corner. There were many opportunities to think about this moment. I thought about Eddie because my wife would leave me a few years later, when things were not as good as they were then.

And I thought about Eddie, because I realized after the fact, after I started coming home to an empty house, that all this time my wife had been lonely. She had been lonely in a way I did not see, in a way that I had not accounted for. And I thought about Eddie, because I wondered how having a dog in our lives could have helped to fill up that loneliness that I had never realized, and that had seeped slowly, but accurately, into the heart of ours.

I had always thought that being a good father meant working hard. I wasn't interested in becoming my own father, a man who had cheated on his wife, and left his children in the middle of the night. So I worked. I worked because it was something my father hadn't done. And in the early evenings I would come home to a house that I had bought, to a family that I supported, kissing my wife and giving my son a hug.

And then one day I came home to nothing. The house was in boxes, the divorce complete. I sat in the kitchen eating leftover pizza. The pizza was cold and I didn't even bother to warm it in the microwave. There was no sound in the house. I heard a few cars passing outside, fathers and mothers like me who had worked all day and now were returning to their families.

The pizza tasted like cardboard and what I really wanted to know was where I had gone wrong. I thought I was good at something and then one day, just like that, I found out the problem I was treating was not the problem at all. I was a good father. I thought I was doing the right things. I played games with my son on the weekend, talked to him about his homework, and drove him to school in the mornings. But what I thought was the solution was really the problem. And I didn't realize it then. I realized it later, that I had forgotten my wife along the way. A woman I loved, a person I thought was as solid as anything in life.

"What are you doing?" I asked once, coming home early to find her putting the last of the boxes in her car.

She kept on walking. "What does it look like?" she said.

And because I was pissed off, and tired, and I had come home early so that I might catch my son at school, before my wife picked him up, I said, "It looks like you're ruining my life."

To which she stopped, holding a cardboard box in her arms. "You ruined it a long time ago," she said.

What I said then was what I had said again and again in court, I said that I was working to make things better, for money, and for a better life for my son, better schools, better colleges, a bigger house for my wife.

"I never cared about that," she said, still holding the box in her arms. "Couldn't you see that I was lonely?"

"Don't do this," I said.

She put the box down in the back of her car. "It's too late."

And I could see then that she had already turned her back to me, that I wasn't even really standing there, and this wasn't her house anymore. I had forgotten about her, I had lost her, and by losing her I had lost my son. I never saw it coming. I thought I was good at something, like Eddie was good at running the fights. But in the end it didn't matter how good I was. I had forgotten about all the other things that come from the periphery to blindside a life.

It bothered me that Eddie had been arrested. It worried me. When I woke in the morning, the house felt as lonely and empty as it had the night before. I checked the news, but nothing was on it about Eddie. It was a Saturday, and for the most part, the news was about the college games, and the weekend weather. It made me think that nothing was wrong in the world, and that Saturday mornings were meant for sitting around without a worry.

But what I got to thinking about was how quiet my house was. And I wondered how quiet it must be in Eddie's cell, if he had talked with anyone, if he had slept? It made me feel guilty, sitting in my big house, with no one to talk to and a coffeepot brewing in the kitchen.

He had done a good thing for me once. In a strange way he had saved me on that field, with the bucket of golf balls in my hand, and a bat in the other, motioning with his hand, saying, "Keep going." I owed him something. Because it wasn't only me he had saved, it was my mother and my family. I knew it when I heard the faith in her voice as we drove out of Long Beach. One way or another, I knew that she had not lost me, that I was more hers than I was my father's. Eddie had been the one to protect us—whether he knew it or not—from all the bad things that were swirling high overhead in the tornado our lives had become.

I drove by the police station three times before I pulled over and switched the engine off. I didn't know what I would do when I got inside. I thought about all the scenes from the movies, the chain tied to the bars and the car pulling away into the night. I pictured the walls coming down, the dust rising off the rubble and Eddie stepping through.

I got out of my car and closed the door. The air had a touch of ocean dew, salty and crisp. The morning was cold around me, no clouds in the sky, and a pale yellow sun in the east. I walked ten steps up the sidewalk toward the station when the doors opened and Eddie walked out.

"Hello," I said.

He looked at me twice and then he said, "Hey," the grin on his face rising off him until all I could see were the round bulbs of his cheeks and a row of his teeth. "How are you?"

"I'm fine," I said, shaking his hand. He was older around the eyes, the worry lines along his forehead more pronounced. But I could still see the boy in there, the way he smiled and the way his eyes lit up when I pressed my hand into his. "I heard about you on the news," I said. "I'm here to break you out."

"Well, I'm out," Eddie said.

I watched him shiver a bit in the morning sun. He was wearing a black silk shirt, open at the neck, with a pair of chinos and leather dress shoes. A group of patrol cars left the station lot, and I could see the officers looking down the block toward us. "Come on," I said. "I'll drive you—" but I stopped and didn't finish my sentence. I didn't know where to drive him. I was going to say that I would drive him home. But I didn't know if he had one, or if he was still living in the back room of the barn, although he dressed like he had a place up on a hill somewhere.

"I'd like that," Eddie said. "Drive out by the ocean," he said after we had gotten in the car and driven down the block away from the police station.

We didn't say anything for a while after that. We just drove and after we climbed a hill and could see the ocean I asked him how he managed to get himself out of jail. I told him about what they had said on the news; how I had known it was him, how even without a name I knew.

"Criminals aren't the only ones who bet on dogfights," he said. "People with money bet on dogfights." We were parked in the thin line of spots along the beach in West Seattle, across the water from the tall buildings of downtown. "These people look after me."

I could see families out on the beach. The tide was out, and the children were looking in on all the pools left behind by the ocean. We got out of the car and walked down to the water. Eddie lit a cigarette and smoked, the wind taking the smoke over his shoulder and blowing it out along the beach. "It's peaceful here," he said.

"Yes," I said. I was tracking the course of a ferry out on the Sound. It made me sad to look at it. Many of my weekends had been spent on one of those boats, traveling across the water to see my son. "Eddie," I wanted to say, "why do you do it?" But I didn't. Eddie smoked the cigarette down to the filter and then flicked it out onto the water, where it floated on the green ocean.

"I like it out here," he said. "It's nice after a night inside."

"Are you ever scared?" I asked.

"I'm scared all the time," Eddie said. "But it's part of it."

The ferry was crossing directly in front of us, and I wondered if it was going across to my son.

"It seems," Eddie said, "that it's part of life. Being scared is just like anything else, you live with it long enough that you don't even feel it anymore. It's still there, but it becomes part of you."

I thought about this. I thought about a lot of things. Eddie took out another cigarette and smoked it down to the filter again. I wanted him to talk more, but he didn't, and after a while, after the ferry disappeared and the children had all climbed up off the beach, I nodded to Eddie and we went back to the car.

There was nowhere for us to go, so I drove back to my house. Eddie did not have a house on a hill. He lived on his land. But couldn't go back just yet. There was still the appearance of an investigation going on. The dogs were gone. He was sure of that. He wasn't worried, though; he said he still had a few matches to run off in the woods somewhere.

I thought he would say more, but when we got to my house I could see that he was tired and that it had been a while since he slept. I set him up in my son's room, letting him borrow a few things from me, a shirt, some pants. We didn't say anything. And as I closed the door to the room, I wondered how to save a man like Eddie or if he was even worth it.

The sky clouded over on the third day after Eddie came to stay with me. It snowed through the morning and into the afternoon, so thick and heavy that the schools were let out early and I could see the children in the fields throwing snowballs as I drove home.

I thought about my son across the water. I saw the flakes drifting heavy onto the ocean and the water absorbing them. I pictured the green and white ferry, the lights along the roof, and the snow falling through the lights. I imagined my son outside his mother's house. I thought of the clean expanse of her lawn, and the tracks they made as they crossed the grass.

It never snowed in Seattle and when I got home Eddie was standing in the living room with a framed picture of my son in his hands, looking out the window. "Look at this snow," he said, thrusting the picture out with his hand. "Can you believe it?"

I was looking at the picture. I couldn't believe it. "Eddie," I said, "what are you doing with that picture?"

"Oh," he said, as if he had just realized he was holding it. "I was looking at it." He tilted the picture up so that he could see it. "I wasn't going to ask."

"I'm divorced now."

Eddie put the picture back up on the mantle with the rest. We both stared out the window and I could see the snow falling and melting on the hood of my car, the ribs of metal beneath the aluminum showing.

"Was it you?" Eddie asked after a few minutes had passed.

I walked into the kitchen and grabbed a couple of beers from the fridge. "Here," I said, giving Eddie a beer and watching the snow come down. It was an almost perfect silence. There was the light flutter of the wind and the soft falling of snow. I heard Eddie crack his beer and we both sat back in the living room chairs watching the snow. And I didn't answer Eddie for a long time.

"Come out with me tonight," Eddie said. The snow had stopped falling and the roads had all been salted and plowed. Outside in the backyard I could see a white layer of snow stretching off into the darkness.

We had talked the whole afternoon, sitting in front of the windows, drinking beers and swapping stories. The snow outside was calm and clean, like polished stone, and where the light fell it shined back at us. It made me feel reckless, it made me feel like walking around all night in the snow, dragging my feet, breaking perfect things. "Yes," I said, "I'll go with you."

"Good," Eddie said. "Wear something warm."

"You're taking me to a fight, aren't you?"

"Yes," Eddie said.

I looked over at him. He was wearing one of the dress shirts I had loaned him, a yellow oxford, which he wore open at the collar. He looked a lot like me, the black stubble under the skin, the creases around the eyes.

"You called it a sickness," Eddie said.

We were in the kitchen, sitting in the nook, a row of beers lined up along the windowsill. I didn't say anything back to him. I just stared out across the table, looking him over, trying to figure out how a man like Eddie could be a man like Eddie. He didn't look like himself. He looked like someone else.

He could have been anyone, someone who led a normal life, who did normal things, capable of anything and nothing all at the same time.

The light was very dim when we pulled off the highway and went down into the woods. And as we drove, it was almost like the stars were absorbing the darkness. The snow opened up ahead of us and I could see as clearly as if it were day. Here and there I saw animal tracks leading off through the woods. They crossed the road several times, then led back into the shadows where the stars did not reach and the snow slipped away beneath the trees.

"Turn your lights off," Eddie said.

We were driving up a dirt road. In between the ruts, the snow was gray from the cars that had passed ahead of us. I turned the lights off and we saw the way the ground drifted away around us. Up ahead, everyone had gathered beneath the trees. Eddie rolled down his window to let the night in. I could hear the ache of the tires on the pressed snow. And as we got closer we could see and hear the popping of a fire in the trees. There was a group of cars. Dark sentinels of metal, waiting along the edges of the forest.

There were more people than I had thought would be at a dogfight. People who looked like me, wearing jeans and a wool jacket, people who looked like Eddie, their hair slicked back, a leather jacket I had let him borrow. There were women amongst the crowd, whites, blacks, Asians, Hispanics. And everyone watched us as we pulled up, our headlights off, the fire burning in the middle of the forest.

"Be cool," Eddie said.

We were sitting in the car. Eddie didn't say anything else. But I realized then that I was an outsider. That Eddie had been arrested and I was coming with him, days afterward, like a cop on the inside. "I'm cool," I said.

We got out of the car. The clap of the doors carried out into the forest. It was mostly birch, the white trunks of the trees coming through the snow, a low moist feel to the land. Once people saw that it was Eddie, they either turned away or kept staring. A few of them whispered to each other, looking at me.

A skinny man, wearing jeans and a padded flannel, walked over and shook Eddie's hand. "Strange weather," he said, looking up into the sky. A few small flakes were falling, dusting everything with a thin sheet of flour. "Is this your friend?" the man said, nodding in my direction, but looking Eddie in the eye.

"Raph, this is the sheriff," Eddie said. "Sheriff, this is Raph."

"You're not a cop?" the sheriff joked, laughing and then looking back at Eddie while he shook my hand. "You the one with the house in Seattle?"

"Yes," I said, realizing that Eddie had been setting this up all along, the sheriff's hands still cupping mine.

"It's good of you."

"He's a good person," Eddie said.

"Not too many of those," the sheriff laughed again. "Are there, Eddie?"

Eddie played with a clump of snow at his feet. "Not in this world, at least."

"You want to get it started then," the sheriff said, turning to walk back toward the crowd.

"Come on," Eddie said, waving his hand for me to follow.

I found a place on the outside of the crowd. The logs were cracking in the fire, red embers near the base where the snow had melted away. I watched as pieces of the fire drifted up into the night until I lost them amidst the stars. It was quiet at first. But then I heard Eddie call out for the money; he was taking it from everywhere, counting it. A shorter man standing nearby wrote down the figures as Eddie told him.

Eddie motioned me up, but I raised my hand and waved him off. The night felt black and limitless behind me, the snow falling across my shoulders and resting in my lashes. I could see the sheriff back in the trees, the thin line of his legs going out into the forest and then the way the crowd parted as he came back, leading his dog by the collar.

All I could see was the way the crowd pushed back to let him in. I saw the faces of the men and women across the circle, the orange light of the fire caught on them. The people in front of me fading out of sight, like the night behind me. They felt like ghosts, every one of them. The dark shadows of their heads drifting from one side to the other, as they watched the dog come through the crowd. I saw them whispering to each other, sizing up the dog for the fight. A man yelled out, his voice lost in the crunch of the snow and the rising excitement coming off the crowd. People were shifting now, the feeling building among them.

I saw another man enter. I did not know from where, but the crowd parted and came back together. I could see them in there together, one man facing the fire, the other with his back to it. Staring off at each other over the distance of the ring. The orange light catching on a face, on a back, each man like the opposing sides of the same man.

There were murmurings in the crowd. People were still calling out, making side bets. Eddie had the money in his hands. I could see it, the silver-green of the bills under the moonlight, snow falling gently amongst us all. The fire popped. I felt the night cold against my neck, the warmth of the crowd bringing me closer in. People were straining to see the dogs, leaning one way, then leaning the other, looking over the shoulders of their neighbors.

Eddie raised his hands. I saw the two men look up. There was a pause. The world slowed down, the snowflakes falling through it all, and then Eddie dropped his hands and I heard the weight of the dogs come together. There was a snarling, a brief sound of something tearing. But mostly, all I could hear was the sound their feet made on the snow, snuffling against each other, their paws scraping at the ground, and the heaviness of their bodies breaking apart on each other.

The dark backs of the crowd shifted in front of me. The light from the fire coming through at different angles until it seemed the crowd was swimming under water. I caught brief glimpses of the dogs moving, circling in on each other. I saw legs and torsos, a bloodied ear, the snow beneath them dotted now with hints of red. But they were quick, little clouds of steam rising off their coats. Little puffs of steam rising off us all, filtering up into the air above.

I looked for Eddie in the crowd. He was there, the fight mirrored in his eyes like a frozen pool. First dark then light, then dark again, as the fire flicked out into the crowd and the dark shapes of the dogs turned around and around in the midst of the ring, the blood dropping like water onto the snow.

Eddie was part of the inner circle, part of the edge of people who made it all. I watched from the outside, knowing that every turn of the dogs brought the crowd closer. I heard the dogs come together, the brief stutter step, fighting for balance, as they went up on each other, chest to chest. The crowd in front of me leaned left then right, a parting of the blackened heads. "Good and evil," my mother had once said, I was thinking about this, feeling daggers of cold at the tips of my ears.

I could see the dogs now, their chests against each other, the veins in their necks bulging as they twisted. It was a certain type of beautiful. A horrible type, a terrible type, but something, nonetheless, that I could not look away from. Something I kept watching although I knew I shouldn't. Watching as the dogs twirled, each one reaching for the other's life.

He that knoweth not good from evil is blameless.
Alma 29:5, *The Book of Mormon*

MORMONS IN HEAT

Don Waters

unlight flashes off chrome fenders, hitting Eli's eyes, blinding him. Eight motorcycles enlarge in the rearview mirror. Hot this morning, and warming up.

"More highway company," Eli says to Sutton, or to the steering wheel—whichever. This latest cache of sightseeing brochures is simply hypnotizing his partner. Sutton holds one by the edges, handling it like a delicate specimen. Splashed across another glossy pamphlet are different types of cacti.

"Forget about those, Sutton. Pay attention," Eli says. "You might learn something."

As the bikes approach, down goes Eli's window. He wants to side-glance that fine Harley craftsmanship. He wants to inhale, for a moment, the freedom.

"Chicks on motorcycles," Eli says, clenching the steering wheel. He can almost smell the armpits.

Leading the charge is a woman wearing square gunner's goggles. Eli clocks her at fifty, maybe fifty-five years old. Her cheeks are as red as her flapping bandana, cinched tightly around her skull, and she commands with her chin, which she holds high, with attitude. She veers into the oncoming lane, and Eli marvels at her glistening biceps.

"Elder Sutton," Eli says. "I am experiencing a vision."

Sutton doesn't say anything, not that the kid would. Eli sets his jaw. Why can't he appreciate this impromptu, middle-of-nowhere, wet T-shirt contest? The woman's custom-made turquoise low-rider has high, wide handlebars, and along with a rib-tight T-shirt, she and her companions wear sleeveless leather vests with cartoonish beavers on the back. Over the beaver's crazed, bloodshot eyes and squared buckteeth is the group's name, stitched in white: The Beaver Rockets.

When the last rider thunders past, she opens her throttle and her muffler explodes. Eli's eardrums palpitate. The women soon disappear into the shimmering highway, and again the desert is quiet, cleansed.

"Now that's the work of God," Eli says.

A bead of sweat disappears into Sutton's thin, wordless lips. If the kid has anything to say about what went down the previous night, in Eureka, he's saving it for the Celestial Kingdom.

"She was eighteen," Eli says, stating his case. "So just stop with your dumb look." And there is, always, a look. Sutton has a sharp, lordly nose that goes up whenever he's disappointed.

Eli, recalling what happened, grows tense and aroused. Desert daughters love opening their legs. He's learned that. He was two nights in Eureka when he met Emily, Emily Something-or-Other. The girl was a threat to any man with functioning testes: strawberry-flavored, bee-stung lips and a stomach as firm as watermelon rind. Last night, he fast-talked the girl out of a pair of rose-print panties. Then, this morning, shocked to realize his bareback, condomless mistake, he unleashed an incoherent but firm speech, insisting that she ingest six blue, oval, morning-after pills. Quite lucky, he lied to the pretty young stranger, he just so happened to work in pharmaceuticals.

"Guilty as charged," Eli says. "She was my Achilles. I admit it. Can we drop it?"

The missionaries flew out of Eureka, coursing along the furnace of Pancake Range. After a wrong turn back on 375, so-called Extraterrestrial Highway, Eli flipped a U and decided on 95 instead. He's aiming for distance, after all. Highway 95 is as flat and coppery as a penny.

Near Goldfield Summit, Eli stops to refuel at a highway gas shack. Prolonged drives make his muscles feel itchy and needled. He scours the trunk for his racquetball, something to squeeze. With all these Books of Mormon they ferry around, there's hardly space for luggage. A canister of motor oil has leaked all over one box. And, thanks to Sutton, the trunk is also filthy with brochures. Hundreds of them! Sutton collects and actually reads the stupid things, front to back. Eli's come across one from every county, an advertisement for Virginia City's Suicide Table, maps of isolated ghost towns. They've never been to Pyramid Lake or the Area 51 Mountaintop Lookout, and, Eli decides, they never will.

"Seen my racquetball?" Eli says, tapping Sutton's window. He mimes like he's rolling down an imaginary window.

Sutton throws a cold glance at him before returning to his brochure.

"Jesus. Let's not rush to the podium," Eli says.

Just look at the kid. Buttoned-up in a starched white shirt and a navy blue blazer. Scarecrow thin, size twenty-eight waist, Sutton could pass for thirteen. And his military-style haircut and glassine features certainly don't add any years. Oh, Sutton is Salt Lake City's foot soldier, all right. On hundred-plus days, during long hauls, he dresses in the required uniform. Even his goddamn name badge is always pinned on, per Church regulations.

Whatever sadist at HQ paired him with Sutton should be fired. After spending an entire year alone, the Church finally delivered Eli a partner. His partner turned out to be a dud. Eli wondered if he could ship him back. He was told that the kid was "shy." But Sutton isn't "shy." He's pathologically withdrawn. Sutton has only spoken a few dozen paragraphs, at most, but the sentences in those paragraphs aren't strung together. Each remark arrives startlingly, unattached to further conversation, each awkward syllable as unlikely as a snowflake landing in Death Valley.

When Sutton isn't looking, Eli scoops up an armful of pamphlets. He deposits them in a nearby trash can.

Eli settles behind the wheel, next to his monkish partner. Eli once read a magazine article about a man with severe epilepsy. Surgeons had to remove half of the guy's brain. When the patient awoke, he learned that the empty side of his cranium was filled with ping-pong balls. Three strands of light blond hair are caked to Sutton's forehead. Eli starts the car, wondering what's in there.

Eli has maintained a steady level of paranoia throughout his tour, sure that the higher-ups are watching him, keeping tabs. Hardwired in his DNA is the fuck-up gene. He understands this. It's always been his way. Surveillance could have started the moment he slaughtered his compulsory vows. Odd the way his sponsor, guy by the name of Jeremiah, never took him seriously after that.

Eli thinks about it from time to time. Perhaps he was a little too eager to enlist in the Church of Jesus Christ of Latter-day Saints. And maybe he was too pushy by insisting on a mission. After all, LDS didn't find him. He flipped open the yellow pages and he dialed them. It was either LDS or the Jehovahs, Eli didn't care, but a nearby LDS Ward called back first. After his endowment ceremony, Church officials must have been stumped. What to do with a thirty-year-old, jobless divorcé who's been living in his brother's basement? Save his soul, yes. But send him where?

Eli excels at putting distance between himself and his problems. Take what happened with Margo, his ex-wife, for example. One affair at his real estate office melted into the next. Margo found out and yeah yeah: divorce. That made *número dos*. Shit, he needed to get his act together. Not long after she walked out (actually, she made him leave), he began paying more attention to the Church's bland TV commercials. LDS appeared to be a wholesome enough choice.

And his decision worked—for a while. The Church kept him on track his first year out in the desert. Eli actually began believing in this stuff. The Books were all around him, so he began to read. Salvation through purity through family seemed okay by him. He was cruising through this missionary thing. He was giving away Books faster than headquarters could ship them FedEx.

Of course, there were a lot of smoky bars amid the brush weed. Also lots of press-on fingernails in those honky-tonks. After pounding pavement morning till night, there was little for Eli to do in those backward towns in the middle of Nevada. The red-haired, bow-legged woman worked for the Bureau of Land Management. Her job, she explained, was exterminating a particular species of invasive thistle. Not that it mattered. What mattered was the morning he awoke next to her, her salty toe lodged in his mouth.

His budding faith incrementally flaked away, bleached by the sun, stripped off by harsh desert wind. Nothing was left for Eli back in Texas, in Houston, his hometown. Rather than abandoning his mission, he stayed the course. He remained in the desert. Besides, everything was all expenses paid. Looked at properly, he was enjoying an extended, two-year vacation.

All he had to do was dispense the Books. The Church was always sending him more, and still more, goddamn Books. He scattered them in places named Jackpot, Battle Mountain, and Manhattan, Nevada.

Highway speed signs read seventy, so Eli goes eighty-five. He wants half the state between him and this morning. That feat in Eureka has that one-two-three strikes ring to it. He thinks the stunt is grounds for excommunication. Eli mashes his heel into the accelerator.

Mud lakes and sand flats skate past the windows. A sea of sagebrush blurs into silver-green fog. Sun fries Eli's knuckles. Augusts are miserably hot. Nevada is long empty roads, etched ridgelines, so much open blue.

Plastic grocery bags trapped by sage introduce the town of Amargosa, a minor highway pit stop cuddled by low hills. Eli slows down when he realizes the town is crawling with bikers.

Eight lady joyriders on a lonely desert highway are a welcome sight. But sixty-plus middle-aged women dangling from ape-hanger handlebars, their modified Hogs parked along the town's half-mile drag, make for an unexpected, discombobulating weirdscape. Amargosa is firing on all cylinders. It's as though he and Sutton have penetrated some sort of menopausal biker pod. Drug-thin gals in tight-tight tees idle next to large-boned women squeezed into jeans. Frontward denim pouches hold beery guts. Some of the women look terrifying, notably the gray-haired lady wearing the "Priestess" T-shirt.

Eli pulls to the side of the road, stunned.

"We have to keep driving," Sutton says unexpectedly. The kid blinks like there's sand in his eyes.

"You work," Eli says. "Did I forget to wind you?"

Sutton reaches for the gearshift, but Eli slaps at his knuckles. "Jesus H," Eli says. So many women, he wants to say. He says instead, "You are the worst evangelical I've ever met." He points out the window. "These are potential converts."

A Hi-Top Motel sits across the street. Three big-breasted women are loitering on the upper balcony. They're huddled around a ripped-open twelve-pack of beer. One of them waves, and Sutton blinks spastically.

Each small, desert town is a slo-mo rerun of the previous dusty stop, full of tedious chitchat and hundreds of miles before interesting new faces. It isn't a hard decision to make.

"We're staying the night," Eli says. "Too many hours behind the wheel," he says. "Plus, my heels ache." He cracks his large toe.

In the motel's air-conditioned office, Sutton plucks brochures from a plastic rack. Not surprisingly, he's holding up his nose. The kid scrutinizes one brochure with a frog across its cover. He swipes several others and slips them into his blazer.

Thanks to the flock of bikers, it's the Hi-Top's last room. Every Hi-Top has the same flavor: bolted down TVs and cheap sunset wallpaper. This particular room smells like a difficult case of athlete's foot. Eli thinks it would be nice, just once, to open the door onto an ocean view. Oh to be able to inhale eucalyptus.

Sutton sheds his blazer and retreats to the bathroom, taking his brochures with him. He slams the door.

Most baby-faced nineteen-year-olds are awarded the primo assignments, two years' traveling around Argentina, Switzerland, the tropics. Eli, on the other hand, knew he was eleven years past the expiration date. A different set of rules applied. On the day he was given his Divine Assignment, he was escorted into a back room of his local Ward. He was handed a worn map of Nevada, keys to a used Toyota, and a credit card good at any Hi-Top Motel in the southwestern United States. The Church, he was quietly informed, was a majority shareholder.

The small parking lot is overrun with custom-made motorcycles. Eli stands gaga at the window. His lips are brackish from the long, face-melting drive, and he feels dehydrated, which always gives him a buzz. Mufflers rumble distantly.

The Beaver Rockets. He's never heard of the motorcycle club, or whatever they are. He spots the woman from the highway, Ms. Biceps, Ms. Red Bandana, holding court from the seat of her low-rider. Her bandana has disappeared, revealing licorice-black hair fashioned into a mullet, business in the front and party in the back. Others listen as she puffs on a cigar. The next time she lifts the stogie to her lips, clutching it, Eli's knees weaken. His thoughts drift. He imagines a life similar to hers, a life beside hers, a life without rules— gnats in his eyes, unpaid bills, arrest warrants with his name on them.

Eli's only successful conversion happened his first week, a Western Hemisphere record. Only one other missionary ever saved another soul within the first seven days. But that was in 1977, in Phuket, Thailand, a different landmass, with completely different standards. So as far as Eli is concerned, it doesn't count. He wins.

For his record breaker, he brought around a copper mine foreman from Cactus Springs named Ted Ringle and his non-English-speaking wife, Tanja. Ted Ringle explained, with a wink, that his new bride was mail-ordered and arrived via Turkish freighter.

Anyway, Eli was out to cut his teeth. He had something to prove. Fresh off a divorce, anointed with a purpose, he was soldier-ready.

For a week he showed up at the Ringles' apartment with Mini-Mart donuts. After reading the usual, best-of, all-time-greatest LDS hits from the

Book, Eli would bow his head and say, "Let's pray." Good-spirited Ted Ringle would nod while his Slavic wife smiled. Bless her heart: she understood nothing. And whenever Ted Ringle posed one of the Big, Unanswerable Questions, Eli would pinch his chin and say, "That is interesting. That is very interesting." Eli learned the importance of validating without answering.

The newlyweds for Eli were a coup. They were everything the Church wanted, a happy, healthy couple on the verge of procreation. But after his first converts, Eli's luck ran out.

So he fine-tuned his advance. He tailored his routines. Each mark required a fresh approach. Conversion was a delicate con. Assumed godliness, thankfully, commanded a modicum of respect. If he had God on his bench (or when others thought he might have God on his bench), they sometimes listened.

Where to find the people, the hearts and minds, the converts? He attended town hall meetings, county fairs, and small-time rodeos. It took patience to sniff out the most attentive audiences.

Lonely old farts were a great discovery. They couldn't hurry away. On Saturday evenings, state-run nursing homes rolled out the bingo and pinochle, and Eli would show up, his face red and raw from having just shaved, and he'd wander around pretending to be a lost grandson.

Naturally, old folks enjoyed their tall tales, too. Eli began to loathe the countless variations on World War II, childhood in Kansas, how-things-were yarns. He was shown plenty of embroidery and too much needlepoint. Then he began noticing the vultures, vultures of all sizes, during his long treks around the state. Their talons were always curled around power lines, perched as though recharging. The ugly birds fed off the weak. They too took advantage of soon-to-be carcasses.

Eli cooled it on the geriatrics. He returned to rural ranches and neighborhood grids. Dressed as he was, in a navy blue spokesperson getup, a square, white name badge over his heart, he was a spot-on giveaway. The sight of him inspired grimaces. Women were nicer than men, and mothers he could talk to. But whenever one of them balked, he'd let loose with the scare routine.

"War, Ma'am," he'd begin. "This is war. And you and your lovely daughter here are in a foxhole. A hot bullet rips through her eye. That creamy scarlet hole is a horror show. That's right. Her eye hangs down her face like some broken jack-in-the-box coil. Bombs are concussing. Your daughter is moaning. So do you take Him into your heart? *Do you then?* To save your daughter's eternal soul?"

Rumor has it there are special departments in Hell set aside for the Sons of
Perdition. If only Eli believed in quote-unquote Hell, if he just believed in
quote-unquote the Sons of Perdition, he might be frightened away from his
boozy mistakes. He was counting on the Church to clear the brush from his
yard. Hellfire scare tactics work on others. Why not him? He knows officials
in SLC wouldn't be pleased with his antics. Hell, they'd probably throw a
few aneurysms.

Eli shuffles across the grubby motel carpet. He taps the wood of the bathroom door with his uncut fingernails.

"We haven't even touched these new boxes," Eli yells through the door.
"What do they expect us to do? Eat them?" He's referring to the latest ship-
ment. "I'm going out. Want me to grab some local leaflets? The usual?"

He hears the sound of a toilet flush. As usual, Sutton doesn't respond. Eli
presses his palm to the door. He doesn't like Sutton. He doesn't understand
him. Still, he feels somewhat protective of the kid. It's the same disturbing
feeling that overcomes him whenever his brother leaves Eli alone with his
retarded, helmet-protected nephew.

In the bathroom of the local Bongo Burger, Eli squeezes out drops of
lingering guilt piss, inhaling the medicinal stench off the urinal puck.

He sets a gold-embossed Book on the toilet's lid in the first stall. He puts
another in the adjoining stall. He leans one more against the faucet. Custom-
ers will have to move them. People love free things, right? Lately, this has
been Eli's general strategy. Who cares if some anonymous face then pops
a Book or two in the trash? Not his problem. He's got all these goddamn
Books. HQ keeps sending him these fucking Books.

There's not a single cloud in the sky, and an eastern breeze drifts in, carrying traces of smoldering sage. Sweat that hasn't absorbed into Eli's sacred
garments settles in a wet sack around his groin. He's in a constant fight against
rashes. He calls the long funny underwear, which wraps his torso and ends at
his knees, his Brigham Sweatbox.

Eli finds two metal newspaper boxes on Amargosa's strip of boarded-
up storefronts. The *Daily Wart* sits beside a national newspaper with week-
old headlines. He shovels a few Books on top of the national paper and the
spring-loaded door slams shut. Yet another lazy tactic—but whatever.

As he's propping the other box open, a motorcycle appears alongside the
curb. Its rim is polished to a mirror finish. Ms. Former Red Bandana, Ms.
Cigar Toker, Ms. Woman of the Highway, holds a bottle of beer.

"Toss me a paper?" she says to Eli. Two lime-green eyes, hooded by wild,
untended eyebrows, overwhelm him. He stares at her like he's stupid.

"A newspaper, please," she says again. She points at the local, the *Daily Wart*.

He fumbles, handing one over. Up close, the woman's triceps are stunning. Deep ravines line the backs of her arms. Her crinkly neck is absurdly out of place with the rest of her, or vice versa.

"Tina Pennybocker," she says to Eli in a rasp. "Tina was born in Amargosa."

She folds back the paper, and he's shown a thumbnail photo of a brunette with spectacular bangs. The brunette's hair crests like a breaking wave. It's a face only a mother could love. Unfortunately for Tina Pennybocker, her photo lies in the center of the obituaries.

"Tina's family plot is down the road at the cemetery," the woman tells him. "A damn shame the nearest minister lives in Tonopah. He called Joanna. Said he can't make it. None of us have much to do in the way of what he's about."

She runs her thick fingers through her mullet and takes a swig of her beer. There's a sudden thirst in Eli's throat. His uvula aches. Dusty goggles hang around the woman's furrowed neck, nestled inside loose cleavage, a soft, flabby, freckled wonderland.

His shirttails aren't tucked. Mustard stains decorate his collar, and his dress shoes are laughably tattered. His LDS name badge is long gone too, misplaced somewhere at Massacre Lake during an all-night bonfire with three Paiutes. He looks anything but pious. Still, getting interested, he glances again at the woman's low-cut landscape.

He says, "Actually, you're in luck." He places a Book on her rhinestone-encrusted saddleback. "I might be able to help," he says. "Eli," he tells her.

The woman's smile shows off a brown front tooth, a shade darker where it meets her gums. Eli always likes people better when they're a little broken.

"Your name?" he asks, and he gently takes her beer bottle. Church doctrine dictates absolutely no alcohol.

"Jane," the woman says. Then she adds, as though it's her surname, "from Wyoming."

Church doctrine also states no fornication outside the sacred bonds of marriage.

"The Lord visits us in unexpected ways," Eli says to Jane-from-Wyoming. He swallows a mouthful of piss-warm beer. That mouthful tells Eli he'd very much like another, and soon.

Nights like this, shrouded by amber lamplight, the idea of a next day does not exist. Jane-from-Wyoming chisels him down to basics. With her, he is just muscle, nerve, and nuclei. All night, motorcycles roam the street, their exhaust notes like Gatling guns, upending Eli's whiskey-sugared dreams.

Their brief get-to-know-you joyride into the tan hills beyond Amargosa segued into shots, cigarettes, and nibbles off of her briny Wyoming neckline. Jane-from-Wyoming smells of seaweed, and when he melts into her large, lumpy breasts, he imagines swimming in an oil slick. Plaquelike odor rises from her decaying tooth, and her expert tongue probes like a lizard's.

In the middle of the night, Eli jolts awake. He sits upright. His throbbing erection pushes against the heavy bedspread. He is insanely thirsty; did he eat a sand castle? The room looks wicked, strange, as though he's seeing it for the first time through smudged blue lenses. Odd, too, the last time his rectum throbbed a doctor was checking for a leaky appendix.

Sutton marches out of the bathroom in tighty-whities. He wears only one sock. A bright fluorescent bulb illuminates steam billowing from the kid's shoulders. Like always, he's been showering, his favorite pastime when Eli's busy. Sutton pulls a cover from the other bed and yanks it into the bathroom.

Eli pinches up the sheet and studies his bedmate's cream cheese body. Varicose veins line her thighs. He might as well be looking at a map of the country's interstate highway system. He is horror-struck. He is so turned on.

A night with Jane-from-Wyoming isn't life changing, but he will have to reevaluate things. At one point, he was sort of tossed in the air and thrown against the headboard, which accounts for his aching jaw. It feels like it's been broken and reset. The floor, strewn with condoms, is a spring break shoreline. Jane-from-Wyoming snores like a trucker.

She rolls over, taking the rest of the sheets with her. Eli freezes. How to turn the troublesome thing off? He needs a switch. She rolls again, and her hand lands on his sternum. As if sensing its animal heat, her fingers wander downward. She steers him like he's a joystick, a game, an object. He is powerless under her weight.

In the morning, Sutton struts out of the bathroom, showered, dressed, and toothpasty. The knot in his tie is a perfect Windsor. The sight of his partner's early morning efforts rouses Eli's nausea.

"We're leaving," Eli says to Sutton. Eli rolls out of bed and begins picking clothes off the floor. There's a window in the bathroom. It's small, but they'll fit through. For some reason, Sutton starts arranging brochures on the other bed, fanning them out, situating them . . . just so. The kid probably read each one—fascinating!

"Are you showing the place?" Eli asks, growing more irritated. He can't find his necklace, a gold crucifix, his Grapapa's.

Jane-from-Wyoming, bless her, tumbled out of the room before dawn. And she never returned. Eli parts the drapes. Beaver Rockets are gathering in the parking lot. He quickly shuts them. Sutton hovers with that nose of his.

"I don't need your jury-foreman attitude," Eli says. "I'm in the middle of a crisis. My grandfather's necklace. It's gone."

"You told her you're giving the sermon," Sutton says.

Eli snorts. How many lies has he used, and with less muscular women? He throws open the end table, and inside is a new Bible. Those goddamn Gideons. Eli's smacked with admiration. They are on top of it.

"That's pent-up sperm talk," Eli says to Sutton. "I'm not giving any sermon. In fact, we're leaving. Right now."

"You said," Sutton says. "I heard you through the door."

"Hallelujah, you talk," Eli says. "A miracle."

This new pain feels like studded plates pressing into his temples. Not to mention, Eli's left incisor is chipped. A quart of Blue Label: just about the right amount for him to tell Jane-from-Wyoming he'd give a sermon. Eli detests public speaking. Anxiety logjams the sentences in his throat before they ever reach open air.

Chewing on the side of his thumb, Sutton paces a figure eight. His willowy shoulders slump forward, and he looks exactly like the teenager that he is. The Church dispatches its lambs when they're only nineteen, the crucial years, when a young man's hard-on is at its hormonal and optimal peak. But Eli doesn't think Sutton ever ties off his own rope. They've shared the same room every night for the past one hundred fifty nights, their pillows mere yards apart, and Eli's never seen movement, or heard rustling, underneath Sutton's sheets.

Eli realizes he's laced his shoes wrong. He skipped holes on both feet. Already it's a horrible start.

Sutton says, "We're going to that woman's funeral."

Another divorce, followed by this missionary charade, barrels of bad decisions, and now that Sutton is finally speaking, he's high-minded. The total prick.

"I like you better when you're broken," Eli says. "Please shut up."

A wolfish glint lights up the kid's eyes. His shoulders pull back and his spine straightens. He charges over. Eli raises his arms in self-defense. But rather than a fist, Sutton comes up with a pair of size 16 panties. They're yellow. He squashes them into Eli's nose.

"I know," Eli says. He sits on the bed. "I know, I know. This is worse than the hooker in Mesquite, isn't it?"

A large contingent of beaver insignias has colonized the Hi-Top's parking lot. Eli's stomach drops when he sees this. More arrived during the night. Sutton shoves Eli out the door, where Jane-from-Wyoming is waiting next to her turquoise bike. Frayed denim cutoffs accentuate her strong, cellulite-padded thighs.

"You clean up," she says. Jane-from-Wyoming looks rested, considering.

"Splashed water in my eyes," Eli says.

Jane-from-Wyoming pats her hump seat. "Minister."

Eli hates her. Eli adores her. He feels chapped bodywide.

"I said," she says. Her lip rises like a curtain, parading her ugly tooth.

As he straddles the seat, Sutton thrusts a Bible at him. It's from the end table, those overachieving Gideons.

The kid says to him, "Do good."

A meandering motorcade has formed on the street. They drive to the front, assuming the lead. The smell of burnt asphalt yields to whiffs of peppermint coming off Jane-from-Wyoming's shampooed mullet.

A beat-up hearse soon rolls into town. Fingers point down the road, directing it to the lead spot, where Eli's afforded a first-rate view, beyond tinted glass, of a plain brown coffin. He's unable to attach any feelings to the thing. To him it's just a large box, nothing more. But he is startled when the driver suddenly leaps out, both thumbs raised, smiling wildly. Short, Latino, the guy's dressed in orange sweats. His socked feet are shoved into a pair of checkered, slip-on Vans with demolished heels. He wears them more like flip-flops, scraping the pavement as he walks. Obviously, the guy is thrilled to be around so much fringed leather and feathered hairdos. Eli's relieved when he sees Sutton, behind the wheel of the Toyota, at the rear of the motorcade.

"I apologize for taking advantage," Jane-from-Wyoming says over her shoulder. She squeezes his knee. "You're a man of the cloth. I understand. But there are times a woman needs a mercy fuck. Tina was a dear friend."

Eli says, for lack of anything, "Glad I could help."

"The bite marks will disappear," Jane-from-Wyoming adds. Before he can respond, she stabs the air with her fist.

Engines rev, the deep reverberations begin. Eli's brain rattles in his skull.

His testicles vibrate on the seat. He imagines this is how war sounds, mechanized and unrelenting.

The deafening swarm follows the hearse a quarter mile and turns down a dirt road, ending at Amargosa's cemetery, nothing more than a powdery scrap of land dotted with scorched weeds. Dominating an acre's worth of headstones is a granite obelisk engraved with the dead woman's name: PENNYBOCKER. It overlooks a sad excuse for a river. Eroded banks hold gray pools of stagnant water. Etched thickly at the base of the monument is the father's generic name, Edward William. Eli does the math on him. Dead twelve years. Her mother, Helen Douglas, followed seven years later. Plenty of room for Tina's four easy letters.

Four women with arms as burly as Jane-from-Wyoming's wrestle the casket from the hearse. They throw it onto a hoist perched over a freshly dug grave. The driver claps, slipping out of his shoe.

Eli can't find Sutton anywhere in the crowd. As the women gather, angling for position, shoulder to shoulder, he wonders how many more predicaments, how many more can he stomach? Deliver a sermon? Eli doesn't even know how, or why, Tina Pennybocker of Amargosa died. He figures he'll just say, Bless this, Bless that, Too bad for Tina, rev the Toyota's four cylinders, and haul ass out of town—next stop Elko.

These expectant eyes might as well be dentist drills. His heart beats in his throat, nearly sealing it. And his stomach squirts up a teaspoon's worth of bile onto the back of his tongue. He is one hundred percent hangover emotional. Noxious exhaust fumes from the bikes swirl, and the glare off some lady's tachometer makes his eyes water.

Eli struggles, and he says, "The sky is hustling with light."

Hustling with light?

He finds faith difficult, if not impossible. Sure, he'd like to believe. When he signed the forms, when he joined the Church, Eli thought it might get the ball rolling. But it didn't. It hasn't.

He peers out over the mob of women. Pale morning light reddens above the hills. It's a commanding land, that's certain. Heat and infinite, forever sky. The West does have the best views. Nothing is more sacred than the sun, he thinks, spotlight on us all.

"Let us look up," Eli says. And a few naive women actually do. His throat catches when he says, "Up at the sky." A sun-glare tear drips down his cheek. Jane-from-Wyoming, misinterpreting, lays her hand between his shoulder blades.

"It's not easy," she says, "I know." Eli briefly recalls the sensation of cold keys whipping his bare ass.

There's a tug on Eli's shoulder, and Sutton steps forward, his sleeves rolled up, lips pursed, his nose raised high. The teenager clutches the brochure with the frog on the cover. He stands before the women assuredly, as if, Bible open, he's behind a pulpit.

"Kid," Eli says.

Sutton stares back at him coolly, and then calmly, reading from his trifold brochure, he begins.

"Amargosa is home to one of the rarest forms of life in the world. Here, along a twelve-mile stretch of river, off Highway 95, down the road from Bud's World-Famous Sausages on a Stick, lives the Amargosa toad." The kid pauses, scanning the vellum paper with his thumb. The sun turns his hair entirely white.

"Amargosa toads are chubby and covered with warts," he goes on. "They're often different colors, beige or olive green, and always have a trim stripe decorating the back. Distinct for webbed toes, for tinted humps, and for black spots on its belly, this ugly but humble creature is truly one of nature's more peculiar sights."

Eli's clenched teeth begin aching.

"I didn't know Tina Pennybocker," the kid says, folding the brochure. "I didn't know there was a Tina Pennybocker until recently. But when I look at you, her friends, the grieving, it's clear that Tina Pennybocker was like the Amargosa toad." One woman releases a high gasp. The kid quickly says, in conclusion, "She was rare. Tina was special."

This draws appreciative sighs. Eli spots the Toyota out of the corner of his eye. He maps out a tiptoe escape route. Nearby, a breeze spins up a dust devil. Space opens up behind him, and he takes a step backward.

Tina's casket is lowered into the grave via steel crank, dusted soon after by fistfuls of dirt. Teary women line up and take turns bidding farewell.

Eli shuffles, he bobs, he weaves. While hiding behind a broad-shouldered woman, a safe distance from all the sobbing, he watches Jane-from-Wyoming tug at her shirt and scratch her collarbone. Wrapped around her thick, dinosaur-sized neck is a gold necklace, a crucifix. His. Grapapa's.

Eli says, "Oh, sweet fucking Christ."

A woman turns and shushes him. There's a chrysanthemum tattooed inside the rim of her ear, the only flower at the service.

Eli snaps his fingers, trying to signal Sutton. Instead, Jane-from-Wyoming notices him hiding behind one of her friends. A look of confusion spreads across her face and then rearranges into benevolence. Jane-from-Wyoming half-smiles. That tooth, so imperfect, so him.

THE BONES OF HAGERMAN

Mitch Wieland

Late afternoon Ferrell and his ex stretch and yawn, finished with their siesta and a little bit more. Ferrell Swan's retirement improved greatly last fall when Rilla drove from Ohio to his cabin in southwest Idaho, her one-week stay stretching through the bitter months of winter and into spring. It's been a tenuous truce to be sure, but somehow each dusk they manage to count small blessings, neat whiskeys in hand.

Clothed, he and Rilla step onto the long covered porch. Beyond the reach of his hundred sage flat acres, lazy white smoke billows on the air, obscuring the craggy peaks of the Owyhees. Ferrell can smell the familiar scent of burning bunchgrass.

"What's on fire?" Rilla asks.

"Places north, like Melba. Each spring farmers and ranchers burn their ditch banks and fields. Gets rid of the weeds."

"Don't people have to breathe?"

Ferrell only shrugs. Over the course of her extended visit, Rilla's love affair with his beloved Idaho has been rocky at best. While struck deeply by his high desert land and its host of wild things, she's found fault with the state's nineteenth-century ways.

"So what now, Ferrell? We've eaten lunch, done the deed, napped for hours. What's left for the day?"

As if God wants to answer personally, Ferrell hears something he can't make out: a faint muffled rumble, a hollow thudding, small and almost lost in all that space.

"What the hell?" Rilla says.

"I have no idea."

To the west, from out of the haze, Ferrell spots a gathering of smoke, hovering low. In short order he realizes it's not fire, but the drift and rise of dust. He squints hard into the horizon, excitement like helium in his veins. His neighbor has long claimed mustangs roam the adjoining public lands, but the only proof Ferrell's seen has been a solitary horse skull on the ridge. *Ghosts*, he says when Cole mentions the herd. *Spirits of the purple sage*. The roiling dust grows closer, and the ground begins to tremble—as if, he imagines, doom itself bears quickly down.

"Speak, Ferrell," Rilla says, her voice more than a little concerned.

"Mustangs," he says. "Coming fast."

Like forming from the dust itself, the horses take shape: wide, white eyes and flared nostrils, flying manes. Their forelegs blur as hooves reach and drive, and Ferrell pictures those big hearts clanging in their sweat-dark chests, that old Spanish blood churning hot. The mustangs gallop straight for the cabin, but veer right at his outer fence, changing direction with a single mind to run lengthwise past the porch. They're ruffians, Ferrell decides, not scraggy drifters like expected. These brutes are bulky and stout, their necks and flanks scarred from hooves and teeth, tails and manes a tangled mess. It's not freedom he's watching but something other, as though these beasts rush toward their own deaths and can't wait to arrive. It isn't grace and glory at all, but the downer Apocalypse.

The last stragglers blister past, blown breaths audible above their pounding hooves. Ferrell takes a final glimpse at sinewy flanks and streaming tails, then just sees dust in the air, the whole thing ending the way it began.

"Good Christ," Rilla says, the air still reverberating though the mustangs have gone.

"More like the devil, I'd say."

Ferrell leans both hands on the porch rail, rather spent after the personal horse stampede. Behind him Rilla sits in her rocker, too stunned, it seems, to offer further comment. He hears the copter before he spots it, the thing coming low and fast, blunt nose angled down. He understands at once why the herd was running.

"What's going on, Ferrell?"

"Bureau of Land Management."

"Tell me they're not shooting them." Rilla shakes her head. "I swear this place is in a time warp. Why don't they just kill everything and get it over with?"

Ferrell has to side with Rilla on this one. He himself has never quite recovered from witnessing coyotes hunted from the air, the drone of the little white plane as it scanned the public lands, the sharp report of the rifle. When the plane had gone he and Rilla hiked the desecrated ground, kneeling at each dead coyote they came upon, offering meager prayers. Up close, the animals were more beautiful than Ferrell could bear, and Rilla cursed openly the concept of shoot on sight. "Fuck the fucking ranchers," she shouted. "This is public land, and I'm part of the public too." Before bed that night she wrote three dozen protest letters, mailed them next morning to all manner of state and government officials, knowing she might as well have asked Ferrell to piss into a gusting wind.

In the distance the low growl of Cole's Dodge diesel, the sun glare bright off the polished black. The truck pulls fast into Ferrell's drive, as if Cole's been out chasing mustangs himself, and slides to a stop.

"Ghosts my ass," he yells, jumping from the cab. "Did you see them?"

"Hard to miss."

Ferrell watches Cole's young wife ease down from the high passenger seat. Before he can offer to help, Rilla is beside the truck. Ferrell knows Melody's due in six weeks and two days, with Rilla set to serve as midwife, but wishes he didn't know the baby's father is Rilla's grown son Levon, the boy visiting more than his mama on his last pass through the state.

Harrison Cole takes the porch steps three at a time. A big, strapping man, he gives Ferrell a bear hug worthy of its name. "Damn, that was something," Cole says. "I bet there was sixty of those sons of bitches, maybe seventy."

"What was that helicopter?" Rilla asks, escorting Melody up the porch steps. Rilla guides the lovely woman to a rocker and helps her sit.

"Once a year, BLM officers round up mustangs and cull the herd. It's part of their management policy."

Ferrell bites his tongue. He cringes whenever the term management is used with nature. In his time out west, he's seen the BLM manage public lands via blanket grazing permits to ranchers, seen cattle and sheep eat the chaparral down to nothing, leave behind trampled desert and muddied streambeds.

"What do they do with the ones they cull?" Rilla asks.

"There's an annual mustang auction, up near Boise. Most go for a couple hundred bucks."

"Let's buy a mustang, Ferrell," Rilla says. "Let's bring one home."

"But you haven't ridden in years."

"But I rode for years, Ferrell. It's not like you forget."

Ferrell gazes across the empty miles stretching from his porch. He sees himself tall in the saddle, riding the range like outlaws of old. It's never dawned on him to actually buy a horse, to roam at will the vistas he so dearly loves. From the cobwebby shelves of his mind comes Ferrell's long-dead father, how the man watched every cowboy matinee ever shown, all those TV Westerns where heroes drew first and bad guys died without bleeding. His father, despite his fascination with horses and the West, never once climbed into a saddle.

"Well, Ferrell?" Rilla says. "Will you buy a girl a mustang?"

"Can you teach a boy to ride?"

As for bloodlines, both Ferrell's grandfathers were farmers, as were his legion of uncles, tough men who worked brutal hours, their bodies busted up bad from life in the fields. In high school, Ferrell's daddy chose the vocational route, figured standing all day at a drill press or lathe beat hustling butt on the farm, beat bucking tons of hay, or plowing from first light to good dark. But his daddy was a flesh and blood contradiction, and despite his denial of the farmer's life, he dreamed daily of the West, of cowboys riding beneath the high, hot sun. At the time it was beyond Ferrell how the poor man could transform a cattle drive into something other than days of heatstroke and an aching ass.

"At least a tractor won't buck you off," Ferrell said once at dinner. "A John Deere won't kick you dead."

"You don't understand the way of the saddle."

"And you do?"

"I've learned much from the old boob tube."

"You're romanticizing those stupid shows," Ferrell said, a notion recently picked up from his ninth grade literature class. "You've seen too many Roy Rogers flicks."

His dad looked down at his plate. "You'll have dreams someday," he said. "You'll understand what sustenance they provide."

Five days after the mustang roundup, Ferrell drives the seventy miles to Boise with Rilla at his side. Having his ex in the truck recalls their enthusiastic college years, all those mornings driving Rilla to campus in his beat-up Ford, the dizzying things she did in the shadows of the cab. Most days he can't believe the decades he's known this woman, how many deeply private acts have passed between them.

Near the airport, Ferrell turns due east across the sage flats, following the handmade signs to the auction. He parks among the other trailers, and follows Rilla to the formidable holding pens, rough-hewn planks bolted onto eight-by-twelve railroad ties.

"Guess they don't want them escaping," Ferrell says.

Rilla peers between the slats of the first enclosure. "Oh, damn, Ferrell, that breaks my heart."

On the far side of the pen, dozens of horses cluster together, looking remarkably less wild than the last time Ferrell saw them. Up close the mustangs seem even larger, capable of doing great harm to his rickety self. Most horses look like the prisoners they are, defeat glazing their eyes, but a few still snort and prance, refusing to believe in the fence between them and the open land. All have big, black numbers dangling from their necks, and Ferrell sees the corresponding numbers on posters nailed outside the pens. He also notes the BLM brand seared onto the left flank of each horse.

The next hour's spent wandering pen to pen, Rilla naming the strengths and weaknesses of the horses, pointing out stifle joints and gaskins, fetlocks and cannon bones, pasterns and the rest. As he studies the mustangs Ferrell recalls the fossil beds of Hagerman, those first nomadic horses now prehistoric bones behind dusty glass. At the last holding pen, five minutes before the silent auction closes, Rilla grabs Ferrell's arm.

"That's ours," she says.

"Which one?"

"The silver sorrel."

"The what?"

"That deep red mare, with the gray mane and tail. Between the buckskin and the paint."

Ferrell finds the one in question, the horse looking much like the other hundred or so he's just seen. "What's so special about her?"

"See how she moves, Ferrell? See how her withers line up with her back?"

"That's good?"

"That's great."

In no time flat Ferrell is a new horse owner, his rented trailer backed against the loading shoot, the horse driven up the ramp and in. He and Rilla shut the gate and climb into the cab.

"Your daddy'd be proud, Ferrell."

On the long drive south, Rilla naps against his shoulder, the radio still picking up Ferrell's oldies station from Boise. With Rilla dreaming the miles away, and the bygone songs shearing time and space, those strange days of Ferrell's childhood fill his head.

When his daddy took to wearing cowboy garb, Ferrell's mama started to worry, telling Ferrell to be ready for anything, come the devil or high water. At breakfast one Sunday, his daddy clomped from the coffeepot to the table, his cowboy boots scuffing the linoleum. He set his white Stetson beside his plate, ran fingers through his mussed hair. When Ferrell's mother put down her fork and stared, Ferrell ducked in his chair.

"What?" his daddy said.

"You know."

"They're just boots, Merle. I like the way they feel."

"Is it me?" his mother said, boldly upping the ante. "Is it your son here? Are you tired of us?"

Ferrell's daddy scooted scrambled eggs around his plate. "I could count myself the king of infinite space," he said, "were it not I have bad dreams. Or something to that effect."

"You're reciting poetry now?"

"It's from *Hamlet*, Mom," Ferrell said. "Dad's been borrowing my English book."

"Well, your father's not a king of anything."

"Nor an outlaw." Ferrell's daddy sipped his black coffee. "I'm just wearing Western wear."

"People are talking, Maynard. The Potters saw you at Beueler's last weekend, pushing your cart down the aisle all decked out. They asked me if they could come ride Trigger. Dobson was very amused."

"Let the bastard laugh. Old fart could use it."

"Ferrell, honey, tell him what your friends are saying."

Ferrell moved his own eggs around. In the past months it had seemed the old alliances had shifted, that new loyalties had formed within his family, the hierarchy upside down. In this curious ordering, Ferrell and his mother were in command, his father the one to be brought into line. "J. R. wondered if Tonto was bunking in my room."

His father put his fork down. "Sticks and stones, son. But I'll tell you what. A man has to do and say what he damn well wants. Otherwise he's not a man."

"For godsakes, Maynard, is that from one of your stupid movies? Or are you babbling Shakespeare again?"

With studied deliberation, his father reached for the Stetson. He rose slowly and ambled across the kitchen to the backdoor. As he turned the knob Ferrell studied the familiar profile, in sharp relief against the window, and for those few heartbeats he saw a stranger passing through town. His daddy put the hat on his head and stepped into the brilliant Ohio sun.

At dawn, Ferrell follows his ex to the barn. He cradles the new English saddle in his arms, the oiled leather smelling sweet and good, while Rilla carries the halter, bridle, and wool saddle pad. By far Ferrell's favorite procurement has been Rilla's tight riding britches, her rearside view stirring his blood in pleasing ways. Hands down, she still has the keys to unlock his safe.

"Oh, quit staring, Ferrell," she says without looking his way.

Northward, Ferrell finds the ditch bank fires going strong. In the rising light, smoke spirals here and there like signals from lonely tribes. To Ferrell's dismay, his Owyhees still loom as faint, ragged cutouts.

"Distant war," Rilla says. "Battles rage."

Inside the corral, Chroma stands watching. Rilla named the horse for her silver mane and tail—like chrome adornments, she said, against the red. Chroma pivots on her hindquarters, lopes to the far corner, faces them once more. Rilla climbs the fence and calmly crosses the sand. During her early childhood, before abandoning his family for parts unknown, her daddy owned a string of horses, and Rilla grew up in the saddle, taking dressage lessons from the time she could hold reins. While at Kent State, Rilla was show-jumping champion of northeast Ohio, a beautiful sight out in the ring, such a slender slip of a girl atop her huge, airborne stallion. Knowing what Rilla looked like beneath her clothes, how her slick skin felt against him, only added to Ferrell's enjoyment of watching her ride.

For the last couple mornings, Rilla's worked her magic. Through diligent groundwork Chroma's learned who's in charge, Rilla becoming lead mare of their herd of two, the new sheriff in town. Before Ferrell's eyes a wild mustang has turned attentive pleasure horse, her ears not back but forward. Now Chroma responds to just a raised finger, to Rilla turning her shoulders, dipping down her head. She's melded minds with the mare, he thinks, his own little horse whisperer of the Owyhee rangelands. His whole life Ferrell's never exerted that much influence, never had any living thing pay him such mind.

Now, after patient minutes to saddle Chroma, and slip bridle and bit in place, Rilla's ready to climb aboard. Ferrell's got the reins, feeling small beside the strongly muscled chest. The sparkling bridle headband transforms the mustang into royalty come to visit their lowly ranch.

"She looks like a princess, Rilla."

"Oh, she is," Rilla says, leading the horse in a few tight circles. She sets the reins in place and it's all systems go. "Look out, Ferrell. She'll probably move the second my butt hits the saddle. I'll bet she just loves to go."

Rilla slips a boot in the silver stirrup, and drumrolls play inside Ferrell's head. Then she rises to the saddle, the horse takes off, and Rilla is an angel with her wings restored. Ferrell resists going romantic on the moment, getting too darn sentimental, but he can't fight it off: Rilla is goddamn beautiful up there, and violins have begun to play. She signals to the horse in some way Ferrell can't see, and Chroma gears up into a canter, practically floats around the corral. His ex circles him in a wide orbit, her flying ponytail a miniature version of Chroma's own. Rilla's face flushes with joy, and the mare's flanks shine with sweat, but still they ride, around and around where Ferrell stands in the center as a fiery sun.

In the months before his departure, Ferrell's daddy built himself a room in their damp basement, just to the right of the tidy workbench. He started one night after supper, the hammering downstairs like he fought some dungeon monster, and the room was framed and drywalled when Ferrell left for school in the morning. By the time the bus dropped him off, his daddy had the door hung and locked, and his mother was nowhere in the house. Ferrell didn't know what else to do but knock. His daddy answered the door with paint specks in his hair.

"You seen Mom?"

His daddy gaped at him, as if he didn't quite know of whom Ferrell spoke. "She's at your grandmother's," he said at last.

"Did she say when she'd be back?"

"When hell grows cold and frosty."

His daddy turned back into the room, and Ferrell followed before the door could close. Inside he found white walls and pale blue shag, an army cot and portable television. Left of the door, their red ice chest sat beneath the folding card table with a hot plate and toaster. The room smelled of paint and new carpet and his daddy's own potent sweat.

"Want a beer?" his daddy said.

"So you're living down here?"

"I wouldn't call it living, but this is my new abode."

"In the basement?"

"Safest place in the house. Come a twister I'd haul ass to my room, no doubt."

"How long you intend to stay down here?"

"I haven't thought that through, son. I just got the idea at supper last night."

"But what will my friends say?"

"They'll say your old man can build a hell of a room. They'll say he's got a way with his hands." He switched the television channel and played with the silver antenna ears. "Besides," he said, fishing twin Rolling Rocks from the ice chest, "once you get a girlfriend, you two can bonk like bunnies down here. After I'm gone, of course."

Ferrell took the offered beer, but drank the cold dripping bottle in his room upstairs.

Toward dusk the big Dodge grumbles into the drive, spooking the horse with its clanking diesel drama. From the porch Ferrell watches Rilla jump the fence to calm the trotting Chroma.

"That thing's louder than a damn bulldozer," Ferrell says as Cole climbs down.

"Uses gas like one too."

Cole circles around to help his wife from the cab. Melody stands shielding her eyes from the low sun, her belly swelled more than seems possible.

"Wow," Ferrell says. "You're enormous."

"Way to go, Ferrell," Rilla says, coming back through the gate. "Make a girl feel pretty."

Together the neighbors line the corral, elbows on the top rail. Chroma faces the foursome, her ears forward and listening, then she comes to the fence and nuzzles Rilla's outstretched hand. In the delicate ruby light, the horse looks absolutely radiant, as fine an equine as Ferrell's seen.

"You've done wonders, Rilla," Cole says. "I didn't think you could even get close to a mustang for weeks."

"Rilla's got a way with animals," Ferrell says. "She could train coyotes to fetch the morning paper."

"So why hasn't it worked with you?" Rilla says.

Bored, Chroma walks off to nibble the remains of her evening hay. Rilla leads Melody to the rocking chairs on the porch, where they sit like frontier women from ages past.

"So how's it going?" Ferrell says.

"Aside from not speaking, we're good."

"That bad?"

"You ever spend time with a pregnant woman?"

"Levon was three when Rilla and I got together, after our practice mar-
riages to other people. I missed these tender experiences—pregnancy and
birth, breast-feeding and diapers, teething."

"Lucky you." Cole slips a Skoal can from his shirt pocket. He renews his
chaw and spits a deadly streak into the dust. "So you were stepdaddy to that
boy for close to fifteen years?"

"Did all I could."

"Think it was enough?"

"Not by a long shot."

"But you still made a difference?"

"Does it look like I did?"

Cole studies Ferrell with his frank, searching gaze. "Surely it seems worth
the effort? Looking back, I mean."

"I'll tell you what, buddy," Ferrell says, wondering how much truth to
offer. "My daddy left my mother and me when I was in junior high. I never
forgave him for that. At least I was there for Levon."

"You think he'll try to see the baby?"

"Levon's ran from responsibility his whole life. I wouldn't expect him to
change now."

"But didn't any of your influence stick?"

"Like water on a duck's ass."

"That's reassuring."

"Ah, don't listen to me, Cole. I find fault with a sunny day, you know that."
Ferrell watches the sun dip from sight, a final winking out of the world. "I
believe it's cocktail time," he says, and leads his neighbor toward the house.

When the tormented man headed west, Ferrell and his mama were mostly
just relieved. His father ended up in Los Angeles, not the open range as far
as Ferrell could tell. He found a job at Lockheed in tool and die, his days
spent beside his trusty lathe. In rare letters home, his daddy would scribble
about plans to visit Death Valley, or to spend his vacation at a dude ranch
in Nevada, but the farthest the man ever got to the West of his dreams was
Anaheim, where he strolled the phony streets of Knott's Berry Farm. That
Christmas he sent Ferrell a picture of him wearing a sheriff's getup, silver star
pinned over his tiny, betraying heart.

Another dawn and Ferrell's in the corral. It's been weeks of daily training sessions, hour upon hour of Rilla taking Chroma through her paces. The pair have learned much about each other, leaving Ferrell odd man out. "Can't we take a day off, Rilla?" he says, his voice whiny to his ears. "This seems too much like work."

"Today's *your* day to ride."

Ferrell feels a sizable jolt of fear. It's been one thing to watch the proceedings, but to climb his fragile bones atop a half-ton animal is indeed another. "Why didn't you tell me sooner?"

"And give you a chance to worry and fret?"

Ferrell wants to protest, but changes his mind. He rarely wins with Rilla, even when she's flat-out wrong. In too few minutes Rilla has the saddled horse before him, the spot he needs to sit quite a ways off the ground. He hears the goofy chortles of herons, and finds a dozen birds high above, headed haphazardly for the Snake. When Ferrell first heard their weird croaking cries he was surprised such humor issued forth from the long, sleek fliers. Today the great blues seem to be laughing directly at him.

"Okay, Hoss," Rilla says, "foot in the stirrup, and swing on up."

Ferrell moves before his mind can figure what he's doing. His leg arcs over the horse's back, and the rest of him follows until he's on top, thighs hugged to the mighty, curving ribs. He looks across the corral, amazed at the unexpected height, at the different perspective from his horsetop view. Rilla stands far down below, smiling like he has done a truly good thing.

"First time on a horse ever," he says.

"I bet you thought you'd run out of firsts." Rilla rubs Chroma along the sweeping neck, whispers into her ear.

"Hey, no secrets down there," Ferrell says.

"Hang on."

And then the complex musculature goes alive beneath him, a tremendous flex and release he feels through the saddle. The horse clops across the corral and Ferrell goes all giddy inside. In some dreamy physical memory he is on a merry-go-round at the fair, laughing with pure kid glee at the lift and drop of the brightly painted pony, the wind against his face, his father blurred with rushing movement.

Rilla leads Chroma across the dusty corral, each step signaled back to Ferrell in that fantastic play of muscle and bone. He remembers not to slouch, his reins held off the withers. He looks over the horse head guiding him through the world, the ears like radar searching. Before them is a western landscape of distance and sage, of mountains hulking in the smoky light. He narrows his eyes to take Rilla and her lead rope out of the picture, and he is for once and all time John Wayne, off to save the world.

When his father's heart gave out at age sixty-two, Ferrell was home grading papers. He'd wanted to outwait the old man, to see if he'd care enough to visit him and Rilla, and wait he was still doing when someone named Charlene called to say his father had fallen halfway across Sepulveda Boulevard, his life finished before he hit the ground. Ferrell held the phone like he was supposed to do, heard the words being driven into his ear, but he was hollowed clean through.

"He's dead," the woman kept repeating, as if Ferrell didn't understand her simple message. "Your father is dead."

Ferrell hung up with her still insisting he know.

The funeral was small, his father gone so long from his birthplace few remembered his birth at all. Without brothers or sisters, with his mother remarried and denying her past, Ferrell and Rilla were the only ones at the lonesome grave. Even the pastor, a man accustomed by trade to burying the unloved and neglected, looked disappointed. Ferrell knocked once on the lid of the coffin, his eyes scalded with tears, and marched swiftly to the car.

In the days after the funeral, Ferrell would be in class when the words would hit—*He's dead. Your father is dead*—and strike him dumb, a stoic schoolteacher wanting to cry out. Acutely, he felt his loss everywhere he went, as if his own feeble heart were about to stop. Some nights, sitting in his den, Ferrell would look up from his papers and stare, his old man keeping just beyond the pool of lamplight.

Like most things in his life, that first ride was pure beginner's luck. In the weeks that follow, Ferrell earns his share of bruised behinds and bruised egos, entering into a squally love-hate fling with Chroma that changes by the minute. For brief stirring moments he rides at one with the mind of the horse god, then he is on his ass with nothing but blue above. He falls off to his left and he falls off to his right, and during one difficult moment Chroma rears like high-ho Silver, sliding him down into that hostile place of horseshoes and hard ground. But he survives the batterings and the days finally amount to some measure of horse savvy and skill. Soon Ferrell knows enough to ride out alone and still come back alive. His favorite place to go is the BLM, those hundred thousand acres unchanged since Butch and Sundance rode through.

One blustery morning, Ferrell rides out into this dazzling world, already tired and the day not half done. Last night his dreams ran too fitful to suit him, and now his mood's gone south on its own fast horse. He gallops through the sharp, clean air, Chroma's hooves kicking powdery dust. Sagebrush reaches for his legs like withered hands, and the distant Owyhees call his name, cast as they are in such odd storm light. Despite himself Ferrell wishes his father could see him now. Here he is breathing air almost fifty years from the day his father left, and he's still waiting for the man to return, but now it would be from the grave and not just Los Angeles.

As Ferrell rides beneath the leaden sky, he feels the stinging hurt of not uttering a word to his father for dozens of years, how his headstrong ways kept him from once picking up the phone, those squandered hours jet-streaming past: Ferrell rushing off to make the morning bell, Ferrell trudging home with ungraded exams, Ferrell and Rilla in brief, sweaty embrace, the ticking alarm clock a time bomb to his fleeting dreams. Entire decades now just a jumbled blur, his thirties, his forties, years spent raising Rilla's wayward son, a career itself to keep the boy from the gates of hell. Home repair and ragged lawns to mow, parent-teacher meetings without end—there was always something to steal his days, to suck away time like an invisible black hole hovered nearby. And while his daddy sat out in L.A., tan and wrinkled in the fabled California sun, Ferrell, stubborn in his pride, drove Rilla and Levon off in every vacation direction *but* west. If his daddy didn't care enough to come see him, well then screw the selfish bastard. After all, it was *his* daddy who left Ohio, not him, left Ferrell and his mama high and dry, as if blood ties were not ties at all, but cumbersome bonds to break.

With the day turning dark and ominous, Ferrell rides the ridge above the cabin. Over his troubled head towering clouds slide heavily past, some gray-white, others black and swollen, one truly nasty storm invading his pristine skies. With speeding heart, Ferrell reins short of the sheer drop-off. He feels purged in body, if not in spirit. Over the tremendous space below a redtail rides the strong currents, eye level to Ferrell and the horse on the ridge. The hawk glides for a spell, then draws hard against the air, its wing strokes the most graceful thing Ferrell knows. Dipping a broad wing, the redtail slides into a hard banking turn, then holds itself in place against the wind, its fierce eyes and hooked beak pointed straight at Ferrell Swan. If he were Nez Perce he'd believe he was seeing some sign just now, an omen from the Great Spirit about the tricky hours to come. Hell, he might as well think so anyway, his Anglo blood be damned.

Ferrell tucks his head and rides, downright buffeted by the wind. He leans into the gusts as if invisible hands push back. At the mouth of the ravine he guides the horse down and the wind dies. As he descends the trail, steep slopes rise on either side, scary sage and strewn rocks, an alien world where he doesn't belong. In this forbidden place he thinks of Melody's child, fatherless already and not even born, then thinks of poor Levon, his own daddy run off when Rilla still carried him around. And what about Rilla and him, her daddy gone when she was just a girl, his taking longer but finding the door? For the moment the world seems crammed with sons and daughters but no fathers. He imagines men everywhere disappeared from villages and towns, from outlying homesteads and packed cities, an entire gang of slackers and bums, riding the badlands while their families soldier on.

Ahead Ferrell spots what he's come to see: the bright white bones of the lone mustang. He found the skeleton soon after buying the property, when home was a tent and a propane stove. Over the years the spot has become eerily sacred, a pilgrimage to make when he needs to be restored. The skull's dark sockets watch Chroma approach. Ferrell dismounts and leaves the horse to graze the cheatgrass. He kneels at the bones, a confounding puzzle of leg shafts and arching ribs, pelvis halves the size of hubcaps. He recalls, as he can't help but do, when Rilla first trekked over with him last fall, how she seemed to slip the skull over her own head, filled that vacant realm with thoughts once more, the sockets with eyes full of menace and desire. Appearing to wear the skull like a sort of demented mask, she told him she was the mistress of the horse god, that she made men beg for things only she understood. Rilla pretended to be joking but Ferrell wasn't fooled: the creature before him meant business, wanted his soul for untame purposes.

Now Ferrell himself lifts the skull from its scattered bones. The thing weighs more than he imagined, dense as stone in his hands. He looks straight into the sockets as if to see something there, perhaps wise eyes searching his weary face. He raises the skull over his head like an ornate helmet, but it doesn't fit. When he lowers the skull to his chest, Ferrell hears the slow shaking of thunder, then spidery lightning threads the dark wisps of rain hung from the clouds. If Ferrell weren't a believer in the supernatural, this would be a good place to begin. He kneels in the sand to make the horse whole again. He points the long snout westward, aiming those hollow sockets toward the rugged country below, where somewhere in the rain-blurred miles its companions still run.

When the phone rings, Rilla lies curled into Ferrell on the futon, their sleeping selves as loving as ever. Rilla tromps to the kitchen to quell the loud jangling, while Ferrell pulls her pillow against him and drifts back down.

"Let's go, Ferrell," she says, standing above him. "Melody's dilating like mad. It won't be long."

Ferrell drives Rilla the pitch-black mile and parks beside Cole's Dodge. He walks with her to the door, the stars flashing messages in arcane code. "A good night to be born," he says.

"Any time is a good time to be born."

"It beats dying, that's for sure."

Cole answers the door in a bad mood. It takes Ferrell just a minute to understand that harsh reality has hit Cole between the eyes: another man's child is about to be born. Seeing his wife sweat and moan, caught as she is in the fierce intimacy of birth, must be a crude reenactment of what she and Levon did in the desert night, halfway between this house and Ferrell's cabin.

With the baby shivering at his mother's breast, Ferrell hands Cole a cheap cigar. The men lean against the far wall, clumsy oafs without a clue. Despite these modern times, Ferrell feels witness to an act ancient and private, and he humbly averts his eyes.

"You boys head out under the stars," Rilla says, shooing them from the room. "This is mommy time."

Ferrell leads the stunned Cole onto the porch, a fifth of Jack Daniels in one hand, two glasses in the other. He holds a match to Cole's cigar, then lights his own, his first in forty years. Anticipating the grand event, he bought Swisher Sweets at the gas station in Murphy, but the celebration now seems a briar patch of emotions, none suited for a Hallmark card.

"What do you feel?" he asks.

"What don't I feel is the better question." Cole drains half the glass on his first sip. "That looked more like dying than being born."

"I won't argue."

"You have any advice for me now?" Cole asks.

"None yet."

"The father's not here," Cole says. "I'd begun to feel it was me, but to-night I'm no more daddy to that boy than the coyotes on the ridge."

Ferrell pours his tumbler full and drinks. He waits a beat for the warm amber glow to reach his head. "But you're the one here."

Come morning, Ferrell wakes a troubled man. All night long his dear daddy wandered his dreams, his physical presence as real as the room into which Ferrell opens his eyes. He wants to tell the sleeping Rilla of his haunted hours, of spending company with a man long since dust. In his dreams his father looked as he had the day he left, young and with swagger, his home and its crushing obligations standing between him and the vast frontier.

"I need to light out for the territories, son," his dream daddy said, straightening the cowboy hat on his head.

"But you're a machinist," Ferrell said, somehow his own age in the dream and not fourteen.

"Well, I'll build me some horses then, make them from polished steel."

Ferrell looked down to find steel-toed work boots on his daddy's feet. "Will I see you?" Ferrell said, knowing he would not, his dream self possessing knowledge of the years to come.

"Sure shooting, son. Hell, we'll still grow old together, buddies to the end."

"But that's not true," Ferrell said. "You'll die before we ever reconcile. You'll return to Ohio in your coffin."

"Well, then you'll visit me out West, son. You'll come ride with me, side by side, our hats pulled low."

"I'll not," he said.

His daddy shook his head. "For a youngster, you don't have much good to report."

Remembering these conjured words Ferrell climbs from bed, careful not to disturb Rilla's own dreams. He dresses in jeans and boots, slips into his Western riding shirt, the buttons bright as coins. He gets his own Stetson off the nightstand, pressing the hat firmly on his head. Downstairs, the kitchen radio reports of flames racing unchecked across the BLM, near Murphy and Oreana, Ferrell's corner of the world. Morning gusts have fanned a burning ditch bank into wildfire seven hundred acres and growing.

Outside blackish smoke hangs thick as fog, his own fence lines mere traces, the sun a cool white star. With his pocket Bushnells he locates robust flames and churning smoke, the whole ugly affair like an advancing evil horde. Swinging his glasses along the fire's lead edge, Ferrell comes upon the mustang herd, not a mile from the blaze. Some of the horses stand guard, their heads raised toward the flames, while others circle nervously about, eager to bolt. Ferrell glances at the house, then looks to Chroma pacing in the corral. The idea strikes him as preposterous, even as he knows it's what he'll surely do. In fits and starts Ferrell saddles the horse, coaxes the clanky bit into her mouth. He ties his red bandana below his eyes and climbs into the saddle.

Beyond the gate Chroma canters on her own accord, heading toward the herd as if magically drawn. Ferrell's blood runs hot and fluttery, and he wonders what the hell he's doing, riding as he is straight into a raging wildfire. Near the mustangs, smoke and dust swirl over Ferrell and the horse, darkening the sky. His eyes sting and water, his breathing labored in the thick air. Chroma drops into a slow trot, then abruptly stops. The mare stands blowing hard, rib hoops heaving beneath Ferrell's quivering legs. She whinnies once, twice, sidesteps in sudden alarm. He senses the herd in the dense smoke ahead, but can't see a thing. Chroma whinnies yet again, louder and with much more fervor, and next comes a whinny from a horse not her. Another horse nickers from the opposite direction. When Ferrell looks this time he finds them in the haze, more mustangs than he can count, edging closer to where he sits the horse, tossing their heads, tails raised. For one peculiar moment he believes the horses of Hagerman have returned, resurrected from the flames.

A buckskin stallion cuts near Chroma, and she throws her head, gathers under Ferrell as if to rear. Another stallion, this one night-black and lathered, wheels close in the smoke and is gone. Soon mustangs circle them until Ferrell goes dizzy with the swirling mass, as if he is the center of a fantastic cosmos. The horses understand one of their kind has finally returned, Ferrell's lanky figure nothing more than a figment of their dreams.

Ferrell holds Chroma in check amid the skittish herd. He closes his bleary eyes to the pounding hooves, to the snorts and squalling cries. He thinks of the mustang skull so bright on the ridge, thinks of his own father's bones beneath the ground, as useless as the bones of Hagerman. When he looks again, his father sits not ten feet away, mounted atop the black stallion. The man's dressed in his finest cowboy attire, a white Stetson on his head. He touches the brim of his hat, and Ferrell does the same. Without a word his daddy turns the horse and disappears into the smoke.

OTHER NOTABLE WESTERN STORIES OF THE YEAR

Helen Jones, "Ghost Riders"
Chariton Review, Volume 30.1 & 2

Richard Lange, "The Death of Various Animals"
Cimarron Review, Volume 164

Peter Levine, "How Does Your Garden Grow?"
Missouri Review, Volume 31.3

Nina McConigley, "Reserve Champion"
Puerto del Sol, Volume 43.1 & 2

Tyler McMahon, "A Pocket Guide to Male Prostitution"
Overtime, Volume 4

David Milofsky, "The Shabbos Goy"
TriQuarterly, Volume 129

David Philip Mullins, "First Sight"
New England Review, Volume 29.2

P. J. Murphy, "The Party"
New England Review, Volume 29.1

Annie Proulx, "Them Old Cowboy Songs"
New Yorker, May 5, 2008

Annie Proulx, "Tits-up in a Ditch"
New Yorker, June 9 & 16, 2008

Elizabeth Searle, "When You Watch Me"
Hayden's Ferry Review, Volume 42

Jackie Shannon-Hollis, "On Their Best Behavior"
High Desert Journal, Volume 7

Al Sim, "Chuy's Truck"
Santa Fe Writers Project: A Literary Journal, May 23, 2008

Al Sim, "Menthol and Smoke"
Greensboro Review, Volume 82

Scott Snyder, "The Thirteenth Egg"
Virginia Quarterly Review, Volume 84.2

Justin St. Germain, "The Last Day of the Boom"
Alligator Juniper, Volume 2008

Lysley Tenorio, "Save the I-Hotel"
Manoa, Volume 20.1

Douglas Unger, "Second Chances"
Southwest Review, Volume 93.1

Urban Waite, "Drown"
Florida Review, Volume 32.2

Mitch Wieland, "God's Dogs"
Sewanee Review, Volume 116.4

The following online and print journals, magazines,
and newspapers were consulted for this volume:

PUBLICATIONS REVIEWED

Abraxas · African American Review · Afro-Hispanic Review · Agni · Alaska Quarterly Review · Alligator Juniper · Ambit · American Literary Review · American Short Fiction · Antigonish Review · Antioch Review · Apalachee Review · Arkansas Review · Arts and Letters · Ascent · Atlantic · Austin Chronicle · Baltimore Review · Bat City Review · Bellevue Literary Review · Bellingham Review · Beloit Fiction Journal · Bilingual Review/Revista Bilingüe · Bird Dog · Bitter Oleander · Black Clock · Black Warrior Review · Bloom · Blue Mesa Review · Bomb Magazine · Boston Review · Boulevard · Brick · Bridges · Burnside Review · Cadillac Cicatrix · Callaloo · Calyx · Canteen · Carolina Review · Carve Magazine · Chandrabhāgā · Chariton Review · Chattahoochee Review · Chelsea · Chicago Review · Cimarron Review · Cincinnati Review · Colorado Review · Concho River Review · Conduit · Confrontation · Conjunctions · Copper Nickel · Crab Orchard Review · Crazyhorse · Cream City Review · CT Review · Cutbank · Cutthroat · Daedalus · Dalhousie Review · Descant (Fort Worth) · Descant (Toronto) · Dialogue: A Journal of Mormon Thought · Dislocate · Dispatch · Ecotone · Elixir · Ellipses · Ep;phany · Epoch · Event · Exile · Exquisite Corpse · Fence · Fiction · Fiction International · First Intensity · First Line · Five Points · Florida Review · Fourth River · Fourteen Hills · Front Range Review · Fugue · Gargoyle · Georgia Review · Gettysburg Review · Glimmer Train · Global City Review · Granta · Great River Review · Great Western Fiction · Green Mountains Review · Greensboro Review · Grist · Guardian · Gulf Coast · Hanging Loose · Harper's Magazine · Harrington Gay Men's Literary Quarterly · Harrington Lesbian Literary Quarterly · Harvard Review · Hayden's Ferry Review · Heat · High Desert Journal · Home Planet News · Hopkins Review · Hotel Amerika · Hudson Review · Idaho Review · Image · Indian Literature · Indiana Review · Interim · Iowa Review · Isle · Isotope · The

Journal · Jubilat · Kalliope · Kean Review · Kenyon Review · Landfall · Laurel Review · LBJ: Avian Life, Literary Arts · Ledge · Legal Studies Forum · Lit · Literary Review · Long Story · Louisville Review · Main Street Rag · Malahat Review · Mandorla: New Writing from the Americas · Manoa · Maple/Ash Review · Massachusetts Review · McSweeney's · Memoir (and) · Meridian · Michigan Quarterly Review · Mid-American Review · Minnesota Review · Mississippi Review · Missouri Review · Narrative Magazine · Natural Bridge · New Delta Review · New England Review · New Letters · New Orleans Review · New Renaissance · New Yorker · New York Review of Books · New Texas · Nimrod International · Ninth Letter · North American Review · North Dakota Quarterly · Northwest Review · Notre Dame Review · Obsidian III · One Story · Ontario Review · Opium · Other Voices · Overtime · Paris Review · Passager · Paterson Literary Review · Pearl · Pen International · Permafrost · Persona · Phoebe · Pinch · Pleiades · Ploughshares · PMS · Porcupine · Portland Review · Post Road · Potomac Review · Practice: New Writing and Art · Prairie Fire · Prairie Schooner · Predicate · Prism International · Provincetown Arts · Puerto del Sol · Quarterly West · Queens Quarterly · RE:AL · Red Cedar Review · Red Ink · Red Rock Review · Red Wheelbarrow · Redivider · Reed · Review of Contemporary Fiction · River Styx · Rock & Sling · Rosebud · Salamander · Salmagundi · Salt Flats Annual · Salt Hill · Santa Fe Writers Project: A Literary Journal · Santa Monica Review · Saranac Review · Seattle Review · Sewanee Review · Shenandoah · Silent Voices · Sinister Wisdom · Skidrow Penthouse · Snow Monkey · Sonora Review · South Carolina Review · South Dakota Review · Southern Humanities Review · Southern Indiana Review · Southern Quarterly · Southern Review · Southwestern American Literature · Southwest Review · Spork · Storyglossia · StoryQuarterly · StringTown · Subtropics · Sun · Swink · Swivel · Tampa Review · Terra Incognita · Terrain.org · Texas Review · Thema · Third Coast · 13th Moon: A Feminist Literary Magazine · Threepenny Review · Tin House · TriQuarterly · Tusculum Review · Upstreet · Vanitas · Virginia Quarterly Review · Walking Rain Review · War, Literature, and the Arts · Washington Square · Water-Stone Review · Weber: the Contemporary West · West Branch · West Coast Line · Westerly · Western Humanities Review · Whiskey Island Magazine · White Fungus · Women's Study Quarterly · Workers Write! · World Literature Today · Yale Literary Magazine · Yale Review · Zahir · Zoetrope · Zone 3 · ZYZZYVA

NOTES ON CONTRIBUTORS

LEE K. ABBOTT is the author of seven collections of short stories, most recently *All Things, All at Once: New & Selected Stories* (Norton, 2006). His fiction has appeared in *The Atlantic Monthly*, *Harper's*, *The Georgia Review*, *Epoch*, *The Gettysburg Review*, and *The Southern Review*, among many, many others. His work has been reprinted in *The Best American Short Stories*, the *O. Henry Prize Stories*, and the *Pushcart Prize* volumes. Twice awarded fellowships in fiction from the National Endowment for the Arts, he teaches in the MFA Creative Writing Program at The Ohio State University in Columbus, where he is a Humanities Distinguished Professor in English.

AIMÉE BAKER has a BA in history and writing from St. Lawrence University and an MFA in fiction from Arizona State University. Her fiction has been published by *The Southeast Review* and *Gulf Coast*, and her poetry appears in *LOCUSPOINT: Phoenix*. She is currently working on a novel and a series of poems about missing women.

SUSAN STREETER CARPENTER has been an antipoverty worker, home health care administrator, independent radio producer, freelance writer, and teacher of writing. For about fifteen years she was involved with the Antioch Writers' Workshop as director, board member, and faculty. Now she is assistant professor of English at Bluffton University, specializing in fiction writing. For her fiction Carpenter has received an Ohio Arts Council Fellowship, a Pushcart Prize nomination, and two first-place Westheimer awards from the

University of Cincinnati. Her second novel won the Distinguished Dissertation Fellowship in Humanities at U.C. She has published stories in journals such as *The Long Story*, *The Beloit Fiction Journal*, *Snake Nation Review*, *Kalliope*, and *Crab Orchard Review*. She has also published essays and poetry.

DANIEL CHACÓN is author of the books *Chicano Chicanery*, a collection of stories, and the novel *and the shadows took him*. He is coeditor of *The Last Supper of Chicano Heroes: The Selected Works of José Antonio Burciaga*. His new book, *Unending Rooms*, is a collection of stories and winner of the 2007 Hudson Book Prize. See his webpage at www.soychacon.com.

JEFFREY CHAPMAN lives in Salt Lake City, Utah, a great city, with Bear, a great cat. He recently completed his Ph.D. in creative writing and literature at the University of Utah. His stories have appeared recently in *Western Humanities Review*, *The Bellingham Review*, and *Fiction International*. His first published story appeared in *Cutbank* in Fall 2000.

TRACY DAUGHERTY was born and raised in Midland, Texas. He is the author of four novels, three short story collections, and a book of personal essays. His most recent book is *Hiding Man: A Biography of Donald Barthelme*. His stories and essays have appeared in *The New Yorker*, *McSweeney's*, *Boulevard*, *The Georgia Review*, *The Southwest Review*, and many other journals. He has been awarded fellowships from the Guggenheim Foundation and the National Endowment for the Arts. He is a Distinguished Professor of English and Creative Writing at Oregon State University.

LOUISE ERDRICH lives with her family and their dogs in Minnesota. She is a member of the Turtle Mountain Band of Chippewa. She grew up in North Dakota and is of German-American and Chippewa descent. She is the author of many critically acclaimed and *New York Times* best-selling novels for adults, including *Love Medicine*, which won the National Book Critics Circle Award, and her latest novel *The Plague of Doves*.

ERNEST J. FINNEY grew up in San Bruno, just south of San Francisco, and lives now in Sierra County, California. His short fiction appears frequently in literary journals and anthologies, including the *O. Henry Prize Stories*, in which his story "Peacocks" was first-prize winner. University of Illinois Press has published two collections of his stories, *Birds Landing* and *Flights in the Heaven-*

lies. His novels include *Winterchill, Words of My Roaring, Lady with the Alligator Purse*, and *California Time*. He is finishing the third of a quartet of novels set in California from 1842 to 1880. A new collection of his stories will be forthcoming next year.

DAGOBERTO GILB is the author, most recently, of the novel *The Flowers*. His previous books are *Gritos*, an essay collection that was a finalist for the National Book Critics Circle Award, *Woodcuts of Women*, *The Last Known Residence of Mickey Acuña*, and *The Magic of Blood*, the winner of the 1994 PEN/Hemingway Award and a PEN/Faulkner Award finalist. He also edited *Hecho en Tejas: An Anthology of Texas Mexican Literature*. Anthologized widely, recipient of awards including the Guggenheim and Whiting, his fiction and nonfiction has appeared in a range of magazines including *The New Yorker*, *Harper's*, and *The Threepenny Review*. Gilb spent most of his adult years as a construction worker and a journeyman high-rise carpenter with the United Brotherhood of Carpenters. Born in Los Angeles, he made his home for many years in El Paso. He now lives in Austin and teaches in the MFA program at Texas State University in San Marcos.

LUCRECIA GUERRERO is the author of *Chasing Shadows*, a collection of short stories, and *Tree of Sighs*, a novel that received a Christopher Isherwood Foundation Grant. Her stories have appeared in literary journals such as *The Antioch Review*, *The Colorado Review*, and *The Louisville Review*. She completed her MFA at Spalding University and has taught creative writing at Antioch University McGregor and the Antioch Writers' Workshop.

ANTONYA NELSON is the author of nine books of fiction, including the forthcoming *Nothing Right*. She is the recipient of the 2003 Rea Award for Short Fiction, as well as NEA and Guggenheim Fellowships, and teaches in the University of Houston's Creative Writing Program. She lives in Telluride, Colorado; Las Cruces, New Mexico; and Houston, Texas.

JOYCE CAROL OATES is the author of a number of works of fiction, poetry, and criticism, including most recently the novel *My Sister, My Love* and the story collection *Wild Nights!*, from which "Papa at Ketchum, 1961" has been taken. A member since 1978 of the American Academy of Arts and Letters, Joyce Carol Oates is the Roger S. Berlind Professor of Humanities at Princeton University.

ANNIE PROULX is the author of eight books, including the novel *The Shipping News* and the story collection *Close Range*. Her many honors include a Pulitzer Prize, a National Book Award, the Irish Times International Fiction Prize and a PEN/Faulker award. Her story "Brokeback Mountain," which originally appeared in *The New Yorker*, was made into an Academy Award–winning film. She lives in Wyoming.

AURELIE SHEEHAN is the author of two novels, *History Lesson for Girls* and *The Anxiety of Everyday Objects*, as well as a short story collection, *Jack Kerouac Is Pregnant*. She teaches fiction and directs the MFA program in creative writing at the University of Arizona in Tucson.

STEPHEN TUTTLE's short fiction has appeared in *Crazyhorse*, *Gettysburg Review*, *Confrontation*, *Western Humanities Review*, *Hunger Mountain*, *Colorado Review*, *Black Warrior Review*, and elsewhere. He is the winner of the *Indiana Review* Fiction Prize, the Scowcroft Fiction Prize, and the Utah Writer's Fiction Prize, and has been recognized by the Utah Arts Council. A graduate of the creative writing program at the University of Utah, he teaches fiction writing and American literature at Brigham Young University. He lives in Provo, Utah, with his wife and two sons.

URBAN WAITE's fiction can be found in *AGNI*, *Hayden's Ferry Review*, *Meridian*, *One Story*, *Colorado Review*, *The Southern Review*, *Gulf Coast*, and elsewhere. A graduate of Emerson's MFA program, he is the recipient of fellowships and grants from the Saint Botolph Foundation, Vermont Studio Center, and Bread Loaf Writers' Conference. *Don't Look Away*, a collection of his short stories, is forthcoming.

DON WATERS's story collection, *Desert Gothic*, won the Iowa Short Fiction Award and was published in 2007. His stories have appeared in the 2009 Pushcart Prize anthology, *The Kenyon Review*, *Epoch*, *StoryQuarterly*, the *Southwest Review*, and other literary magazines. He lives in Santa Fe, New Mexico.

MITCH WIELAND is the author of the novel *Willy Slater's Lane*. His short stories have appeared in *The Southern Review*, *The Kenyon Review*, *TriQuarterly*, *Shenandoah*, *The Yale Review*, *The Sewanee Review*, *Prairie Schooner*, and other journals. He teaches in the MFA Program in Creative Writing at Boise State University, and serves as founding editor of *The Idaho Review*. He is the recipient of a Christopher Isherwood Fellowship and two literature fellowships from The Idaho Commission on the Arts. "The Bones of Hagerman" is from his collection of short stories, *God's Dogs*, forthcoming. He is currently working on a novel set in Tokyo, where he lived for several years.

CREDITS

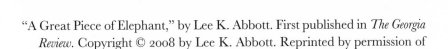